Praise for *Storm Front*

"Warren's stalwart characters and engaging sto[...] Montana Rescue series a must-read."

Booklist

"This exciting penultimate book of the Montana Rescue series will please Warren's large fan base."

Publishers Weekly

Praise for *Troubled Waters*

"This book stands on its own, combining faith, action, romantic tension, humor, and emotional depth into an adventurous love story."

Publishers Weekly

"*Troubled Waters* is a story that will not be easy to forget and one that you will read again."

Fresh Fiction

Praise for *A Matter of Trust*

"Warren captures both the beauty and danger of the life of a competitive snowboarder, transporting readers through vividly detailed descriptions to a treacherous world of snow-covered mountains and daring displays."

Booklist

"Everything about this story sparkles: snappy dialogue, high-flying action, and mountain scenery that beckons the reader to take up snowboarding."

Publishers Weekly

"Warren excels at creating flawed characters the reader cares about, as well as building a suspenseful adventure. She draws vivid word pictures in her stories, with a faith element that is present but not preachy. Readers will be engaged from the first page until the last."

Christian Library Journal

Books by Susan May Warren

MONTANA
RESCUE
✦6✦

WAIT FOR ME

SUSAN MAY
WARREN

Revell

a division of Baker Publishing Group
Grand Rapids, Michigan

© 2018 by Susan May Warren

Published by Revell
a division of Baker Publishing Group
PO Box 6287, Grand Rapids, MI 49516-6287
www.revellbooks.com

Printed in the United States of America

Library of Congress Cataloging-in-Publication Data
Names: Warren, Susan May, 1966- author.
Title: Wait for me / Susan May Warren.
Description: Grand Rapids, MI : Revell, a division of Baker Publishing Group,
    [2018] | Series: Montana Rescue ; 6
Identifiers: LCCN 2018020849 | ISBN 9780800727482 (paper)
Subjects: LCSH: Women air pilots—Fiction. | Helicopter pilots—Fiction. |
    Rescue work—Montana—Fiction. | Man-woman relationships—Fiction. |
    GSAFD: Christian fiction. | Love stories.
Classification: LCC PS3623.A865 W35 2018 | DDC 813/.6—dc23
LC record available at https://lccn.loc.gov/2018020849

This book is a work of fiction. Names, characters, places, and incidents are the product of the author's imagination or are used fictitiously. Any resemblance to actual events, locales, or persons, living or dead, is coincidental.

18   19   20   21   22   23   24   7   6   5   4   3   2   1

HE WASN'T LOOKING FOR TROUBLE, but if Pete didn't act right now, at least one person was going to die.

And more than anything, SAR incident commander Pete Brooks was sick of failing, of seeing lives destroyed. Especially on his watch.

"You should wait." His co-rescuer, Aimee, grabbed the back of his shirt, as if to keep him from sliding down the slope into the churning black floodwaters of the Meramec River. The 218-mile river had overflowed its banks two days ago under a torrent of rain caused by the tail end of a Cat 4 hurricane that ravaged the Gulf Coast, then traveled northward. All six Ozark highland counties, nearly three thousand square miles, sat under grimy waters, and the rain continued to fall.

Pete and his disaster team had spent the past twenty-four hours hauling people off roofs, pulling them from debris, and searching for the unaccounted.

Now, heading back to their hotel in their SUV, they'd come upon a washed-out bridge. And in the frothing waters, a caravan, drowning fast in the swift current.

Please, let there not be a family inside.

"We don't have time. We need to move, now." The SUV's head-lights scraped over the bridge, most of which was submerged, having taken a hit after an old railroad bridge from upstream slammed into the girders.

Pete had watched it happen, wanted to scream at the caravan edging its way over the swollen waters. He'd pumped his brakes, slammed the SUV into park, and was halfway out when the bridge collapsed.

"You can't go in there alone," Aimee said, scrambling up the bank after him.

"I'm not an idiot," Pete snapped, and instantly regretted it. It wasn't Aimee's fault he'd had barely four hours of sleep in the past day and a half. Everyone on his team was functioning on raw, serrated nerves, their veins pumping more coffee than blood. "Sorry." He turned to Jamie Walsh, who was climbing out of the SUV. "Walsh—throw me that rope and tie it off."

The recruit, ex-navy, all muscle and get-'er-done, pulled the coil of line from the back end and secured it to the jack. He tossed the rest of the coil, plus a harness, to Pete.

Pete pulled the harness on, one eye on the gray caravan as Aimee shined the Maglite on his movements.

"Don't lose them!" he said to Aimee. He could buckle on his gear in his sleep, for Pete's sake.

She directed the light across the frothy waters.

He clipped on the carabiner, buckled on a helmet, and grabbed the life jacket Walsh handed him. "Give me two more."

Walsh loaded him up, and Pete also grabbed another harness.

The roar of the river drowned the thunder of his pulse.

Maybe he *should* wait. Going in the water was always the last choice. The waters frothed, choked with debris and who knew what lethal underwater booby traps.

But now the caravan lay on its side, half-submerged, trapped

6

fifty feet downstream against a cement pylon that could give way at any moment.

"Turn the truck and keep the lights on the river," he said to Aimee, then glanced at Walsh.

Good man. He'd anchored himself in with webbing to a nearby tree and would belay Pete into the wash.

Don't let go. He wanted to say it, but it sounded, well, weak. Afraid. As if he expected disaster.

Although, with his recent run of luck . . .

Instead, "Call for backup," he said to Aimee, because, well, he *wasn't* an idiot. His simple plan in this torrent was to get whoever was trapped in the car out and wait for help.

The night sky was dark as ink, the drizzle insidious as it soaked his shirt, his canvas pants, and sent a shiver down his back.

He waded into the wash. The current nearly swept his feet out from under him.

He should wait. He nearly turned back, except for the voice lifting from the vehicle, haunting across the waters.

"Help!" A man had crawled out of the van and was waving his arms, screaming, the words eaten by the violence of the storm.

Pete still made out the word *child*. Went cold.

"Stay put! I'm coming for you!"

A tree with stripped arms twisted past him. Pete let it go, then plunged into the frigid water. It rose to his shins, then his knees. When it hit his waist and higher, he sprang out, swimming hard for the other side.

He'd always been a strong swimmer, but he was no match for the flow as it caught him up, tumbling downstream. Walsh belayed out his line, and twenty feet from the vehicle, Pete turned onto his back, feet downstream, and let the current have him, paddling hard with his arms for the right trajectory.

The river had yanked the caravan around, and the passenger

side was downstream, submerged. Pete slid by, grabbed the bumper, and wrestled himself around. He jammed his feet against the carriage as the water crested over him, filling his eyes, his mouth.

Gulping a breath, he forced himself up onto the vehicle's side. A man lay on the side of the car, reaching inside. He didn't look at Pete. "I can't get them out!"

A woman was wedged inside against the dashboard, her belt pinning her, her mouth just above the rising tide.

A toddler screamed in a seat just behind the driver's side, still above the rising waters, but—

"I got 'em." Pete pulled the man up and buckled his life preserver around him. "You need to get to safety."

"Not without my family!"

Okay, Pete understood that tone. And didn't have time to fight him. "All right. But put this on." He unhooked the second harness and handed it to the man. Then he took his belay rope and hooked it to the harness. "Stay put. I'll get your wife."

The man obeyed, his face grim in the shadows.

Shouting came from shore, probably from Aimee.

Pete unbuckled his helmet, shoved it into the man's hands, took a breath, and climbed in, submerging himself next to the woman. His hands scraped over her writhing body. Her grip clawed into his arms as he searched for her buckle and the other debris that imprisoned her.

Her legs were pinned against the dashboard, but if he could unbelt her, move the seat back—

His lungs burned, and he came up gasping.

The man was screaming. "It's over her head!"

Pete took another breath and plunged back into the depths. She clawed at him, frantic.

He found the buckle, popped it, and she floated up.

But not enough. Her feet were still trapped. He came up for air, gasping, as her hand clutched his shirt.

"You have to let me go, ma'am."

"I'm scared—"

"I know—trust me!"

She shook her head, but he grabbed her hands, wrenched them away—yeah, he probably hurt her, but it was better than dying—and plunged back in.

The seat was electric. Foolishly, he tried to move the seat back, then, in desperation, grabbed her and tried to tug her out.

His lungs turned to fire before he surfaced. The water had crested over her again.

Above him, into the night, the man was screaming, his hands entangled with his wife's. "Save her!"

Pete went back under.

He couldn't open his eyes and cursed his lack of equipment. But he'd see nothing in this darkness, and maybe damage his eyes in the dirty water and debris. Feeling his way around her body, his hand landed on the seat tilt-back lever. Miraculously, it was manual.

He popped it and gave the seat a push. It fell back.

She released, just enough for him to grab her around the waist.

He pulled with everything inside him.

Please let him not be breaking bones.

She came free and he propelled her up.

He surfaced, the water now at the level of the driver's seat. The woman kicked him in the face as her husband dragged her out through the window. Pete shoved the second life jacket at her. "Put this on!"

She coughed, doubling over. "My baby!"

Below, in the depths of the car, the baby was screaming.

He spotted more lights panning across the water, heard shouting. A glance toward the lights suggested more vehicles had arrived.

The tumult rocked the van.

"You both need to get to shore. I'll get the baby."

The man pulled his wife into his arms. "He'll get her," he said to his wife, talking of Pete.

And yeah, he would. Because when he said he'd do something

. . .

Pete unclipped his harness and worked it over her legs, around her waist. "Belt her in and clip her to yourself," he told the man.

He climbed into the back. The water lipped the bottom side of the car seat, rising fast. The child—maybe less than two years old—was wedged into the seat, facing backward, arching her back, screaming.

Pete found the buckle and unlatched it, pulling the child free and holding her above the rising tide.

The entire van shook as he climbed to the front. Pete shoved the child into waiting arms, and when he followed, he discovered that another man wearing a life vest and rescue gear had reached them. Pete recognized him from the private crew of volunteers out of Minneapolis. Somebody Jones. Military build, a grim set to his lined face.

A guide rope strung along the opposite bank. Another man from their team was maneuvering a raft into the water. Walsh still had hold of the belay attached to the husband.

Jones had unhooked the wife from her husband and was re-hooking her onto the rescue line, not an easy feat with the husband clutching her.

Pete climbed up onto the seat, tried to reach for the baby, to hold it while Jones hooked the woman onto the line. "Trust me, ma'am. We've got her." She trusted him. He saw it in her eyes as she loosened her hold. He started to ease the child from her arms.

And that was when the cement pylon shifted.

The current caught the vehicle, tearing the child from his grip. *The baby!*

The woman jolted from her perch as the van jerked hard into the current. She crashed into the water.

The van rolled over.

Pete was suddenly trapped, half in and half out of the window, under the car.

How he'd managed a breath, he didn't know, but the vehicle pinned him as the force of the water corkscrewed the vehicle into the wash.

And then he was slamming against boulders, darkness and water filling his eyes, his nose, his throat.

Not. Like. This!

He wouldn't die with blackness choking him, the river twisting him, pummeling him.

And not without seeing Jess one more time.

Even if the sight of her with another man might drown him more than this moment.

Pete kicked against the car, straining to shove himself away, his lack of breath searing his lungs.

Air. He ached for it, the burn compelling him to take a breath, draw in the lethal water.

Not . . . yet . . . His hand dragged against something firm, a pole—maybe rebar from the cement pillars that had buttressed the bridge. He gripped it.

The momentum of the vehicle, carried away in the torrent, tore Pete free.

His feet found bottom, and he surged to the surface with everything inside him.

Sweet, glorious air. He drank it in even as he fought the churn of rapids surging him downriver. The frothing water roared in his ears as the gulf crested over him, swamping him. His shoulder sparked as his body slammed against a boulder.

He'd break a leg like this. Or worse.

Lay back. Defensive swim.

Pete fought to get his legs around, to sit back, to turn his body to ride on top of the water.

He'd never been good at surrender.

Calm down. He willed himself to take even breaths, despite the water sloshing over him, burning his eyes. *Float.* Just for a moment, to get his bearings. The roar filled his senses, the surge of it turning his body to ice.

He'd been in enough training scenarios to know that if he just kept his head, he could find a way to shore.

But wow, he was tired. The kind of fatigue that poured through him, turned his body to a rock. Probably the adrenaline of wrestling his way to the surface now dropping hard.

Or maybe the fatigue went deeper. The kind that seeped through his bones to his spirit. The weariness of striving. Wanting. Failing.

Of trying to break free of his broken heart.

"I choose you, Pete."

Jess Tagg. Her voice had the audacity to linger in his head, and he hated it.

No, no she hadn't chosen him.

Not that he should have been surprised, really, in the end. He didn't know why he'd let himself believe in happily-ever-afters.

Ahead, a great shape burgeoned in the darkness, lights on it reflecting out onto the river. A bridge. Which meant submerged girders and lethal footings.

He'd break every bone in his body.

"Pete!"

The voice echoed over the rim of wave and froth, lifting then bouncing into the night.

He searched for it, thrashing. The roar of the river deepened.

"Pete!" A light skimmed across him, and he followed it.

A raft. Speeding down the river in pursuit. A man—he recognized him from the other team—knelt at the helm, swinging a rescue throw bag.

The orange bag arched over Pete and dropped into the water past him. The rope shifted over him, the roughness against his legs, and he grabbed it.

But his frozen hands couldn't grip the slippery line. It ripped at his skin as it reeled out, the current wrestling him away from rescue.

Don't let go!

Maybe someone shouted, but the words rooted, found his bones. Galvanized him. He rolled over, kicking, winding the rope into his hands and tightening his grip.

"I got you!" The man on the raft was reeling him in toward shore. "Roll over! Put the rope on your inside shoulder."

His training kicked into his brain and he obeyed, letting the rope ease him to shore. The earth scraped his legs, and as he bumped onto the rocks, he rolled over to grip them.

The raft motored up to assist.

But Pete had already crawled his way into the mud and grass to pillow himself on land.

He rolled over, breathing hard.

The man piled out of the raft and kneeled beside him. "You okay?"

Pete put a hand to his chest. Alive. Yeah, his heartbeat confirmed it.

In fact, it might be the first time he'd felt it beat since the woman he loved walked out of his life into the arms of another man.

He just needed to lie here awhile and try to figure out how to get back up.

———— + ————

Jess Tagg had nowhere else to run.

But it didn't mean she couldn't try. Except for the grip her fiancé, Felipe St. Augustine, had on her hand, she would have already been fleeing out the front door of the seven-story mansion located in the heart of what used to be called Billionaires' Row on the Upper East Side of Manhattan.

Right into the throng of paparazzi just waiting to pepper her with questions, trail her every move, splash her grimaced face onto Page 6, and turn her into clickbait for a syndicated slew of tabloids that lit up the internet.

So, no, she couldn't flee out the gold-gated front door.

And she'd already tried escaping to the red-tiled roof patio earlier, where more guests had gathered for cocktails. Unfortunately, she'd spotted a couple cameras from the high-rise across the street. That was what she got for attending a fund-raising event that also included the likes of George Clooney and Ivanka Trump.

Thank you, Vanessa White and her philanthropy-minded superstar chums.

"Champagne, *ma chérie?*" Felipe set his empty glass on one of the skirted tables and motioned for a gloved and tuxedoed waiter to swing by with his tray.

"No, thank you," Jess said, her stomach too empty for anything bubbly. Or any of the canapés. The wasabi shrimp and avocado on the rice cracker churned in her gut.

What she wouldn't do for a ham sandwich.

Felipe glanced at her, his dark brown, nearly black, eyes running over her, a crease in his brow. "Are you all right?" He lifted his other hand, as if to touch her cheek, and she gave a quick nod.

"I'm fine."

His hand dropped away, just a flicker of something she couldn't

14

place in his gaze. He squeezed her hand, however. "I'm sorry about earlier. We'll go out the back, or—"

"It's okay, Felipe. I'm used to it."

His mouth tightened, but just then a woman slid up to him, her hand finding his tuxedoed arm. A tall drink of water, the brunette probably walked the runway for one of the haute couture houses in Paris. She wore a dress that gloved her body, black, with a slit that hit her high on the thigh. The high neck made of sheer lace only added to her regal demeanor. Jess felt a little garish in her red strapless asymmetrical sweetheart gown. Nor was she in possession of the fluent French that rolled off this woman's elegant tongue. Jess hadn't a hope of understanding the words, but she did notice Felipe's strange expression, the way he kept glancing away from her, anywhere but on the woman's face, on her curves, even as he answered her.

His hand heated, slicking with just a hint of sweat, in hers. Weird.

Or maybe he hated being here just as much as she did.

They both needed air. Room to breathe. Think. Sort out the whirlwind of events over the past year that led them to today. Trapped in a room filled with socialites, billionaires, athletes, doctors, investors, aka the rich and famous of New York City.

Living a lie.

The weight of it could drown her.

The main ballroom of the 1917 mansion added to the suffocation, with its heavy dark paneling, ornate coffered ceiling, and parquet flooring. Oil paintings of bankers and cotton owners who had owned the twenty-thousand-square-foot home presided over the event. The home was now in the possession of a former basketball player for the Knicks. An athlete turned celebrity sportscaster who was into raising money for Doctors without Borders, a charity she could certainly get behind. Not that Jess had any money to invest, but Felipe did, which kept them—him, but yes, because of the lie they perpetuated, her too—on social rosters and highbrow guest lists.

It also kept her conveniently in his folded grip. Not that she minded Felipe's hand tucked into hers—he'd been more than generous this year, sacrificing more than she ever intended or expected.

But that was Felipe. Surprising. Charming. Loyal.

Safe.

Not the kind of guy who'd ask her to dangle over a cliff with him. Or tell her to hold on as they drove a four-wheeler through a forest fire. Not bossy or flirtatious or impulsive.

Not dangerous.

"I'm sorry, *chérie*, I should have introduced you. This is Gabrielle Martinique."

Oops. Felipe had taken her silence for annoyance.

Wait. Gabrielle Martinique?

"Gabrielle," Jess said, finding her socialite smile. She held out her hand.

"And this is Selene Taggert, my fiancée," Felipe finished without a hiccup in his voice. She glanced at him, and he too wore a socialite smile.

Jess tried not to wince at the name of his friend or the relationship title. Or at the flicker of surprise, even hurt, that crossed the woman's face. So, the poor woman didn't know.

Apparently, the gossip hadn't yet traveled overseas.

"Nice to meet you," Gabrielle said, her voice a smooth ribbon of chocolate. "Felipe is a lucky man."

Jess wanted to cringe for Felipe, to take the woman aside and rescue his breaking heart. Because one look at his tight-lipped smile and the bob of his Adam's apple told her he was as trapped as she was.

What a mess she'd made for both of them.

"As am I," Jess said. "Although you can call me Jess."

Gabrielle frowned, and why not? No one on this side of her Jekyll-and-Hyde life knew her as Jess Tagg.

No, she'd always be, no matter how far she ran, Selene Jessica Taggert, heiress to the estate of former billionaire Damien Taggert, the man who had bilked thousands of investors out of their life's savings.

More precisely, she was his turncoat daughter who put him away to save her own hide, and maybe—according to a few websites she'd made the mistake of reading—squirreled away her own billions in fraudulently gained funds.

Never.

She'd left it all, money, name, and reputation, gladly behind and fled to Montana to rebuild her life with only pocket change and her own two hands. Had purchased a house for a dollar and remodeled it with every extra dime she earned as the EMT for a private rescue team called PEAK.

How she missed her house, the redolence of sawdust, fresh paint, and stain, the ache in her bones from a day of painting or sanding or even sheetrocking. With the memory came the image of Pete Brooks, dusted in white from sanding sheetrock or splattered with lime-green paint, grinning at her as they took a donut break.

She was suddenly ravenous.

"Felipe, you must take her to Paris again," Gabrielle said now.

Oh. So Gabrielle *did* remember her. Interesting.

"There is nothing like strolling down the gardens of the Palais-Royal in September," she was saying, her tone a little husky, inviting, her gaze on Felipe. "The entire city becomes a watercolor painting, especially the gardens of Versailles. And they have the most delicious *vin chaud*. Don't you remember, Felipe?"

He nodded, his smile pained even to Jess's eye, and she wanted to throttle Gabrielle. What was her game here?

Perhaps now might be the time to end the charade.

If it wasn't already too late.

"It sounds divine," Jess said and eased her hand out of Felipe's. "In fact, I think Felipe would very much like to return to Paris, wouldn't you, darling?"

Felipe frowned. Gabrielle glanced at him.

Jess met his gaze. *It's okay. Really.* "I'm going to go find a sandwich." She gave him a smile, something that hinted of the friendship, the truth between them, and left him there to have a real conversation with the woman he loved.

Her heart could break for all of them.

A cellist played in the corner, a Bach solo in G minor, and she stopped by the marble fireplace for a moment to listen before she spotted a waiter and followed him.

There had to be a kitchen somewhere in this mansion.

The stairwell circled up the middle of the seven stories, lit by a stained glass dome. She'd read that the place had fourteen fireplaces, an indoor pool, and a squash court, not to mention the elevator and the three terraces that overlooked 69th Street.

The waiter headed down to the main floor and she suspected even farther, to the original kitchen, located in the basement.

But no, he circled around to the back of the house, through a narrow hallway. She followed and emerged into a working culinary kitchen lined with stainless steel surfaces, a massive chop-block counter, and a kitchen brigade attired in chef's whites. Assistants filled trays with canapés and aperitifs while waiters unloaded their empty trays.

The general buzz of conversation and activity halted when a chef in a *toque blanche* looked up and cleared his throat. His mouth drew tight a moment before he forced a smile. "Can I help you?"

18

Oops. Running away and hiding in Montana for five years had made her forget the rules.

"I'm sorry. I'm just . . . I was wondering if you had something simpler than the . . . well, they are delicious, but . . ." She glanced at the canapés. "I'm so sorry. Thank you."

She shook her head and turned to leave, but a waiter banged through the door behind her, blocking her path.

Maybe she wasn't hungry at all.

She just needed air.

Turning, Jess made for a door across the room, the one propped open to let the steamy air of the kitchen escape.

The night might not be layered with the pine-laced, musty autumn scent of the Rocky Mountains, but at least outside she might momentarily escape the choices that left her hungry and raw.

"Miss—"

"I'm fine," she said as she stepped into the alleyway alongside the house. Narrow, maybe ten feet wide, the alley smelled of diesel oil, dirt, and not a little refuse.

But a cool breeze tickled her skin, and she descended the stairway, aiming for the private parking lot behind the house.

Where hopefully their driver waited in the Taggert family Cadillac.

The sickly sweet scent of cigarette smoke clouded the air, and she coughed, then put her hand over her nose—more for the combined scents of the alley than the secondhand smoke.

A garish whistle arrested her attention, followed by, "Selene Taggert. Making a run for it. As usual."

She glanced around for the voice and spotted a man, midthirties maybe, leaning against the opposite wall, half-hidden in the shadow beyond the luminance escaping the kitchen door.

He had dark hair, with enough of a thatch of whisker to be called a beard, and wore a black T-shirt, a pair of jeans, and a baseball hat on backward. She recognized a logo on his shirt but couldn't make it out. Probably with the catering company.

The char from his cigarette glowed red in the darkness.

She ignored him, walking away.

"Oh, you're too good to talk to me?"

She glanced over her shoulder. "No. Just . . . please leave me alone."

"How's Daddy?"

She drew in a breath. "He's fine, thank you." Considering he'd had a heart attack and was serving 101 years in federal prison.

"Of course he is." The man had pushed off the wall. "Because even in jail, your type gets first-class surgeons and a fancy room."

She whirled around. "He's in prison. He didn't get—"

And she stopped herself. Because it didn't matter what she said. The public thought what they wanted, despite the truth. At every event, there were a few who showed up with signs, banners, and once even mud. She shook her head and turned around to keep walking. "I don't want any trouble. I'm just looking for my driver."

"Oh, your *driver*."

His steps quickened behind her, and she picked up her pace. But she was wearing five-inch stilettos and clearly he was wearing something more substantial because he moved around her, blocking her path. She stopped short.

"What are you doing?" she said, her voice more surprised than panicked.

"Scared?" he said, and smiled. With her heels, she was about his height, but he had a good hundred pounds on her. His eyes held something dangerous.

It lit a flare of panic inside her. She swallowed it down. "Please get out of my way."

"You smell good." He leaned in, as if to catch a whiff.

Hot panic flashed through her, and she slapped him. Oh, she

knew better—had been taught better, but sometimes she just . . .
well, she reacted.

And then regretted.

The story of her life. Not anymore. Now she took pains to make
sure people didn't get hurt. At least if she could help it.

He touched the back of his hand to his jaw. "Really? A man
pays you a compliment and—"

"Please, leave me alone." Shoot, now her voice shook.

Noises from the kitchen, the traffic on 69th, the hum of air
conditioners, and a thousand other city sounds spilled out into
the street. But if she screamed, certainly someone would hear.

And then, oh joy, she'd land in the papers, again.

Better to flee. She turned, her eyes on the kitchen door.

He grabbed her left arm, snatching her back. "I thought you
were heading to the parking lot." His fingers dug in, a vise grip
on her flesh.

"Let me go," she said. "Or I'll scream."

He jerked her close to him, his breath on her skin. "Scream.
Do you really think anyone would rush to save *you*?"

It happened fast, but she'd worked it out a second before she
acted. She pivoted and used her momentum to slam her palm
into his face—one, two, three hard hits that snapped his face back
as she ripped her arm from his grip.

The man jerked away from her. "What the—"

She turned to run just as he gave a shout of fury and lunged
at her.

Her beginner Krav Maga moves fled from her mind. She
screamed, threw her hands over her head.

The rest she didn't figure out until later, after the cycling lights
of the patrol cars, the ambulance screaming into the city, after
Felipe drew a sane breath and she found her voice.

Her driver, a man named Kais, had saved her.

New to the family and hired by Felipe, Kais was dark, broad-shouldered, and had thick arms, as if he spent his off time at Gold's Gym. However, he attired himself as a driver, in a plain black suit and matching tie, and Jess had never given him any mind—until he grabbed her attacker and shoved him against the limestone wall and slammed his fist into his face.

Her attacker howled as blood spurted from his nose onto his shirt. He railed out, but Kais towered over him a good four inches, and in a second, he had the man cowed. He drove his knee into his chest.

"You're going to break his ribs!" Sure, the man had assaulted her, but the violence drove her into the fray. "Stop!"

Kais lifted the man up by his shirt and delivered an uppercut into his chest.

She could practically hear the bones crushing, see the bruises forming. "Stop!"

Her driver let him go. Just like that, Mr. Menace had turned into a victim, crumpled in the fetal position in the alleyway with blood pooling beneath him.

"What's wrong with you?" Jess glared up at Kais even as she knelt next to the man. "Lean forward—you don't want to choke."

A few of the kitchen staff gathered on the stoop.

"I need towels! Right now!"

"Ma'am," Kais started. "He was—"

"I know! Just call 911. We need an ambulance."

"You're going to be okay," she said, her voice pitching low. "What's your name?"

One of the female prep chefs had run down the steps and now shoved towels into her hand. "That's Ryan," she said, her voice shaky.

Jess pressed the towel against his nose and helped him sit up. "You gotta lean forward, Ryan."

He moaned, his hand across his stomach. "I can't breathe—I can't—"

"Shh. Don't talk." She looked up at the crowd. "I need help moving him against the wall."

She said nothing when Kais stepped in and dragged him under the armpits to the wall where only moments earlier he'd been dismantling the guy.

"Get me some ice," Jess said, kneeling again in front of him. "Selene!"

She looked up as Felipe pushed through the crowd, practically falling down the steps to her. He took her by the shoulders.

"It's not my blood."

He seemed to take that in with a rattled breath, his dark eyes wide in hers, so much emotion in them she could probably give her heart away to him.

If it didn't already belong to someone else.

Someone from the crowd ran down the steps and shoved a bag into her hand. Cold and clammy, it was filled with crushed ice.

She turned to Ryan and pressed it to his ribs. "Hold this in place."

Sirens cut through the trauma, and it seemed everyone took a breath.

Ryan groaned, catching her hand on the ice pack, squeezing. His grip shook. Then, in a different voice than the one a few minutes back, this one broken, on shards of pain, "Why're you helping me?"

She looked at him, his wrecked, bloody face, her bloodstained hands, the tragedy of his behavior raw and ugly and nearly fatal, and had only one response. "Because you're hurt." She sighed, her throat thickening with so much truth she wanted to scream. "And I can't stand seeing people hurt."

———— + ————

"You're a very lucky man to have gotten out alive, Mr. Brooks."

Pete had heard that before—from his teammates, from his boss, from fellow incident commanders. Heard it after he'd survived a cave-in last year while digging out survivors in a fallout shelter. Heard it from Jess after they'd outrun a bear in Glacier National Park. Even heard it from his fellow teammates on his hotshot wildland firefighting team.

But hearing the words from the ER doc, a pretty woman named Hensley, who was dressed in scrubs and wearing the tragedy of today's events on her face, made him look up, gave him pause.

He didn't believe in luck—just guts and training and maybe a little good timing, but today . . . Pete's gaze flickered over to the man sitting across the hall in the opposite ER bay.

Pete had learned his name from Aimee—Roger Ellis. They'd had to sedate him when he first arrived.

Pete supposed they'd have to sedate him, too, if he'd watched the woman he loved drown.

"I'd like to keep you overnight, just to make sure your lungs don't develop a bacterial infection from the water—"

"I'm fine," Pete said and pushed off the table. "Discharge me. I have work to do."

Doc Hensley frowned at him. "Only if you promise to come back if you develop a cough or a fever."

"Yeah, whatever." He reached for the jacket he'd worn trying to keep warm after he and the team finally gave up the search for the woman.

They'd rescued the baby, however—a miracle, right there. She'd gone into the drink, but one of the boat rescuers swept her up and managed to revive her.

She lay in ICU, still fighting for her life.

"I'll send a nurse back with your discharge papers," Doc Hensley said. "Try and stay alive, okay?" She touched his arm, smiled, a nod to the fact that she knew why he'd gone into the river. Why he'd shown up here nearly hypothermic.

"Thanks," he said quietly.

She left him and he stood for a moment, then gathered up his courage and walked over to Ellis. Took a breath. "I'm sorry for your loss."

A beat passed between them, then Ellis looked up. He bore the wreckage on his face.

His mouth opened, then closed, and he simply stared at Pete.

Pete swallowed, his breath brittle in his chest.

"She had her," Ellis said softly. "She had her, and then you took her away."

Pete frowned, trying to sort out the man's words.

Ellis released a hot, shaky breath and stared past him. "Have you ever been married, Mr. Brooks?"

"No," Pete said softly. Almost, but . . .

Ellis made a sound deep in his throat. "Then you don't know what it means to love someone to the marrow of your body. To pledge to protect her, to hand over everything of yourself gladly knowing you never want it back."

Pete said nothing.

Ellis looked at him, his gaze raw with grief. "You don't know what it feels like to try and hold on to her, only to have her ripped out of your hands. Only to watch her disappear." He closed his eyes.

Pete had been among the men who'd had to drag Ellis from the water, thrashing, kicking. The man had landed a few blows, and Pete had the bruises to prove it. But now he said nothing, his jaw tight.

"You don't know how it feels to lose the love of your life," Ellis whispered.

Another beat, and Pete didn't know what to say, how to reach out and help. He shifted his feet, his jaw tight. Bowed his head.

"Don't you have *anyone* that you love?"

The question emerged harsh, almost accusingly, and Pete's head snapped up. He simply reacted. "Yeah, actually, I do. Her name is Jess."

Ellis met his eyes, something in them Pete couldn't quite read. But the man's grief blew through his defenses, and he found himself putting a hand on Ellis's shoulder. His voice cut low. "And I would be destroyed if anything happened to her." He considered his words and realized he meant them, even now. "So when I tell you I'm sorry we didn't save your wife, I mean it."

The man stiffened under his touch. "She had her, man. She had the baby, and if you hadn't tried to grab her—".

Pete withdrew his hand.

Ellis started to sob.

His throat thick, Pete finally eased away, his eyes burning. He could blame fatigue and perhaps the residual trauma of the night, but the man's words churned through him.

"You don't know how it feels to lose the love of your life."

Yeah, he actually did know how it felt to lose the person who made you feel whole. To have that person in your arms, only to let her slip away.

In fact, he still bore the bruises. Still harbored the regrets that chased him from sleep.

So, yeah, he knew what grief felt like. He was still locked inside it, and with little encouragement, Pete could crawl right back into the hospital bed, curl into a ball beside Ellis, and weep with him.

But it wouldn't help. Pete just had to keep moving.

He emerged into the ER waiting room to find Walsh waiting for him.

"They said they might keep you overnight," Walsh said as he rose from a chair.

"Just get me back to the hotel," Pete mumbled.

He followed Walsh out to the van, under the relentless drizzle, and got in, staring into the darkness.

"A bunch of us are having dinner in the hotel bar. There's karaoke."

Pete just shook his head.

A buzzing in his pocket made him dig out his cell phone.

A text from Ben King, country music star and part-time rescuer. His wife, Kacey, flew the chopper for the PEAK Rescue team back in Montana.

> Pete! Are you coming to my wedding reception?
> Your invitation came back Return to Sender.

The last thing Pete wanted to do was attend the gala wedding reception of his buddy Ben King.

He should have never given that verbal RSVP back this summer when Ben showed up married and announced the party after a SAR operation in Minnesota. Pete had clearly been suffering from a case of desperate hope that Jess might also decide to show up.

Pete texted back.

> Oops. On the road a lot. Address forwarding
> must have expired. Sorry. I don't know. Maybe.

The return text came back almost immediately.

> Don't let me down, bro. Bring a friend!

Pete tucked away his phone. He stared out the window at the wind and the rain.

"Everything okay?" Walsh said as he turned into the parking lot of the hotel.

"Yeah. Just the past, trying to find me." Reeling him back home. Back to the place where it all began.

The place, maybe, where finally it could end.

2

THE ODOR OF CHAR EMBEDDED NED'S SKIN, his hair, and he could nearly taste the soot in his teeth. The smoke filled his nostrils, burned his throat, the fire a roar as it closed in around him.

Don't stop! Run.

The words pulsed inside Ned Marshall in time with his own heartbeat.

They were right—if he quit now, people could die.

He could die.

Heat. It enflamed his skin, his own sweat coating his body, running in rivers down his face, blinding him. But it wasn't the burn of the forest fire licking at his neck but the agony in his knee that had him nearly roaring in pain.

His twisted, nearly torn ACL threatened to send him into the dry, pine-needled soil.

"Ned! Keep up!" The voice cut through the layer of fog and smoke that haunted the trees and cut off visibility from the rest of the team. The voice of Jed, his jump boss, the one guy Ned had to impress.

He was already crying from the smoke, so he might as well let the pain erupt through him, give in to the wail building inside him. His grunting became audible as he pushed himself, his boots crushing branches, the straps of the ninety-pound pack he carried digging into his shoulders.

It didn't even help that Jed had chosen a downhill path for their escape, because with every jarring step, Ned's knee wanted to quit.

Jed came barreling through the smoke. "You're nearly a half mile behind the rest!" He grabbed Ned's shoulder strap and hauled him forward.

That did it.

Ned's knee buckled—might have even gone sideways—and he crashed, skidding face-first into the roughened soil.

Jed nearly came down on top of him, his hand just barely breaking free of the pack.

For a second, Ned simply lay there, writhing, the pain coiling through him.

"What the—are you injured?" Jed knelt beside him, his face grubby, his helmet dirty and banged up, such fury in his expression that Ned nearly lied.

Again.

Except he could hardly deny the way he wanted to curl into the fetal position and howl, clutch his knee like a child and weep with frustration.

"You were injured on the training jump, weren't you?" Jed said, hauling him up without mercy. He pulled Ned's arm over his shoulder, tucking his own around Ned's waist.

Ned didn't answer.

Jed shook his head, and right about then, Reuben, the big sawyer for the Jude County Smokejumpers, showed up, took one look at the situation, and came in for the assist.

They dragged his sorry carcass out of the burning training fire to bench him.

And not just for this op but for the rest of the season. It had felt like for the rest of his life, frankly.

"Ned. What are you doing?" A kick to his boots and Ned raised his arm off his burning eyes and blinked at the outline of his father standing at the foot of his bench. "Are you sleeping?"

"No. I'm . . ." Well, *regrouping* might be the right word, but he didn't want to say that to his father. Because that would mean telling his father the truth.

Including his failures.

Garrett Marshall didn't know the meaning of failure, or the word *quit,* not when he took over the family farm and converted it to a very rare yet successful Minnesota winery. He hadn't quit when the vines froze, year after year, hadn't quit until he found the right grapes to survive the northern frosts. He'd taught his sons not to quit—starting with his oldest, Fraser, now a navy SEAL, and then the middle, Jonas, who had the propensity to drive right into the middle of a tornado just to watch it spin. He'd even passed the concept down to his adopted son, Creed, who'd survived three days buried underground this summer after a tornado hit their school.

Even their sister, Iris, had no-quit in her. She had to, being the only woman referee in the NFL.

Apparently, the only one who failed was Ned, and even then, he'd gone down with a fight.

But his strained ACL had kicked him in the teeth, sent him home to recuperate and become, well, a farmhand.

He would have rather been left in the sooty soil for the fire to consume him. Everything he'd worked for had gone up in smoke the day Jed disqualified him from the smokejumpers team.

Well, he'd show Jed. He'd show them all.

No more quitting, ever.

He wasn't going to end up a farmhand, either.

As if he might be reading Ned's thoughts, his father reached out his hand to help him up. "No quitting now, son. We have three more barrels to finish toasting. I need to rack off this wine and get it into the barrels tomorrow."

Ned ignored the offer of help but sat up. "Actually, I already finished them."

Garrett's eyebrow raised. "All three?"

"Just finished toasting them," Ned said. "They're ready for new wine."

Garrett sat down beside him, glanced over at him. And for a second, he actually looked impressed.

"You took the barrels apart and sanded all the staves?"

Ned nodded.

"Replaced the hoops—"

"And roasted the barrels over the fire. Yes. If it's one thing I know how to do, Dad, it's tend a fire."

That got a sideways smile.

In fact, that was all he'd done for the past two weeks. Unhooping the barrels, taking apart the staves, sanding them back down to the grain, reassembling them, tending the fire that would toast them, then setting the barrels over the flame. Giving them a light roast to re-season the wine, then rinsing them off, rehooping them, and finally restacking them in the barn for refilling.

Tedious, tiring, and sooty work, although those exact words could describe his summers as a smokejumper.

Somehow, however, it felt different. Smokejumping included jumping out of a plane, camaraderie, and not a little adrenaline.

He couldn't bear the thought of being a farmer for the rest of his life. Still, it was a job, for now. "They're back together, rehooped and ready to go."

Silence, then, "I had always hoped that one of my sons would go into the family business." He gave Ned's leg a pat. "Apparently, it's you."

Aw, wait. "Dad—"

32

Garrett held up his hand. "Just think about it, Ned. It's not like you have anything else on your radar, right?"

Right now. He could run a defensive play right now and tell his father.

I'm going to be a SEAL.

But somehow unfolding that hope from where he'd tucked it inside his chest . . . no.

Because he might not quit, but he could *fail*. So many hoops to jump through to get from sitting in the barn with his father to that trident being pounded into his chest on some sandy beach. Each hoop, from qualification to boot camp, to pre-BUD/S to Hell Week to SQT, meant more strain on his knee, which was still achy from today's five-mile conditioning run. He should probably ease up on his training.

It was simply embarrassing to fail in a family of overachievers.

So he just nodded, and it was a spear to his chest when his father grinned, his expression so full of hope Ned just had to look away.

"Tomorrow we start racking off the wine." Garrett clamped his hand on Ned's shoulder. "First day of vintner apprenticeship."

Oh brother. Never mind that he'd helped his father rack off wine into barrels for the past fifteen years, since he was eight years old. But he nodded, a sigh building inside.

Even though he couldn't tell his father, or any of his family, not yet, he still ached with the news, needing to tell *someone. I joined the navy. I'm trying to become a SEAL.* Someone who wouldn't look at him like he was crazy for wanting to dream so big. Someone who wouldn't compare him to Fraser, his superstar brother, or probe around his reasons why.

He didn't have a why. He just had a want.

And right now, that want included telling someone who might be, well, impressed.

Someone like Shae Johnson.

His father had left for the house, and Ned followed slowly, flicking off the lights in the barn. With the stars spilling into the velvety darkness overhead, he tucked his gloves into the back pocket of his jeans and pulled out his cell phone. Opened his text app.

Read Shae's last message.

> I really miss you. There's a wedding reception this weekend for Ben King, and I've decided to go. But I could use a date . . . No pressure, but if you decided to show up and take me dancing, I'll let you show me those two-step moves you keep bragging about. Did I mention I miss you?

I miss you too, Shae.

He hadn't expected to fall in love—and he wasn't sure he was in love, really. Just knew that meeting Shae this summer had changed everything, for a while. Maybe he'd put too much into their two-week whirlwind romance, but a tornado and the stress of searching for Creed added an intensity to a relationship that threw down roots, rich with emotion and promises that usually took years to bloom.

He blamed her beautiful, misty, pale sky-blue eyes. They were the first thing he'd noticed about her. Crazy, since they'd been hiding in a building that had been threatening to come down around them, a tornado blowing over them that shattered windows and overturned cars. She was bravely trying to staunch the flow of blood on country music singer Benjamin King's arm, a tear he'd received from breaking a window. Ned hadn't stopped to think, simply pulled off his shirt and pressed it to the wound. Mumbled something about being an EMT and a smokejumper, but really . . .

He'd been caught by those eyes that looked at him as if he could stop the chaos, save the world—and heaven help him, he wanted to believe her.

Over the next few days, during the desperate search for his

brother, he'd told her things in the wee hours. Things that he hadn't even known about himself until she flushed them into the open. Things that she hadn't laughed at.

Like the fact that his training injury had wrecked him more than he'd expected. Or the truth that—and he hadn't admitted this to anyone until somehow, lying under the stars, Shae's hand in his, he'd let his dreams spool out—he even thought about joining the navy, becoming a SEAL, being a bona fide hero.

She hadn't laughed. And he'd rolled over, propped his head on his hand, and traced her beautiful face with a curious finger. With her cute nose, silky blonde hair, and the Milky Way shining in her eyes, he couldn't stop himself from kissing her. The summer wind played a melody in the apple trees nearby, the sweet smell of cut grass and ripening grapes stirring the sense of freedom and youth, and it didn't take long before he'd had to roll away, breathing hard, grasping at a few vows to himself.

So yeah, him joining the navy wasn't world-altering news, but he'd wanted to tell Shae first.

In person.

And preferably on a dance floor with her arms hooked around his neck, those sky-blue, believing eyes in his.

He headed into the house, upstairs to his room. Took a shower. Packed a bag.

Left a note for his father.

Then, in the wee hours of the morning, he got into his truck, pulled out, and set his GPS on Mercy Falls, Montana.

———— + ————

"One more." Pete shoved his empty glass toward the bartender. And while he wanted to fill it to the brim with something stronger than the tonic water from the bar tap, he knew himself.

Or at least the man he'd been.

Still, there was something about nearly drowning that made a man thirsty. Parched right to his marrow with the emptiness of needing more, so much more. Every time he closed his eyes, the caravan pulled him down, turning his breath to fire in his lungs. Trapping him. Drowning him.

Shoot, his stomach just might erupt, and it wasn't from the bar fries and his half-eaten burger.

He buried his head in his arms on the bar.

On stage, a couple had queued up a karaoke machine and were belting out, of all things, one of country music duo Montgomery King's covers. Oh swell, now Ben was haunting him.

> *Golden tan, a laugh for the band*
> *I see you in the crowd, waving your Coke can*
> *I like your smile, stay for a while*
> *Huddle up around the fire*
> *It's all right, stay for the night*
> *Let's chase away the cold and do it right*
>
> *C'mon, baby, let's start a fire*

Yeah, that was hardly fair. Too easily he conjured up the sweet image—a longing more than a memory—of swaying with Jess on the dance floor at the Gray Pony Saloon back in Mercy Falls. Could nearly feel her body against him, curves and heat and the sense that she belonged to him. Her fingers twined through his formerly long hair, and he could lose himself in her blue eyes, the way she looked at him like he might be her hero.

Wow, he was in trouble. His fatigue and near miss had clearly turned him into a brokenhearted Hallmark movie character.

He should get it through his head that Jess wasn't going to walk back into his life and fling herself into his arms, beg him to take her back, declare that she'd chosen the wrong man.

Really, she wasn't. Because he'd read the article Ty had forwarded him last month on his phone. A gossip column, yes, but he couldn't deny a picture of Selene Taggert on the arm of, yep, the Frenchman. Selene *Jess Tagge*rt—although he barely recognized the former EMT whom he'd taught to climb and rappel and even survive in the wilderness on pine sap and berries. He hated to admit it, but of course she looked like she belonged with the European, with her dressed in a body-hugging black gown, her blonde hair up in couture tangles.

Pete leaned up, feeling woozy. Turning in was probably the right idea. The teams worked on tight, round-the-clock shifts right now and he needed some z's before the 5:00 a.m. wake-up to search for more of the stranded and lost.

A hand clamped him on the shoulder just as he was about to rise, and he looked over to see the man who'd helped rescue the family from the river. He wore a black T-shirt with a team emblem of some sort, and was the same size and build as Pete, with maybe a little more military in his demeanor.

"That was some crazy out there today. You okay?" He held out his hand to Pete, who took it. "Hamilton Jones, people call me Ham."

Pete nodded. "Pete Brooks. We met once before, I think. In New York City?"

The eyes narrowed slightly, then a nod. "Right. That was you."

Pete made a noise of assent but had gone far enough down memory lane, especially if he wanted to keep Jess's memory at bay. "Thanks for the assist." He let a sigh escape. "I'm sorry about the wife."

"She was struggling and making it hard to hook her in. I should have taken the baby from her before I tried to hook her in, but she wouldn't let me." Ham shook his head. "They found her body past the bridge, in a tangle of roots and downed trees. I stopped in to check on the husband. He's . . . well, I'm not sure why he blames you, but he had a few choice words to say about you. I'd keep my distance in case you were entertaining ideas of swinging by the hospital."

Yeah, well, he'd borne the brunt of misplaced anger before. Years of it, actually, from his brother over the death of their father. Still, it didn't stop his grief over the man's loss.

"I already saw him," Pete said. He scrubbed a hand across his jaw. "I should have waited for help."

"They would have all died. At least the man has his child." Ham motioned to the bartender, who came over. "You got chocolate milk?"

The bartender nodded.

Ham offered no explanation but turned back to Pete. "The fries any good?"

"Soggy now, but yeah."

Ham caught the barkeeper's attention and pointed to the fries, adding them to his order.

"You been doing this long?" Ham asked, reaching for some bar nuts and a napkin.

"About two years. Before that I was with a private rescue team in Montana, called PEAK—"

"Oh sure. I've heard of them. One of my guys' family was in a tornado a few months ago. The PEAK team helped find his kid brother and a bunch of other missing kids."

Small world. "Yeah, I was there. Little town in Minnesota. Who's your friend?"

"Fraser Marshall. I used to work with him on the teams."

Teams. "You were a SEAL?"

A bare nod, and Pete figured that was all he was going to get on that topic. He'd met a few former navy frogmen over the years, and they kept their pasts tucked tight to their chests.

The bartender delivered the milk and set the glass on a napkin. Ham thanked him, then took a drink. Grinned. "Yeah, that's what I needed."

Okay. Pete liked him. And the fact he hadn't trailed back around to their previous meeting in New York City. A fancy shindig for the Red Cross. By that time in the evening, Pete had been trying to find a way to escape. He didn't remember a word of that conversation at the dinner table with Ham. Might have even left before dessert.

"How'd you end up down here, in Missouri?"

Ham set down the glass. "My team volunteered. We saw the mess, decided to take a drive down, pitch in."

"Your team?"

"Jones, Inc, out of Minneapolis. We're private international medical relief and SAR contractors. We also do danger assessments and occasionally help with emergency evacs. We go to the places nobody wants to talk about, although we occasionally are hired to track down college students who've taken off to Cancun with Daddy's money. That's real fun."

Pete couldn't tell if he was kidding. "Well, thanks for pulling me out of the drink today."

"It got a little dicey there when you went down, but you were doing everything right. You probably would have found shore downriver."

"If I hadn't been skewered by a tree first."

One side of Ham's mouth lifted. "What-ifs. You can't let them roll around in your head or you'll never get any sleep."

Pete looked at his refilled glass of tonic water. Yeah, the what-ifs.

The bartender delivered Ham's basket of fries. He took it and eased off his stool, the basket in one hand, his milk in the other. "Join us if you want." He nodded toward a group of men now walking into the bar and commandeering a table. They all wore the same black shirts.

"Thanks," Pete said. "I'm heading up to bed."

Ham nodded. "Stay alive."

Pete lifted his glass in agreement, then set it down on the bar.

The what-ifs. Like what if he hadn't just stood by and watched another man steal the woman he loved?

And with that thought, Pete was standing at the edge of the Hall of Ocean Life in the American Museum of Natural History in NYC, stuffed into a tuxedo, a glass of champagne sweating in his hand, watching Selene Jessica Taggert glide in on the arm of the man Pete most wanted to strangle.

Pete knew he'd lost his mind a little when he'd agreed to attend the Red Cross gala event last fall. But that was what happened when you gave someone your heart and they walked away with it, all the way to NYC. You eventually had to go chasing after it.

And oh, Jess looked good. Especially under the glow of the blue lights that illuminated the dome of the glass ceiling, made to resemble the ocean and highlight the giant blue whale that arched over the expanse. A band played in the center square, and around it, round tables were set with golden centerpieces and placards that detailed the highlights of the activities for the year. The crowds gathered in the cocktail area.

He'd gone in with a set of social instructions from Alena, his director, but all thought flushed away when Jess floated into the room.

Suddenly, he couldn't breathe.

She wore her blonde hair down, a golden waterfall that he could nearly feel between his fingers. Diamonds glittered at her neck and ears, and a creamy white lace dress hugged her, from low-cut bodice down to the floor.

He knew she had curves, but she usually wore them under layers—a T-shirt, sweatshirt, jeans, a PEAK jacket. Now, his mouth turned a little parched, and he downed the glass of champagne while watching her.

She smiled as she greeted someone, offering an air kiss with those lips that could set his entire body on fire.

He set his drink on a tray and barely refrained from grabbing another.

Then he took a breath and headed across the room, weaving around tables and chairs, moving past conversation groups, smiling at his boss, a woman who believed in him more than he believed in himself sometimes. She chatted with Aimee Boomer, who glanced at Pete with a look in her eyes that he probably wore himself.

Hungry. Desperate. Aching.

And right now, he just didn't care what kind of raw expression he wore. Yes, Jess had a lot on her plate with her return home, from her father's recovery from open heart surgery, to helping her mother sell her apartment. He was trying to be patient, but his patience was starting to turn into panic. A month of communicating through texts, a couple short phone calls that were cut off too soon, and even a desperate email that he regretted sending from Ty's Gmail account told him that something wasn't right.

He was losing her.

Jess had practically vanished when he'd kissed her good-bye in Florida and gotten on a plane. He hadn't expected that he would need to chase her down. Not with the words "I choose you, Pete" embedded in his head.

And now his expression probably reflected a hint of the anger, the frustration churning up inside him. The fear that despite her words, she'd somehow ended up right back in her former fiancé's embrace.

Pete shouldn't have downed that champagne quite so quickly, on an empty, roiling stomach.

41

He was close enough to hear her laughter, to spot the way the Frenchman—Felipe St. Augustine—secured his hand on the small of her back. Possessive. Familiar.

Pete deliberately flexed his hands. No fists here.

He took a breath, searching for the right—the calm, not-reeking-with-hurt—words.

That was when she turned.

When she spotted him.

When her blue eyes widened, her mouth parted, the expression on her face flushed to horror. Panic.

Pete's jaw tightened as he broke into the conversation circle, which had dropped to silence, despite the hum around them.

She swallowed, her hand pressing to her chest, perhaps over her heart to see if it was still beating. He was wondering that himself.

"Pete?"

A hand on his shoulder broke him from the memory, and he came back to the seedy hotel bar just as Aimee slid onto the empty stool next to him. Someone was singing another country song, something twangy and sad from an up-and-coming singer.

> Looks like it's just me and the whiskey
> 'Cause you ain't here to kiss me . . .

"You okay?" Aimee asked. She wore an off-the-shoulder black sweatshirt, faded jeans, and flip-flops. Her short blonde hair, freshly washed, lay in tousled layers, and she smelled good—fresh and clean with a hint of something floral.

But it was the soft look in her eyes that had him answering, "Rough day."

"I'm sorry about the wife." Her hand went to his arm and squeezed. "We tried to get her."

"If I hadn't fallen in, maybe—"

"Stop. You saved the father. And you nearly died in the process."

He lifted a shoulder.

"Pete, no really. You scared me." Her smile had fallen, and with it any veil hiding how she felt about him.

In truth, they'd been dancing around this moment for the better part of two years. They'd gone out for dinner a few times, and once he found himself on the doorstep of her long-term hotel room late at night, lingering. But they'd simply ended up hanging out on the balcony overlooking Lake Michigan.

Because between them always hovered the ghost of Jess Tagg. And that was even before he'd returned to PEAK, given away his heart to Jess, asked her to marry him.

Oh, that had been a great idea.

And even months later—okay, even now—he couldn't seem to shake her out of his system. Break free of the crazy idea that they belonged together. That he was a changed man, a marrying kind of man.

A man worth coming home for.

"Sorry," he said to Aimee. "I didn't mean to scare you."

She touched his face, drew her thumb through the rough scrub of his whiskers, something tender in her eyes. "You're too brave for your own good."

He swallowed.

Her hand dropped to his arm, trailed down to his hand, and squeezed.

What-ifs. He saw them play out before him.

What if his hand closed around hers, and he tugged her close? Pressed a kiss onto those lips that parted just a little as his gaze roamed her face.

What if she kissed him back, maybe emitted an enticing sound of desire?

And what if he followed the loneliness and hurt right down into the past where the old Pete lingered, dormant, forbidden.

The old Pete who took all the anger, all the longings, all the hopes of who he wanted to be and shoved them behind a veneer of charm, husky flirtation, and short-term promises.

That Pete knew how to live with the hurt, the ache, the wounds. That Pete knew how to survive. That Pete just might be able to shake free, just for a while, from the grief that held him captive.

And, Aimee smelled freshly showered, something floral on her skin.

Pete tightened his jaw, seeing the promises—perhaps also short-term—in her eyes and took a breath.

"I need a shower," he said quietly. Which wasn't an answer at all, but rather a weird sort of reply to the question on her face.

"Mmmhmm," she said, her eyes—pretty, hazel with hints of blue—in his.

What if.

He finished his tonic water. Set it on the counter, his hand tight around the glass. Picked up his phone, the text message still on the screen: *Bring a friend.*

Bring a friend.

He glanced at Aimee. Heard Jess's voice replay in his head from that night in New York City.

"Pete! What are you doing here?"

No "I'm so glad to see you." No "I should have called you." No "I miss you desperately."

Right.

Pete gave Aimee a smile. "I . . . uh. I don't suppose that you're free this weekend. To go to . . . well, a wedding reception for my buddy Ben King?"

Her eyes widened. "The country music singer Ben King?"

44

He nodded.

"Are you kidding? Yeah. I'd love to go with you."

He liked the smile he lit in her eyes.

Maybe it was time to stop drowning and breathe again.

"Great."

She hadn't moved. Her gaze hung on to him, and he heard her words pulsing inside. *"I'd love to go with you."*

Right.

Oh boy.

"It's been a long day. I guess I'd better turn in," he said quietly. Slid off the stool. Considered her a long moment.

Then he held out his hand.

———— + ————

Joy to the world, she'd made the front page.

Jess folded the paper with a shake of her head and tossed it on the sofa table.

"At least it's below the fold," she mumbled, more to herself than to Felipe. She sank down on the arm of the leather Chesterfield and ran a hand across her brow. "Did you have to use the word *fiancée*?"

"What else would I call you?" Felipe stood with his back to her, one hand braced on the sash of the window, his fingers whitened. And she didn't have to stand close to him to see the tremble still vibrating through him.

Through her, too, honestly. *"Do you really think anyone would rush to save you?"* She shook her head to dislodge Ryan's voice, the way it raised gooseflesh on her skin.

Ryan's blood stained the front of Felipe's tuxedo shirt, a two-thousand dollar Stefano Ricci with French cuffs and crystal-trimmed silk. The fact that she even knew that made her a little disgusted.

Not that Felipe couldn't afford it or shouldn't be allowed to wear whatever he wanted, but she knew he'd probably throw the shirt away without a thought. And maybe that gave credence to the accusations that people like her family hadn't a clue how her father's crimes had decimated the working class. Something the *Times* loved to point out on a regular basis.

And with every mention, they included her supposed upcoming nuptials to millionaire Felipe St. Augustine.

Oh, the mess she'd made.

"I'm tired. I'm going to bed," Jess said.

"He could have killed you." Felipe's voice pitched so low she had to force herself to hear him over her still-thundering heartbeat. "You *do* realize that."

They'd spent half the night at New York Presbyterian Hospital—Felipe's crazy insistence that she be examined, not to mention her own need to know that Ryan would be okay.

She'd finished her gala evening by giving her statement to the NYPD.

She'd also changed out of her soiled dress and into a pair of hospital scrubs.

"He was just . . . angry, Felipe."

"He attacked you!" Felipe rounded on her, his dark eyes red-rimmed. He'd ripped his tie off and tucked it into his pocket, opened his collar at the neck, and spent a good portion of the night running a shaky hand through his now unkempt dark hair. He hadn't shaved, either, of course, which only added to his ruffled exterior.

Oh, if he could only see himself. Clearly he didn't care. "Did you not hear the police? He has a record of assault. If it weren't for Kais, you would be—"

"Kais could have *killed* him." She pushed up from the chair, the memory of her driver's attack now unraveling her own slim hold on her composure. "Wicked ninja skills for a driver, don't you think?"

Felipe stared at her. "He's former French Green Beret."

"Of course he is. He's not a driver, is he? Be honest—he's my bodyguard."

Felipe's mouth tightened as he stripped off his jacket and began to unbutton his soiled shirt. "It's about time."

"This is why I enrolled in those self-defense classes. I can take care of myself."

"Right. You against a two-hundred-pound man? That's laughable." He stripped off the shirt to the white undershirt beneath.

She just stared at him. "So now I get to lose my freedom along with my reputation."

He sighed. "Do you expect me to just let my future wife walk around unprotected?" Felipe threw his bloodied shirt onto the sofa and advanced on her. "Every day outside this window, there's at least one protester. You get mail constantly from someone asking—no *demanding*—you pay them back what your father stole. We've been ousted from at least three private restaurants because they can't handle the security needs of our visits. And don't tell me that you're sleeping because I see the hours you're putting into studying for your boards. And it's not because you're worried about passing them. It's because you have to do something to fill the nights, don't you?"

She drew in a breath. "If I don't pass my Step 1 boards, I can't apply for residency. I can't finish my medical degree."

"Finish it in France. After we get married."

Twice. She drew in a breath. Twice in the last minute he'd alluded to their supposed marriage. "Felipe, I'm not sure what you're thinking, but we're not actually . . . I'm not *really* marrying you."

She said it low, in case the words carried out into the marble hallway and bounced down to the bedroom where her mother convalesced. Or rather, deteriorated, because no one actually recovered from her condition. But she'd had good days recently. Good enough to make Jess believe that the lies were worth the cost.

Worth breaking Pete Brooks's heart.

I'm sorry, Pete.

He'd blocked her calls long ago. She'd have to track him down somewhere in the US and get on a plane if she wanted to explain.

It might not matter anymore, even if she did.

Felipe drew in a breath at her words, his jaw tight. "Unless you find the courage to tell your mother differently, we *are* getting married, Selene."

He glanced out into the hallway, where the sun had begun to gild the parquet floor through the tall windows overlooking Central Park and the Manhattan skyline. Jess had finally convinced her mother to sell the eleven-room penthouse and had spent the past six months packing boxes and trying to downsize.

Mostly, she hoped to hide the fact that despite her father's crimes, her mother still had her blue-blood income and assets. That's what happened when you came into a marriage with money and when your husband moved his resources into your name.

Jess hadn't touched her own trust fund principal and had donated the interest proceeds since she'd escaped the limelight. Frankly, it felt like blood money. But she'd need it now to finish medical school. Maybe do something to pay back humanity for her family's crimes.

Although, even Jess had to agree that the collective sins of her family might simply be too great. The Taggert name was now synonymous with the destruction of other people's lives.

Which was precisely why she'd changed it. Moved to Montana.

Fallen in love with a man who didn't know anything about her life in New York City. Who loved the woman he knew as an EMT, a rescuer, a home remodeler. A simple girl without a past who just wanted a clean slate.

Felipe took a step toward her. "Darling. Selene—"

"Jess."

"Selene." His eyes darkened. "You are Selene Jessica Taggert, and it's time to stop running. Yes, I was the one who suggested the arrangement, but you agreed. Because you knew in your heart who you really are, and it's why, ten months after our agreement, you still haven't told your mother the truth. Because you know your old life is over. Because you belong with me, and you've always known that. Embrace it. Let this romantic fantasy about Peter Brooks go. There is nothing left for you in Montana. It was . . ." He touched her cheek. "It was an adventure, ma chérie, one you needed. But you've found yourself now, and it's time to return to me. To *our* future."

His finger traced her jaw, and he stepped up to her, tipped her chin to face him. "I love you. I want to marry you."

She closed her eyes, fighting the urge to lay her head against his shoulder. "And what about Gabrielle?" She kept her voice soft so as not to sting.

He swallowed hard. She opened her eyes in time to see the answer linger in his gaze. He shook his head sharply. "She has . . . a different life."

Oh Felipe. She knew how it felt to wait for the one you loved to return that love. To hope, pray . . .

Poor Pete. She'd pined for him for three years, watching him self-destruct under the weight of his own past. And just when he opened his heart, found peace, and got a glimpse of a happy ending, she'd run off to New York City.

Done to him what he'd done to her. Made him wait. Made him watch her self-destruct.

But she wasn't the only one. "Felipe. You know you love Gabrielle. You always have, and you always will."

"I love you."

"You love her more."

He drew in a breath. "I love you enough." He rested his hand on her cheek. "And you love me enough also."

She considered him. He wasn't being unkind. He did love her, and she saw the memories in his expression. He'd been her first love. Her only love.

Until Pete.

"I may not be a cowboy, but I will protect you." Felipe drew her close, and his lips whispered across her cheek.

Pete was hardly a cowboy, but of course that's what Felipe saw in Pete's swagger, his Western drawl. Pete had Montana embedded in his cells, a rugged, get-'er-done aura that had spilled out of him and engulfed her. Somehow, with Pete she was brave.

She was Jess Tagg, rescuer.

Without him . . .

"Your mother longs for us to set a date and see us married. Before . . ." Felipe leaned back. "It is time to admit the truth, Selene. You belong with me."

He kissed her. His touch was so achingly familiar. Soft, but still a jolt went through her. The taste of the cigarette he'd smoked while waiting for her to finish with the cops. The lingering cologne, something exotic mixed with the scent of the street. The cotton of his undershirt beneath her hand, the hard planes of his gym-honed chest. His arms curled around her, tugging her in, and for a moment, she surrendered. She softened her mouth to him, let him linger. Call it fatigue or simply loneliness, but she could admit that being with Felipe felt like she'd unearthed a piece of herself that she'd buried so many years ago.

The Selene Taggert who lived in an insulated world of happy endings and nothing-ever-goes-wrongs.

She knew better now.

No. She was shaking her head even before she broke the kiss and pushed away, out of his arms. "No, Felipe—I can't—"

"Yes, you can!" He stepped back, his hands raised in surrender. "Make a decision. For all our sakes, Selene. We've waited long enough." His square jaw ground tight. "Marry me. This weekend, this month, I don't care, but marry me and let us get on with our lives. No more charades."

"What charades?"

The voice tumbled out on a hint of strength borne from years of scrutiny and scandal.

Jess caught Felipe's bowed head, the tiny shake of resignation even as she turned to face her mother.

Just because her illness confined her to a wheelchair didn't mean that Caroline Taggert had surrendered to disarray. Her personal assistant Helene had already coiffed her mother's graying hair, dressed her in a pantsuit, and applied enough makeup for her to appear, if not well, then far from ghastly.

Indeed, the disease had crept through her mind more than her body, although her mother had lost weight over the past year.

Not stature, however. Or the ability to make Jess choose her words.

Now, as her mother's assistant pushed her into the room, Caroline repeated, "What charade?" She pronounced the word like Felipe had, as if she might be British.

"It's nothing, Mother."

"Is that blood on your shirt, Felipe?" Her mother's glance had evidently fallen to the bundle on the sofa. "And what on earth are you wearing, Selene?"

"We had an incident," Felipe said, crouching by her chair. "But it is over, and everyone is all right."

Not entirely true, but . . .

Her mother's blue eyes cast over Jess, then back to Felipe. "I wish you two would move to Paris. It's so much safer."

"Your doctor is here." Jess sat on the arm of the Chesterfield.

51

"I am aware of my medical situation, Selene. I can find another doctor in France. But more importantly, what charade?"

Jess glanced at Felipe, who met her eyes.

Perhaps she'd been a fool to suggest—

"Wait. It's the wedding, isn't it? You're planning to elope, aren't you?" Her mother raised a groomed eyebrow. "This is why you've put off the date—because you're trying to circumvent the fanfare of a St. Augustine-Taggert wedding and scurry off to some Caribbean island for your nuptials."

Oh.

Jess closed her eyes, the lie too easy to perpetuate.

"Of course, I can't blame you, but . . . we still have friends in this town, you know."

"We know," Felipe said softly. "And in Paris. And perhaps it's simply too much. The mayhem a society wedding would cause." He slipped his hand over her mother's, squeezing. "An elopement is easier, don't you agree?"

Oh, he had a way with her mother that smoothed her rough edges, turned her mother into someone Jess once knew, before the scandal, the bracing headlines, before the accusations, the anger. Felipe had healed them all, in a way, with his grace.

Maybe she *should* marry him.

"You're probably right, Felipe. I just . . . I wanted more." Her mother offered a tight smile, so much unspoken in it. Indeed, they'd been cast into the no-man's-land of her father's betrayal, his sins, and no one had emerged unscathed.

Felipe pressed a kiss to her mother's forehead. "I must get out of these filthy clothes." He rose, then came over to Jess, pitching his voice low. "We will talk later, *non?*"

She nodded. He kissed her, softly, just a caress, then crossed the room and picked up his jacket and shirt. "Don't go anywhere. Not without Kais. Or me." He held her eyes until she acquiesced.

"Who is Kais?" her mother asked as Felipe left.

"You met him, Mother. He's our driver."

Caroline Taggert nodded, her gaze caught on the view out the window, or perhaps further, in a time, or a place. A muscle spasmed in her arm, another in her shoulder. She rarely went out anymore; her lack of coordination and occasional overactive reflexes were too hard to explain.

Besides, no one really understood Creutzfeldt-Jakob disease, the terminal illness that resembled Huntington's disease.

Jess had a few adjectives, however.

Cruel.

Insidious.

Heart-wrenching.

Her mother had progressed slower than most—but still, the insomnia, the muscle spasms, and most of all, the memory loss, inched her toward death each day. Worse was the anxiety and the depression that, despite her society upbringing, she struggled to hide.

So yeah, Jess had agreed to get engaged.

But she'd never meant for it to get this far, for the news to find its way to Page 6, for pictures to land on the internet.

Never meant for Felipe to put a ring on her finger.

"Perhaps you would consider wearing my dress," her mother said quietly, clearly coming back to herself. "I could get it refitted for you."

"Of course, Mother."

Helene came into the room. "Ma'am, your breakfast is ready." She wheeled her out, and Jess was going to pick up the hospital bag holding her soiled red dress when her cell phone rang.

She paused only a moment at the caller ID before she answered. "Hey, Ty."

Ty Remington, who had gone to college, even roomed with

Felipe, who knew her friends in New York City and the life she'd left behind.

Ty Remington, who had become her ally, her confidant, and even her cohort in crime as he helped her build a new life in Montana, hiding her secret for years.

Ty Remington, teammate of Pete Brooks, and the guy who had accidentally outed her secret to Pete while trying to protect Jess from his zealous reporter girlfriend, Brette Arnold.

And most importantly, Ty Remington, who knew that she still loved Pete to the marrow of her bones.

"Hey." The deep timbre of Ty's voice rolled through her, tugging her back to Montana, to the rugged beauty of the Rocky Mountains and the two-story Victorian she'd remodeled. A simpler life, with simpler goals. Rescue people. Fall in love. Live happily ever after. "Are you okay?"

His question stilled her. "Um . . ."

"Brette is subscribed to about a bazillion Google alerts, and one is for you. Were you attacked last night?"

Oh. Jess sighed and sank down on the sofa, her head in her hand. "I'm fine. It's just . . ."

"You sure you're fine? You sound tired."

"I was up all night. But . . . yeah. That about sums it up."

"We miss you out here. I'm not sure if you got Kacey's invite, but Ben and Kacey's wedding reception is this weekend. Come back to Montana."

His words made her ache. *"Come back to Montana."*

"I got the invite, but . . . I don't know. My mother—"

"This isn't about your mother, and we both know it. But don't worry, he's not coming."

He. As in Pete. Jess didn't know how to describe the darkness that crept through her at Ty's words. Relief—no. Disappointment, perhaps, but maybe just dread. Except . . . "Are you sure?

Because . . ." Well, frankly, a desperate part of her hoped that he might be there. "Sierra said he'd RSVPed this summer, when Ben announced the event."

"Oh. Maybe. Ben said his invitation came back Return to Sender. Ben mentioned that he was going to text him, but Pete's working search and rescue in Missouri, at the flooding there."

She'd seen the flood on the news. Half the state was under water, the result of one of the many hurricanes tracking inland.

"It doesn't matter what Pete does," Ty said. "Come to the reception. Everyone misses you."

Everyone misses you. She got up and walked to the window. Stared down at the hustle of 62nd Street. Yeah, she missed herself too.

"Okay. Just for the weekend." And if Pete didn't show up, she'd take it as a sign.

Or an answer. Whatever. Because it was time to make a decision.

3

NOTHING QUITE SPOKE TO THE TAMED RENEGADE in Pete like the arch of the blue Montana sky over a bejeweled range of Rocky Mountains. He could practically smell the freedom, taste the endless expanse in his veins as he stepped out of the Kalispell airport into the sweet autumn air. Rimmed on every side by the craggy scape of mountains, the Flathead Valley streamed with the crimson, amber, marigold, and deep greens of the season, the finest hint of wood smoke seasoning the breeze.

Sam Brooks leaned against his pickup idling at the curb. He wore a dress shirt rolled up to above his elbows, jeans, cowboy boots, and a pair of shades, clearly in his off-duty attire. "Bro!"

Pete slung his duffel bag—and Aimee's carry-on—in the bed of the pickup, then met his brother in a handshake-slash-man-hug. Sam plunked him on the back, soundly, then turned to Aimee. "Hey there. I didn't know Pete was bringing a friend."

"We work together," Pete said quickly. Because he didn't know what they were after the fiasco in his room two nights before. He could barely look at her.

What kind of guy invites a girl back to his room to, well . . . as it ended up, to watch a rerun of the Alabama-Clemson national championship.

It wasn't for trying—he'd intended to quiet the ghosts and let the old Pete take over.

Unfortunately, the moment he'd taken Aimee in his arms, Jess appeared in his mind, with her blue eyes in his and making those sounds he liked, and suddenly everything felt wrong and ruined and he'd ended up backing away from Aimee, plopping down on his ratty in-room sofa, and reaching for the remote.

And sure, there'd been some snuggling after that, but his heart wasn't in it.

He needed to get back in the game, figure out where the fun and easy Pete he relied on had disappeared to.

But, until then, he hadn't known how to back out of this weekend.

"This is Aimee," he now added to Sam, who took her hand and gave him a sidelong, eyebrows-up look even as he welcomed her to Montana.

She climbed in the back seat, and Pete slid into the front as Sam went around to the driver's side.

"Are you sure you want me to be here?" Aimee whispered, leaning up before Sam opened the door.

They'd gone over this a dozen times, and each time Pete tried to sound more convincing. To Aimee. To himself. "Of course," he almost snapped, but then he turned and, because he was desperate for this to go well, he kissed her, fast.

Her eyes widened, but she smiled.

Sam caught the kiss as he got in. His gaze skimmed over Aimee and landed on Pete a second before he grabbed his seat belt.

So he was moving on. Everybody could just get used to it.

"How long are you sticking around?" Sam pulled out onto the highway.

"Just the weekend. Our team is still helping with relief efforts."

Sam drummed his fingers on the steering wheel, a crazy weird smile touching his lips.

"Okay, what?"

"It's just . . . I have some big news, and I was hoping you'd stick around for it. We're announcing it Sunday night, at the Gray Pony."

Their old hangout, a barbecue place that also hosted some of the hottest country artists in the nation, thanks to their local superstar and the groom of the weekend, Benjamin King. He had opened his own record label and liked to try out talent on the local crowd.

"What's the news?"

Sam glanced at him, then Aimee. "Can you keep a secret?"

"Yes," Pete growled.

Sam cut his voice low, as if there might be others in the car who could hear them. "I popped the question. Willow and I are getting married."

"It only took you a *year*."

Sam frowned. "Thanks for that."

Aw shoot. He didn't have to be such a jerk. "Sorry, bro. Ignore me. I'm just tired. And peeved. It's been a long week."

"He nearly died," Aimee said.

Pete cringed. "No, I—"

"What?" Sam glanced over his shoulder at Aimee.

"Yeah. He was saving a family from their overturned caravan trapped in a river, and the current grabbed it and pinned him. He nearly drowned."

"I was fine." Clearly, he needed to go over a few ground rules with Aimee. Like no harrowing stories to his overly protective big brother.

Sam's mouth tightened.

"You almost weren't, though. It was the bravest thing I ever saw," Aimee said and put her hand on his shoulder.

Now he really was a jerk, because she deserved a guy a lot better than him. The kind of guy who wouldn't invite her back to his room in the first place. A guy who actually wanted to spend time with her.

What was wrong with him?

Pete put his hand on hers and gave a little squeeze. Glanced over his shoulder and smiled.

Aimee had a cuteness about her, with that blonde hair pulled back in two tiny braids, her face tanned from so many hours outdoors this summer. She wore a brown tank top, a pair of jeans, and flip-flops and had challenged him to the crossword puzzle on the plane.

In a different world, one that didn't include his scarred heart, they might have had a chance.

"You okay?" Sam asked, glancing at Pete. "Because to my memory, that's the second—"

"Leave it." He should have guessed that Sam would be keeping tabs on his way-too-frequent-for-his-own-good brushes with death.

Sam glanced back at Aimee. "So, do you know Ben King?"

"I'm a huge fan," Aimee said, and Pete let go of her hand. "When Pete invited me, I was thrilled. I didn't know he was married."

"He eloped this summer with Kacey. They just got around to holding the reception. Too many festivals and gigs this summer got in the way."

Pete listened to them exchange favorite songs, and Sam filled her in on Ben's involvement with the PEAK Rescue team, Pete's home for too many years. Years that he stuck around because of Jess.

He stared out the window as they drove toward Mercy Falls. To the grassy pastures, the rim of ragged mountains, the cattle and horses that gave the town an Old West feel. A small town that sat under the shadow of Glacier National Park, Mercy Falls hosted everyone from climbers to cowboys to country music wannabes.

Even firefighters and national park workers. Pete had been the former before he was a rescuer.

In fact, he'd been risking his life for as long as he could remember. Only recently had he lost his grip and seen the odds turn on him. It left him with a chill, his mistakes piling up against him in the middle of the night to haunt him, wring him out in a cold sweat.

With Jess in his life, he hadn't lived quite so recklessly, maybe.

He listened to Aimee and Sam chat, his mind churning. Please, please let Jess *not* be here this weekend. He hadn't worked up the courage to ask Sam, but the thought of her showing up sat in his gut like a live coal, burning a hole through him.

And if she showed up with Felipe, well . . .

Yes, this was possibly a very, very bad idea.

———— + ————

There would be no catastrophes on her watch. Not anymore.

Not that anyone would die at the gala wedding reception of Benjamin and Kacey King, but Esme Shaw—now Shae Johnson, thanks to her alias for the past five years—was tired of trouble.

Of running. Of hiding.

Frankly, of thinking about her past in general. She was ready for fresh starts and new tomorrows, and Ben and Kacey's party of the year seemed the right place to make her comeback. Or reset.

Whatever. After five years, it was simply time for her to come home, to face her mistakes, her grief. To start over.

Maybe even join the PEAK Rescue team.

Although she never expected to be attached to a climbing harness, balancing on a ladder some three stories above the floor, hanging paper chandeliers. Gage Watson, a team EMT and world-famous snowboarder, belayed her from below.

"A little more to the middle," said Ella, resident lawyer and Gage's girlfriend, who stood next to him, directing the process.

"We have three more to hang," Shae said. "And the center chandelier. Let's leave some room."

Ella considered her comment like she might be dissecting the testimony of a client. Shae had seen that exact look yesterday when Ella sat her down in the kitchen of Sierra and Ian's new bungalow and asked Shae if she was ready to file her statement about the crime she'd witnessed five years ago. The crime that included watching her boyfriend being beaten to death.

The crime perpetrated by a man still at-large.

And that fact, the fear he'd find her and finish what he started—no, she wasn't ready to relive it all again. She just wanted to erase the past and start fresh.

"Okay, you're right, we need to leave more room. Good call, Shae," Ella said. She wore her auburn hair tied back, along with a black dress and leggings tucked into a pair of cowboy boots. She'd made the transition from state senator in Maine to county prosecutor in Montana without a hitch.

Or maybe that was simply what falling for the right man did. Changed your perspective.

Certainly being around Ned Marshall this summer had pivoted Shae from victim to . . . well, someone who wanted to take control of her life again. If she could just figure out how.

Ned was brave and strong, and even with his hurt knee, he didn't stay down. Although, she had to admit, the fact that he hadn't gone back to smokejumping helped edge her heart his direction. Brave was one thing. Reckless, with a head for danger and risky jobs, was another. Frankly, he had an idyllic life—his family's vineyard in Minnesota was exactly the place she might dream of, if she were dreaming of a life with Ned. Safe. Peaceful.

She could easily picture Ned on a tractor, the sun skimming his dark hair, bronzing his skin. She could even picture him working on the vats, his broad arms sanding the staves, as he'd explained to her in their chat two days ago. She'd texted him today, but he was probably still helping his father put the wine into barrels to age.

The whole thing sounded painfully fetching, a Hallmark movie kind of life. She hadn't exactly allowed herself to dream of a happy ending, not since she'd fled Montana.

But when she was with Ned, tucked into his arms, leaning against his muscled chest, staring at the stars . . . yeah, it ignited something she'd thought was dead inside her.

Hope.

And wasn't that a new perspective borne by love? Or something like it? For a moment, the thought of her hasty words, texted during a tired, raw moment, slipped through her. *"I could use a date . . ."*

She hadn't really meant it—how could she? Ned was busy in Minnesota.

And how serious were they, anyway? A two-week summer romance . . . yeah, that had the staying power of a warm autumn day. Something to be savored but not counted on.

Still, she'd try not to be jealous of Ian and Sierra, and even Gage and Ella and Ty and Brette. In fact, she'd even heard a rumor that Sam and Willow had gotten engaged.

Well, she was a few years behind them. And had a few loose ends to tie up in her life. Namely trying to break free of her nightmares to a new day.

Shae finished attaching the chandelier, climbed down the ladder, and unclipped herself from the belay line. Gage helped her move the ladder to the next spot. "Are you sure you don't want me to hang this?" he said as he handed her the next paper chandelier.

"And give up my handy tool belt? Never." She climbed up the ladder again.

"Where do you want these twinkly lights?" Brette Arnold, their photographer and Ty's girlfriend, came into the barn. She slid the box of lights on one of the nearly thirty round tables that already occupied the expansive area that once housed the PEAK team chopper.

"I was thinking of draping them around the rafters." Sierra came up, holding an armful of tulle. "I'm going to wrap the tulle around the columns."

She stopped and surveyed the array of decorations. Shae finished tacking in the chandelier, then came down to stand beside Sierra.

"Can I offer an idea?"

Sierra nodded.

"Let's wrap the twinkly lights around the columns, and tuft the tulle along the beams. It'll be easier to plug in the lights and make the ceiling not quite as soaring." Why Ben and Kacey had decided to hold their gala event in the PEAK barn, Shae couldn't quite comprehend. Not when they had Uncle Ian's beautiful former home, now theirs, to accommodate their three hundred or so guests.

And okay, maybe even the palatial log home wasn't large enough, but certainly they should try to impress the A-list country stars due to arrive. Then again, Ben and Kacey were down-home people, local Mercy Falls residents who had gotten married in a very private ceremony in front of a waterfall in Minneapolis. And since then declined offers from *People* and other magazines to buy their wedding photos. Even tonight's reception locale had been under the radar, with only the locals suspecting the location. Some of the guests were even staying at the ranch with Ben and Kacey.

But even though they were trying to keep it simple, Ben and Kacey had waited nearly three years to get married, to celebrate their future with their friends, and more than a handful of Nashville royalty were attending. So, while the party might be held in a barn, Shae intended to make it as glittering as she could.

A smile tipped Sierra's lips. "You're brilliant, Shae. Those designer skills are making a home run, again." She winked.

Shae tried not to feel like Sierra was trying too hard. Treating her like she might be skittish and about to bolt. "Thanks."

She directed Gage to move the ladder, took the final chandeliers, and headed up the ladder. The first she hung without a problem, but the second meant moving the ladder, and she didn't want to climb back down, then up, and if she just . . . leaned . . . out . . .

The ladder tipped, and her feet kicked it out, and in a blinding second, she had dropped the chandelier and was gripping the beam as the ladder careened away from her.

Gage just barely dodged it as it crashed to the ground with a bang that reverberated through the barn.

"Shae!"

Only it wasn't Gage's voice, or even Ella's or Sierra's, that echoed through the room.

Low and powerful, the voice could slip under her skin, fill her with warmth.

No. It couldn't be—and it wasn't like she could look, because she had a pretty firm grip on the rafter, both hands around it as she dangled over the three-story drop.

She'd forgotten to reclip in her belay line.

"Stay there!" Again, the voice, and it rippled through her, adding just a little oomph to her hold.

"Not going anywhere," she said to everyone below. "But someone better hurry up and get the ladder back up here."

Her hands were starting to sweat. And no, she wasn't looking down, because it was a long, long way with a hard welcome onto the cement floor.

She heard scraping, then the ladder landed beside her, nearly unseating her hold on the beam. And when she tried to get her foot around it—

Nope.

"Just hold on!" said the voice, and steps shivered the ladder.

64

And then he was there, like he'd materialized out of a dream. She nearly let go with the shock of seeing him. Dark hair flattened under a baseball cap that he wore backwards, those amber-brown eyes, and the kind of shoulders that suggested he hadn't stopped working out since the last time she saw him.

He wrapped a piece of webbing around the beam and hooked her rope through the double carabiners. Then, he met her eyes and smiled. "Just reach out and hold on to me."

Seriously. It suddenly *felt* like a Hallmark movie, with the hero showing up to save her. Except she couldn't let go. She shook her head.

He laughed, a strange response, but she liked the way his eyes lit up. "It's okay, Shae. Just let go."

She hazarded a look down. And there was Gage, holding her on belay, and Ella with her hands over her mouth, and Sierra, looking pale.

She let go and practically leaped for Ned.

He caught her easily, holding her hard to his body. She hadn't realized she'd been shaking until she felt his firm embrace holding her tight.

"I got you."

She found a rung for her foot and balanced on it, the harness also supporting her weight. He directed her hand to a rung, closed his over hers. "You okay?"

"Are you kidding? What are you doing here?"

His smile dipped then, and oh, she hadn't meant it that way, so she kissed him hard and fast, with her other hand gripped into the front of his shirt, pulling him to herself.

He tasted of chocolate, like he'd eaten a Snickers bar, and a touch of coffee and smelled of twenty hours on the road, but his arm tightened around her waist and kept her secure against him on the ladder. When she leaned back, she met his eyes. Smiled.

"So, I'm hoping that's a yes to taking you dancing tonight," he said.

"Yes." And oh, she could stay on this ladder in his arms for the rest of time.

Except, they had a party to finish decorating for, and . . .

"I'm hoping you'll introduce us to your friend," Sierra said, and when Shae glanced down, she could see that Sierra's arms were folded, her posture turning wary aunt and protector on her.

But Gage was grinning at her, his eyes twinkling.

She climbed down the ladder first, then Ned, and after she introduced him as her, um, friend, to her aunt Sierra, she found his hand in hers, squeezing.

"You do know how to show up at exactly the right time, don't you?" she said.

"Apparently, I'm here to rescue you," Ned said, and winked.

"That's the last trouble I'm getting into, thanks," Shae said. "But I'm glad you're here anyway."

"No more kissing," Sierra said, walking by. "We have a party to put together."

But when Shae looked at Ned, at the grin on his face, well, she wasn't making any promises.

———— + ————

So, for a while there, Pete thought he could relax, just a bit, into the gala.

First of all, his team—*former* team—acted like they actually missed him. Snowboarder and EMT Gage, with his attorney girlfriend Ella, met him with a hug at the door of the huge PEAK barn, normally the home of their chopper but tonight the venue for Ben's whopper of a party.

The PEAK administrator and organizer of the soiree, Sierra, acted like she knew he'd make it all along, even had a place set for him at the PEAK table. Said nothing about the addition of Aimee, scooting in a place for her.

And then there was their other chopper pilot, fancy-pants cowboy Ty. Whose eyes widened just a second before he took his hand. "Great to see you, Pete," he said, and it didn't sound at all a lie.

Inside, Sam, who clearly couldn't keep even a hint of a secret, was showing off Willow's massive solitaire. Apparently they weren't waiting on the announcement after all. The guy had turned sappy on him.

To Pete's view, it seemed that Ben and Kacey had invited all of Nashville, from Brad Paisley and his cute wife and their two little boys, to Keith and Nicole, to Tim and Faith, and even a few new-comers—he thought he recognized Brett Young, a singer whom Ben had tried to woo to his label, Mountain Song Records. Pete remembered a conversation with Ben this summer, long after they rescued a group of teenagers, about his weariness at chasing the country music festival scene.

Ben seemed sufficiently recovered now, dressed in a tux, two-stepping with the bride, who wore a short white dress, probably reminiscent of her wedding day attire. It hugged her body, sparkled under the globe lights that hung from the heavy overhead beams. The barn was filled with white round tables adorned with cen-terpieces filled with what looked like oversized daisies, and on a table near the front, a gorgeous five-layered cake.

A male crooner on the front stage entertained the crowd with a cover of one of Ben's songs. Gage and Ella two-stepped along with Ben and Kacey while Ty and Brette swayed in the corner. Sam and Willow seemed content to stare into each other's eyes, and Pete had to avert his gaze.

Even his mother, now openly dating Chet, was on the dance floor, grinning at the old man like he had just saved the world.

"I'm not sure what's eating you, Pete, but shrug it off and let's dance."

Aimee had changed clothes at his mother's condo and emerged in a very non-grubby black dress that not only showed off her petite curves but stirred inside him the memory of taking her in his arms. Which only made him remember exactly how the night had ended, which set in his gut a frustrating mix of embarrassment and shame.

He should have listened to his instincts and stayed in Missouri.

Wow, he was a mess. And it wasn't just Aimee and the memory of their near tangle, but all of it—the desperate search for his brother so many years ago during which he'd first kissed Jess, the time they'd hidden from a grizzly, teaching her how to climb and rappel, finding her in the middle of a forest fire, and later, asking her to marry him.

He should be on the dance floor, happily swaying with—

"Please, Pete?" Aimee put a hand on his arm.

Yes. Time to move on. He dug deep and found a smile for her, took her hand, and led her right out into the middle. "Hang on to me and let me lead," he said before hitching his hand on her hip.

"I always let you lead," she said, winking.

Huh. And he wasn't so stupid as to not hear the suggestion there. So he might actually salvage this night. He found the beat and counted just a smidgen for her—quick, quick, slow, slow—and added them to the circling dancers.

She had light feet and a smile that should heal the fraying parts inside him. And when she tripped, he caught her around the waist, set her right, and she laughed.

It loosened the darkness inside, just a little. In fact, he'd managed to live without Jess in his life for nearly twenty-seven years. He could probably figure out how to survive again. If she wanted Moneybags and his French accent, then . . .

And this wasn't so bad. Maybe the best he could hope for. Aimee was a good partner for him. Fun.

The music had slowed, so he curled his arms around Aimee, drawing her close. She hung her arms around his neck, pressing her lithe body to his, and that's when Pete saw Jess Tagg walk in.

She wore a little black dress that flared out at her waist, hit just above her knees, and, shoot, just like in New York City, his heart simply stopped. Those legs. Under the dress, she wore a white blouse with puffy sleeves, and in theme with the event, a pair of cowboy boots. Her blonde hair flowed down her back, thick and full and shimmering in the light. When his heart restarted, he realized that she stood at the doorway, her arms tucked around her waist, her gaze scanning the room.

As if searching for him.

No. That was just his broken heart, hoping, getting him into trouble. He turned Aimee, his back to the door, but the coal inside him had burst to flame, searing through him.

"Pete? You okay?" Aimee leaned back. "You're breathing funny."

He nodded, managed to swallow, then bent his head, hiding it in her shoulder.

And that sent all the wrong signals, because Aimee pressed a kiss to his neck, molding her body to his.

Not a good idea . . .

Except, so what? He was tired of being the guy with the broken heart. So he lifted his head, found Aimee's eyes, and when she read his meaning and smiled, he kissed her. Something sweet but with enough ardor to suggest that whatever had gone wrong before wouldn't be a problem now. She tasted tangy and bright, and smelled of the lingering hint of summer, and when she tightened her hold around his neck, kissing him back, he knew she wanted him.

And shoot, that felt pretty good.

He smiled, one side of his mouth lifting up, a bit of Western charm in his voice. "Wanna get out of here?"

"Mmmhmm."

He took her hand, and out of the corner of his eye, he spotted a crowd around Jess—Sierra, and Gage, Willow, and of course Ty.

He tried not to feel betrayed.

His hand tightened on Aimee's as he led her off the dance floor toward their table.

"Wait here. I need to snag some keys." Pete glanced around for Sam. Spotted him talking with Ned Marshall. He knew Ned from his last year as a smokejumper for the Jude County Smoke-jumpers. He'd seen him this summer when he'd helped rescue Ned's brother. Pete had a hunch his appearance had something to do with Esme—no, Shae Johnson—who sat at a nearby table.

Pete stalked over to his brother. Leaned into his ear. "I need to get out of here."

Sam frowned at him. "Really?"

Pete lifted a shoulder.

"Aw, bro, just go talk to her." Sam glanced past him, and Pete didn't have to think hard to figure out at whom.

"No. It's over, Sam. I'm not that dense."

But Sam's eyes had widened, and when he glanced back at Pete, it was to take a breath and offer a smile. "Jess!"

Shoot.

Pete turned then, his jaw tight, bracing himself.

Not expecting in the least for Jess to come right up to him, her eyes glistening, and take his hand. "Hey, Sam," she said as an aside, but she met Pete's eyes, something of agony in her own.

What did she have to be so hurt about?

"We have to talk," she said.

"No, we don't," he retorted, but she had a grip on him and

70

was pulling him away from Sam. And what was he going to do, tussle with her right there?

"Fine, Jess. If this is how you want it to be, we'll do this." He didn't know where the words, the clipped tone came from—because inside his head, there was screaming.

And maybe just a smidgen of an urge to pick her up and simply run. Get her alone and find a place where he could look her in the eyes and ask why.

Because the last time he saw her, she'd told him she loved him. That she'd marry him.

And like a fool, he'd believed her.

So he let her drag him outside, and even stood dumbfounded when she rounded on him in the pocket of the shadows behind the barn.

They stood just outside the rim of lights but close enough for him to see the tears cutting down her face, the glistening of her blue eyes. "I realize I owe you a conversation," she said, "but . . . what, are you dating her?"

Seriously? He yanked his hand away from hers. Stared down at her, stupefied and slightly shaken at the fury on her face. Too many words rushed to his brain, accusations and even incredulous laughter. So why he decided to clarify, he hadn't a clue. "No . . . she's just a friend—"

"That you were kissing!"

This couldn't be happening. He held up his hands in disbelief. "You're *engaged*, Jess." He shook his head. "What was I supposed to do—wait forever? You made it pretty clear what you wanted."

"I'm not engaged, Pete." She ran a hand across her cheek, a violence in her action that had him stymied. "You can't believe everything you hear or read on the internet."

She stared at him, her expression fierce, as if he should have an answer for his actions.

71

And that was just enough.

"Yeah, well, I *didn't* just read about it. Ty told me. And frankly, he's a pretty reliable source when it comes to your secrets. And by the way, I can hear *silence* pretty well. I haven't heard from you . . . in almost a year, isn't it? And you show up tonight, hoping that I'll just sweep you into my arms, like nothing has happened?"

She stared at him. And deep inside his chest he heard his own pitiful *yes*.

Because he was on the verge of stepping in, pressing her against the barn, and kissing her like she *belonged* to him, with an edge of anger and plenty of desperation and a whole lot of broken-hearted *whys*.

He might not even care about any answers if she would just kiss him back, tell him—

Oh, he was a pitiful man.

He shook his head and was about to stalk past her when she undid him with her words. "You promised you would."

The words pieced like a blade between his ribs. And the pain, the anger went straight to his voice. "Let's talk about promises, shall we? Because the last thing you said to me was . . . I'm coming back, I *promise*."

She stared at him, swallowed. "And? I'm here. Right now. I'm here. And you're kissing someone else."

His mouth opened, but nothing emerged, not a retort, not a defense.

She whirled and headed off into the night, past the parked cars, into the darkness.

And clearly, out of his life.

Finally.

For good.

His eyes burned, his heart hammered, his entire body felt battered.

"Pete?"

The voice emerged from the front of the barn, and in a moment Aimee appeared, thin and small, worry on her face. "There you are. I couldn't find you, and for a second I thought you'd left without me." She came up to him and caught his hands. "So. Do you still want to get out of here?"

———— + ————

She'd handled *that* like an emotionally unstable thirteen-year-old.

Jess hadn't talked to him for nearly a year, despite her attempts. Really, a sane person couldn't hold on to the belief he'd wait for her, that he wouldn't have moved on with his life. He didn't deserve her anger, and she knew it. But oh, it had felt like a punch to her heart when she'd seen him kiss the blonde on the dance floor. And she'd clearly lost control of her common sense, not to mention her mouth.

Just keep walking. Don't look back.

Jess wrapped her arms around her waist in a feeble effort to hold herself together, barely stopping herself from fleeing into the darkness in a full-out sprint. A pale moon had risen, the rays parting the clouds and puddling on the ground. Wind stirred the autumn scent of loam and the hint of pine off the mountains. She cleared the parking area, not sure where she might be headed.

Home. She needed to go home.

Except, where exactly might that be?

"Come to the reception. Everyone misses you."

Her breath hiccupped out of her and she emitted a sound so pitiful she just wanted to cringe. She'd only rehearsed a thousand other conversations in her head on the five-hour flight this morning. Conversations from a casual "Hey, Pete, how are you? Can we talk?" to . . . well, none of them had gone over the edge, with her grabbing Pete and dragging him outside into the shadows to attack him.

He was with someone else now.

Petite, cute, the kind of girl Pete Brooks would definitely be kissing.

And from the look of it, who knew what else.

She closed her eyes, her teeth grinding so tight her jaw ached. No. That wasn't Pete—not anymore.

Please.

Although what did she expect, really? She knew the kind of free-spirited, broken man Pete had been before she'd fallen for him. Not the dating kind. And for sure not the marrying kind.

Maybe she'd expected too much from him.

Except, that wasn't fair. She'd been the one who ran back to New York City.

She'd been the one who hadn't kept her promise.

A glow from the porch of the PEAK-house-turned-HQ tugged at her, the memories brutal as they slashed through her. Pete, bending over the map in the middle of the room, charting out a potential search grid, his blond hair tied back in a bun, a two-day grizzle on his face, his T-shirt stretching across his broad shoulders.

Pete, sitting on a stool at the counter, his blue eyes watching her across the room. Pete chasing her out to the equipment room to watch her pack an emergency bag. His hands on hers, checking her knots before they climbed. If she really wanted to torture herself, she'd let her memories drag her back to the time he'd protected her with his body, tucking her close under him as they'd hidden from a bear. Or even made her climb on his back, front-rappelling down a mountain on the craziest ride she'd ever taken.

No, loving Pete, handing over her heart to him, might have been the craziest ride. Exhilarating but dangerous.

She became a woman she didn't know when she was with him. Brave. Resourceful. And apparently one who didn't live in reality.

She angled away from the house, a hand over her mouth, staring at the ground as she passed a couple kissing on the back of a tailgate.

They broke the kiss and she mumbled an apology.

"It's okay," the man said.

But the woman slid off the tailgate. "Jess, you okay?"

Jess stopped. Frowned. *Shae?* Long blonde hair, slim and pretty, the woman wore a dress, leggings, boots, and a jean jacket. What was she doing here?

By Shae's worried expression, Jess knew she must look a mess. She'd given up any hope of not crying, and probably her nose was running, and who knew what wretched noises had escaped, despite her efforts. Worse, she still hadn't gotten control of her mouth. "I'm an idiot. A complete fool."

Nice, Jess.

The man had turned now, slipping his arm around Shae. Handsome, lean, and tall, he looked like the kind of man who stuck around. Kept his promises.

"Sorry," she said again and pressed her hand over her mouth to stop herself from completely unraveling right here.

Oh, who was she kidding? What else was she going to do? Because although Ty had suggested just a weekend trip, if she were honest, a too large part of herself had hoped that Pete might be here, alone, pining—yes, she was that foolish to believe he hadn't moved on—waiting to pull her into his arms.

That one thought had made her slip off Felipe's engagement ring and leave it on the bureau.

And no, she hadn't figured anything out beyond that.

Clearly now she had her answer. Even if she loved Pete, he no longer loved her.

"Can we help?" This from the man, who wore a genuine expression that fortified his offer.

She just stared at him, her brain scanning through her options. A ride to the airport? No . . . not yet. "No. I just need to see if Willow will let me take her car home. She met Sam here, and . . ."

"I'll drive you," he said. "C'mon."

Shae smiled up at him, and the look she gave the man pinched Jess's heart.

Once upon a time, she'd looked at Pete that way, she was sure of it.

"Are you sure?" Jess said.

"Yes." This from Shae, who headed to the truck and opened the passenger door to the back seat. She left it open in invitation while she hopped in the front.

Maybe this was simply the easiest answer. Go back to her house in Mercy Falls, find her footing, wait for daylight, and figure out what to do with the shambles of her life.

Jess got in.

The man introduced himself as Ned Marshall, from Minnesota. Jess had a faint memory of a PEAK Rescue operation that took place there this summer after a tornado. But she was too tired to chase it all the way to Ned and Shae.

Instead, she looked out the window, at the darkness, refusing to weep. Aloud.

Silence pulsed against the engine and road noise until Jess couldn't ignore it. "I know you heard the fight." They weren't so far away that they wouldn't have heard the raised voices.

Shae glanced at Ned, but she said nothing.

Jess didn't know why she felt the need to defend Pete. "It's not his fault—not really. Pete didn't know I was going to be here. I was planning on . . . well, stupid me thought I'd surprise him. I wasn't sure he'd even be here, but when Sierra said he'd RSVPed . . ." Jess took a breath. "Sorry. I'm just babbling."

Ned turned onto the highway toward Mercy Falls.

She looked out the window, speaking more for herself than her audience. "It wasn't fair, what I did to him. I just . . ." She sighed. "I am two different people, and each version of myself loves a different man."

She'd never said that out loud, but hearing it made her close her eyes.

"So, are you engaged?"

The question speared through her. She ran a thumb over the indentation in her left finger. "Not right now."

Silence. And in it Jess heard Felipe's voice. "*No more charades.*"

"What's the matter?" Shae's voice, talking to Ned.

"I think that truck is following us."

Jess's head came up at his answer. What? She turned to check out the lights behind them. "Well, he is behind—oh. It's going to—" Jess reached for her belt.

The truck ramrodded them, and she threw her hand out to brace herself against the seat.

In the front seat, Shae screamed.

"What the—" Ned shouted as he sped up. "He's trying to run us off the road."

"Who is it?" Jess turned back around, clipping in her belt. For a crazy second, she imagined Ryan, his breath on her face.

But here, in Montana?

The truck was moving up beside them.

She fumbled for her phone, yanked it from her cowboy boot. *Please, Pete, please.*

She couldn't bear to stop and think about how sad it might be that he was still her first call.

The pickup revved, and she didn't want to know how fast they were going. The call went to voice mail, and she hung up.

Called her second option. The headlights peeled back the

darkness, and she spotted the Mercy River running alongside the opposite side of the road, silvery and bright.

"Selene?"

The voice on the other end answered just as Ned shouted, "Hang on!"

The truck came at them again.

Metal crunched, and Ned hit the brakes, tires squealing. Jess screamed and dropped the phone. They rutted into the ditch, bouncing hard in the dirt. The truck sped out ahead.

Ned did a hard U-ey and floored it back along the highway, putting distance between them and the truck.

Her shoulder ached where she'd hit it against the door. And somewhere from the darkened floorboards, she could hear Felipe's voice shouting. She bent over, searching, her fingers finding the phone.

"Ian's not picking up!" Shae said.

She'd accidentally hung up on Felipe. No, no—she opened her app and hit speed dial. "Pick up, please."

"I don't know what he's driving, but it's got more under the hood than I have." Ned glanced in the rearview mirror.

Shae jerked around.

Jess couldn't help it—she too turned. The headlines seared into her eyes, and she looked away, heard the voice just as the truck hit them again. *"This is Pete. You know what to do . . ."*

Ned hit the brakes, fighting for control, but the truck pushed them forward and over to the ditch.

"Hang on to something!" Ned yelled.

Brakes squealed.

Jess dropped the phone again, pressed one hand to the roof, the other to the front seat even as the truck shifted weight and lurched over.

They went airborne. A scream—Jess's or maybe Shae's, she didn't know—and her heart left her body.

They landed passenger side down, and the world turned into bright lights and splashes of pain as they bounced. Rolled.

And rolled.

Jess's head hit the window, her body jerking as they tumbled, the truck catapulting toward the Mercy River.

And somewhere in the back of her mind, she heard the message playing out. *"Leave me a message and I'll get back to you as soon as I can . . ."*

4

PETE MIGHT AS WELL FACE IT.

Jess had wrecked him.

And it wasn't just her words, although they had the power to strip his thoughts, his actions, and leave him standing like a fool in the star-strewn darkness. *I'm not engaged, Pete. You can't believe everything you hear or read on the internet.*

Not engaged.

No, that couldn't be right. He'd read an article in the paper—or at least an internet version of one forwarded to him by Ty.

He'd never seen Jess so unraveled; her words practically shook out of her. And it undid him a little too, her final words turning him raw. *"You promised you would."*

Promised that he'd wait for her. Promised that he wouldn't stop loving her.

Yeah, well, he'd kept that promise, despite his best efforts.

Which was why he was now leaning against the Mercy River bridge, staring at the moonlight tracing a luminous finger through the dark waters, silvered now and again by the waves.

"Pete, what are we doing here?" Aimee asked quietly.

Good question. Because after he'd taken Aimee's hand, after he'd gone back inside the barn and snagged Sam's keys, he'd driven almost in empty, rootless desperation to anywhere but where he wanted to go . . . Jess's fixer-upper Victorian.

Somehow, he ended up at the romantic arch of the town bridge. With benches and twinkle lights, the bridge held a few memories of pre-Jess romantic walks with faces he could barely remember.

He'd hoped his old instincts might kick in, because he needed the Pete he'd once been. The Pete who kept his emotions soundly tucked away, who lived off his charm and humor. That Pete helped him survive, fooled him into believing he had enough in his life.

Apparently, it wasn't enough anymore, because the old Pete refused to emerge, replaced by this pitiful version who couldn't shake free of a sick sort of roil in his gut.

Aimee wrapped her arms around his waist.

His hand went down to wrap around hers. Lifted her grip away from him. He turned to meet her eyes. "I'm sorry," he said softly. "I . . ." He drew in a breath and shook his head. "I can't."

Her smile fell. The moonlight had turned her hair to gold. Yes, Jess had certainly wrecked him because Aimee was a good catch.

"I guess I knew that." She touched his arm. "You're not even here, are you?"

He frowned.

"A girl knows when she's the replacement, Pete. And I think I've known that for a while now." She raised her gaze to him. "Right?"

He swallowed, his throat tight. "I don't know what's wrong with me. I'm probably the thickest guy around because I should have seen this coming. She's never . . . well, she said she loved me, but . . ." Pete shook his head. "I guess not like I loved her."

He tightened his jaw before he did something really stupid and started to tear up. Sheesh.

He needed to be over her. "I'm sorry. I know I dragged you out here, and I thought we could have a good time, but . . ."

"Pete." Aimee touched his chest. "I never wanted a one-night

stand with you. I admire you. And respect you, and sure, you're
. . . worth waiting around for. Even going home with." She gave
a chagrined smile. "I'm not going to say that I'm not that kind
of girl, but I'm starting to get the feeling you're not that kind
of guy."

He gave a harsh laugh. "Yeah, well, you don't know me that
well."

"I know what I see. There's a kindness in you, Pete, beyond the
risk-taker, the hero, even the stubborn jerk who sometimes nearly
gets himself killed."

"Is that some kind of weird compliment?"

"I'm not sure." She had such pretty eyes that he wanted to like
her enough to be the guy she saw. "Maybe."

He let out a sound of frustration. "I don't know what's wrong
with me. Because honestly, I used to be that guy. I *was* fun."

"You're still fun. Just the kind of fun that prefers a football game
with a girl over breaking her heart in the morning."

Oh. Well. His face heated in the darkness.

"By the way, that night in Missouri? I thought you were a gentle-
man."

Huh.

"Pete, you're more than you see. And I wish I could be the one
to convince you of that, but I think you're only going to hear it
from one person."

He drew in a breath. "She doesn't want me."

Aimee had a hold of a button on his shirt, not opening it, just
rubbing her thumb on it. "I wish I could believe that, because I'd
be after you hard." She patted his chest then, and dropped her
hand. "But that's why you can't really look at me. Why when you
kiss me, you hold back. Why right now, you're wishing you could
just drop me off at the airport."

"Aimee—"

82

She held up her hand. "Like I said, a woman knows when she's the replacement."

The wind took her hair, and he had a crazy urge to tame it, tuck it behind her ear. Run his hand down her face in a caress.

But that's where his desire ended. He kept his hands tucked in his pockets.

"Track her down, Pete, and convince this woman who has so devastated your heart to give you another chance."

He gave a wry chuckle. "Yeah, well, I've been there, done that. Remember the cave-in last summer? Out in Dawson?"

The memory flickered in Aimee's eyes, and of course she remembered it. She'd nearly leaped into his arms after she and the team had pulled him out of the earth and to safety.

"You took time off."

"I came home to propose to Jess."

She blinked, and he hated his bluntness. But she recovered well. "And?"

"She . . . well, it's complicated. While I was home, I found out that she had been engaged to someone else before, and then he walked back into her life. I told her that I would wait for her while she went back to New York and ended it." He sighed. "And I did wait, for an entire month."

"A month?"

He drew in a breath. "We texted at first, and talked a couple times, but she got swept up into her family's problems, and . . . I don't know. Maybe I read too much into it, but I got desperate and went to a charity event in New York City in the hope of talking to her."

"Desperate doesn't sound good."

"It wasn't . . . at first."

At first.

When he'd walked up to Jess and the circle of blue bloods, his heart in his hand. When she'd looked up, a hint of panic on her face and said, "Pete, what are you doing here?"

Yeah, he'd wanted to turn and run. Or maybe plow through the crowd, grab her up, and steal her back to Montana where maybe he had a chance of winning back her heart.

He was considering both options when the horror on her face slid away and a smile broke through, something sweet and incredulous but oh so overpowering that it flushed away his frustration, his anger. "I'm so glad to see you."

He'd stood stymied as Jess came over and kissed his cheek, like she might an old friend. Then she took his hand, her fingers soft in his, and turned to the group. "This is Pete Brooks. He's an incident commander with the Red Cross and a dear friend from Montana."

Pete managed a smile.

And then his gaze had fallen on Felipe's expression. Feigned smile, a tightness in his eyes. And it fueled a swell of possessiveness that Pete thought he'd tamed. His hand tightened on Jess's and he turned to her. "Can we talk, in private?"

She nodded and sweetly excused herself, as if they might be slipping away to discuss a financial contribution.

He refused to release her hand as he searched for a quiet place, finally dragging her into a room with the giant fossilized remains of a T. rex. It felt like the right place to discuss their decaying relationship.

She'd followed without a word. Only when he found a quiet, shadowed place behind a towering pillar did he take a breath and let her go. He swallowed hard to find the words.

When she turned to face him, her eyes glistened. "You came to New York."

"Of course I did. Jess, I've barely heard from you since you left."

"I . . . I called you."

"Twice, yes. But both times we got cut off and . . ." He wanted to touch her, to put his hands on her bare arms, that smooth skin. To pull her to himself, smell the fragrance of her hair, convince himself that the woman he loved hadn't somehow walked out of his arms into another's.

"I'm so sorry, Pete. It's been . . . complicated." Her face tightened. Shoot, he hadn't come here to make her cry. "I've been so busy . . ."

"What, going to parties with Felipe?" He didn't mean for the anger to return or to ignite her defenses, but . . . *busy*?

Her eyes darkened. "No! But yes, I've taken over my mother's social schedule. One that is quite exhausting, I might add."

Oh, cry him a river. "Why? You were supposed to come back and break up with Felipe. Not resume the life of Selene Taggert!"

"But I am Selene Taggert!" She drew in a hard breath, cut her voice low. "Too. I'm Selene too."

He didn't know what to do with that, except, "Of course you are. But I thought—" He reached out, unable to stop himself, and touched the smooth skin on her arm. Softening his voice, he tried to cull the anger from it.

"I thought, at best, you'd come here and then two weeks later, you'd be saying yes to me. Maybe that was crazy, but . . ." He touched her cheek. "Was it crazy?"

She shook her head, and the texture of pain in her eyes tore at him.

"Then what happened?"

Her eyes filled. "I think my mother is sick, Pete. She's tired and forgetful and even unsteady on her feet. She's fallen a couple times. I'm trying to get her in to see the doctor . . . I'm worried."

Oh.

"It might be just the strain of my father's surgery. We've been flying down to see him while he recovers, staying at a local hotel. It's been stressful."

"You saw your father."

She nodded, and he couldn't stop himself from reaching out to her, pulling her to himself. And breathing in the smell of her as she wrapped her arms up around his shoulders, as she rested her head on his chest.

This was his Jess. She was still here, still holding on to him. His voice softened. "Are you okay?"

She sighed. "My brother still isn't talking to me—he's in London, reinventing his life. But yeah. I'm okay. Felipe has been— oh . . ."

He'd tensed, despite his promise to himself not to go there, not to envision Felipe with his arms around her. Because then he'd have to fight the urge to take Felipe by the throat and throw him from a tall building.

She leaned away and met his eyes. "We're just friends, Pete. He's . . . yeah, he missed me, but it's not like it was. It won't be."

He wanted to believe her.

She caught his gaze, moved her hand inside his jacket, to smooth across his heart, and he couldn't stop himself from surrendering, from drawing her close.

He kissed her, forcing away the coil of fear in his chest, sinking into the sweet taste of her. Losing himself in the touch of her hands on his chest, the smell of her, something expensive yet decidedly familiar.

Yes, he would wait for her.

He backed up against the wall, leaning against it, drawing her to him in a lingering embrace until she finally pressed against him, breathing hard. "I need to get back to the gala."

"Jess—"

"Felipe will come looking for me."

He drew in a breath. "This—us—shouldn't be a surprise to him."

"It's not. It's just . . . we're going to Paris in the morning, and he was hoping to leave early."

He'd blinked at her, trying to untangle the words. "Paris?"

"It's a horse race called the *Prix de l'Arc de Triomphe*, and his stables compete every year."

He tried to ignore how easily the French rolled off her tongue. Never, not once, had she spoken French in the three years of knowing her.

"You have to go?"

She nodded. "I promised. It's . . . nothing."

"It's *Paris*." The crazy inside began to stir. "I wanted to bring you to Paris."

Actually, he hadn't thought it, but he would have, if she'd even hinted at wanting to go.

She smiled, shook her head. "What would you do in Paris?" And the little laugh she emitted sent a sliver deep into his heart. Drew blood.

His smile dimmed, his throat tightened.

"I promise to come back," she said softly. Then she kissed him again.

And he did everything he could to believe her.

Then.

Now, Pete came back to himself, standing on the Mercy Falls bridge, the water churning below him.

Aimee repeated his words about the encounter. "It wasn't good . . . at first? What do you mean?"

"She was surprised to see me. But then she told me she loved me. And I thought everything was going to work out."

"So, what happened?"

Oh. He couldn't unravel it all without sounding wretched and pitiful, so he forced a smile. "We both know that I'm not the marrying kind, right?"

87

Aimee frowned. "I think you're *exactly* the marrying kind, Pete Brooks." Then she rose up on her toes and kissed his cheek. "Now, bring me back to your mother's condo so I can pack and take an Uber to the airport in the morning."

He shook his head, but she nodded. "And I know it's late, but you go over to Jess's house and demand a few answers."

Answers. The kind that might destroy both of them. But maybe, finally, he could let her go.

Start over.

Pete gave in to the urge to catch Aimee's hair, let it twine between his fingers. "Thanks, Aimee."

"Don't break my heart, Pete. And don't make me change my mind. A girl can only take so much charm before she gives in."

He grinned, but her words lodged inside.

Apparently.

"I don't know where this will lead, Aimee. I can't promise—"

"Pete. I'm okay. Really." She patted his chest. "You're not the last man on earth."

He didn't know why that didn't make him feel any better.

———— + ————

Jess hadn't come 2,500 miles to die.

She'd outrun a grizzly, lived through a forest fire and a chopper crash, and even managed to climb the Eiffel Tower in high heels.

She wasn't going to die in the back of some seedy pickup.

And she certainly wasn't going to let anything happen to Shae. Not when the woman had finally found a way to come home.

But first Jess had to get free. She lay with her hands secured behind her, with what she assumed was duct tape strapping her wrists and ankles together. More tape pasted her mouth shut. She guessed they were in the bed of a pickup, given the hard stripes of metal pressing into her back and hips. With the wan moonlight pressing in through grimy side windows, she added a topper to her assessment.

Bodies edged up next to her, and she prayed with everything inside her they were Ned and Shae.

They weren't moving fast, and the road was bumpy and rough, jostling her hard, digging the planes of the truck bed into her hips.

Get free. The thought pulsed inside her, focusing her, and she stretched out her arms, pulling her shoulders down to get her bonded wrists past her backside. Contorting her body, she moved her arms down her legs, sitting up to bring them around her feet.

Her fingers found the edges of the tape over her mouth, and she worked it free, finally ripping hard. Her skin burned, raw where the tape dragged off a skin layer on her lips. But she gulped in a full breath, then moved her hands toward the bodies next to her.

Please be alive.

Her hands found a leg, then a torso and Ned's heartbeat, alive and thundering under her hand. She felt her way to the tape over his mouth and ripped it off.

He grunted. Then, "Where's Shae?" Ned kept his voice low.

She matched it. "Over here. Get your hands in front of you."

While he writhed, she found Shae, then her mouth, and worked the tape free. Not a hint of movement, and Jess felt her way down to her carotid artery. A steady thrum under her fingers.

"She's alive but unconscious."

Next to her, Ned had wrestled his arms in front of his body. "We need something to cut off this tape."

"Raise your arms above your head, then bring them down hard—the tape should break." She lay back, found room, and obeyed her own instructions. Please . . .

The tape broke free of her wrists.

Beside her, Ned had done the same. "How did you know that trick?"

"Self-defense training. Long story." She scrambled over to Shae, rolled her to her side, and began to work on her bonds, unwinding them from her wrists. Freeing her, she set her back and ran her hands down her arms, across her body, then down her legs. "Her ankle is really swollen, and I felt some sponginess in her ribs, maybe even blood. I can't tell in the dark."

They were still bumping through the forest, and a dip in the road jarred her hard into Ned. He caught her but grunted.

"You're hurt?"

"I'm fine. We need to get out of here." He moved to the back of the truck and, from the sound of it, tried the latch.

She guessed his words even before he hissed, "We're locked in."

Meanwhile, she tried to find her bearings out the window, her focus on the wan headlights peeling back the forest. But she saw only a knot of pine and poplar, a tangle of woods.

"We're not anywhere near Mercy Falls," she said. "That's all flatland and fields."

"Do you think he took us into the park?"

Glacier National Park, her stomping ground as a search and rescuer on the PEAK team for three years. She shook her head, then added, "No," because of course he couldn't see her. "Most of the roads in the park are pretty well maintained. This feels like a logging road."

"I was a smokejumper in the Kootenai National Forest. It was like this."

"So is the Swan Range, where we found Ty."

That brought a rush of swift, aching memories of the team's reception tonight. The way Sierra and Willow greeted her like a lost sister. Gage swinging her into his arms. Ty, his green eyes holding warmth.

It felt like coming home.

Until, of course, she'd spotted Pete, and then everything turned to poison.

"The Bob."

Ned's words brought her up cold, and she drew in a breath. "No."

"Why not? Who is this guy, and what does he want? If it's to kill us and hide our bodies, then where else but the Bob Marshall Wilderness? Even if we manage to get away, we'll never find our way out. We could be injured and eaten."

"Thanks for that."

"I'm just being honest."

"Be less honest."

"Let's find a weapon."

She heard him scrounging around the bed of the truck as she returned to Shae and held her hand above her mouth to confirm breathing.

They had to stop the truck. Anything short of that would injure Shae further.

She roused, groaning, and Jess moved close to her ear. "Shh, Shae. You're okay. You're with me and Ned. Don't move, don't talk."

Shae's hand came up to grasp her arm. "Jess?"

"I'm here. I know you're hurting—"

"What happened?"

"Do you remember the car crash?"

Silence, then, "Yeah. Where are we now?"

"A truck. Somewhere in the wilderness." She hoped Ned would keep the extras to himself.

"Jess . . . I think it's Blackburn who took us. It has to be."

Sheriff Blackburn? The name buzzed inside Jess's head, stirring a memory.

"Somehow he found out that I'm still alive."

And with those words, the memory focused. Randy Black-burn, the man who had killed a woman in the park five years ago, who had tracked down the only witnesses—Shae and her boyfriend, Dante—and killed Dante in front of Shae's eyes. Somehow Shae escaped to Minnesota, where she'd hidden for the past five years.

Until Sierra had found her and convinced her to come home just in time to search for her missing uncle Ian, lost at sea.

The PEAK team had found him, reunited him with Shae, and the last part of the story Jess remembered was Shae's fear that Randy still wanted to kill her.

"Why did you come back?"

No, no, that wasn't the question she really cared about—it just popped out.

"Blackburn left town a month ago, and I thought . . . I thought my uncle could protect me . . ." Her voice wavered. "I was just tired of running." Her voice hitched. "I'm sorry—I'm so sorry—"

"Shh." Ned had come up beside Jess and now leaned over Shae. "Shh, babe. It's going to be okay. I'm going to get you out of this, and you're going to be just fine." His voice betrayed a calm that Jess longed for, the kind of solid assurance she might find in Pete's—

Stop. He wasn't here to rescue her this time, and frankly, after their fight, he never would be again.

So . . . *think.*

Ned was thinking too. "These toppers are usually latched with clamps at the corners. If we can unlatch them, maybe we can kick it off. Then we can jump out."

"And Shae?"

"I can do it!"

"Shh." Ned moved close to her. "We'll do it together."

"Hold on to me!" Pete just couldn't help but be in Jess's head,

this time in his words to her as he'd burst out of a forest fire on a four-wheeler to save her life.

Stop it.

Jess ran her hand down the edge of the pickup, searching for the clamp. Found it rusty and unmovable. "I can't budge it."

"I got mine to move," Ned said. "Let me see if I can—"

The truck jerked hard, and Jess slammed into the side of the pickup. Shae cried out even as Ned reached for her.

"He's going to kill us," Ned hissed. He held Shae in his arms. "Hold on to her while I work on the bolt."

Jess crawled over to Shae, pulled her into her arms while Ned worked on another clamp. He stifled a sound of pain as the pickup rammed through ruts and runnels.

"Are you okay?"

He dropped the nut onto the bed of the truck. "Peeled back a fingernail." He moved over to the other nut and began to work on it.

They hit another bump, and Shae, brave girl, only grunted.

"Got it," Ned said as he scrambled back to them. "The last one doesn't want to budge, but I think if we lay on our backs and kick with our legs, we can rip the top free. Only, we'll have to be quick about it."

Shae groaned as Jess set her down and settled herself next to Ned on her back.

"Ready? On three."

He counted and she kicked up with everything inside her. The top lifted, popping free on three sides. The fourth stuck tight, but they'd managed to move it off its grid.

"Again!" Ned said.

The driver slowed, sliding them forward, but they kicked again, and this time the fiberglass cracked around the mounted point.

Ned scrambled to his feet, set his back to the topper and lifted the mass off its moorings, moving it sideways on the pinned axis point like a sliding door. "We'll have to jump!"

The night air crested inside, and for a second, Jess sat paralyzed. Jump. From a moving truck.

"Jess!"

The truck skidded to a stop. She fell hard against the cab, fire shooting through her shoulder and down her arm. She bit back a cry.

"You gotta jump, Jess! Go. I got Shae."

Right. She felt her way toward the opening and ducked under the open edge.

Jump.

A curse sounded on the driver's side.

Ned had pulled Shae into his arms.

Just jump. She didn't know where the voice came from—it simply sounded familiar, bold, and not stopping to think, Jess leaped from the truck, off the passenger side. When she turned to help, Ned was right there, landing beside her with Shae clutched to him.

"Run!"

She whirled around and headed for the tangle of forest. A shot cracked through the air, ripping through the darkness.

She ducked, her hands up to protect her face.

Another shot shredded the forest.

"Keep running!" Ned plunged into the wild, a step behind her.

She hadn't a clue where she might be going. Her footsteps landed in soft loam, then cracking roots and fallen trees. She tripped over logs and bramble, cut her face on random snapping limbs, and nearly plowed into a tree. A panicked run into the wilderness that had no direction, propelled only by the shots behind her and Ned's labored breath.

The earth fell beneath her and she pitched forward, landing on her hands. Heat speared her side and she cried out. She could run right off a cliff and not know it until she was in midair.

Ned's hand in her jacket collar pulled her up. She bit down against the burn in her side as another shot bit at the trees.

"He's not stopping," Ned said, breathing hard.

No, he wasn't.

Jess held her hands straight out and kept running.

———— + ————

He'd landed wrong on his knee, and now Ned's only thought was, *Don't drop Shae.* Because although he knew she was light—he'd been surprised how light when he'd caught her earlier today on the ladder—he struggled to hold her.

It didn't help that his knee barked with every step, taunting him, as if it might suddenly give out and pitch them both into the brambles.

A branch slapped him hard across the arms. Although he could barely make her out, Jess ran a few steps ahead of him, plowing through the forest. And the word *run* might be generous when it came to him—his was more of a crazy Hunchback of Notre Dame jog. They weren't being quiet about their escape either, crashing through the forest like buffalo. No wonder they hadn't shaken whoever was firing at them.

Shae moaned, but like a trooper, she kept her arms locked around his neck.

Another shot, this one rebounding through the padding of night farther away, as if their pursuer might be headed in the wrong direction. Jess must have sensed it because she slowed, then stopped, breathing hard as she braced herself on a tree.

Ned stopped behind her, the sweat dripping down his back. "Don't stop," he said. Because if he did, he might collapse. And if he did that, he harbored slim hope of getting Shae back up into his arms.

Besides, right now, his knee seemed to be working. If they stopped to rest, it would swell up.

Except Shae moaned in his arms, something bone deep and grating on his heart.

"Hang in there," he said and pressed a hard kiss to her forehead.

"I'll be . . . okay," she managed. But her eyes closed and she winced.

"We need to find someplace to hide," he said to Jess. Because when he did stop to rest, he'd need to stay put and regroup.

Another shot. Shae stiffened in his arms.

"Apparently, I'm here to rescue you." He didn't know why those stupid words filled his head. Arrogant. His attempt to impress her, maybe. But he'd done a stellar job of *not* rescuing her. If he'd been a little smarter, seen the truck sooner, maybe not let the guy catch up to him, they wouldn't be running through a tangled, lethal woods.

Not that it was his fault, but . . . well, it was hard not to assign some blame, even to himself.

Jess grabbed his arm. "This way." She pointed toward what looked like a clearing. "There might be a river or something. Maybe a cave."

That could work.

She took off, and he followed.

Except his foot came down on a hollow log, breaking through hard. He pitched forward, all his weight to bear on his bad knee.

Just like that, they were down. Shae fell hard out of his arms and cried out, a horrible shrill sound of agony as she hit the ground.

"Shae!" Jess reappeared, knelt beside her.

Shae was curled into the fetal position. "I'm okay, I'm okay."

"I don't think you are!"

Another shot, and this time it echoed through Ned's soul.

"He's found us," Jess hissed.

Ned pushed to his feet. He knelt, gritted his teeth, and pulled Shae into his embrace. Sweat broke out on his forehead. "Run," he growled to Jess.

She turned and fled.

He followed, refusing the ache, the wobble in his knee, and strode hard after Jess, his head down, his jaw tight.

Shae grabbed his jacket. "I'm sorry."

"Not your fault," he said. "Sorry I dropped you. It won't happen again."

"I know," she said and turned her face into his chest, her other arm around his neck. "I trust you."

And nothing could have galvanized him more than her soft words.

So he plowed ahead, following Jess, catching up until her branches slapped him, until he could hear her breathe.

The ground smoothed out, turned firmer, no longer the spongy loam to cushion and capture his steps. And yes, like Jess had predicted, the tangle of forest thinned as if they might be headed to the open.

Jess picked up her speed as they burst from the forest, and he followed her, his feet scraping over rock, finding purchase.

Before him lay a dark pane of granite. Jess looked back at him, seemed to pause, then grabbed his jacket as if to help him.

He glanced down at Shae. "Hang on. We're going to be fine."

She nodded and managed a smile.

Then the world dropped out from beneath him. His body careened into midair as Jess's scream rent the darkness and they fell, and fell . . .

5

Of course, Pete ended up alone, stifling a shiver on Jess's front porch.

Waiting for the woman he loved—no, *once* loved, thank you—to show up.

Oh, who was he kidding? One look at him would confirm that he had turned into a sappy golden retriever.

Pete shoved his hands into his pockets and leaned against one of the columns of Jess's 1903 fixer-upper Victorian. Overhead the half-moon glowed, eerie and pale as the clouds boxed out the stars. Crispy leaves tumbled down the gutter, a crackle and rush that made him think of the late-night simmer of a forest fire, popping and snapping as it fought for life.

He should get in his car, drive to his mother's condo, wake up Aimee, and ask her to be his girlfriend. Finally let the wreckage of his relationship with Jess sink into the sand and disappear. He and Jess were over, forever and ever amen.

If only Aimee hadn't been correct. *"A girl knows when she's the replacement."*

Maybe *he* was the replacement. The rebound, the guy filling in for Jess's true love.

Oh boy. He hadn't even considered that. No wonder she hadn't come running back to him.

Except, *"I'm not engaged, Pete."* Those words tunneled through him and rooted him to the cold, abandoned front porch. Maybe, if he knew with clarity and 100 percent surety that Jess didn't want him . . .

He just needed a collar and a bone to gnaw on.

He'd knocked on the door, not just a few times, in case she'd gone to bed. He had even entertained the idea of climbing up the outside of the house to the Juliet balcony just outside her room.

But that just might get him arrested. And the last thing he needed was to end up in county lockup, with Sam shelling out bail money with a shake of his head.

Pete wanted the old version of himself back, but not the angry, hurting, trying-not-to-care jerk who'd gotten his father killed.

So no law-breaking tonight, if he could help it.

Headlights flashed at the end of the street. He watched as they strafed the road, the houses. The bulk behind them finally formed into a familiar pickup truck. Sam pulled into the drive, and Willow emerged from the passenger side. With long brown hair and a free spirit, Willow was everything Sam could never be—easygoing, sweet, sunshine in the darkness. She had probably saved Sam's life in every way that mattered.

Willow caught Sam's hand as they came up the walk. "Pete, what are you doing here?"

Pete wanted to get up, shrug, and run.

"I was . . . ah, shoot. Is Jess still at the reception?"

Willow frowned, gave Sam a quick glance. "I didn't see her after . . . well, after your fight."

Perfect. "It wasn't a fight."

"At one point, you were shouting," Sam said. "But don't worry—just the few of us standing near the doorway caught it." Sam moved past him, up to the porch. "No flowers? That's bold."

"I'm here, aren't I?" Pete got up, wiped the dust from the back of his jeans. "I sent Aimee home."

Sam opened the door, held it open for Willow. Considered Pete, his gaze enigmatic.

"What?"

"I'm just . . . sorry. That it didn't work out between you and Jess."

Pete pushed past him. "We're not done quite yet."

He came inside, and Willow turned on the lights. Like a magnet, his gaze went to the sofa, and the memory of comforting Jess when she found out about her father's heart attack over a year ago engulfed him. *"I love you, Pete. I choose you."*

Yeah, right. He walked into the kitchen and pulled out a chair at the table. "Mind if I wait?" he asked Willow as she opened the fridge.

"Not at all. Ice cream is in the freezer." She pulled out some chocolate milk and a glass.

"Did Jess say anything today . . . about . . ." He winced, looked away.

"About you?" She poured herself a glass of milk, another for Sam, who appeared in the doorway, his jacket off. "Sorry, no."

Pete's mouth tightened. The futility of camping out at Jess's in a blind hope that she'd take him back had him shaking his head. "Right. This is stupid. I should go." He stood up.

"Whoa—bro." Sam had taken the glass Willow offered. "Listen, I'm not sure what happened between you two, but now that you're here, stick around and give her the chance to explain herself. There had to be a reason she got so hot about you being with Aimee. That says that she hasn't given up on you two."

"Except for her being engaged."

Every time Pete said it aloud, the word landed in his gut like a fist.

"Then why would she care that you kissed another woman?"

100

Willow's mouth tightened around the edges, her eyes flashing. "Nobody missed that, Pete."

He looked away. Shook his head. "I can't believe I did this again." He pushed past Sam.

"Did what again?" Willow followed him into the hallway.

He rounded on her. "Chased her down. I just keep running back to her like a freakin' lost puppy." He pressed his fingers and thumb to his eyes, as if to scrub away the image lingering in his brain. "Last year I even followed her to Paris."

Silence, and he looked up to see Willow staring at him, Sam with his eyebrows up.

"Paris?" Sam said.

"Yeah, Paris," Pete snapped. "I got on a plane and followed her across the Atlantic Ocean."

"Why?" Willow whispered.

"Because I'm an idiot! Because I thought—" He took a breath. "Because I thought I could convince her to come home with me." He looked away, back to the living room, his jaw tight. "Because she said she loved me."

Thankfully, Sam didn't make a sound.

Willow, however, moved toward him. "What happened in Paris, Pete?"

He drew in a breath. "A lot. Everything. I proposed, again, and she said yes. Again."

"But . . . then how did she end up engaged to Felipe?"

"I don't know." He looked at Willow and tried not to break down weeping. "I left her in Paris. She was going to talk to Felipe and then come home. Instead, she refused my phone calls for the next two months. I'm such a fool."

"Or, a romantic," Willow said.

Pete frowned.

"What?" Willow said.

Sam laughed. "Right. Okay, honey, let's leave Pete alone." He hooked her hand and pulled her into the family room. Settled down on the sofa.

Pete wasn't romantic. Had never been romantic.

With a wince, he got it. At least enough of it.

And sure, she probably had real feelings for Pete, but as soon as he left her radar, she reverted to her real identity as Selene Taggert. Who belonged with Felipe St. Augustine.

Felipe was everything Pete wasn't. Sure, he hadn't spent the past five years saving lives with her, but maybe Jess didn't want that, not really. Maybe she wanted to be wooed with the lifestyle of the rich and famous.

Except none of that sounded like the Jess he knew, the woman he'd fallen in love with, who'd remodeled this very house with her own hands, played football with him in the backyard, enjoyed pizza on the porch watching the sun sink behind the mountains.

"You can't believe everything you read."

A car pulled up outside, the lights scraping across the door, and he took a breath.

He'd give her a chance to explain, unwind the tangles.

Footsteps sounded on the porch, and he was at the door, pulling it open, an apology on his lips. "Jess, I'm sorry it's so late but—"

Not Jess.

Pete easily recognized the man, with his cropped and gelled dark hair, square jaw, and dark brown eyes, the polar opposite to Pete's usually long, unruly blond hair, blue eyes. He wore a jean jacket over a black dress shirt and a pair of black jeans and stood on the stoop, bearing what Pete guessed might be his exact expression.

Startled.

And not a little annoyed.

"You," Felipe St. Augustine said. "What are you doing here?"

"Me?" Pete didn't move. "What are *you* doing here?"

"Selene called me."

It took Pete a half second. Jess had called Felipe. After she'd left Pete.

That ignited a tiny lick of fury inside him. "She called you. And what, you dematerialized in France and beamed here?"

Felipe's jaw tightened. "No. I was in America."

"Still. That's amazing timing, pal, even for Superman. Got a little windburn there?"

"We had a fight. I was worried, so I followed her to Montana. I was in-flight when she called."

Oh. A fight.

The flame flickered.

"I'm not engaged, Pete."

He grabbed ahold of her words with everything he had. "She clearly doesn't want to be with you, so turn around and—"

Felipe hit the door with his palm, slamming it open. "Where is she?"

Pete longed to grab him by the scruff of his dress collar. Instead he fisted his hands at his sides. Stepped back to allow him room. "Not here."

"She was upset when she called." His gaze landed hard on Pete. "And she sounded scared."

Seriously? "I'm not the one who's held her captive the past year." And suddenly, his word—*captive*—registered.

Felipe hadn't . . . *threatened* her, right? Scared her? Hurt her? Made her feel like she couldn't return to Pete?

"You want to tell me what happened after I left Paris?" Pete said quietly, carefully.

Something sparked in Felipe's eyes, a challenge met. He considered Pete, his jaw hard. "I would admit it was a gallant effort, chasing her down at the *Prix de l'Arc de Triomphe*, but you are a smart man, Mr. Brooks. Certainly you could see, even then, that Selene

103

doesn't belong in this life." He glanced around at Jess's home. "She panicked—I understand that. And you were here. But she has come to her senses, and this game is over. Now, where is she?"

Sam had come into the room, stood beside Pete. "She's not here."

Felipe's eyes narrowed at Pete. "She'd better be okay."

"What's that supposed to mean?"

"Because I know she came to see you—"

Oh. Maybe his expression shut Felipe down, the one that said how much he wanted to hurt him. But Pete just shook his head. "Whatever, man. I'm going to look for her."

He headed toward the door, but Felipe didn't move. So Pete pushed him aside.

Felipe jerked back, against the doorframe.

Pete ignored him, stepped out.

He saw Felipe's movement in his periphery, but not fast enough to get a hand up, to stop Felipe from slamming into him.

Then he was off the porch and in the soft grass, in a sort of brawl that had him hearkening back to his teenage years.

Felipe, on top of him, slamming his fist into his kidney in a blow that turned his world splotchy and gray. What the . . . ?

Pete used the twenty or so pounds he had on the Frenchman and threw him off. Scrambled to his feet.

Felipe rushed him.

Pete met him with a fist to his face. The sound of the impact exploded, along with pain in his fist. Felipe swore, stumbled, but stayed on his feet.

His nose gushed blood.

Pete couldn't stop himself. It wasn't Felipe's words that lit him aflame, but all of it, starting with the moment he'd stood on Jess's porch nearly two years ago and begged her for a reason not to walk away.

She'd given him nothing.

And since then, he'd done nothing but run back to her, hand over his heart, to fall at her feet.

Let her go.

He couldn't—*please, no*—be the rebound replacement for this skinny Frenchman.

Pete launched himself at Felipe.

Sam tackled him into the grass. Pete writhed beneath him, but Sam had him in a submission hold.

A few feet away, Felipe stood, a litany of French spilling from him that Pete didn't want to interpret. "You don't deserve her." He held his nose, tipping it forward, the blood dripping from it onto the grass. "For the life of me, I don't know what she sees in you."

His words stopped Pete cold. They raked through him, stole his breath, stopped his heart.

Because—*oh, please, yes*—he got it.

Felipe had run to Montana, had tackled him, angry and jealous, because maybe Jess's words were true. *"I'm not engaged."*

"Get off me, Sam," Pete growled.

"Not until you calm down."

"I'm calm. I promise."

Sam eased off him and Pete turned over, climbed to his feet. Stared at Felipe.

In the distance, a siren sounded. "You called the cops?" he said to Sam.

"Not me. Probably the neighbors," Sam said.

"Good," Felipe said, trying to staunch the bleeding from his nose. "Because I'm pressing charges."

Pete stared at him. "You started it!"

The lights hit the street, blood red on the house.

"If anything has happened to her, it's your fault," Felipe snarled as he sank down on the porch steps.

"*My* fault—what are you talking about?"

"Because she came to see you. And something terrible has happened to her. She was screaming when she hung up."

Screaming. Like a punch, the word took Pete's breath.

"What do you mean, *screaming?*" Sam said, not so quietly.

"That's all I heard. Then the line went dead, and when I tried calling her back, it just went to voice mail."

Pete stared at him. For crying out loud, the man could have *led* with that. "Why didn't you say that?"

The cruiser pulled up to the curb, and Sam went out to meet it.

Pete pulled out his phone, intending to pull up Jess's number, and only then did he notice the voice mail message. He retrieved it, and the voice on the other end emerged muffled, then a man's voice. "*Hang on to something!*"

A screech in the background, probably brakes.

Screaming, more than one voice, and then a cacophony of random sounds, as if the phone might have been thrown or trampled.

The message ended.

Pete stared at Felipe, and now he too trembled.

Sam returned with an officer. "I told him the story. You both have to go down to the station and make a statement."

Pete looked at Felipe, then back to Sam. "Sorry, bro, I'm not going anywhere but to find Jess."

———— + ————

Jess had led them right over a cliff in a spectacular crash and burn.

They lay broken at the base of what she could only imagine was a huge glacial boulder, maybe ten feet tall, one padded with enough of the forest floor—overgrown with moss and loam and the litter of downed trees—for them not to have perished in the fall.

106

She'd led with panic and propelled them into midair, flying off the edge, feet pedaling, arms flailing.

Despite the cushion, she landed hard in a brain-exploding, body-jarring crash, bracing herself with her outstretched palm that only earned her a burning up her arm that she dearly hoped wasn't a broken wrist.

Next to her, Ned hiccupped, as if fighting for breath.

"Ned! Are you okay?"

Her eyes had dissected the shadows and forms from the darkness, and she finally made him out. He lay on his back, Shae still in his arms. It seemed he'd protected her from the fall, sacrificing his body to do it. He must have lost his breath because he lay gasping like a fish on land.

Then a groan, low and deep as if he was trying—and failing—to stave off a cry of pain. His voice emerged on a broken wisp of breath. "What . . . about . . . Shae?"

Jess crawled over to them. Shae was awake and pushing herself off Ned. "I'm okay."

Just how far into the forest they'd escaped, Jess hadn't a clue. They seemed to have fallen into a dry riverbed, or perhaps just a ravine, maybe twenty feet wide given the arching shadow looming over them. She hadn't even suspected the gap in the rock.

Overhead, the treetops webbed the wan light from a half-moon and stars shone so bright she couldn't believe she hadn't seen the gap. A breeze blew and rustled the leaves, and the scent of night and the dank loam thickened the air. An owl hooted, and in the distance, a howl lifted, raising gooseflesh on her skin.

"We need to keep moving," Ned said, forcing himself up.

Shae shook her head. "I'm . . . I'm bleeding." She held her hands away from her side. "I think I punctured something in the crash, and now . . . it's worse."

Please let it not be a rib protruding from her chest cavity.

Especially since Jess could do nothing about it until they found help. "Let me feel," she said to Shae and reached out to her.

She found the wound under her rib cage, and despite Shae's groans, she examined the injury. A puncture wound, too deep to tell. "The bleeding seems to be slowing. Just keep pressure on it. Anything else?"

"My side burns when I breathe," Shae said. "And my ankle feels fat."

"Yeah. It's pretty swollen. It might be broken. I'll try to splint it somehow in the morning."

"We can't stay here. Whoever is after us is still out there," Ned said. "We need to find help."

"We have no idea where we're going," Jess said. "We could be running deeper into the Bob for all we know."

"And no one knows where we are," Shae whispered. She backed up to the wall of the ravine. With the darkness hooding them under the lee side of the boulder, they might stay hidden.

"Let's just catch our breath," Jess said.

Ned considered her a moment, then moved next to Shae, his groan rumbling out from deep inside.

"Ned, what's going on?" Jess asked.

"I think my shoulder is dislocated," he said through clenched teeth.

Jess moved over to him, holding her wounded arm close to her body. "I'm going to check, okay?"

"Mmmhmm."

Her thumb eased between the bones and he stiffened, cutting off a noise from deep inside him.

"It's an anterior dislocation. I think I can move the bone back in. Can you lie down?"

He positioned himself beside her, and she took ahold of his arm. "This is going to hurt. I'm sorry."

"I'll be okay."

No, he wouldn't. None of them would be unless they got help.

This would be easier on a table, using weights, but they were out of choices. She moved the arm out at a ninety-degree angle. "I'm going to have to counter leverage against you."

He might have nodded, but she didn't wait, just pressed her feet into his side as she pulled, her teeth gritted against the burn in her wrist.

He choked off a grunt.

"Just a little more—"

Please don't let me be tearing ligaments, damaging nerves and blood vessels.

The humerus slid under the shoulder and back into place with a soft clunk.

Ned gasped, let out a breath, almost a hiccup of relief.

"It'll still hurt."

"Yeah, but . . ." Ned blew out a breath, sat up, and ran his other hand across his forehead as if he might have been sweating. "Thanks." Then he used his uninjured arm to pull Shae against his chest. "We need to huddle together, try to stay warm."

Jess sat next to Shae, the cool rock against her back, and pulled her arm against her body, trying not to shiver. "I'm so sorry, guys."

"What are you talking about?" Shae said. "This wasn't your fault. If anything, it's mine. I should have never come back. Blackburn wants me dead, and you guys got pulled in."

"We don't know it's Blackburn." Jess stared at a dark clutter of clouds. "Right before I left New York City, I was attacked by a . . . well, a protester. People hate my family. Who knows but it's someone who wants payback."

"For what?" Ned said.

Jess sighed. "My dad was a Wall Street investor who master-minded the biggest Ponzi scheme in history. He stole billions from everyday people, defrauded them out of their retirement funds, their kids' school savings, their nest eggs. He destroyed tens of thousands of lives."

Silence.

"That's why I came to Montana. I had to testify against my dad in order to keep my brother and myself out of jail, and I needed someplace to run. So I changed my name to Jess Tagg—it was Selene Taggert, if that rings a bell—and tried to start over. And for three years, I did. I bought a house, started working for PEAK . . . and met Pete."

Understatement. Because she'd fallen hard and fast and forever with Pete Brooks. Even if it had taken him leaving the first time for her to realize it.

Truth was, he'd stepped inside her heart long before she admitted it to herself, and he had never left. She looked away, her eyes burning.

"Then your past showed up in Florida," Shae said.

In spades. "About a year ago, we were rescuing Shae's uncle Ian," Jess said, "whose yacht had wrecked in the Gulf of Mexico, and one of the passengers recognized me. She was from New York City, and she knew my former fiancé, Felipe. So she called him, and he came to Florida."

She closed her eyes. The image of Pete's face when she came upon him and Felipe confronting each other in the hospital hallway could still send a spear of dread through her.

Choices. And wretched timing because Pete had just proposed. Oh, she'd wanted to turn and run. Again. Because no matter who she chose, someone was going to get eviscerated.

Of course, Pete had fallen on his sword and told her to return to her life in New York City. At least long enough to reunite with her family and set things right with Felipe.

She'd promised him she'd return. "Poor Felipe thought I was dead."

"But you weren't," Ned said.

"No, I wasn't. And I had to go back to New York City and face the mess I'd made. Or thought I made. When I got home I realized that I'd overreacted to my own fears. I thought my family didn't want me around. But my mother was . . . well, she had her own troubles and needed me. Sure, my brother still hasn't spoken to me—he still hates that I testified against our father, even if I did save him from his own run in prison. But Felipe, well, it's complicated. Let's just say that Felipe still wanted to marry me."

"But do you love Pete?" Shae asked.

Jess nodded, her movement hidden in the darkness. "But it doesn't matter. I've hurt Pete so much, there's no way he wants me back."

"You show up tonight, hoping that I'll just sweep you into my arms, like nothing has happened?"

Yes. She'd hoped it with everything inside her. And no, even if she *could* figure out how to break it off with Felipe and not hurt her mother, she had no right to expect Pete's forgiveness, to even ask for it . . . but it was Pete.

Pete, who showed up to rescue her from a forest fire, from her crazy, money-pit house repairs. He'd even gotten on a plane and shown up in Paris.

Her hand curled around her bruised wrist and clutched it close to her. She sucked in a tremulous breath, longing with everything inside her to turn and see him standing there, her rescuer.

If she closed her eyes, he could be. She could almost picture him, determination in his eyes, the same fierce expression he'd worn when he'd shown up in France, of all places, two days after she'd left him in New York City.

Pete?

How he'd gotten past the gates of the historic Château de Chantilly, where Felipe's family held their postrace celebration in the formal garden, she hadn't a clue, but apparently he knew how to dress the part of an aristocrat. In the back of her brain, she recognized him, sure, with his long blond hair queued back, the cut of his wide shoulders, the slightest hint of golden whiskers, rich with copper highlights along his chin. But every other inch of him moved her off her axis, and she was completely taken by the splendor of a man who knew how to wear a suit.

A silk navy-blue suit, with a vest and a vintage white shirt. The collar of his shirt was opened at the neck to give a hint at the golden tan that betrayed his summer activities.

Twice now, Pete had shown up fitting into her world better than she did.

Except, what was he doing in France? More specifically, in Oise, fifty kilometers north of Paris? In the small town of Chantilly?

He lifted a glass of champagne from the tray of a white-gloved waiter and fixed her with a look that turned her boneless.

Pete Brooks, in France. Just when she thought she understood the man.

She shot a glance around the gathering and spotted Felipe standing next to his winning filly, Lady Anne, one hand on her withers, talking to a gorgeous brunette who stroked the filly's nose. For a moment, Felipe's smile, the glitter in his eyes . . . it sent a jolt through Jess.

Felipe hadn't looked at her that way in, well, *years*.

Maybe, in fact, never.

"This isn't Paris." Pete's voice had the power to tunnel under her skin, turn her to flame. She turned, only to be caught in those blue eyes that shucked from her mind any thought of Felipe.

Pete. "How . . . how did you find me?" She hadn't meant to phrase it that way, but sometimes Pete's mere presence held her brain captive, reducing her to instincts and rash statements.

Or nothing at all.

For a second, his smile flickered. Then, "It's what I do, baby. Search . . . and find." One side of his mouth tugged back up.

Oh no. Because she wanted to grab him by the hand and run. Still. Because from the second he'd shown up in New York City and pulled her into his arms under the shadows of history, she longed to simply flee back to the life she loved, in Montana.

How she ended up wearing a white, wide-brimmed derby hat, flounced with feathers, a white pencil dress, and heels that sank into the grass with every step still befuddled her. One yes at a time, she supposed. Or perhaps she simply hadn't said no.

She just didn't want to hurt anyone else. Except, Pete had gotten caught in the cross fire. She'd meant what she said—she loved him. Planned on returning to him.

Just wasn't sure when. And she knew that wasn't fair, but . . . oh, how she'd made a mess of everything.

And yet Pete still showed up. Here. In Paris.

She knew that she didn't deserve him. And that made it all the worse.

She took a drink of her lemonade, swallowed, and found her voice. "You look good."

He grinned then, a full-on, show-stopping smile that added to his stunning physique. "When in Paris, right? Besides, when I called Ty for the lowdown on this fancy race, he read me the riot act and told me not to embarrass you. How am I doing?"

She'd noticed a few women in the crowd giving him the eye

and stepped up to him, closing the gap. "Well, you do know how to draw a crowd, Pete Brooks."

"The only crowd I'm after is you." He winked and finished off his champagne. "Now, how about I rescue you from this soiree and you show me Paris?"

Yes, please. "I can't. Felipe—"

"Felipe is fine." He glanced at the man, now leading the filly away and walking with the brunette. "I know the look of a man who has one thing on his mind."

"Pete!"

"What? I'm telling you, your boy Felipe there isn't just interested in his horse."

And she didn't want that to burn, but his words left a mark.

Still, maybe, yes. Time for her and Felipe to face the truth, to move on.

For her to return to Pete like she promised.

"My mother will kill me if I leave."

"Blame me. A lost tourist in France." He took her hand.

"You don't look lost."

He found her eyes then. "Jess, without you, I'm always lost."

Ho-kay. She let her hand tighten around his.

Paris, with Pete.

Because he'd followed her, wouldn't let her go. She could still feel his hand in hers as he led her out of the château grounds and back to his hired car. Still smell his cologne, feel the heat of his embrace as they traveled back to Paris.

Now, in the damp, renegade darkness of Montana, Jess clamped her arm around herself and listened to the night sounds, the rustle of wind, the mournful howl of a coyote or wolf. The quiet breathing of Ned and Shae.

And the truth settled into her bones.

This time, Pete wasn't coming for her.

———— + ————

Blackburn was winning. Because deep inside, where the lies couldn't hide, Shae knew she was dying. Her injuries had to be fatal for her to hurt this bad.

She thought she just might pass out—longed for it, really—as Ned ran with her. But she'd gritted her teeth and held on with everything inside her to the fine edge of consciousness, driven by the deep determination not to let Blackburn get away with his crimes. Not again.

In sleep, Ned's arm jerked and tightened around her, and she bit back a cry, choosing instead to breathe, to settle against his chest, smell the forest on his skin, lean into the meager warmth radiating from his body.

Moisture burned her eyes. She refused to let whatever had begun between them result in his death.

He would not be Dante, another casualty wrought by her choices.

Ned's chest moved steadily beneath her, and she stilled her own to hear his heartbeat. His arm slipped down, falling behind her as exhaustion finally overtook him.

She longed to lift her head, to study his face in the moonlight. But she only had to close her eyes, remember the way he'd looked at her that night in the apple orchard at his family's winery in Minnesota.

Two days into the search for his brother, who was lost after a tornado hit southern Minnesota. If it hadn't been for country musician Ben King's quick thinking—the way he grabbed her out of the audience and made her follow him to safety—she might also have gone missing. Instead, she ended up huddling for safety in an office, trying to staunch the blood flowing from Ben's arm.

Like the hero he was, Ned appeared, right there, to help her.

Theirs was a relationship borne out of stress and desperation, but something about Ned tunneled right past her defenses, made her trust him.

She'd told him about her past. Told him about being on the run for five years. Told him about Dante being beaten to death at the hands of a murderer who had already killed someone before her eyes.

Told him that she hadn't felt safe—still didn't.

Until . . . until she lay in a field, under a spray of stars, Ned's hand in hers. He'd been telling her about his family, the winery, his life as a smokejumper. His brothers, Fraser, a navy SEAL, and Jonas, the storm chaser.

She'd been watching a star cascade across the sky when Ned rolled over onto one elbow and touched her face, probably to push a stray hair out of her eyes.

She should have pushed him away. Should have told him that being with her would only get him hurt. Should have never let him trace his finger down her cheek, to let him light inside her a fire she'd long banked, desperate to forget.

But he had the most beautiful amber brown eyes, the kind that seemed to peel away her fears, find the place inside that longed to be held. Five years of running did that to someone—turned them raw and desperate and painfully needy, and when he leaned down to kiss her . . .

Heaven help her, she kissed him back. Simply surrendered as if she belonged in his arms, softening her lips, breathing him in to her embrace, her heart.

She wanted to love again.

She wanted to love Ned Marshall.

The thought, the desire welled inside her, took possession of her and turned her kiss urgent. Maybe he felt the same thing—or perhaps it was simply the romance of the night, the desperation of the search for his brother, the unshed emotions of grief, but he kept up, moved them from a place of sweet exploration to hunger and fire, and she was breathing hard, caught up in the rush of desire when he suddenly leaned away from her.

He too was breathing hard. He stared at her, something almost akin to panic on his face, then rolled over onto his back, his chest rising and falling.

The next time he'd kissed her, it was to say good-bye when she left for Minneapolis. But they'd texted. Called.

And she saw the longing in his eyes tonight when, after dropping her off at home, he'd arrived two hours later to pick her up for the reception. He wore a pair of black jeans, cowboy boots, a white dress shirt, a brown leather jacket, and a smile that she felt down to her bones.

She could too easily fall for brave, handsome, sweet Ned Marshall and the life he embodied.

But clearly she needed to wake up and take a hard look at her life. Because she might be the worst thing that could ever happen to him.

"Shae?"

A whisper, and she lifted her head, found Ned looking at her in the moonlit darkness.

"I heard what you said earlier. This isn't your fault."

"I shouldn't have come back to Montana. If I hadn't—"

"Your past doesn't get to hold you hostage for the rest of your life. You escaped. Started a new life. Changed your name. You are not Esme Shaw, runaway, anymore."

His words slicked moisture into her eyes. "I don't want to be. But . . . you don't get it, Ned. I cause trouble, even if I don't mean to."

"Shae—"

"No. Listen. It's not just tonight, or even Dante. It's my . . . entire life. I wrecked my mother's life by even being born."

Ned drew a breath, stiffening in her arms. "You can't actually believe that?"

"It's true. She told my father she was pregnant with me, and he left her. And from that day on, I was baggage. Every time she met someone she loved, I got in the way."

"Shae—"

"I was there, I remember. She'd bring a guy home, and the next morning . . . well, I tried to stay quiet. Once, I even thought—I'll make breakfast. So I made bacon and nearly lit the kitchen on fire. I think my mother was hoping child services would take me away." She attempted a rueful laugh.

Ned kissed the top of her head, smoothed his hand down her hair.

Her chest thickened, her laughter choking out, leaving behind only the raw, unadulterated truth. "I was just trouble for my mother. Without me, she wouldn't have had to . . . well, do what she did to support me. She would have found a man who loved her."

"She should have found someone who loved you both."

Shae pressed her hand to Ned's chest, feeling the muscles beneath his shirt, the steady thrum of his heartbeat. "I liked your family. Your mom is really great."

"They liked you."

She closed her eyes. "I'll never forget the day Uncle Ian came to get me. Mom had been arrested, again, this time for possession, and I was sitting in the office of some social worker who hadn't a clue what to do with this angry, rebellious kid. Suddenly, the door opened and in walked Uncle Ian. I just stared at him, thinking he looked like some kind of superhero. Something inside me just broke when he looked at me and said, "It's going to be okay, Esme. You're safe now.""

Her voice had softened, and she realized she was crying. Oh

118

well. It was dark, and beside her, Jess seemed to have fallen into fatigued unconsciousness. "I realized then that I'd never really felt safe."

Ned's embrace tightened around her.

"He took me back to his enormous ranch. Gave me a room of my own. A horse. A life. A future. And what did I do with it? I fell for a troublemaker kid who had beautiful eyes and told me he loved me."

"You were a kid."

"I was my mother's daughter. Ravenous for love but unable to believe it when it reached out and accepted me, no strings attached. I broke Uncle Ian's heart." Her breath hitched. "And I keep breaking it. He's going to lose his mind when he discovers we're missing."

"Which only means he'll get the PEAK team out looking for us. I've seen them in action."

"They have no idea where to find us."

"Doesn't mean they won't. God knows where we are, right?"

Oh, she'd forgotten this side of Ned. The guy whose family prayed, who hung on to faith even when life told them to let go.

Or maybe she hadn't forgotten, because his words roused something inside her, freshly seeded, cultivated this summer. "Right," she whispered.

"We are not alone, Shae. And we are still safe." Ned touched her chin, nudged it up, and she lifted her face to his.

Then he leaned down and kissed her. A whisper touch, so sweet she ached with the control, the gentleness behind it. His lips were cold, but his touch held promise.

Hope.

He leaned away, and his gaze found hers. "And you are not a troublemaker."

Oh.

She offered him a smile, then put her head back on his chest. Listened to his heart, beating a little faster now.

Yes. Oh yes, she was.

But this time, she wasn't going to let the man she loved die, no matter what it cost her.

HE JUST WANTED TO PUNCH SOMETHING.

Pete sat at the edge of the metal bench in the county lockup, his head in his hands, watching the dawn wax blood-red shadows over the cement floor.

His body buzzed with fatigue, and just under his skin a shout kept building, a rush of heat and fury. And yes, he'd like to hit something very, *very* hard.

Like perhaps Felipe St. Augustine.

Or even his brother Sam.

Resisting arrest? Thanks, bro, for that one—a potential charge that Sam flung at him as Pete headed toward his truck. And two seconds before his uniformed cohorts shoved him against that same truck, cuffing him.

For assault.

A charge thrown at him by Felipe, who gave his statement to the cops right there in the yard. And okay, maybe if Pete hadn't decided that he had other priorities, things wouldn't have gotten physical with his own interrogating officer. He wouldn't have found his face against the hood of a car with accusations of assaulting a police officer being shouted in his ear.

Hello. Said police officer was his own annoying brother.

Pete had just barely escaped the resisting arrest charge but tried to turn his brother to ash with a look as one of Mercy Falls's finest led him to their cruiser.

Sam stood tight-lipped in the yard, wearing that big brother expression that suggested he knew what was best.

No, what was best was letting Pete follow his hunches, or at least his panic, around Mercy Falls and the surrounding countryside to find the woman he still loved.

Instead, Sam had poked his head into the car and promised to figure out a way to calm everybody down. Which meant Pete cooling off in a nine-by-thirteen cell. He might have preferred padded walls.

"Why isn't Felipe arrested too?" Pete had shouted after his brother's retreating back.

Sam ignored him while Felipe accepted Willow's offer of a towel and let her usher him into Sam's truck, where they left, no doubt, for the ER.

Pete hoped he'd demolished the man's nose, left him permanently disfigured.

Okay, maybe not quite that, but close. Because Pete knew he'd never recover from the wounds Felipe had rendered on him.

Especially if Jess ended up seriously wounded or . . . worse.

He got up, hung his hands on the cell bars. "Hey! C'mon, anybody! Sam! I shouldn't be in here!"

Nothing, and he closed his eyes, leaning his head on the bars, letting the cool metal brace him.

"Take a breath there, Brooks."

Pete looked up and frowned at the sight of Ian Shaw heading his direction. He wore a Minnesota Twins baseball cap over his dark hair, a T-shirt and jeans, hiking boots and a jacket, as if he planned on a jaunt into the woods.

Pete met his hand through the bars. "What are you doing here?"

SUSAN MAY WARREN

"I heard you got a call from Jess early this morning."

"Late last night, actually. And I didn't talk to her. She just left a message—and it sounded like she might be in trouble."

"What kind of trouble?"

"I don't know. There was a male voice. Shouting. And . . . a crash. Get me out of here, man, and I'll replay it for you."

"Working on it," Ian said, and blew out a breath. "I got a similar voice message from Shae. Screaming. What sounded like a wreck. I didn't pick it up until a bit ago when I got up and realized she wasn't home." He wrapped his hand around the back of his neck. "I know I'm being paranoid. Probably she's with Ned, although that is an entirely different conversation. However, with Blackburn still missing . . ."

Pete stepped back. "You think Blackburn found her and ran her off the road?"

Ian lifted a shoulder. "But I'm worried. I called Chet, who called Sam, who told me about Jess. I think Shae and Jess must be together. Chet called the rest of the team—they're coming in to look for them."

"I have to get out of here."

Ian nodded. "Okay, so I talked to Sam. Apparently Felipe has filed assault and battery charges."

"He assaulted *me*! He should be sitting in the cell beside me!"

"He says you started it. That you pushed him. And he says he's got some pretty heavyweight lawyers ready to add civil damages, so while you're probably right, this isn't going to go your way, Pete."

Pete backed away from the bars, holding up his hands as if he might like to strangle someone. Blew out a hot breath. "I did not *push* him. I . . . nudged him. He was in my way."

Ian gave him a tight nod.

"I gotta talk to him."

"He's pretty hot. Sam and Willow brought him back from the

hospital. He's at Jess's house. He blames you for Jess flying out here."

Pete closed his eyes against Ian's words, not wanting to sort them out to find the hope. Or the guilt. "Jess makes her own decisions. Or not, depending on how you look at it. But trust me—I'm not the reason she came back here. I haven't been her reason for anything for a long time. He might want to take a look closer to home. After all, *he's* her fiancé, not me."

"I'm not engaged."

Sure looked like it, from his vantage point. Still, the question lingered. Felipe was here because something wasn't right in Jess-and-Felipe land, and maybe—*oh, please*—it had something to do with Pete.

He might have said that aloud, because Ian held up his hand. "I've talked to Felipe, told him we need your help. He's agreed to drop the charges, but he has a couple conditions."

That Pete not murder him immediately? Done.

That Pete find Jess and let them sort this mess out later? Yep, that too.

That Pete walk away and never talk to Jess again? Not a chance.

He folded his arms over his chest. "What conditions?"

"He wants to help us search."

Pete gritted his jaw, looked away. "He'll need new shoes."

Ian looked down, and when Pete glanced at him, he caught Ian's grin.

"Fine. What else?"

"He wants a public apology. In front of the team, and Jess. Or Selene, as he calls her."

Pete shook his head, more in disbelief than refusal. "Of course he does."

"Listen, we all know the story. Who cares?"

"It wasn't my fault!"

Ian held up his hand. "I get it. And I know you hate taking the blame for something you didn't do. But suck it up and let's find Shae and Jess. And probably Ned too."

Pete shucked his hands down his face. His gut growled, a mix of frustration and hunger. He needed a shower. And coffee like his life depended on it.

Mostly, he needed to talk to Jess.

"Fine."

"That's a yes?"

He nodded.

"Okay, sit tight. I'll be back, hopefully with the keys."

Pete sank again on the bench, closed his eyes, and listened to Ian's steps fade.

Please, Jess. Be okay.

Be alive.

I promise, I will find you.

———— + ————

The sunrise could murder them where they sat.

Jess watched the hues of dawn slide into their enclave, the narrow cleft between two looming boulders, and tried to sort out the what-ifs.

What if they stayed here and just hid, waiting for rescue?

Except, no one knew they were missing. Of if they did, how would they ever deduce where they were?

They could run, but a glance at Shae's face—pale and wan in the gray wax of morning . . .

Jess curled her fingers around Shae's wrist and found her pulse. Faint, slow, but steady. Shae leaned against Ned, asleep on his chest, the brambles and leaves of their frenetic flight through the woods littered in the tangles of her blonde hair. Jess moved Shae's jacket to get a closer look at the wound.

Still seeping, just a little, but the blood was mostly dark, old and clotted. The wound was just below her rib cage, as if she'd landed on something hard enough to impale her. Most likely her ribs also took the brunt of the fall. Which meant they might be cracked, with possible internal bleeding. Jess needed to take a look at the skin surrounding the wound and search for bruising.

And then what? Movement would only make it worse.

Ned groaned as he shifted, his head leaning against Shae's. A handsome man, dark hair, and a dark smattering of whiskers across his chin. Wide shoulders. But how he'd carried Shae through the darkness . . .

Yeah, well, she'd seen the type before, the kind of guy who didn't think twice about telling a girl to hold on, that he wouldn't let her go.

Her throat tightened, burned.

"How did you find me?"

She closed her eyes, leaned back into the warmth of Shae, and sank into the memory of Pete in Paris. Let it warm her.

"Really. How did you find me, Pete?"

She sat in the nook of his arm, the lights of Paris glittering in the distance. The sun hadn't yet set, and streaks of green and blue hovered over the city, the glorious Eiffel Tower alight and sparkling over the spillway of the Seine.

"I looked up the horse race on Google and found out it had been moved this year. Then I took a cab out to Chantilly and asked around for the St. Augustine stables. I walked in like I knew what I was doing, and it wasn't long before I tracked down your little party. You texted Felipe, right?"

Pete had made her send Felipe a message as soon as they climbed into the car, the responsible rescuer in him not wanting to start a panic in her fiancé.

Maybe. Or perhaps he just wanted to win. He seemed to wear

126

something of a smug smile, and she didn't want to chase it down, dissect the meaning.

She just wanted to escape into it.

"You're not mad that I came, are you?" he asked suddenly.

"No—of course not. It's just . . ." She caught her lip. "Nothing."

"What?"

"It's funny how you think Felipe is in love with someone else." And oh, she probably should have thought long enough to pull those words back. "It's not a big deal—I mean, of course he might be. I was gone for a long time, and he . . . he should have moved on. It's just . . ." She lifted a shoulder. "I'm glad. Really glad."

"Really? Because you don't sound glad."

"I just . . . I didn't want to break his heart."

Pete didn't move. Just kept his gaze in hers. "But it's okay to break mine?"

She took a breath. "No! I—Pete, I . . . listen, I am coming back to you. I am. It's just . . . I didn't realize how much my family needs me."

He touched her face. "And you need them."

Her eyes burned, and she looked away, leaning into Pete's touch. "Maybe." She pulled his hand away but held it. "Thank you for . . . for sending me back here."

His thumb moved over her hand, but he said nothing. When she looked up, he was staring at her, his jaw tight, so much emotion in his eyes she couldn't move.

It cost him. The distance, the letting her go and all of it ranged across his face, in his gaze. "I missed you," he said, his voice low, a little husky. "So much, Jess. And yeah, if you need time, you got it. But . . . and I know this was crazy, coming all the way to Paris, but I had this feeling that if I didn't . . ." He shook his head, turned away, ran a hand across his chin. "I guess I just wasn't sure . . ." He took a breath, glanced at her. "I'm not Felipe St. Augustine. I know that. I don't have fancy horses or the kind of money to jet you off to Paris. I mean, I spent way too much on this stupid suit trying to impress you."

"It looks good." She touched the lapel.

"It's too tight."

She unbuttoned it. "It fits you perfectly. And no, you're not Felipe."

He drew in a breath.

"But I don't want Felipe."

He swallowed. "I want to believe that."

They had entered the city from the east, past the Bastille, along the Rue de Saint-Antoine, turned on the Rue de Rivoli. Pete leaned up as they passed the Hotel de Ville, the nineteenth-century city hall square. "Let us out here." He glanced at her. "Let's catch the sunset over the Seine."

He caught her hand and helped her out of the cab.

Paris turned into a postcard under the glow of the fall colors, crimson and golden leaves littered along the square, the tang of something roasting in a nearby boucherie.

Pete folded her fingers into his. "Tell me about Paris."

She cupped her other hand around his forearm, felt the sinews there. "I really can't believe you're here. I mean—"

"When was the first time you visited Paris?"

"When I was twelve. We came in the spring. My mother made us tour the Louvre for days. If I never see another ancient, naked statue again, it'll be too soon."

He raised an eyebrow.

"We went to Versailles too. Room after room of ornate tapestries, scrollwork, and history. My mother made us stop at every exhibit and read every plaque. Ask me anything about Louis the Fifteenth."

"Really?"

"Oh yeah. And then we visited the Bastille, and I learned about the French Revolution and Marie Antoinette." She pointed toward the Eiffel Tower, rising from across the river. "Napoleon is buried not far from there."

"Noted."

"My mother thought it was a sign of good breeding to know history. We also visited Shakespeare and Company, the 1920s bookstore not too far from here."

He shook his head.

"It's where Hemingway and F. Scott Fitzgerald hung out."

He tugged her across a bridge. "How about some ice cream?"

"Always."

He bought her a single cone, and they wandered around the island of the city, standing for a long moment in front of Notre Dame, the lights illuminating the grand cathedral.

How could she not choose this man over Felipe?

Pete had opened his jacket but stood with the cool fall wind playing with his blond hair. The suit matched his eyes, so blue she could sink into his gaze and never come up for air. Especially when he turned it on her, reached out, and caught a strand of her hair in his grip, tucking it behind her ear. "You're so beautiful, Jess. I don't tell you that enough."

Oh.

He stepped closer to her, whispered his fingers across her face. "I need to ask—"

"Yes."

He frowned. "You don't know what I'm going to ask."

"It doesn't matter. The answer is yes. It's been yes, and it will be yes."

"What if it's run away and marry me tonight?"

She grinned, stood on her toes, and found his ear. "Yes."

He caught her as she moved away and put her face in the cradle of his hands, his eyes in hers. They glistened, thick with emotion. "Jess," he whispered. "I don't have horses or a house in Paris, or really, *anything* to give you but myself."

She could hardly breathe through the squeeze of her chest. "It's enough, Pete. It's all I want."

And then, finally, he kissed her. So sweetly, right out there in the middle of the square. A whisper of a touch, as if he might be trying to keep from losing himself, pulling her into his arms and deepening his kiss.

But that was the Pete she knew. The man who longed to get it right. To be both the charmer and the protector. The man who put himself second.

She was reaching up to touch his face, maybe grab his lapel to draw him closer when he eased away. His eyes were closed, the brush of his eyelashes golden against his skin.

He opened them and smiled. "Ever been on top of the Eiffel Tower?"

Of course. But she grinned, shook her head.

"You're lying to me."

"Show it to me, Pete. Show me Paris."

He took her hand, and they crossed to the west bank. He caught them a cab, negotiated them down to the Champ de Mars, and out onto the parkway. Under the shadow of the tower, he paid their tickets and kept her warm as they stood in line, his arms around her. She sank into the heat of his body.

When they took the elevators to the top, she buried her head into his chest. And clung to him as he led her out to the platform.

"What, are you scared of heights?" he said as she closed her eyes and gripped the back of his jacket as they shuffled toward the grated lookout.

"Terribly. And you know it."

He laughed. "I do. Hang on to me, babe." Then he turned his

130

back to the railing and wrapped his arms around her, backing toward the edge. "I got you. Open your eyes."

She'd seen it before, but during the daytime, and through the press of her fingers. But holding on to Pete, she allowed herself the view.

Paris arrayed before her in glittering glory. He moved behind her, clasping his arms around her shoulders. "See Notre Dame?"

She wove her hands into his forearms, gripping them against the sway of vertigo. "And there's the Arc de Triomphe." Below and glowing, at the far end of the Avenue des Champs-Élysées.

The Seine wove through the city, a dark ribbon of history, and the Champ de Mars jutted out like a runway beneath them, lit up and inviting.

"I bet you'd like to base jump from here," she said.

"It's been done, but it's illegal," Pete said.

"Really? You checked into that?"

He kissed her neck, sent shivers through her body. "Maybe. Just out of curiosity."

She grew silent, still.

"What is it?"

"You make me want to do brave things, Pete. There's a part of me who loves the person I am with you. But then . . ." She turned in his arms, met his eyes. "You were right. I'm also Selene. And I can't forget that part of me."

He didn't flinch. "I know. And I . . . I guess I showed up here to see if I could fit into that world too." A smile tugged up one side of his mouth. "I know—crazy. But . . . Jess—Selene—I love—"

She couldn't wait for the rest; her body took over her thoughts. She moved her arms around his neck as she took his mouth with hers, her heart so far out of her body she thought it might have taken flight over the glittering cityscape of Paris.

He tasted of the night, of the soaring heights of danger, and yet, as his embrace tightened around her, she'd never felt so safe. A tiny groan emitted deep inside his chest, and whatever he'd held back in the square he released into the cover of the night, deepening his kiss. Giving himself to her, sweeping her to himself.

Pete. She should have run back to him. No—taken him with her.

He moved away, breathing hard. Pressed his forehead to hers. "You. I love you."

She nodded and realized her cheeks had wetted. "I love you too."

"Marry me, Jess. I know it's not the romantic proposal I promised, but—"

"We're on the Eiffel Tower. It's romantic enough."

He kissed her again, and she lost herself in his touch and how, right here, she was exactly where she belonged.

He eased away, "So, is that a yes?"

"I . . . I need to tell Felipe."

He frowned. "Of course you do."

"No, really, Pete. He's been good to me. I will tell him. And then . . ." She smiled, her fingers dragging in his soft whiskers. "Yes. Of course I will marry you."

He met her gaze. "Please don't break my heart. You have to make a choice, Jess. If you want me, it's time to come home."

She stared at him, her heart thundering. *Yes.* "You go home. I'll follow in a couple days."

His mouth tightened.

"I'm coming back, I promise," she said and kissed him again.

But she knew his smile was forced. Because he'd clung to her, his chin on her head as they stared out into the night. *Please don't break my heart.*

"Jess, wake up."

The hand on her shoulder jostled her awake, and she came to fast and hard into the brisk, bright morning.

Just Ned, reaching over to roust her back to reality, to the cold dew on her body, the tremble deep within. "Are you okay? You were whimpering in your sleep."

She looked at him, at his breath emerging in chilled clouds. "I was?"

He nodded.

"I'm fine. I . . ." She looked around. "We need to get out of here. But your shoulder is too weak to carry Shae."

"I'm *fine*." His outburst made her stiffen, but his mouth tightened even as Shae roused. He cut his voice low. "Yeah, it hurts, but we don't have a choice."

"I could go," Jess said. "Find my way out—"

"No. I know my way around the woods. I've spent the past four summers as a hotshot and a smokejumper. I know how to read the forest, find service roads—I can get to help."

Ned met Jess's eyes, the unspoken truth in them.

So, she voiced it. "It would be faster without us."

"Yes. I'll get help, and I'll come back."

She took a breath and pressed her hand to Shae's head.

"I promise," he added.

Yeah, well, sometimes even the most heartfelt promises got broken.

———— + ————

"You're a Marshall, Ned, and Marshalls don't quit."

Of course big brother Fraser had to enter Ned's head and drive him crazy as he tried to get himself past the primal urge to lose whatever he'd put in his stomach last night.

He'd hit the ground too hard—holding on to Shae, trying to protect her from the blow. And in doing so, he'd slammed into the rock and had probably broken or at least cracked a rib, because every time he took a breath he wanted to howl.

The bone-deep ache in his shoulder and radiating through his torso didn't help, either. He clutched his arm to his body, his jaw clenched tight as he worked himself through the corridor into which they'd fallen, on his way to help.

They'd tumbled off a wall of boulders settled like bowling balls in the thick, tangled wilderness. He guessed that in the spring, the crevasse acted as a glacial run, because as he followed it, the gully turned slightly downhill. He picked out his steps on the path cluttered with boulders and moss, as well as lethal shadows. The trees arched overhead, still thick with foliage, enough to dapple the morning light against the rumpled terrain.

Sweat slicked down his spine as he stopped and braced himself against a thick birch. The sun had begun to burn the chill from the air, but his injuries took more out of him than he could afford. He tucked his arms around himself and tried to get his bearings.

Sun to the east. And he should probably be going up, not down, to get the lay of the land.

From there, he might be able to orient himself toward civilization. He might even glimpse a service road.

But he worried about Shae and Jess in the open. Better would be to find them a dry, safe place to hide while he hiked out. So he'd headed downriver, to where the spring rush would have thickened and carved out gullies and trenches into the rock.

The trees were thick with a bejeweled autumn, and in any other circumstance, the lush glory of an aspen, larch, and poplar forest, ripe with ruby-red maples and sunny oaks, might be romantic.

Thankfully, he knew the shape of these Montana forests pretty well. He knew how to survive in the bush, knew how to read the run of a fire, knew how to spot a *V* in a skyline that might lead to a forest road, or a peak that might promise a lookout tower.

So yeah, he wasn't about to quit, not when he'd just gotten started. Not when he'd made a promise.

Not when Shae depended on him.

He gritted his teeth, managed a breath, and kept moving. The riverbed turned rutted, rimmed with shards of granite cut with tongues of glacial ice and rammed into the ground. Here, the water had scooped out pockets, some deep enough to hide a body.

Or two.

He trekked nearly a half mile before he found a cave big enough to hide them, a cavity that arched over the dry riverbed, littered with branches and crispy leaves, and big enough for Jess and Shae to tuck inside, secure until he could return.

And he *would* return. With help.

He turned around and stifled a moan as he headed back the way he came.

Jess and Shae hadn't moved, of course, still fighting for heat and life under the grimy shadow of last night's enclave. Jess looked up at him with so much hope in her eyes he wanted to wince. She held her wrist close to her body, her body language hinting at pain. Shae had roused too, and he forced himself to offer a tight, grim smile.

Shae had lost more blood, her face pale and her eyes even bigger. Her death grip around his neck as they ran still radiated through him, the way she'd returned his kiss last night, a tentative, sweet touch that had him breathless.

"I cause trouble, even if I don't mean to."

Oh Shae.

Truthfully, he still couldn't get his brain around the events of the past eight hours—the crash, the flight through the forest, the fall, the huddle for warmth.

Yeah, when he showed up at the reception, Shae on his arm, he'd had vastly other ideas of how last night might end. Nothing more than G-rated, but they certainly resembled a different reunion with Shae. He'd even found a romantic location, a recommendation from Sam Brooks, who was apparently the local law. He liked the guy—reminded him a little of Fraser. A little bossy, although maybe that gene ran strong in the Brooks family. After all, his brother Pete had been Man-in-Charge last summer during the search for Ned's brother. And Ned remembered him from his rookie summer with the Jude County Smokejumpers too. A get-'er-done guy who didn't quit. He hoped Pete was helming the search, if they'd started one.

But any search would probably start with the abandoned bridge Sam told him about. Which was probably miles from here.

And meant that they hadn't a sliver of hope that someone would point this direction. So it was up to him to hoof it out of here, ASAP, regardless of a couple broken ribs, a wounded shoulder, and his stiff knee.

Leaning over in front of the ladies, he kept his voice down, despite the stir of the wind. "I found a cave a little way down the wash. I think you two should hide there while I hike out. It's less exposed than here, and . . . well, I'm not sure how long it'll take."

He left unspoken the suggestion that their kidnapper-slash-assailant might still be searching for them.

"Okay. We can carry Shae together," Jess said.

But as she climbed to her feet, he had to catch her, grabbing her jacket. "You okay?"

She nodded, but moisture slicked her eyes. "Just—my arm hurts. It's making me a little sick to my stomach."

Her too, huh? "Try not to throw up. It'll make you weaker. I got Shae."

He hid a wince as he crouched in front of her. "How are you doing, babe?"

Shae made a noise, something that suggested the pain was winning. He touched her face. "I'm going to go for help while you stay with Jess and keep breathing, okay?"

She nodded, her skin practically translucent, and he caught her hands, held them against his chest to warm them.

"I mean it, Shae. I'm going to find help and then . . ." He leaned close. "Then I'm going to teach you how to two-step. That little sway we did earlier is not a true country dance."

He longed for a smile.

She swallowed, her face hollowing. "I'm so sorry—"

"No," Ned said. "We're not going there again. This is not your fault."

"It is—Blackburn had to be the one who ran us off the road."

Wow, she was fixated on that. But maybe her pain spiraled her thoughts into a hard, focused ball. "Stop. We don't know anything for sure. Except that we need to get you some help." He put his arms around her. "Hold on to me."

She looped her arms around his neck, her hold flimsy at best. He drew in a breath, got his feet under him.

He couldn't hold in the groan as he pulled her up, couldn't stop himself from stepping back, once, twice, trying to find balance. He did manage, however, not to cry out in some sort of pansy scream. But a knife had gone straight through his shoulder, scraping down his chest, and sweat broke out across his forehead.

Jess's hand went to his back to steady him. "Ned, are you okay?"

Shae tried to meet his eyes, but he looked away.

"Mmmhmm."

"I can walk," Shae said.

"You can't," Jess answered. "Your ankle is wrecked, and you'll start bleeding again."

"I'm okay," Ned said to Jess. The pain had stepped back, the sudden light-headedness and flash-bang of agony quelling to a deep throb that radiated through his body.

He turned and looked at Jess. "Go in front of me." He didn't add anything like "Because you might have to catch us both" because he was *not* going to fall.

Shae rested her head on his chest, and he concentrated on the feel of her body, small and tucking close to his.

Okay, so his intentions last night might have been more PG, and the way she held on to him roused some of that to life. She even turned her face into his neck, let her lips settle there, probably an accident but for a second it took his mind off the ache thrumming through him.

Yeah, he was going to get her to the cave, find help, save them all, and then . . . prove to her that she wasn't trouble. That she just might be the best thing that ever happened to him.

In fact, he might even ask Shae how she felt about someday being a navy wife.

Hooyah.

7

PETE'S BREATH CONGEALED IN THE MORNING AIR, a fog of frustration and all-out horror as he stepped back from the over-turned truck. It lay half-in, half-out of the dirt-brown and angry Mercy River. The glass from the windshield had shattered and lit-tered the mud and grass like pale-red tears as it reflected the dawn.

Pete had clambered down to the crash, slipping on the dew-slicked grasses uprooted and torn from the vehicle's descent, his entire body coiled with the fear of what he'd find.

Empty. He had braced himself on the frame, breathing hard, keenly aware of the chill in the air. And he couldn't take his gaze off the blood splattered on a twisted mangle of metal door that was sharpened like a spear. They had to have taken a header off the highway at an alarming rate of speed to incur this much damage.

They'd rolled, and the roof dented in as if the Almighty had put his fist into it.

Please, let God have also pulled them out, rescued them.

"You need to sit down and put your head between your knees." Gage had come down, a little less quickly, not falling on his back-side and wetting his jeans through in a full-out, sweat-slicked panic.

139

Behind him, Felipe had also picked his way down, and now, grim faced, searched the truck.

"I'm fine," Pete said, but he crouched anyway, braced his hand onto the ground just to keep himself from going over. "Are we sure this is the truck they left the wedding in?"

The skid marks on the pavement had alerted a morning driver who'd spotted the truck down the embankment on its side and called Mercy Falls 911. Ian had confirmed that Ned had picked up Shae in a late-model Ford F-150, and when patrol read off the Minnesota plates, Pete followed Sam's lights out to the accident location.

"Yeah, this is the same truck," Ian said, his jaw tight. He'd dropped Pete off at Willow's house to retrieve his truck, had presided over the terse apology Pete offered Felipe, who waited for him at PEAK HQ. Felipe had shaken Pete's hand and glared at him like he wanted to have another go-round.

Pete shook off the urge to offer up a time and place.

It wouldn't help find Jess. And no doubt, wouldn't help Pete win her back.

At the moment, he just wanted her alive. He'd figure out who got the happily-ever-after later.

"They must have rolled, at least twice," Gage said. "I hope they were belted in."

"Except they're not here, are they?" Pete rose, still woozy.

"Maybe they got out, tried to find help?" Felipe suggested.

Sam treaded down the hill toward them. On the highway, a convention of patrol cars churned bright red lights into the sky, and criminal investigators examined the scene. "It looks like they might have been forced off the road."

Pete pressed a hand to his gut.

"There is another set of tracks, and it looks like whoever ran them off also stopped to check on them. There's a set of tire prints in the ditch, with a few sets of footsteps leading down the embankment."

"And back up." Pete found them now, imprinted deep into the mud. "Although they look like the same person." He crouched, pointed to an overlapping set. "And they're deep. As if he might be carrying someone."

"Or all three, one after the other?" Felipe asked, coming over to stand by Pete.

Pete stood up. "Yeah. Maybe." He turned to Sam. "Show me."

Sam led him up the hill, and Pete stood for a long moment staring at the indentation of truck tires, wide-set wheels. Older tires, given the smooth grooves between the raised seams in the mud. He followed them along the ditch, then stopped, stared at the other side of the road. "The driver turned around."

He crossed the highway and found the curved, muddy path that led away from the ditch. "He took them away from Mercy Falls."

Sam came up, stood beside him. Silent.

And really, what could he say? We'll find them? Yeah, well, that was a given.

Jess will be fine? Pete couldn't hear that right now.

Sam put his hand on Pete's shoulder and squeezed. "Let my CSI guys do their job. You get back to the ranch, set up a search grid, and get Kacey and Ben in the air."

Pete wanted to weep at the comfort of a to-do list. He nodded and nearly sprinted to his truck.

Gage slid onto the seat beside him, while Felipe got in beside Ian. Ian followed Pete back to the ranch.

Sierra had coffee brewing. Ty, Chet, Ben, and Kacey were leaning over a giant map in the kitchen of the old ranch-house-turned-search-and-rescue HQ. Even Willow was on-site, helping Sierra stir up breakfast. Breakfast burritos in tinfoil piled on a plate.

Ian, Felipe, and Gage came in behind them. The sun had cleared the mountains to the east, fingers of light peeling back the shadows, lighting the grasses afire. Dark indigo clouds cluttered the sky, and Pete suspected Kacey had already downloaded the weather report, one that included winds, if not a storm front. He braced himself for the worst.

Instead, "The clouds are headed east, over the mountains, and we already know the vehicle carrying them headed south on Highway 2, so we can start there." She met Pete's eyes. "I'll fly as long as I can see, Pete. I promise."

He noticed she didn't look at Felipe.

Selene might belong to Felipe, but Jess was his.

Except, no she wasn't. And that thought still had the power to put fingers around his throat, squeeze. Still, he *knew* Jess Tagg.

Jess Tagg was a survivor.

Pete nodded and moved over to the map. "We have a number of side roads to search too. I have no idea what we might be looking for, although from the tire bed, it looks like an older model pickup with worn tires, so my guess is that the body might be a match. And we probably should check any of the local clinics, including Kalispell Regional, just in case we're reading this wrong and what we have here is a do-gooder who brought them to the hospital." Please, *please*.

"I've already put in a call to the local hospitals," Sierra said, walking over with the plate of food. "No one matching Jess, Ned, or Shae's description came into the ER last night."

The silence pitched about the room.

Who would run Jess—and Ned and Shae—off the road and steal their bodies?

No, not bodies. Because they were alive.

They had to be.

"This is a kidnapping," Pete said finally. "We'll break into teams and search the back roads. Ian and Felipe, you take Pioneer Road and Helene Flats Road and the surrounding areas. Ty, you and Sam take the roads on the other side of the highway—Rose Crossing and Trumble Creek. Gage and I will head down to 35 and work our way north on the other side of the river."

"We'll do a scan of the entire area," Kacey said, taking a burrito and heading out to the barn that only the night before had been filled with tables, twinkly lights, happiness, and forever-afters. Pete followed her out, along with Ben.

Ty had already checked the batteries on their two-ways in the equipment room, and handed them out, along with emergency medical bags.

"I'll touch base with dispatch and see if they've gotten any 911 calls." Sam had come in behind them. He glanced at Pete.

We'll find her. He saw the words in Sam's eyes and didn't want them sitting inside him, churning up hope to intermix with the fear, to make him crazy.

"Don't say it," Pete said with a shake of his head. Because he didn't need hope.

Not when he had resolve. Yes, he would find her. And if God was merciful, she'd be alive.

Pete climbed into his truck, and Gage slid in beside him. Handed him a foil-wrapped burrito and a travel mug of coffee.

The clouds rolled over the horizon as he drove south, along Highway 2. The Rockies edged them to the east, a hazy, razor-edged blue. Green pasture rippled out from the pavement, cordoned off by barbed wire. Bungalows, ranch houses, and lodges sat back from the road, on the bank of the Mercy River. The air smelled of wood fires, evidence of last night's cold snap.

"It's supposed to get below freezing tonight," Pete said, setting his coffee back into the cup holder.

The burrito sat unwrapped. The last thing his gut could handle at the moment was food, especially with his brain flirting with horrendous what-ifs. He'd seen enough tragedy over the past few years to have a too-honest idea of what might have happened.

Or be happening, right now, to Jess. And Shae. And okay, even Ned.

Kidnapped.

No, no food for him.

He might even lose the coffee.

Gage said nothing, bringing his binoculars to his eyes occasionally. But really, they hadn't a clue what they might be looking for. Not until they got an ID on that mysterious truck.

They needed a lead, and desperately.

The morning waxed long and quiet as they drove, cutting east on Highway 35, then north up 206, searching the dirt byroads and paved crossroads, working their way back to Mercy Falls.

Around ten o'clock, they gassed up, and Sam checked in with a no-go report.

At noon, Kacey and Ben returned for fuel. They picked up Brette, Ty's girlfriend, and set back out, with her snapping aerial photos for them to examine later.

By two, Ian and Felipe had finished their grid and returned to the ranch house. Ian grabbed lunch, and they hit the highway north, just in case Pete read the tracks wrong.

Pete made his way to Mercy Falls, turned around, and backtracked. Gage ate his burrito.

Sam called in around 3:00 p.m. with a report of the tracks. "The tire cast showed cracks at the edges. Something that can happen when a vehicle hits a pothole or debris."

"On any number of the undermaintained dirt roads around here." Pete had pulled over onto the side of the road, watching as a V of Canada geese flew south, the pattern interrupted by a few stragglers.

"Could be a hunter. There was also evidence of cupping or

scuffing. It's a diagonal pattern of curves that occurs when you carry heavy loads in the trunk or cargo area. The weight changes the geometry of the suspension and it shows in the tire pattern. But it often happens in lighter vehicles."

"So, an older model, off-road truck, not one of the heavy F-150s, but a lighter model. Like Dad's old Ford Ranger."

"And the weight—could be a topper."

A topper.

"There's more. The CSIs found specks of light blue paint on the pavement near the skid marks. They think it's from the truck. They're putting it through an analysis to determine the paint type, maybe get a make and model."

"Thanks, Sam."

A beat. "Breathe, Pete. We'll—"

"Yeah." Pete hung up and put his truck into gear. "Blue truck, maybe a topper. Older model."

Gage nodded and lifted his glasses.

The setting sun poured out despair as Pete headed north, back to PEAK. Back to nothing. The sky turned eerily orange, the mountains aflame with the debris of autumn. The wind littered shorn maple and oak leaves across the road.

Pete pulled up to the house and parked next to Ian's truck. Gage got out. Closed the door.

Pete didn't have the heart to follow him inside. Instead he found himself walking over to the chopper. A new one, courtesy of donors after the crash that had nearly killed Jess over a year ago.

She'd been lost in the forest, a fire consuming the world around her, the team unable to get to her.

Not on his watch. Pete had gotten out his map, ignored the closing of the forest service roads, and found a back way on his four-wheeler into Dawson's Creek, where she'd been hiding out at a forest service cabin.

If he closed his eyes, he could still see her standing at the edge of a cliff, about to jump into blackness, the flames around her.

He'd been ready to burn with her, if it came to that, because he wasn't going to leave her to roast to death. Instead, he'd reached her in the nick of time.

And the look on her face—yeah, he could have died a happy man seeing her sheer, amazed disbelief. The way she clung to him, her body pressed to his as they careened off the cliff into the dry creek bed below.

Not unlike how she'd held on to him as he'd rappelled them away from a grizzly only a year earlier.

But it wasn't just the fact that, inadvertently, she made him feel like her hero; it was the way she took him seriously. Believed in him.

"Pete. How you doin', bro?"

Pete wiped a hand across his cheek before he turned to his brother. Sam stood in the driveway, his hands in his pockets. "Sierra made some chili."

"I'm not hungry."

"Of course not. But eat anyway."

Pete's mouth tightened, and he walked over to the bench near the door of the hangar and sat down, his head against the cool metal siding. "It's going to freeze tonight."

Sam came over, sank down next to him.

"She called me." He looked at Sam. "When she was going off the road, she called me."

Sam nodded, understanding in his eyes.

Pete looked at the sky, now streaked with fire. "It's the waiting. It's the not knowing. It's the helplessness. It's the fact that right now, she needs me and I'm not there."

"It's Dad, all over again," Sam said softly.

Dad. Who had gotten lost on a ski hill following Pete off trail.

146

He'd fallen in a tree well and frozen to death while a blizzard closed in on the mountain. And Pete hadn't even noticed. Had skied all the way to the bottom without a backward glance, just one, that would have saved his dad's life.

Sam had forgiven him, finally, two years ago.

Pete hadn't found it quite so easy to do the same. And that had led him down a path that . . . well, he could easily put the blame for his behavior on not a little self-hate.

But that behavior insulated him, made him focus on the immediate shame and not the deeper, embedded inability to face himself in the mirror.

The old Pete had saved him. Until, of course, it nearly destroyed him.

Pete closed his eyes, the burn in them turning his jaw tight. "I royally screwed up, Sam."

He let the words sit there in the shadows.

Because Sam had no idea what he was talking about. Couldn't know. Because Pete barely could face it himself.

He didn't deserve Jess, even if he found her, even if she wanted him back.

Sam didn't retort, just sat in silence.

And the rest of it burned in his chest, aching for air, for release.

"I told you I proposed in Paris."

"Mmmhmm."

"She said she loved me and promised to follow me back to Montana. So I got on a plane." He shook his head. "I should have never gotten on that plane."

Sam leaned forward, his arms on his knees.

"After a couple days, when she didn't call, I called her. My call went to voice mail. And the next one, and the next one. And then a couple weeks had gone by and I started to get mad. I stopped calling . . . and she never called back. I realize she was overseas, but . . . two months, Sam," Pete said. "I didn't hear from her for two whole months. It was like . . . like I'd been deleted."

The smell of smoke curled out into the night.

"Nothing?"

"Not until New Year's Eve. Late. I was out with friends and I got a call. I stared at the number, recognized it as Jess's and . . . I . . . I was just so angry. And trying to figure out if I was supposed to live without her. And . . ."

"What did you do, Pete?" Sam had glanced over, his jaw hard, and Pete winced.

Because shoot, his brother knew him.

"I declined the call. And the next one. And then I . . . I blocked her number."

He wanted to wince at his own words, and even what he was omitting. But he had been hurting. Needy. And the old Pete had revived, trying to save him.

Thankfully, Sam said nothing to probe deeper, unearth the rest.

"I unblocked it a month later, but . . . she never called back."

Sam leaned back. "Why didn't you call her?"

"Because I was hurt. And I thought . . . okay, I don't know what I thought. Maybe that she should want me a little too. That maybe if she didn't hear from me, she would hop on a plane and track me down too." He leaned forward, his hands over his face. "And then last night . . ."

He got up, strode away. Stood staring at the sky. "If she's dead, Sam, I'll never forgive myself."

Sam didn't move. "This isn't your fault, Pete."

He rounded on Sam. "She was in that truck because I pushed her away. Because I let my pride get in the way. Just like it did with Dad. And now she's missing, probably hurt, and I'm not there to save her."

He wanted—*needed*—to hit something. So when Sam got up,

Pete held up his hands in surrender, backing away. "I'm not in a good place, here, Sam."

"Take a breath, Pete. I get it. But I repeat. This is not your fault. And neither was Dad's death."

Pete shook his head.

"Maybe it feels easier to blame yourself than to simply admit that stuff happens and you have no control over it."

The truth just spilled out, fast, harsh. "I might be less apt to blame myself if I actually believed that God was on my side, that I wasn't a screw-up that had it coming. That somehow the people I love aren't going to pay for my mistakes."

Shoot, he didn't know why he'd decided to strip it all away and stand practically naked in the cold in front of his brother. But Sam didn't flinch. Just looked at him and shook his head. "So that's why you spent the last ten years driving me crazy."

Pete frowned.

"Because you thought if you acted like a jerk, like you didn't care about the world or anybody else, then when bad things happened to you, you deserved them."

Pete swallowed. Yeah, well . . .

"Guess what, pal? God doesn't create a blizzard because he's trying to punish you. Or cause a crazy man to force your girlfriend off the road because you slept with some girl—"

"If you're referring to Aimee, I didn't sleep with her." Not that the clarification really mattered, but . . . okay, maybe it did.

Sam raised an eyebrow.

Pete looked away. "I couldn't."

Sam cocked his head.

"I mean, I could. Of *course* I could." Now he might be going overboard because a smile ran up one side of Sam's face. "But I didn't. Because I *chose* not to. Because . . . I don't know. I . . ." Pete ran the back of his hand across his mouth. "I'm broken, Sam. I

. . . I lost the old me." He gave a burst of laughter that had him cringing. "Oh, you have no idea. I'm clearly a mess."

"No, bro." Sam grinned at him. "You love Jess. And that changes everything, doesn't it? When you meet real love for the first time? You want to be worthy of it. Want to pursue it with everything inside you. And that means leaving behind the guy who ran after the cheap. You want to be the guy who deserves it."

"But I don't deserve it." Pete turned away, the words, the truth again pulsing, fighting for air.

Sam, perfect, honorable Sam couldn't possibly understand the impulses that made Pete . . . well, undeserving.

"Probably not," Sam said quietly. "But love says it doesn't matter. True love—unconditional love—declares you worthy just because it chooses you. And there's nothing you can do about it."

The words settled in Pete's gut, made a fist.

He didn't know that kind of love.

So, he forced out something easy, anything to change the subject. "Since when did you turn into a romantic?"

Sam said nothing, as if debating his answer. Then he shrugged, letting Pete off the hook. "Engaged, bro. Or did you forget that part?"

Jerk. "Right."

"I am right. And oddly, suddenly, for the first time in your life, so are you. Taking the chance to be a different guy. To lean into love. Because that's the *right* direction. And the next step is to start trusting that love. To believe in it and truly let it change you."

Oh, no problem. Except . . . "You've been hanging around Willow too much. Because I have this feeling we're no longer talking about . . ."

"Yeah. I'm talking about God's love, Pete. You gotta start trusting in God's love for you. For Jess. Lean into it. Let it change you. Let it set you free."

Pete held up his hand. "Listen, how about we revisit this *after* God hears my prayer and saves Jess's life."

Sam considered him. "He'll find her, Pete."

Pete just blinked at that. "No. I'll find her." He had to. Because he knew the truth.

God might love Jess—of course he did—but Pete knew himself. Knew the darkness that resided inside.

He turned and walked toward the house.

Ned had never, not once, jumped fire into the Bob Marshall Wilderness. If this *was* the Bob Marshall Wilderness. Frankly, it could be any of the millions of acres of protected wildland areas of Montana. But they must be deep into some untamed forest, judging by the narrow deer trails, the cluttered, old growth of Douglas fir, larch, and shaggy black spruce. A looming escarpment, over 1,000 feet high, that walled the east as far as he could see suggested that they had driven at least ten, maybe twenty miles into the wilderness.

Still, he knew enough about the rugged Montana landscape to know that if he headed west, he'd find a road.

But first, he found a river—a fast-flowing, waist-high river that spanned twenty or more feet in places—and he realized that he could either cross the river and head southeast, along the ridge of whatever jagged peak shadowed the valley, slicking it with a late afternoon chill, or walk due west, along the creek, and hopefully to civilization.

Problem was, in order to get a cell phone signal, he also had to get to high ground. And, if he got higher, he'd also get the lay of the land.

He muscled his ache into a hard ball, crossed the river, and headed up the ridge. It led him out into the open, through a meadow filled with purple crow garlic. He picked the heads and ate them. As he ascended, he walked through fireweed, and white, gold-nectared pearly everlasting. He spotted evidence of wildfire—maybe two or three years old, a vast acreage of barren, blackened trees—that brought to mind the hours and years trekking through burning forests, just a Pulaski and a chainsaw to stop the wave of destruction.

He missed that—the gritty, dirty battle against nature. And he missed his boys—the Jude County hotshots, and later smokejumpers. The crew that worked with him. The camaraderie.

Another reason for his decision to join the navy.

No, if he were honest, the navy sign-up had to do with the fact that he simply couldn't sit around the farm one more minute.

Ned reached the ridge, sweat slicking down his spine, and stood for a moment, trying to find his bearings.

The sun had sailed past the apex of the sky, heading west, and sighting it, he turned and examined the valley behind him, divided by the river.

Beyond that, miles in the distance, he made out what could be a road winding through the trees.

But first, he pulled out his cell phone. Got a flicker of a bar. Dialed 911.

Please.

The connection struggled, and he pulled it away from his ear, watching the icon spin. *Connecting . . .*

Then, abruptly, he got a hit. "911 . . . will . . . hold?"

"Are you kidding me? No!" But the call clicked off, and when he looked, the connection had died.

Seriously.

He held up his phone, and not only did the bar flicker, but his battery beeped down to three percent. Nice, just perfect.

He dialed the only number he could think of. *Please, someone be home.*

SUSAN MAY WARREN

The voice that answered rocked him back. "Yo. Bro. 'Sup?"

Fraser? But he didn't have time to ask his SEAL brother what he was doing home, or where he'd been this summer when they'd really needed him. "Fraser," he said. "I was run off the road last night and someone is trying to kill us and—" No, no, make it easier. Quicker. "I'm in Montana. In the middle of a forest, and Shae and Jess are hurt—"

He attributed Fraser's cut-to-the-chase response to his military training. "Where in Montana?"

"I think I'm south of Glacier National Park, but I could be wrong. Maybe the Bob Marshall Wilderness, but it could be anywhere."

His phone beeped, another bar down.

"Landmarks, bro."

Right. "I see a lake to the southwest. And . . . there's a big peak to my east."

"That's all of western Montana!"

"Okay, there's—wait. A bunch of switchbacks in the valley below, dirt roads. And to my northwest, about eleven o'clock, there's a crow's nest. A lookout tower."

The phone beeped again.

"I'm losing you—call Shae's friends. The PEAK guys, see if—"

"Stay warm and find shelter. Stay alive. We'll—"

The phone died.

Find you.

That's what he imagined Fraser was about to say. But really, what echoed in Ned's brain was Fraser's previous words. *"That's all of western Montana."*

Oh, he'd done a stellar job of pinpointing their location.

But the crow's nest—that might still be an active fire lookout, with a working radio.

And if he could get back to the river, he could follow it west . . .

Or, he could keep hiking along the river, toward the clearing he'd spotted in the trees, maybe a trail, or even one of those forest service switchbacks.

But the ridge on the other side offered a path to the lookout tower.

The sun chased him down the ridge, and by the time he reached the river, the sweat was threatening to turn to chill. With no resources save his leather jacket—which he probably should have left with Shae and Jess, come to think of it—and his body achy, he needed to find shelter before it got dark.

He crossed the river and found hoofprints indenting the spongy grasses. And farther down, in the dusky light, he spotted the remains of a campfire, the ash dry and white but recent enough for him to conjure up a crew of hunters.

Deer season in the backwoods. He'd spent one autumn in Ember, Montana, after hotshot season and had gone out hunting with Reuben Marshall, a Montana cousin.

Deer season meant hunters. And maybe walkies. Or cell phones with transponders. He followed the trail up along the ridge, squinting in the wan dusk of light. The path arched above the river, back into the trees. He guessed himself maybe four miles from where he'd left Shae and Jess—his route memorized by the lay of the land, the peaks and ridges.

Maybe he should go back, stay safe and warm, like Fraser said.

But he'd never been very good at staying put. Something his brothers had taught him. Both of them, but especially Fraser, the hotshot, the football star, the golden child.

And shoot, Ned did want to follow in his footsteps. Prove that he was every bit the man Fraser was. More perhaps, because Fraser had never jumped out of a plane from 3,000 feet into an inferno, armed with only a Pulaski and a chainsaw.

Hooyah.

154

Ned's body had started to work out the ache and he'd found his rhythm, the forest speaking to him as he listened to the rush of water to his right, the creak and moan of the trees arching over him. The sun simmered in the west, turning the sky a tufted orange and lavender, the valley below a deep, burning umber, the trees nearly black in relief against the flame.

And ahead, just an outline, the crow's nest rose from some unnamed peak, a dark sentinel. He guessed it six miles away, maybe more.

Maybe he'd find the hunters first.

He stopped, looking back along his route, just another moment to memorize the dent of forest, and . . .

Through the trees, back along his route, on the other side of the river, a light flickered on.

A porch light, or maybe a front light.

A cabin. Peeking through the woods, maybe two miles down-hill.

Thank you, *thank you*. He turned, and his footfalls sent rocks tumbling down the slope.

A wolf howled in the distance, the echo lonely and dissipating into the breeze.

Ned picked up his pace to nearly a jog.

When the shot rang out, he jerked at the report. The explosion echoed down the river valley, ricocheted against the cliff wall, and slowed him.

Hunters.

Or . . . worse.

Ned took off in a run.

The second explosion spun him around, flashed fire through his body. He gasped, the pain blinding, crumpling him to his knees.

His momentum sent him over the edge of the ridge. He skidded down the cliff, his body aflame as he jerked and howled, scrabbling for purchase. Writhing, he tumbled and slid and burned and *landed*, a hard jolt at the bottom that emptied his lungs.

Sucking wind hard, he fought for breath like a drowning man.

His vision finally cleared, and the world returned to him in hard, brutal planes.

Someone had shot him.

Maybe in the back. Maybe the leg. He couldn't tell. But his heartbeat whooshed in his ears as he lay there, gathering himself. Assessing, trying to locate the source of his injury.

But for the moment, he could do nothing but lie in the darkness, whimpering.

————— + —————

Jess would surrender her entire trust fund for a fire. It didn't even have to be big. Just a trickle of flame from a tiny mound of twigs, enough to heat her fingers back to life, maybe touch her core with a lick of warmth.

And mostly to keep Shae from shivering herself into hypothermia. Jess sat against the cave wall, Shae's back to her chest, Jess's arms and legs wrapped around her to keep her from losing too much body heat. The temperature during the day hadn't exactly been frigid, but being half-exposed to the elements and sitting on a hard rock enclave had done nothing to add precious heat to Shae's body.

Jess had left long enough to find pine boughs and drag them back to the cave in an effort to create a sort of bed off the floor. Although the spines of the boughs dug into her backside, left indentations and bruises, it got them off the damp rock. And with the sun setting, they needed any advantage as the chilly air crept in through their flimsy clothes.

Shae wore a pair of leggings and a dress, her jean jacket more decoration than outerwear. And Jess rued the thought—the one that had her wanting to attract Pete's attention should he be at the reception—that made her don her black dress.

So, they needed each other. Jess periodically reached down to check Shae's pulse. It had slowed, dangerously so, Jess thought, and a touch to Shae's forehead suggested she didn't shiver from cold but from the temperature she ran.

"Shae, how are you doing?"

Shae groaned, and Jess jostled her awake. "Tell me about Ned. Where did you meet him?"

Outside, the sunlight had shrunk back into the forest, leaving the night to seep into their enclave. Please, let Ned have found help. Because if he hadn't made it back yet, she hadn't a clue how he'd find his way back now. Only with flashlights and SAR equipment and guys like Pete who—

No.

"C'mon, Shae, wake up. Tell me about Ned."

Shae moaned, but she opened her eyes.

"You met this summer, in Minnesota?"

"Mmmhmm."

"How?"

"He was . . . at the country music festival when the tornado hit. We hid together."

Oh. The tornado that destroyed the tiny town of Duck Lake, Minnesota, where Ben King had been playing. His father, Chet, had gone missing, and the PEAK team deployed to hunt him down.

"His brother was lost in the tornado."

"Oh no."

Shae drew in a breath. "He lived. Because PEAK found him."

Right. True to form, Chet had managed to save the lives of five teenagers on the local track team. "Was his brother on the track team?"

"No. He was trapped with the other half of the team. I helped with the search."

And apparently, hit it off with Ned. "Are you two dating?"

"I . . . I don't know. We got . . . close. During the search."

Yeah, well, high trauma and stress did that to people. Brought out their worst. Or best.

When it came to Pete, definitely his best. His heroic, I-will-show-up aura that made a girl believe that he might, at any moment, poke his head into the cave and tell her that everything would be okay. That she didn't have to be afraid. That no one was getting hurt today, not on his watch.

"I don't know why he came to Montana," Shae said softly. "Not that I'm complaining. He's . . ."

"Cute."

"Yeah. And kind. And patient. He used to be a smokejumper. He knows Pete from a few summers ago when they jumped fire together."

That information sent a sliver of hope through Jess. It meant that maybe Ned was cut from the same cloth. The never-give-up fabric.

"Except, after this, he'll probably run back to Minnesota as fast as he can." Shae shook her head.

"What are you talking about? I saw the way he carried you, the way he talked to you. He's not running away."

"He should. I just cause trouble, everywhere I go. And some-day he's going to get hurt—he already is." She shook her head. "I should have never come back to Montana."

Yeah, well, Jess understood that sentiment. All the same, "Give the guy a chance to prove you wrong. He might do something . . . well, amazing." Like show up in Paris.

Like propose at the top of the Eiffel Tower.

Like become Mister Romantic when she least expected it.

"And if he does, don't second-guess it. Just believe it. Hold on to it. Because a man giving his heart away is a rare and beautiful thing."

"Is that what you meant in the car? When you said that what you did to him wasn't fair?" Shae asked. "What *did* you do to him?"

Oh. Jess closed her eyes. "I broke his heart."

"How?"

The last thing Jess wanted to do was take a trek down the most painful year of her life. Well, not exactly the most painful, but watching your mother be diagnosed with a terminal illness, watching her deteriorate, it was right up there with having cops show up at your door and drag your father to prison.

Or maybe, walking through hordes of haters, listening to them call you and your family names, dodging epithets and sometimes even worse.

"It's a long story."

"I have a date later, but I could pencil you in for now," Shae said.

Jess gave a sad smile. "I don't know where to start."

"You said you went home to New York City."

"Yes. Right. Well, I returned home to more than I imagined. Between visiting my father in prison, packing the house to move, and her social calendar, my mother needed help. So I started filling in, going to events with Felipe, and that included a trip to Paris. Problem was, with everything that was going on, and Pete's callouts, we kept missing each other. Pete finally came to New York City for a fund-raiser and found me. But I was on my way to Paris. The last thing I ever imagined was that Pete would follow me."

"To *Paris*?"

"I know. I couldn't believe it when Pete showed up at the country estate where Felipe's family was holding a party. I mean, Pete Brooks, Montana cowboy, dressed in a silk suit, showing up at a horse race, drinking champagne . . . it was surreal."

"Pete did that? He's so romantic."

Huh. Funny. She'd never thought about that, but maybe, in his own way, Pete was devastatingly romantic. "We drove back to Paris and eventually ended up at the Eiffel Tower. Where he proposed."

And for a moment, she was there, sinking into his arms. *"Of course I will marry you."*

"What did you say?"

"I said yes. And I intended to follow him stateside . . ."

"Don't break my heart." Oh Pete, I'm sorry.

"And then . . . then, well, let's just say that everything crashed around me. And Felipe was there to help pick up the pieces."

"Your former fiancé."

"Yeah."

"If you had Felipe, why did you choose Mercy Falls to escape to?"

"Because . . . I was afraid I would destroy Felipe's life with the scandal. I knew Ty Remington. We skied together as kids, and he was Felipe's roommate."

"So he hid you."

"He helped me get a job. Start over." And live the lie.

"Did he introduce you to Pete?"

"Pete joined PEAK, and we started out as friends. But, well . . ."

"It's Pete. He's hard to ignore."

"I fell hard. I had changed my name, wanting to leave that life behind. I didn't want anyone else to get hurt because of me. But Pete is a true hero. He rescued a group of kids, and the press was all over him. He wanted to give me the credit and I just . . . well, I freaked out. I didn't want anyone to find me." And because she'd been desperate, she'd turned to Ty.

Ty, who stepped between her and Pete.

Ty, who pretended to be her boyfriend, until he fell hard for his own true love.

"I hurt Pete and he left town." All because she feared telling him the truth about her past.

160

Because who would love a woman who betrayed her family? Apparently, Pete.

"He came back about a year later, told me he couldn't forget me. That he loved me. And he proposed for the first time."

"He's proposed to you *twice*?"

The words hit her exactly as they should. Because yes, Pete had proposed twice, and frankly, she didn't deserve a third chance. Which she'd never get anyway.

"It was bad timing. My dad had a heart attack in prison, and suddenly I feared losing him and the life I'd had, although I had walked away from it. Pete figured out that I wasn't ready, and right about then Ian and Sierra went missing—"

"Wait. I remember this. I came to your house, and Pete answered the door . . ."

That's right. Shae had walked back into their lives, and suddenly Jess had realized she was tired of running, of hiding. So she'd told Pete she chose him. Wanted him.

"You were there for the rest. When we found Ian and his shipmates, I knew one of them. She called Felipe, and he showed up at the hospital."

"And you left for New York City."

And she left for New York City. "My mother was . . . well, I had read it all wrong. She was thrilled to see me. My brother had moved to England, so she was alone. We visited my father often as he recovered, and then . . . well, I started to notice that something wasn't quite right. She kept forgetting things, and her hands shook. I took her to the doctor for tests, but they couldn't find anything. And then . . . then Pete showed up at a fund-raising gala in New York City. I couldn't believe it. I was so . . . shocked. And thrilled to see him. Because although Felipe wanted to get back together, I . . ."

"You still loved Pete."

Jess leaned her cheek against Shae's head. "I've never stopped."

"What happened in Paris when everything fell apart?"

"I went back to Felipe's chateau prepared to tell him that I was ready to move back to Montana. And discovered that he'd been trying to get ahold of me." She closed her eyes. "My mother had a seizure."

"Where have you been, Selene?"

She opened her eyes. "Felipe met me at the door, and he was panicked and angry. He told me that my mother had collapsed at the reception. He was crazy with worry. I'd texted him, but he'd never gotten it—I found out later that my phone plan wouldn't work overseas. Felipe took me to the hospital, and I was there for over a week as the doctors tried to figure out what was wrong. And Felipe—he was so sweet the entire time.

"I was upset about Pete—of course Felipe knew I'd been with him. He let me use his phone to call Pete, but he didn't pick up. I called twice, then again, a couple days later. My life was consumed by doctors and tests and . . . pretty soon a couple weeks had gone by. I thought we'd head home, so I decided to talk to Pete when we got stateside.

"But a couple weeks stretched out to after Christmas, and by the time we got home, well, nearly two months had gone by since Pete had left. I know it was selfish . . . I guess I thought he'd understand. And he probably would have, if I'd tried harder and actually got ahold of him."

Shae had reached out, taken her hand. Squeezed. "I get it. I should have told Uncle Ian I was alive. The longer I waited, the harder it was to face the hurt I'd caused him."

"Yeah. And I was also trying to figure out how to tell my father that my mother was—is—dying."

"Oh no."

"Yeah. We found out that she has a disease called Creutzfeldt-Jakob. It's a fast-acting, degenerative brain disorder."

"Oh, Jess."

"Yeah. I'm so thankful Pete told me to go home." The words just spilled out, a realization she hadn't quite formed before. Because of Pete she got to say good-bye.

"When Mother got out of the hospital, she had one request—that Felipe and I get married before she died."

Shae leaned over and looked up at her. In the barest of fading light, Jess met her eyes. "I wanted to tell her no, but . . . she was hurting and scared and I thought I'd eventually find a way to tell her that I didn't love Felipe that way anymore. But, at the moment I didn't know what to do."

"What *did* you do?"

"It was Felipe's idea to tell my mother we were engaged. He . . . well, he had his reasons. Namely, a woman he was desperately in love with who he couldn't be with. At first, I thought he was trying to make her jealous. But it's more complicated than that. And now . . . he seems to really want to marry me."

"What do you want?"

"I don't know . . . I don't want to hurt Felipe. He's a good man. When he suggested the engagement, I thought we'd simply go through the motions, make my mother happy until we returned to America and she was more stable, maybe even a little stronger and I could tell her that . . . I don't know. That I didn't want the life she longed for me to have? She'd mapped out a happy ending for me, and it felt so cruel to shatter those dreams. But I also knew I couldn't break Pete's heart." She sighed. "I know it sounds devious and morbid, but after everything, I just wanted her to get better. I thought maybe it would help if we said we were engaged."

She shook her head. "My mother announced our engagement. I think my mother's secretary wrote up the announcement, but that's when everything got out of control. I tried to call Pete on New Year's Eve, right after we returned, to explain, but he didn't pick up. And after the media got ahold of the news, I feared he'd find out, so I tried again. But he never took my calls. I even texted, but all my texts said 'sent,' not 'delivered' and I figured it out . . . he'd blocked me."

"He *blocked* you? Oh boy."

"Of course he was angry. I didn't blame him, but I was devastated. Felipe found me crying and told me everything would work out. I didn't realize he meant that he truly intended to marry me."

If she hadn't been quite so heartbroken, she might have understood his plan. She heard her voice, plaintive, broken. *"I know he's with someone else, Felipe. I just . . . I just know."*

Pete hadn't deserved that. But in her aching heart, her worst fears found daylight. "Truth is, I feared that Pete was with someone else." Of course he was, and the memory of Pete kissing the blonde burned through her. "I know it wasn't fair, but I remembered the Pete I knew, the one who filled up his loneliness and hurt with company, and I couldn't blame him, but it hurt too much to call him. So, I didn't."

"Then why did you come back this weekend?"

Desperation? Hope?

"I don't know."

Except she did, didn't she? She'd even said it earlier. "I never stopped loving him, I guess." Jess drew in a breath. "Which I suppose is why I freaked out when I saw him with someone else. Kissing someone else."

Because she'd been right.

Shae nodded. "Her name is Aimee. She works on his Red Cross team."

Of course she did. Jess blinked back the burn in her eyes. "He deserves someone who won't hurt him."

"He deserves to be with someone who loves him," Shae said quietly.

Jess would love him until the day she died. "Pete is . . . the most amazing man I've ever known. And he deserves to be happy. To be loved by someone who won't break his heart."

"So, stop breaking his heart," Shae said.

Jess stilled.

"You've told me twice that you have made decisions because you don't want to hurt someone. Pete, your mother. Even Felipe. And especially you. Someone is going to get hurt here, Jess. And right now, it's everyone. Make a choice."

She drew in a breath. "You're right. I made this mess. I need to fix it."

8

"A LOOKOUT TOWER. A mountain, a river, and a few switchback roads? That could be all of Montana!" Pete braced his arms over the map in the middle of the room, studying the landmarks Ned had described to his brother, Fraser Marshall.

Who had called the PEAK team shortly after sundown last night with a message. Ned, Shae, and Jess had been run off the road, but they'd managed somehow to escape and were now lost in the wilderness. His words lit a fire under the team.

Especially when he added, "Ned said Shae and Jess were hurt."

Yeah, that did wonders for Pete's ability to focus. He'd stayed up most of the night with Ian and Kacey routing out possible locations.

At one point he'd wandered out to the porch to stare at the stars and listen to Sam's voice. *"You gotta start trusting in God's love for you. For Jess. Lean into it."*

He didn't know how to lean into God's love. What that even looked like.

The stars blinked in and out of a cluttered sky, the air crisp. He'd smelled snow in the air, and it turned him brittle.

God, I know you probably don't want to hear from me, but I need you to keep them alive. Long enough for me to find them.

166

He'd finally trudged back inside, found the lights off, everyone trying to get some shut-eye before dawn. He'd forced himself to lie on the sofa, to close his eyes.

And all it did was scrape up the image of Jess, backlit by flames, grimy and wide-eyed as he emerged through the forest on his four-wheeler. Or Jess, nearly falling as she rappelled during a training op.

Or even Jess, the wind in her hair, shivering as he held her, as he handed over his heart to her in Paris.

Stay alive, honey. I'll find you.

He wasn't the only one thinking about Jess—and Shae. Ian hadn't gone home, either. He'd spent the night upstairs in the bunk room, tossing away the night.

And Felipe. They'd all sort of forgotten about Felipe, who stood back, arms folded, face grim as he listened to them talk. He'd also retired upstairs, to the men's bunk room.

The rest of the team had peeled away to regroup, catch some winks. Kacey and Ben left for their lodge home just down the road. Sam had brought Willow home. Sierra had stuck around in the women's bunk room. And Gage and Ty returned to their condo, dropping Brette off at the apartment she shared with Ella, Gage's girlfriend.

At the first wax of gray light, Pete was up making coffee.

Sierra came down soundlessly and pulled some pancake batter, already mixed, from the fridge. She said nothing as she retrieved a griddle.

Ian emerged, donning a thermal shirt. He walked over to Sierra, wrapped his arm around her neck, and kissed the top of her head. She turned in his arms, curled hers around his waist, and set her head on his chest.

Pete turned away, his gut twisting, a longing rising through him so thick he couldn't breathe. He went outside, let the crisp air peel away the frustration and loosen the coil in his gut.

The rim of Rocky Mountains to the east was still shrouded in the royal blue cover of night, the sunlight beyond just burning it away with a glorious ribbon of gold and salmon. A pale layer of snow evidenced the cold night in the higher elevations.

Pete shoved his hands into his jeans pockets, blinking hard against the chill that swept in under his T-shirt—a change he'd gotten from Gage, who stashed a small wardrobe upstairs.

The door opened, and Pete stiffened to see Felipe walk outside. He handed Pete a cup of coffee. Met his eyes.

Pete's mouth tightened, but he accepted it.

A truck pulled up in the gravel drive, and Kacey and Ben got out. Kacey touched Pete's arm as she ascended the steps. Ben nodded to him, then Felipe.

Apparently, no one was taking sides today.

Neither was Pete. Because right now it didn't matter whom she chose.

He turned, looked at Felipe, whose gaze was now fixed on the mountains. The Frenchman looked rough—dark whiskers across a weary face. Red-lined eyes. So maybe he too spent the night fighting demons.

"We're going to find her today," Pete said, and then, not sure why, he clamped a hand on Felipe's shoulder.

Felipe's jaw tightened, but he met Pete's gaze and nodded.

Pete headed inside, the room now thick with the smell of frying bacon and flapjacks.

Kacey was printing off the updated weather report.

Ben and Ian stood over the map, debating.

Pete's phone buzzed from where he'd plugged it in to charge last night next to the sofa. He picked it up and tried to swallow back his disappointment that it wasn't Jess.

"Sam."

"We got a break," his brother said. "A couple hunters called in just a few minutes ago. They apparently tried to track a deer they shot last night, but it got away. When they took another look this morning at the tracks—well, they think they shot a person."

Pete wrapped his hand around his neck, kneading a muscle there. "And?"

"They couldn't find him, but they found blood. And boot tracks. Possibly male, from the size."

Oh no. Pete closed his eyes. "What did they call on—a sat phone?"

"I don't know."

"If it was a cell, maybe they called from the same pocket Ned located. Do you know where?"

Pete had raised the attention of everyone in the room, maybe by his voice, perhaps his posture, but Sierra turned off the heat on the flapjack griddle and bacon pan, and Ian walked over to the map. He braced himself over it, staring at Pete, as if he could somehow hear the conversation with his Superman ears.

"Just east of the Bob Marshall Wilderness," Sam said. "Not far from the Squeezer Creek Lookout tower. It's about fifteen clicks south of Swan Lake, toward the Bob."

Pete set his phone down on the map and clicked it on speaker. "Tell us again, Sam."

Sam repeated the information, and Pete pinpointed the tower. "It's west of Swan Peak."

"The mountain to the east," Kacey said, repeating Fraser's words. "And if the lookout tower was to the northwest, around 11:00, that puts him in this area." She pointed to a ridgeline.

"He mentioned a lake to the southwest," Ian said. "Could be Van Lake."

"And there are switchback roads all over Swan Mountain."

"Kacey, let's get a chopper up there, see if we can spot anything," Pete said.

"I'm pulling in," Sam said and hung up. Outside, his truck hit the gravel lot.

"I know that area," Ty said. Pete looked up to see Gage and Ty crowding around the map. "That's not too far from where the chopper went down."

Ty pointed to a campground maybe ten miles northwest of Swan Mountain. "We were headed here, to pick up a wounded skier. Ended up north of there about eight miles."

Sam had entered and now came over to the map, Willow behind him.

"There's no way you're going to get four-wheelers in there," Ty said. "Horses, maybe . . ."

Horses. Pete drew in a breath, his hands breaking out in a sweat.

Sam gave him a tight-lipped shake of his head.

"Fine. Okay," Pete said, ignoring him.

"I'll call my brother and we'll get some of our pack horses loaded up." Ty pulled his cell phone from his pocket.

"I'll ride with Kacey," Gage said. "More eyes."

"I can ride," Ian said.

"As can I," Felipe said.

Sam was still looking at Pete, but he didn't meet his gaze. He *could* ride.

Mostly.

Pete wiped his hands on his jeans. "We all need maps, and I'll head out to the barn for a few first aid packs. If Ned is injured—"

"Ned is injured?" Ian said.

Pete glanced at him, but Sam filled in the blanks. "A couple hunters called in fearing they'd shot someone last night. They couldn't confirm until this morning."

"He's *shot*?" Ian's words silenced everyone. Ian took a breath, and Sierra covered her mouth with her hand, turning away.

"We don't know that," Sam said, using his cop tone. "But maybe." He turned to Pete. "You could stay here, run ops—"

"Have you lost your mind?" Pete rounded on him. "I'm not staying here while the woman I . . ." He swallowed, amended, "When Jess is out there, hurt and terrified and possibly hunted by the person who ran them off the road."

"But—"

Pete held up his hand. "Don't, Sam—"

"He hates horses. Got bucked off once and broke his leg."

Pete shot his brother a look. "Thanks. We all needed to know that. Yeah, I hate horses. But seriously, I also hate airplanes, but that doesn't stop me from flying. Sheesh, Sam."

"I'll run coms," Sierra said, sweetly rescuing him. "And Chet is on his way in."

No, Chet was already there, the wind whisking in behind him.

But really, they could use someone professional at the helm, running operations.

Not Pete. Not today.

In fact, a part of him would like to never run operations again, maybe. The thought slicked through him, tightened in his gut. Lately, he hated running operations. The responsibility, the mistakes . . . even though he mostly got it right, the times that he got it wrong sat in his gut, took hold, and held him prisoner.

This is your fault.

He hadn't really realized before how much he carried those words with him. "Sorry, but I'm not staying behind." Pete grabbed his jacket. "Meet me in the barn for coms and maps. If Ned is shot, we're running out of time."

———— + ————

The good news was that Shae had stopped shivering. Sometime during the night, her body simply began to shut down, sink into the cold and the pain, and now she just felt numb.

As long as she didn't move. Because when she moved, pain wrapped tentacles around her, cut off her breathing, and threatened to make her shrill out a scream.

Jess curled behind her, her arm around her waist, pulling her in close to conserve body heat, her breaths steadily rising and falling. She knew because she'd been listening, depending on that steady breathing for the better part of the night, her gaze peeled on the entrance to the cave.

Praying.

Keeping at bay the brutal thought that Blackburn had found Ned. Killed him.

Left him to die in the woods, like he had Dante.

Shae's eyes burned, and she blinked away the moisture. It trickled across her nose, dripped onto her arm. Sweet, heroic Dante. Her first real love. He'd wanted to join the military, to be a soldier.

Even had a plan to ask Ian if he could marry her.

"Run, Esme!"

Her breath hitched, Dante's shout like a flash in her head, reviving the past so vividly that for a second she was caught up in the smells of that summer day, the feel of his hand in hers as they hiked down the path, away from the campfire. Away from Uncle Ian and his watchdogging.

He'd caught them, just the night before, in a pretty G-rated clench that he'd completely overreacted to, losing his mind and ordering her into her tent like she might be a grade-schooler and not an eighteen-year-old woman who'd just gotten accepted to Yale.

So, she'd sneaked out that morning to find Dante and talk about . . . well, yeah. Running away. Being together.

"Es—just wait. Let's think about this." Tall, wide-shouldered, lean and tough, Dante had all the markers of trouble. A tattoo that banded his arm, a half-hitch smile that made her heart flip in her

chest. Dark hair that fell over his beautiful brown eyes, and despite the renegade spirit he exuded, he possessed a way of looking at her that shut down the chaos and fear in her head. Safe. Dante made her feel *safe*.

And right then she got it—Dante, for all his trouble-making history, had reminded her of Uncle Ian. Brave. Confident. Creative.

She'd woven her fingers around his neck, leaning against him. "I have thought about it. I want to be with you."

Even in memory she wanted to shake her head. Poor Ian—and even Sierra—had tried to talk her out of giving away her scholarship, but she'd been so focused on the immediate, she hadn't given one thought to the future.

Not again. Shae refused to live by her passions. If she lived through this, she'd listen to her uncle. Let him come up with a plan. Obey it.

"I love you, babe. We'll figure it out, I promise." Dante had kissed her then, so sweetly, his hands on her waist to keep their passion at bay.

As the golden dawn streamed light through the forest that fateful morning, he'd pushed her away and taken her hand, walking her down the path. "We'll figure out a way to make it work. You'll visit me after basic, and when I get leave, you know I'll find you. And you can come down to wherever I'm stationed for spring break."

He'd been drawing a picture of their future, enough for her to start to see it, when he suddenly stiffened and pulled her down, behind a scruff of bushes.

Across the river, in a clearing, a man yelled at a woman, clearly scaring her because she held her hands up, as if for protection. Shae made out words that she'd heard before, back when she lived with her mother, and it made her want to cover her ears and run.

Dante's arm locked around her waist, and he held her to himself.

"It's Sheriff Blackburn," he said. He would know, of course. More, she too recognized him as one of Uncle Ian's friends. Blackburn had sparred with her uncle in his home gym.

Dante leaned over. "Shh. It's okay. Let's just go back to camp."

She'd started to rise, her gaze stuck on the altercation when, to her horror, the man hit the woman so hard she cried out, tripped backward, and fell right over the edge of the cliff.

Twenty or more feet down, into the river below.

Shae spotted her crumpled at the base of the cliff, her blood pooling into the water a moment before the rapids gobbled her up.

Shae had screamed. A high, loud shriek that echoed through the canyon and alerted the man across the river.

Dante's hand clamped over her mouth, but the man had already spied her. Shut her down with the look in his eyes.

"Run!" Dante's hand closed around hers, tugging.

The man had already taken off into the bush.

She just stood there, stupidly, unmoving. Just like she had when her mother's boyfriends started screaming at her. She couldn't think, couldn't react. Just mentally retreated, leaving her body behind.

Unable to fight back.

Precious moments during which Dante actually picked her up and started to run with her. Stumbling, really, because he too was freaked out. She finally pushed against his chest, coming back to herself. He looked pale and terrified as he put her down.

She made the mistake of looking behind her, down the trail.

And screamed again. Because the man had found a place to cross. He barreled up the trail after them.

She turned, and this time her legs worked. But the trail was rutted and old, the path broken with roots and boulders, and she fell, skinning her hands, her knees. Dante hooked his arm around her waist and hauled her up, pushing ahead.

Then he yowled, stumbling, and landed on his hands and knees. He was bleeding behind the ear.

The man had thrown something—a rock probably—and it nailed Dante in the head.

She whirled around just as another rock whizzed past her head.

Then the man was on her. Or would have been had Dante not gotten up and lunged at him, meeting him in the path with a feral, wounded cry.

She'd shattered, right there, watching the man take Dante down. He was big—probably had sixty pounds on Dante.

Even as Dante fought back, Shae knew.

Dante would die for her.

"Run!" Dante was screaming. Blood ran from his nose, his ears, but still he fought.

Run, Esme!

Yes, run. The words clicked in and found her synapses, her muscles, and suddenly, just like that, she fled. Down the path and the direction where they'd come.

Run away. Into the forest. Run away as fast as her legs could take her. Run away and hide! Hide until dark, until Dante stopped screaming, until she knew the truth, and then keep running.

She'd found a cabin in the woods. A woman who recognized trauma in Shae's wide eyes and garbled words. A woman who put her in her old truck and drove her to a lodge on the other side of the park where Sheriff Blackburn would never think to look for her.

Stupid her had thought, after five years, she could actually stop running. What had she been thinking? That Blackburn would simply forget the girl who'd seen him beat the boy she loved to death?

And now . . . Shae closed her eyes and put a hand to her mouth. Which only made her release a groan and elicited a shiver. The tears took her, bending her in half as she sobbed, her hands pressed to her mouth to keep from waking Jess.

Blackburn was going to take more people from her.

Dawn waxed gold along the riverbed, peeling away the shadows, and Ned was still out there.

Probably dead.

"Shae, are you okay?"

Jess had roused behind her, and Shae heard a quick intake of breath as her friend moved. A chill stole through her as Jess sat up. She pressed her hand to Shae's forehead. "You're a little warm."

No, actually, she just might be freezing to death. She couldn't seem to stop shaking.

"Ned isn't back yet," she whispered.

Jess said nothing. But she stood up and walked out to the edge of the cave as if assessing their situation.

Which, to Shae's math, felt dire. No food, no water, and now her teeth chattered. Jess held her arm to her body, but even as Shae watched, Jess worked her wrist in a circle. So, maybe not broken like Jess had feared.

They had to get out of here.

"We can't wait for Ned," Shae said quietly.

Jess didn't move.

"He's not coming back."

This got a reaction. Jess turned, frowned. "He's coming back."

"Not if he's dead."

Jess just stared at her. "He's not . . . he's . . . no." She turned back to the entrance. "He's coming back."

Jess made a noise, something of a hiccup, then in a moment she stumbled out of the cave, climbing over the rocks and disappearing.

"Jess?"

Shae bit back a moan and rolled over onto all fours. Reached out for a grip on the rock. A sweat broke out as her entire body clenched, but she bit down on the pain and found her feet. She leaned hard on the rock. "Jess!"

Bracing her hand along the cave, she took a step toward the entrance, then another.

Rocks spilled, footsteps scrabbling toward the opening.

She stilled, held her breath.

Jess appeared, her arm around . . . *Oh, Ned!*

He was limping, half-dragging one foot, breathing hard, his jaw clenched so tight Shae thought he might break molars. He leaned hard on a stick, and the other hand reached out to brace himself on a boulder.

Fatigue and cold stripped the color from his skin, and his dark hair was matted, his clothes sodden and grimy.

"Ned!" Shae reached out for him but couldn't hide a wince as she lifted her hand.

He caught it. Wove his fingers between hers, dropped his walking stick, and curled his other hand around her neck. "Shae."

"What happened?"

He didn't answer her. Instead, he kissed her, hard, his lips crushing hers, holding her there as if he might be unraveling, as if only her touch kept him together. He backed off, his body trembling, his voice falling. "Shae."

Then his knees buckled.

"Ned!"

He slid down to a ball at her feet.

Jess crouched beside him, her hand to his forehead. "He's burning up."

"I'm fine."

"You're not fine! You're hurt!" Shae slipped down to her knees.

He closed his eyes, leaned forward on both hands. Then, slowly, he put his head in her lap, letting his body fall to the side.

"Ned?"

"I just need a second. Just . . . a . . ." He drew in a breath, let it go.

"Ned!"

Jess pressed her fingers to his carotid artery. "Just sleeping. Or maybe in shock." She was examining his leg. "He's been wounded," she said. "His pants are bloody."

"I was shot," Ned said from the catacombs of slumber.

Shae stilled. Looked up, met Jess's eyes.

"Don't get excited," Ned mumbled. "I'll be fine." He sighed, a deep growl in his chest. "He hit me in the bum. It's just a graze."

Shae leaned down, ignoring the flash of pain, and kissed Ned's cheek.

"What's that for?" he mumbled.

"For being alive," she said. "For coming back."

His hand squeezed hers.

Then he was out.

———— + ————

What would Pete do? Jess didn't always want to default to that position, that thought, but Pete Brooks was the smartest rescuer she knew. He always knew the right answer and wasn't afraid to do something crazy. Like the time he'd spider rappelled down a cliff, facedown, her on his back, to escape a mother grizzly.

Those kinds of risky decisions were exactly what Jess longed to be able to reach out and grab.

Instead, she stood at the mouth of the cave, watching the sky open up and pour down despair and death, the temperature skimming just above freezing.

If they stayed, Shae—and maybe Ned too—would die. Shae was fighting a fever, and Jess feared internal bleeding from her wound; the blood was black and the wound red and inflamed with infection. Jess had taken Ned's proffered undershirt and wadded it into Shae's wound, using his belt to hold the makeshift compression bandage in place. Shae simply closed her eyes, her breaths short, her hand whitened in Ned's as Jess tended to the wound.

As for Ned, poor guy had been shot in the backside. The bullet had grazed across his upper buttock, leaving an ugly, probably agonizing, but not life-threatening wound. She was more worried about possible internal bleeding from the fall he'd taken down the hill, aggravating the already cracked ribs from yesterday's crash.

"I crawled over to the river and just sank into it, letting the coldness slow the bleeding and numb me," Ned told them after he'd slept on Shae's lap. Not long, but enough for life to return to his face. Enough for him to shut down the pain that cut off his breath when she examined his wound. What she would give for thread, or even fishing wire. Something, anything to close it.

"I can't believe you walked on this," Jess said.

"Crawled. Lots of crawling. I finally found a stick, but I stayed to the river, sitting in it to numb myself when it got crazy."

Jess could see what Shae saw in him. The guy was brave and dedicated to haul himself all the way back to their cave. In the dead of night, no less.

"There was a half-moon. And the clouds gave way halfway through the night. I followed the river, then managed to find the dry creek. It took me longer after that. I . . . well, there was no river to . . ."

Numb the pain. Jess pressed her hand on his shoulder, squeezed.

"I'm good now," Ned said, but the grit of his jaw and the finest squint around his eyes betrayed his lie. "We need to get out of here. I saw a cabin about four miles from here. We can make it. And then . . . well, at least we'll be safe and dry and warm."

That was when she rose and walked to the mouth of the cave.

As if God had heard them and decided to add more tragedy, the sky opened and sent the deluge. The water trickled into the riverbed, running through stones and rivulets down into the cave.

"You can't make it, Ned," Jess said, her breath reforming her words. "You can't walk."

"I can walk, Jess." He said it calmly. "What I can't do is carry Shae."

She turned, and his gaze caught hers, his Adam's apple dropping in his throat. It cost him to admit that—she saw it on his face.

Shae had curled next to him, and he had his arm around her. She'd stopped shivering, and Jess knew without touching her that her skin was clammy and hot. "I don't know how much internal bleeding she has, and if we move her, it could open up again and . . ." Jess shook her head.

What would Pete do?

"But if we stay, no one will ever find us." Shae's voice emerged in a mumble. "I can make it."

Jess wrapped her arms around her waist.

"We need to make a decision, Jess," Ned said.

"I know!" She drew in a hard breath. "I know, okay? But if we go, Shae could die. And if we stay . . ."

"We could all die of exposure. Not to mention I'm still bleeding, aren't I?"

Her mouth tightened. She gave a sharp nod.

"You could go," he said softly.

"That's a great way for us all to die. I don't have a compass or a map and I've never been a pro at navigation. Wilderness medicine, yes. Bringing us home . . . well, that's always been Pete's job."

And that memory only made her ache. She came over, crouched next to them. "It's getting colder out there."

"I know they're looking for us," Ned said. "I talked to my brother and I know he'll call PEAK."

"But we're not anywhere near where they're looking. And they won't have the faintest idea where we might be." Jess ran her hands up her arms, trying to stir heat into them.

Ned just looked at her.

"Every time I make a decision, someone gets hurt." She met his gaze. "I can't . . . I don't . . ."

"You don't want someone to die on your watch," Shae said. "I get that."

Ned frowned, but Jess nodded. "Last time I made a hard decision, my father was sentenced to 101 years in prison and my brother stopped speaking to me."

"That wasn't your fault," Shae said.

"It feels like it. It feels like I took the easy way out."

"What are you talking about?" Ned said. "The Ponzi scheme your father went to jail for? How is that your fault, in any way?"

And, well, what did it matter anymore? "When I was sixteen, I found my father collapsed at the bottom of the stairs. I thought he'd fallen, but really, he was having a heart attack. I called 911, and while we waited for the EMTs, he told me that he probably deserved to die. That he had done a terrible thing and that this was God's justice. I didn't know what he was talking about—and afterward, when he lived, he never said anything again."

She scrubbed her hand down her face. "And maybe I didn't want to know. My brother and I both interned for him, but I was mostly working PR. My brother came to me with questions. Said things didn't add up. Investor statements that pulled from accounts he'd never heard of. And overseas accounts that had no evident funding. But I was on my way to medical school and I . . . I just didn't want to know. So, I said nothing.

"The worst day of my life was when the FBI showed up at my school and marched me out for questioning in front of Felipe. I just wanted to run. To hide."

She closed her eyes against the shouts of her brother, clawing through the memory to terrorize her. *"How could you?"* "They told me that they had enough to put both my brother and my father—and even me, because they'd tracked my brother's emails to me—in prison for a very long time. And then . . ."

She opened her eyes, watched the sky weep. "I didn't want

to, but I was scared. I wasn't sure they could actually put me in prison, but I didn't know. And I don't know why they needed my testimony—maybe they didn't have enough evidence for all their charges. Maybe I should have said no and called their bluff. Believe me—I've blamed myself for not being stronger for years. It didn't help that my father's lawyer gave me a letter from my father. In it, he told me to testify and detailed exactly what I should say. All the proof the FBI needed to put him away." She sighed. "I think he might have been afraid of what might happen to my brother and me too. So I did what he asked."

She turned to Shae and Ned. "I memorized exactly what I needed to know, got on the stand, and convicted my father with my words. I made it emotional and real and couldn't meet his eyes once. Nor he, mine. He stared down the entire time, even when I finished. Then I sat in the gallery and listened as they took away the rest of his life."

She looked away. "I love my father. And I deliberately hurt him to save myself. And I can't do the same thing to my mother."

"That's why you're still engaged to a man you don't love," Shae said. "Deliberately hurting yourself to keep from hurting your mother. And Felipe."

"But I can't win. Because I destroyed Pete."

"You're just like your father, Jess," Shae said softly. "You believe somehow that you don't deserve to be happy. And that's why you don't choose the one person you know you want to be with."

"Not everyone gets to live happily ever after, Shae," Jess said.

Shae's mouth tightened. "I know that, Jess. Better than most. But it doesn't mean we can't try."

Jess felt like a jerk. Because Shae did understand, and she did deserve to live.

For Jess to try. "Sorry."

Shae simply met her gaze, gave her a nod.

"Okay, listen," Ned said. "Meanwhile, this cave is filling up with water."

She hadn't noticed that, but as they talked, the rainwater seemed to pool in the recesses of the cave, already five inches deep.

Jess climbed to her feet. *"It doesn't mean we can't try."* She turned to Ned. "You want to get out of here?"

"No, I'd like to stay here and build a summer home."

"Funny. Give me your jacket. I'm going to make a stretcher."

Ned unzipped his jacket even as Jess stepped out into the rain. "Stay put. I'll be back. Then we're making a run for the cabin."

9

THE CABIN WASN'T WHERE NED HAD LEFT IT, and now they were going to die.

All because he'd been shot in the backside. What a hero. Ned gritted his teeth against the burn that leached out his breath with each brutal step.

As least he was done throwing up, although that probably had more to do with whatever was going on inside his gut. Because he'd seen blood in his bile.

Thankfully, over the past two hours, the pain in his backside had lessened its grip, or maybe he'd simply gotten accustomed to gritting his teeth and bracing himself. He hardly noticed the ache in his knee anymore, although if he gave it any mind, it might shut him down.

But he could hardly lie in a ball and give up now. Not with Shae so soundless and unmoving on his back.

"Let me carry her," Jess said.

"We'll find a spot to rest," Ned said. Admittedly, he needed a break.

He just wanted to carry Shae as far as he could. The sight of Jess nearly tripping, fading, exhausted after carrying Shae on her back for the first part of their journey had dug a fist through him.

He hadn't liked her plan from the first—let her carry Shae like she might be a backpack. But Jess had found a sturdy four-inch-thick branch and had wound the arms of his coat around the stick and secured it around her waist, with the brace across her back. Then, with Ned's help, she'd positioned Shae on the floor, secured her toes, then in one smooth move, pulled her up and around her back, holding her arms in front of her.

Ned had lifted Shae's legs onto the stick, resting at least half her body weight on Jess's hips. Shae barely grunted, although her eyes opened and her mouth tightened. "I'm sorry I'm so heavy."

Hardly. The woman probably weighed 120 soaking wet. Still, he remembered carrying her through the woods. Suddenly, 120 became 300, especially for someone who hadn't eaten for thirty-six hours.

"Come on, Jess. Let me do this." He hadn't been blind to the fact that she was staggering under Shae's weight. "I'm not that hurt—"

"You *are* hurt, so stop trying to be a hero!" Jess had rounded on him with a little more oomph than necessary.

She cut her voice down. Took a breath. "Sorry. I'm freaking out here. What if . . . what if we don't find the cabin? We're in real danger of our body temperature dropping in this rain."

"But if we don't find real shelter and get help, Shae could die."

"Then we'd better get moving." She'd stood at the edge of the cave, her expression wan and hollow before he squeezed her arm and headed out into the storm.

The wind had died down and the rain eased for the first hour of their hike. He'd followed the now-filling stream, helping to steady Shae as Jess studied each step, until they finally made it to the river, now dark and frothy.

By his calculation, the ridge that led to the lookout tower was just up ahead. But he'd seen the light in the forest in the valley near the river.

That was when he found a shaggy pine tree with thick branches some eight feet off the ground. He ripped off the lower limbs to create a pocket of protection for them. Then, he helped Jess ease Shae off her perch. Jess checked her pulse, and Shae roused long enough to flash her "we'll be okay" grin at him, as if she could see the knot of worry in his chest.

Wow, he liked her spirit.

Shae's eyes closed, her breathing shallow. Jess took off the coat and sat beside her, leaning against the tree, her eyes closed.

He tried to get his bearings. How he'd found his way back in the dark—although, admittedly, sheer panic had propelled him up the river to where he'd found the creek bed. Why he didn't head straight for the cabin—well, again, his first impulse told him to get back to Shae, to Jess.

Just like the impulse to drive to Montana to see Shae. To show up at the wedding reception and . . . impress her.

"Stop trying to be a hero."

The words stuck inside him like a burr. However, Jess couldn't last another mile. And according to his math, he was all they had.

He tied the coat to his waist.

Then he walked over to Shae and knelt before her.

When she opened her eyes, he kissed her forehead, then, using Jess's technique, pulled her onto his back.

Jess roused, and in a second found her feet. "What are you doing?"

"Calm down. I'm not trying to be a hero, I'm just giving you a break."

He'd used her own words against her, and now her mouth pinched tight. "I just don't want you getting any more hurt."

"My choice. My body. And you're hurting too." He gestured to her wrist, which she still held a little gingerly.

"It's not broken," she said. "Maybe sprained, but I'm fine."

"Good. Get Shae's legs up, then lead the way. The cabin is a couple more miles down this river."

Except, it wasn't. Because two hours later, and no, maybe they hadn't gone four miles, but it felt like he'd walked a marathon, sweat streaming down his back, despite the rain that soaked through his dress shirt and raised gooseflesh. They'd long ago passed the ridge from where he'd been shot and fallen into the stream.

Jess stood next to him, her grip on his arm. "You need to rest. Your wound is bleeding again."

He gave her a look. "I know. But we need to keep going."

Jess looked like she might cry. The rain had stripped all the color from her face, and her hair was plastered to her head. Her white blouse had turned nearly translucent under her grimy and snagged dress. And she was shaking from the cold.

Shae, however, lay like the dead on his back.

"How much farther?" Jess said.

"I don't know. I expected to find it by now. To see something . . . but . . ."

"You don't know where we are?"

"No. I don't know, okay? I haven't exactly been here before. I didn't write a map on my hand."

"Well, maybe you should have!"

He stared at her, and inside a voice said that Jess was simply unraveling, a by-product of fear and maybe even regret for following his stupid idea to try to find a cabin he'd only glimpsed in the waning light.

What had he been thinking? "Yeah, maybe I should have," he snapped, not unaware that he might be coming unglued too. "But I didn't think of that. All I could think was that whoever forced us off the road, tied us up, and followed us into the forest might have found us. And I was crazy with worry that I'd come back and find you two shot in the head. So yeah, I sort of just reacted. Made it up as I went along. It was just another stupid decision, okay?"

She was staring at him. He hadn't quite meant for all that to spool out.

"Let's keep moving, okay?"

He took a step, but of course, he was angry and hurting and tired and his foot didn't quite land squarely on the slippery river rock. His knee twisted and he pitched forward, stumbling hard as his hand went out to brace himself.

Instead it glanced off a boulder and he landed on his jaw, scraping it raw before collapsing next to the boulder on his knees.

Somehow, by the grace of God, he still held onto Shae, but she'd roused and started to thrash.

"Shae, shh," Jess said, her arms around her, behind him.

He clutched the rock, fighting to summon what he had left to get up.

His legs wouldn't work.

They collapsed on him, and thankfully Jess was behind him to grab Shae before she spilled on the rocks. Jess peeled her off him as he crumpled into the rocky shore, breathing hard.

Trying not to cry.

Because oh, he longed to simply put his head down into his hands and wail. With pain, yes, but also with the dark frustration knotting inside him that turned him inside out.

Yes, they were going to die.

He closed his eyes. *"Stop trying to be a hero."*

He didn't know why those words rose inside, took root, but when Jess crawled over to him, put her hand on his back, and said, "Stay here. I'm going to walk upstream and see if I can spot anything," he didn't respond.

Just let her walk away like the coward he'd become.

"Ned?"

Shae's voice nudged him, and when he turned to her, he saw that she was crawling over to him. And despite the urge to hide, he took her in his arms and held her against him, mostly to stop her shivering. "How are you doing?"

"No," she said softly, her hand on his chest. "How are *you* doing?"

He looked away from her, into the gunmetal sky. The worst of the storm had blown over and now just the cold wind and an irritating drizzle remained, and he pressed his lips to her head, the best answer he could give her.

"What did you mean by another stupid decision?"

Oh, she'd heard that? He shook his head.

"You meant me, didn't you? Coming out here to see me—if you hadn't come to Montana, you wouldn't be sitting here, shivering, shot in the—"

"No." He pushed her away far enough to find her eyes. "No, Shae. That's not what I meant. Trust me, coming to see you was not a stupid decision." He put everything he had into his gaze, more than he was ready to say aloud. "I came out here because I did something and I wanted . . . I wanted to impress you."

"Impress me? How—okay, yes, showing up to take me dancing, I get it—"

"No. That's not it." But now his news didn't sound so impressive. "I joined the navy. I'm going to try to be a SEAL."

She just stared at him. No smile, no "That's amazing, Ned." Nothing.

If anything, she blinked, drew in a breath.

"Shae, are you okay?"

She nodded. "Yeah. I'm just . . . wow. I didn't realize . . ." The smile she gave him looked like something she'd dug deep to produce, almost a grimace. "That's great. If anyone can do it, you can."

It suddenly didn't feel great.

"What's going on, Shae?"

"Nothing. So . . . a SEAL. Why?"

Why. He didn't really have a why. Just followed an impulse.

No, that wasn't exactly true.

"I wasn't completely honest this summer about . . . well, the truth is, I wasn't just injured. I got kicked off my smokejumper team."

There, he'd said it aloud, and it hadn't dismantled him, hadn't caused him to look into the sky and howl. Just closed a fist around his heart, cut off his breathing for the briefest of seconds, and still filled his throat with a burn he couldn't quite swallow away.

"What?" Shae said.

"I got kicked off the smokejumper team."

"For getting hurt? That's crazy." She leaned up, a little spark in her eye that reminded him of this summer, her determination not to let him give up on the search for his brother when all else seemed lost.

"Not for getting hurt," he said, finally meeting her eyes. "For . . . endangering the team."

"How did you—"

"I got hurt."

She cocked her head.

"And I didn't tell anyone." He leaned his head back on the boulder. "I knew I'd wrenched my knee pretty badly, but I didn't want to tell Jed, our jump boss. He was in the middle of selection, and I didn't want any other person to take my place, so I just . . . I just took a bunch of painkillers and taped up my knee and kept going. But I only made it worse. And there we were, out in the bush, needing to hike back with all our gear during a training fire and I . . . I couldn't do it." He closed his eyes, the rain slicking his face. "Reuben and Jed had to practically carry me back to camp."

"So? It's a dangerous job."

"I was the weak link." His jaw tightened as he looked at her. "Jed chewed me up and spit me back out, and he was right. If we'd actually been deployed, and I'd gone out hurt, I could have gotten someone else hurt. They would have had to babysit me instead of doing their jobs . . ."

He looked away. "He sent me home to recover. That's why I was home when the storm hit. After we found Creed, I called Jed and asked him if I could come back. He told me to get my head on straight and he'd think about it . . . in a year."

"My guess is you didn't take that well."

Huh. He thought he had taken it very well. Had gotten in his car and driven to the nearest navy recruitment station. "The navy has this SEAL recruitment program that allows people to join the navy, and before you report for boot camp—which is usually about six months after you sign the papers to join up—you can try to qualify for the Special Ops program. They give you about six months to qualify, but if you do, you can go right to BUD/S after basic. I still haven't qualified, but I will . . ." He looked away. "I hope."

"You will, I know you will."

There they were, the words that he'd come to hear. "I don't know. I'm not getting any faster. To qualify, we have to swim, run, and do push-ups in a limited amount of time, and I'm a strong swimmer, and I can easily do the push-ups, but my run time is . . . it's bad."

"Your knee."

He nodded. Sighed. Looked at her. "I don't have my final recruitment physical until I actually show up at what is called MEPS—the military entrance processing station. But I need to be operational before that to qualify for the SEAL program."

He froze. Her eyes had filled. "What's the matter?"

She closed them as if in pain, and looked away.

"Shae?"

"I've always known you were a hero, Ned."

Huh. Because despite her words, he suddenly didn't feel like one.

"I know it was an impulsive decision, but it feels like the right one, you know?"

She nodded, gave him a tight smile, hued with sadness, as if somehow he'd broken her heart.

What . . . ?

"Ned!"

Jess half jogged, half tripped up the shoreline, shouting, "I found it!" She came closer, breathing hard as she slowed. "I found a trail from the river and it leads to a hunting cabin. I spotted it through the trees. You were right." She leaned over, grabbing her knees.

Huh.

"We're going to make it."

Maybe. But, as he wrestled himself to a stand, as he leaned down to pull Shae up, fighting to find his footing, he had a feeling that maybe the happy ending he'd come to Montana to find had just perished.

They just needed a little mercy. A smidgen of heavenly intervention. Because although Pete wasn't going to admit it, not aloud, and not even to the tiny screaming voice inside, finding Jess and Shae and Ned in the near-freezing mist that saturated the wilderness would take a miracle.

Pete stood in the riverbed, his feet soaked through as the rain coated his rainsuit, examining the crushed brush and tree limbs caused by the fall from the trail some twenty feet above.

Whoever had been shot—and the sixteen-year-old kid who described his target, in between assertions that it looked like a deer in the dimming light—had been wearing a brown jacket. Pete had found a soggy ripped piece of soft leather. And, judging by the destruction wrought on his tumble down the slope, the victim had enough weight and girth on him to crush brush, to break poplar branches and skid pine needles from the boughs of low-hanging evergreens.

The rain had destroyed everything else. Blood, footprints. All of it, washed away in the increasingly frothy river.

He glanced up to where Felipe, Ian, and Ty waited on horseback.

"Anything?" Ty yelled. They'd interviewed the hunters who'd brought them to the trail, on a ridge overlooking the river. A father and two teenaged sons on horseback. They'd chased their prey without results last night, but this morning had found enough blood and boot prints to put the cold hand of horror on them. The father had followed the destruction down to the riverbed, found evidence of more blood on the rocks, but that was where the trail ended.

They'd trekked along the ridgeline, down the river, but when the rain started, they turned back to their camp and drove out, calling in as soon as they hit cell range.

There weren't cell phone bars on the ridge where they thought they shot the victim, either, which only meant that this wasn't where Ned had called his brother.

Pete grabbed the brush and trees to anchor himself as he climbed back up the slope to where Ty sat astride a chestnut stock horse, holding the reins to Pete's sturdy, sweet—Ty's description—mare named Lulu.

Pete could jump from a peak with nothing but a backpack strapped to his shoulders, dangle over a cliff with one hand, but getting on the back of an animal . . .

So he'd had a few nightmares. It wasn't fun to be eight years old and in a full leg cast.

Pete took Lulu's reins and stood looking out over the horizon. A fog hung low, a ghost through the trees and along the valley that held the river. "How far to the crow's nest from here?" He lifted his glasses and sighted it, just barely, through the haze.

"Maybe six miles? More?" Ty said. "The river runs at least that far. He could have followed it until he found a deer path, or even a horse trail."

Pete turned, scanning the area. From here, the wilderness dropped off into a mass of shaggy pine, gray poplar, and black-and-white birch. Thick and tangled and menaced with bobcats, mountain lions, wolves, and grizzlies.

Not to mention, if they kept following the river, a fifty-foot waterfall and a spectacular hike for anyone who wasn't hypothermic, hungry, and needing help.

"Are we guessing that he came from the opposite direction? Walking toward the crow's nest? Because if he'd seen it from any point beyond this, wouldn't he have gone straight for it instead of walking this way?"

Felipe sat in his saddle as if he'd been born there. He backed up his filly, turned it. "If I were looking for help, I'd want to get high, find a place that might pick up my cell phone signal."

Ian was nodding. "Except now that he's located the crow's nest, he'll have headed there."

"And what about Jess and Shae?" Ty said.

"You're assuming they weren't together," Felipe said. "Maybe he climbed up here, looking for a signal, got shot, and they helped him down the river."

"He said they were hurt," Pete said. "I would have gone for help."

Thunder rolled, and a tremor went through Lulu. Pete put a hand on her withers. Just what he wanted, to be in a rainstorm on a cliffside with a skittish horse.

"So, what are we going to do, Pete?" Ty asked.

Of course they'd look to him. Pete pressed the binoculars to his eyes. "I don't know."

"We should split up," Felipe said. "Two of us head to the crow's nest. The other two follow this ridge, see where it takes us."

Pete glanced at Ty, who was still watching him. "It's not a terrible idea. Check your coms."

They ran a check and Pete mounted Lulu. She skittered back, and he refused to grab the saddle horn. She wasn't going to buck him off, or worse, pitch him over the side of the cliff and land on top of him, crushing him.

He still preferred motorized vehicles, thanks.

Or himself. His own two feet.

Ian turned his horse, also easy in the saddle. Well, that was what happened when you actually wanted to be a cowboy. "I'm headed to the crow's nest. Pete, Ty?"

"I'm behind you, Ian," Ty said and rounded his mount to follow Ian.

Which left, oh joy, Felipe with Pete.

Thanks a lot, Ty.

Especially since Ty *knew* Felipe. Had roomed with him in college. But it wasn't like they were picking teams.

They had a job to do.

Felipe eased his horse forward. Pete managed to follow, not quite as gracefully.

They chased the ridge down a half mile until it met with the river. There, the land flattened out and Felipe fell back.

"This is what she did? Selene? On your rescue team?"

Pete looked over at Felipe. He'd changed clothes before leaving, also taking advantage of Gage's extra stash of clothing. He also wore a navy-blue PEAK team rainsuit, the emblem on the breast, reflective lettering on the back. And cowboy boots, courtesy of

Ben. With his hood up and a woolen cap under it, Felipe looked like he actually belonged on the team.

"Who?" Pete asked.

"Selene—Jess. You know who I mean."

Yeah, okay, he did. It was just that every time Felipe said *Selene*, it reminded Pete that he might have been the second choice, the rebound guy, the fling on the other side of the tracks, or country, as it were.

Pete was a temporary fix for Jess.

Felipe knew her as the woman she'd been, and had become again.

"Yeah, Jess did this," Pete said. "Not on horseback that I can remember, but she was on plenty of callouts for missing campers, hunters, and hikers. She helped in the search for a bunch of kids about two years ago, around this time. Their van went off the road in the mountains of Glacier National Park, and she wouldn't give up until she found them." Of course, she'd had help. Ty and Gage and even Pete.

In fact, that had been the first time he'd realized that Jess Tagg had gotten under his skin. First time he'd realized that he might be falling for her, hard.

"She's an amazing EMT. Always knows what to do. Steady under pressure. Once she sets her mind to something, it happens. Like her house—she bought this wreck of a house for a dollar and fixed it up, room by room. Redid the plumbing, the electrical, fixed the foundation, sheetrocked the walls, painted—she even installed new cabinets."

"You helped her, didn't you?" Felipe's voice eased out light, as if just making conversation, but Pete heard the jealousy in it. So, it went both ways, huh?

"Yeah. But she did plenty by herself."

"Is that how you met?"

"Chet hired her on the team before I joined up. We met while I was working as a smokejumper out in western Montana. She rescued a girl who'd been mauled by a bear. Saved her life."

Felipe nodded. "She always wanted to be a doctor. She had just finished her second year at Columbia when the scandal began."

That was what Felipe called the complete derailing of her life? A *scandal*?

"I knew that," Pete said.

"I'm very proud of her. She's applied to start her internship at CUMC, but of course, she wants to wait until . . ." He trailed off, his gaze on the surroundings. "You should know, it wasn't easy for her to stay in New York. She missed her life here very much."

Pete frowned at him. "So then why . . . No, I guess I don't want to hear this. She made her choice."

"Yes, she did, Peter. But it wasn't without heartache. And you didn't make it any easier."

"What are you talking about?" Stay calm. "It was *my* idea for her to return to New York City—"

"Then you chased her down, and even followed her to Paris. The desperate cowboy who couldn't let her go."

Pete wanted to dismantle the man on the spot. Instead, he cut his voice low. "I proposed. And she said yes. *Yes.* I wasn't desperate. I was her fiancé."

Felipe's mouth tightened around the edges.

"Did you know that I proposed? Did she tell you?"

"Yes, she told me," he said quietly.

Pete just blinked at him, the hot coil tightening. "And then what? Did you get angry? Did you . . . scare her? Threaten her?"

Felipe rounded in the saddle. "Don't be rude. I love her. Let us not forget that I asked her to marry me first."

"And then you left her."

"I never left her. She left *me*." Felipe took a breath, as if he too

197

were fighting a rise of heat. "It might occur to you that she did the same thing to me as she did you. Ran. Never looked back."

His words flushed Pete of a response. No, he hadn't thought of that.

"Of course, it was a fragile time for her. She was afraid that I would reject her, so I understand why she ran. She didn't believe that I would have helped her. Stayed with her. I am *still* staying with her." Felipe drew in a breath. His voice returned to the calm, cool tone. "Selene and I care very much for each other."

Pete's chest tightened.

"Let's be honest here. You're exactly . . . well, you're not the kind of man Selene should be with. You are a . . . well, she needed you, I suppose. But you're not the kind of man she should marry, have children with. Spend her life with. I know you cared for her. But it's time to be honest."

Pete didn't even know where to begin to dissect Felipe's calm, scalpel-precise words.

Except for: "I care. Present tense." He wasn't going to declare his undying love for Jess to Felipe, but the truth rose up to strangle him.

Yeah, he cared. More than cared. Because just the thought of Felipe knowing her, comforting her, laughing with her, kissing her . . . spending the rest of his life with her.

Now Pete couldn't breathe.

Because like it or not, he was still desperately in love with Jess. And had wanted exactly all those things.

The very last thing he wanted to do was get over her.

Worse, if he was being brutally honest, he would do just about anything to get her back.

Pete urged his horse forward.

"If you care for her, then you'll do what's best for her."

"And that's you?" *You little French jerk.*

"At best, you're just confusing her. If you keep chasing her, she'll never accept the life she should have." He glanced at Pete. "Can't you just admit that you're not right for her? That you've already done enough damage? Leave her alone."

Damage?

Pete turned in the saddle, stared at Felipe. "What are you talking about? She's the one who did the damage. She *destroyed* me after Paris. I called her repeatedly, and it went right to voice mail. Not one return call. I lost my freakin' mind."

"Until New Year's Eve."

That shut Pete down. He sat there, his heartbeat thumping. "What?"

"New Year's Eve." Felipe's dark eyes landed on him, no mercy. "Selene called you."

Pete's mouth tightened.

"I found her weeping. She wanted to explain—"

"Explain what, exactly?" Pete knew he was shouting, but it was better than launching from his saddle and choking the man.

No, no it wasn't, but Pete stayed put. "Explain how she cut me out of her life—?"

"Explain that she'd been in France taking care of her dying mother!" Felipe was shouting too.

"Her dying mother?" Pete said, Felipe's words finally taking root. "What are you talking about?"

Felipe managed to rein himself in, his jaw tight. "The night she was out with you in Paris, Caroline Taggert had an episode."

"What is that . . . an *episode*?"

"A seizure. She collapsed and we had to rush her to Paris. She was hospitalized for two weeks and spent another month recovering before she was allowed to return home. For pity's sake, man, get email or Facebook or something. Selene's phone didn't have an international plan, so I let her use my phone to call you, and you didn't pick up."

A roaring had started, a low hum in the back of Pete's head. "I don't take calls from people I don't know." But yeah, he'd probably declined a couple calls he thought might be telemarketers. "But she could have figured out a way to contact me."

"While sitting by her mother's bedside? Give her a break, Peter. We were in and out of the hospital until Christmas. She was exhausted. We got to New York shortly before the New Year, and she called almost immediately. She wanted to talk to you about . . ." Felipe gave him a sidelong look, then a shake of his head. "Well, you should have answered her call, Peter."

"Talk about what," Pete said softly, the roaring getting louder.

"About why we needed to get engaged."

"Needed?" His chest tightened. *Needed?* "Was Jess pregnant?"

Felipe mouth tightened. "Of course not."

Pete probably should be ashamed of his question, but he just felt a crazy, momentary relief.

"There were other reasons," Felipe said. "Which you would have discovered if you'd bothered to answer the phone."

Pete couldn't breathe, the roaring too loud, the darkness closing in.

"I was busy."

"Mmmhmm. That's what Selene thought too." Felipe eased his horse forward, picking up the pace.

Why didn't he answer? The thought burned through him.

Because she'd hurt him for two long, agonizing months and . . . and now he wanted to punch something, anything, until the roaring stopped. Until he destroyed the memory of his phone buzzing in his back pocket, annoying him as he leaned into . . . well, he couldn't exactly remember her name, but she was blonde, wore a sweet smile, and lit a fire through him as she ran her finger down his chest.

Of course, he hadn't exactly been operating on all cylinders.

He *had* been coherent enough to pull the phone from his pocket. To see Jess's number.

And didn't that shut down any New Year's romance? A call from his ex.

He'd thumbed away her call. Shoved the phone back into his pocket. Turned back to the blonde. But his heart wasn't in it. In fact, he could pinpoint that night as the start of his current run of brokenhearted failure to revive the old Pete.

Still, it wasn't what Jess—or Felipe—thought. Not entirely. "Wait one doggone minute." Pete caught up to him. "It was New Year's Eve. I hadn't talked to Jess for nearly two months and—" His chest tightened. "It's none of your business what I was doing."

"Agreed. We're all adults here. And Selene knew what kind of man you were—are, apparently. But that's why you need to let her go."

Their fight outside the reception rushed at him, the wash of tears in her eyes. *"I'm here. Right now. I'm here. And you're kissing someone else."*

No wonder she'd turned and run.

He wanted to weep for the timing, the injustice.

The truth.

The rest of their fight played out in brutal clarity. His angry words. *"And you show up tonight, hoping that I'll just sweep you into my arms, like nothing has happened?"*

And her response. Broken. Quiet. The power in her words could shatter him. *"You promised you would."*

He had. Maybe he had plenty of reason to be angry, to walk away, to find someone else. But he hadn't. "It wasn't what you think."

Felipe ignored him.

"I'm not letting her go," Pete said.

"It doesn't matter, Peter," Felipe finally said. "She's already gone."

———— + ————

Jess wouldn't exactly classify the cabin as paradise, but right now, it felt pretty close. Made of timbers, it sat nestled more than a hundred yards back from the river, in a clearing surrounded on all sides by forest. A light blazed from the front door stoop like a beacon calling them hither as Jess helped Ned carry Shae between them up the path.

A covered porch, Adirondack chairs, and a metal fire pit suggested hunters or at least vacationers who knew how to enjoy the wilderness.

Please, let the door be open.

Shae eased herself into one of the Adirondack chairs, and Jess tried the door. Found it locked.

Ned appeared with a poker that was probably used to stir the fire. He put it into the frame of the door and used it as a fulcrum to wedge it open. The door broke free of the frame and swung in. "I'll fix it later," Ned said as he returned for Shae, picked her up, and brought her inside.

He'd scared Jess when he'd fallen to his knees and stayed there, moaning on the shoreline. In a way, Ned reminded her of Pete. A darker but still broad-shouldered, teeth-gritted version of the man she hoped might be searching for them.

Yeah, they were cut from the same cloth. The way Ned looked at Shae . . . Pete had looked at her that way, once upon a time.

If Pete Brooks was out there, he wouldn't stop looking. That gave her pause, and for a moment she stood on the deck, looking out into the forest, half expecting him to emerge out of the woods wearing his navy-blue PEAK rainsuit, a baseball cap, and a pair of hiking boots, his blue eyes zeroed in on her as if she wore a homing beacon.

It was just wishful thinking because . . . well, yes, he might be looking for her. But only because it was his job.

She headed inside and found the place small but homey. Shae lay on a sofa made from rough-hewn timber, the fashionable log-cabin style popular in rental cabins. Unstained birch cabinets and a Formica countertop formed a U-shaped kitchen in the corner. In the center of the room, firewood was stacked near a wood-burning stove.

A door to another room revealed a double bed. She walked into the room—a simple bed, a table, a gas light. Off the bedroom, a tiny bathroom with toilet and sink. She opened the cabinet, hoping for a first aid kit, but found nothing.

All the same, most definitely paradise.

"Ned, can you get a fire going?" Jess said as she came back out to the kitchen.

He'd been standing near Shae—probably not eager to sit down, Jess guessed—and now moved into action, opening the stove and filling it with kindling and other lighter material conveniently stashed in a nearby tin bucket.

She did a quick search of the kitchen supplies. The fridge contained a six-pack of beer, some bacon, and a tin of coffee. In the cupboard she found three cans of pork and beans, garlic powder, salt, but still no first aid kit.

Shoot.

A drawer of plastic ware, a few plastic bags, and some plastic wrap. Matches. She dug those out and handed them to Ned. "I'm going to see what I can do about Shae's wound."

She sat down on the coffee table in front of Shae. "Okay, let's take a look at what we've got here."

Shae's hands caught Jess's wrists the moment she made a move to remove the belt.

Jess paused. "Be brave."

Shae's eyes widened, but she nodded. Removed her hands.

Be brave. Her own hands shook a little as she reached again for Shae's wound.

Take a breath. Think. Airway, breathing, circulation.

She unbuckled the belt, and Shae let out a gasp as the pressure eased.

In a second, Ned was kneeling beside her. "It'll be okay."

Maybe. Or not. Because the congealed blood had glued the cloth to the wound. Jess needed saline to loosen the dressing if she didn't want to tear any skin away.

Worse, if there were exposed intestines, or even a tear in the omentum, it could be excruciating to remove the bandage.

But at the very least it needed to be cleaned.

"Get that fire going," Jess said to Ned and headed into the kitchen. The pots were under the stove and she filled one with tap water—probably well water, but she wasn't taking any chances.

She put water on to boil, added a tablespoon of salt, then went over to help Ned with the fire.

He already had a tiny blaze crackling.

"You're next, tough guy. I need to see that backside. If you want, we can go into the bedroom for you to drop your drawers."

He just looked at her. Raised an eyebrow.

"That was supposed to be an offer for privacy."

He added a grin. "I know. I was just giving you a hard time. Yeah, privacy would be nice. But I'm not leaving Shae, so, let's just do this." He toed off his cowboy boots and unbuttoned his jeans. "No laughing."

"Dude, you had a bullet go through your backside. Two more

inches and you wouldn't be walking. I'm not laughing, I'm relieved. And—"

Oh boy. He'd turned and shucked his jeans down one side, to reveal the wound that tore through the outer left side of his buttock. It separated his skin in a thumb-wide gash that looked about an inch deep and ran across his backside and up to his hip. Blood still oozed from it, from all his exertion.

She was right. Two inches closer to the right and he wouldn't be walking. Or jumping out of airplanes. Or dancing at his and Shae's wedding.

Because the way Ned kept glancing at Shae, Jess was sure that the man had serious, never-let-go feelings for Shae Johnson, aka Esme Shaw.

Otherwise, why would he travel a thousand miles to attend a wedding?

Yep, just like Pete. Following his emotions across the globe. *Please, Shae, don't break his heart.*

"I need to irrigate this and then figure out a way to close it."

The water on the stove was boiling, so she returned to it and shut it off.

"You're just going to leave me here, in the wind?" Ned said.

She laughed. "No. I need to get some pine resin. You button up and stay with Shae while the water cools. Then I'll get you both fixed up."

Somehow, just saying that seemed to sink heat, courage, even hope into her bones. "Stay put." She grabbed a kitchen knife, something with a sharp point, and found a bowl in the cupboard.

She could just about hug the person who stocked this little place.

Ned already had his britches back on and was kneeling next to Shae as Jess left the house.

The sun refused to emerge from the soggy sky, and wind whipped into the trees. The air smelled of loam and carried a nip. Next on the agenda, food, because her stomach clenched as she trekked into the rim of forest.

She needed a pine tree, preferably wounded, where resin would form as a scab. It didn't take long to find a towering white pine, ages old, the bark gritty and thickened. A divot rankled the trunk about five feet up, and she used the knife's point to chip off beads of hard orange resin into the bowl.

"Resin is the tree's effort to heal itself. It makes a great glue if you melt it down. Or, add it to a fire to keep it going."

Thanks, Pete.

One of his many survival tips, offered in casual conversation some nondescript time they trained in the wilderness, as if it might be something she already knew.

He never made her feel like a city girl—although, for his part, he hadn't exactly known she was from New York City. But the last time they went climbing, he'd taught her how to rappel without a safety line. Just in case she ever needed to.

Scared her to her core.

But he'd kept her on belay, secured to himself and feeding out her safety line with those amazing arms, shouting encouragement to her. *Jess! You got this.*

She could almost hear his voice in her ear. *Jess!*

She stilled, her breath caught, listening to the echo against the trees, perhaps lifted from the river.

She walked to the middle of the yard and yelled, "Pete!"

No response, and she suddenly wanted to cry with the absurdity, the crazy hope of it all.

Wow, she missed him. It wasn't just that she hoped with every breath that he might be looking for her, but that . . . she missed the woman she was with Pete cheering her on.

Felipe was safe. Predictable. Downright perfect.

And Pete was a storm. Bold. Impulsive. Dauntless. But with Pete she wasn't a second choice. Wasn't a good decision. Wasn't a family expectation.

With Pete she wasn't afraid. Or if she was, she did it with his arms around her. *Hang on to me, babe.*

Pete made her believe that the crazy was possible.

So, she stood in the yard, and with everything inside her yelled again. "Pete!"

Her voice echoed against the soggy ceiling, then fell back to earth. She closed her eyes, but the only answer she heard was her heartbeat against her ribs.

"Jess? You okay?" Ned stood at the door, and she turned, slightly chagrined.

"I just thought, since I was out here . . ." She lifted a shoulder and headed inside.

The stove had shaved an edge off the cold in the house.

Jess found a cast-iron pan and a cutting board. After cleaning off the bark from the resin, she dropped the pieces into the pan and turned up the heat.

"What are you doing?" Ned said.

"Making glue. The resin will melt, and after I irrigate your wound, we'll close it."

His eyes widened. "Uh . . ."

She turned a hip to the counter. "Pine sap is antibacterial and an antibiotic."

"Who are you, Survivor Man?"

"You can thank Pete Brooks." Of course.

The resin had started to soften, and she took a spoon and separated the bark from the pitch as it melted and turned into a jelly. She took it off the heat.

She emptied the heated water from the pan into a bowl and

207

pulled out a baggie from the drawer. "Okay, Ned, let's close that wound." She poured water into the baggie, then cut a tiny hole in one end.

He made a face.

"Don't be a baby."

"You're going to glue my skin together with hot pine sap and you're calling me a baby? I'm a wildland firefighter, Jess. Pine sap is like Greek fire, it holds heat like napalm."

"I promise not to burn you."

He pursed his lips and walked over to the table.

"Lie down."

"I feel like I'm being operated on."

"You are. Drop your drawers."

"Not even." But he hiked down his jeans just enough for her to have access to the wound.

She used a towel to catch the liquid as she irrigated it, the water warm but not too hot. He closed his eyes, his breath even and thick.

"Sorry if that hurts."

"Just do this."

The resin had turned pliable, and she touched it, testing it.

"I'm going to draw the edges together and use this as a bonding agent."

"I don't care if you sear it shut with a glowing ember, the sooner you get this done, the sooner I'm hiking out of here and getting help."

Maybe her words had galvanized him too, because as he positioned his head on his hands, he met her eyes. The guy who'd fallen on the creek bed was long gone. His gaze flashed over to Shae.

Jess didn't argue with him.

It wouldn't be pretty. But the pitch worked like she'd hoped as she used one hand to close the wound, the other to dab the resin onto his skin. Still warm, the resin bonded quickly, creating a glue that hardened into a firm bandage. When it dried, she found a cloth and secured it over the wound.

He said nothing as he slid off the table and put himself back together.

"Now let me see your back."

He gave her a look.

She raised an eyebrow.

"Fine." He turned and lifted the back of his shirt. A bruise the size of her hand darkened his back on the lower right-hand side. She pressed on it and he stiffened. "Have you vomited any blood?"

He said nothing, and when she looked up, he nodded his head.

"You could have a cracked rib or even a bruised kidney, but there's nothing I can do about it. Just go easy, okay?"

He lowered his shirt. "Talk to me after we're safe." He nodded toward Shae. "Now her."

Jess retrieved her baggie and refilled it with water. Ned took Shae's hand, and Jess wet the cloth and used the saline to loosen the cloth from the wound.

Tears ran from Shae's eyes, but other than a whimper that raked through her body, she didn't move. The heat in the room seemed to add more color to her skin, however, and a sweat broke out across her forehead.

The cloth eased away from the wound, and finally Jess got a good look.

A puncture wound, but the damage had been more extensive than Jess first thought, with spongy, yellowish tissue emerging from the wound, along with pus and dried, blackened blood. A new trickle of blood formed, bright red around the edges from the removal of the cloth.

Her best guess was a lacerated small intestine, with damage to the mesentery, which would account for the flood of blood from a penetrating wound. And the infection Shae seemed to be fighting.

209

Jess rolled up Shae's dress—glad that she also had leggings—and found bruising through her lower body. "No more moving her," Jess said, glancing up at Ned. "Shae might have a broken rib or two, along with this wound."

What she wouldn't do for the PEAK chopper right now.

"All I can do is try to keep it bacteria free."

"With more pine sap?" Ned said.

"Not on this." Jess got up and retrieved the plastic wrap, ripped off a piece, and brought it back to Shae. Wetting the surface with the saltwater solution, she covered the wound with the plastic wrap. "Ned, get me a towel from the bathroom."

He returned moments later with a thin brown towel. She folded it and placed it over Shae's abdomen. Then she retrieved two dish towels from the kitchen, folded them diagonally, and worked them around Shae's body, tying them above and below the wound to secure the towel. She folded the dress back over the wound. "Don't move."

"I'm thirsty."

"You can have something to moisten your lips, but no swallowing, Shae. I don't know what is perforated."

Shae nodded, but another tear dripped down her cheek. Sweet Ned used his thumb to brush it away.

Jess went to the sink, moistened a towel, and handed it to Ned.

He touched it to Shae's lips, so gently it might have been a kiss.

Jess turned away, walking to the window to stare out. Shae needed immediate medical attention. But with the wind stirring the trees and the drop in the temperature, snow could be on the tail end of this storm, just waiting to gather.

Either she sent Ned out to freeze, possibly to get lost in the woods and perish, or they stayed here and watched Shae fade away.

Jess ran her hands up her arms, needing more fortification than the beans in the cupboard.

SUSAN MAY WARREN

Because once again, no matter what she chose, someone was going to get hurt.

She closed her eyes. And maybe it was silly, but she was raw and desperate and frankly too tired to do anything but unleash the cry of her heart.

Find me, Pete. Please, find me.

10

SHE JUST MIGHT BE THE MOST SELFISH PERSON SHE KNEW. Shae watched Ned ease over to the stove and hide a wince as he leaned over and put another log inside.

All she could think about were his words "I'm going to try to be a SEAL." And how they'd turned her cold. He'd seen right through her pitiful attempt to act like it didn't matter, saying that she was behind him, thrilled for him—and with every word, biting back a tiny wail.

Shae couldn't love another man who could die. Sure, he'd told her this summer that he'd thought about being a SEAL, but . . . oh, why hadn't she taken him seriously? He had such an amazing life on the farm, she'd thought—maybe hoped—he was just dreaming. She didn't know why being a SEAL seemed so much worse than being a smokejumper. Statistically, smokejumping was one of the most dangerous jobs in the world. Next to bomb disposal. And perhaps Alaskan crab fisherman.

But those jobs weren't designed to put a man in front of a bullet.

And with that thought, she had the image of Dante leaping at Sheriff Blackburn, to the background noise of her scream.

"Shae?" Ned's warm hand slid onto her arm and brought her back from the abyss. "It's going to be okay. I'll go for help—"

"No!" She grabbed his hand, ignoring the flash of pain that cycled through her. Since Jess had removed the wadded shirt and eased the belt, the pain had flattened out and spread through Shae's stomach, the sharp edge blunted. At least now she could breathe a mostly full lungful. "Please, stay here."

He crouched next to her, caressed her cheek, then pushed her hair away from her face. "Shh. I'm not going anywhere. Not yet."

Now she wasn't just selfish but a coward because of course someone needed to go for help. And probably sooner than later. "I'm sorry. I'm just . . ."

"Scared. And hurt. I get it."

"No, that's not it." She eased herself up.

"Stop, Shae. Don't move, you'll hurt yourself."

"Oh, believe me, I've been perfecting that move for about five years, and look where that's got us."

He frowned at her.

"Don't you see—all my hiding, all my trying to protect the people I love, and here you are, wounded—"

"Don't worry about me. I'm fine."

"You're not fine. I know you think it's no big deal to be shot in the butt, but it is. It's a gunshot wound, and I happen to know that you're in tremendous pain, Ned."

His mouth tightened. "It's no big deal."

"Because you refuse to be the weak link."

His face didn't move.

"Well, me too—but I am, and I hate it. I hate that Blackburn has been haunting me for five years, that he's so in my brain that I can't close my eyes without seeing him pinning Dante, beating him to death. I only really started sleeping through the night about two years ago, and even then, I still jump when someone comes up on me too fast. I live with the ghost of Blackburn in my shadow, and now he's finally found me. Us. And the last thing I want you to do is go outside so he can hunt you down and kill you too!"

Ned just stared at her. "I'll be fine."

"Maybe. Even if you are . . . then . . ." She closed her eyes. "Then you leave for the military, and the nightmares start all over again."

She hadn't wanted to say that, but she was tired and raw and it just sort of spilled out.

Ned said nothing for so long, she finally dared to look at him.

His mouth had turned to a grim line. "That's what the weirdness was back there on the river. You're afraid I'm going to get killed."

She met his eyes. "Dante wanted to be a soldier. And he died protecting me. I realize that it's a little different when you're in the military, saving the world, but . . . but it feels the same. I'll still lose you."

They hadn't quite taken steps that far into their relationship, but yeah, there it was. "I . . . I care about you, Ned."

He looked away. Closed his eyes, as if in pain.

Please, tell me I'm not reading this wrong—

"I'm in love with you, Shae."

He looked at her, those brown eyes holding hers, so much emotion in them she couldn't move. "I know it's fast, but I probably fell in love with you this summer, and I just can't . . . I can't stop thinking about you. You're so amazing. Brave and sweet and—"

"I am *not* brave." The retort just rose up, spurted out. "I'm the furthest thing from brave. I'm a coward!"

He recoiled. "You're not a coward, Shae."

"Blackburn was beating my boyfriend to death and I ran. I *ran*. I didn't pick up a rock and try to defend him. I didn't run back up the trail to get Uncle Ian. I ran away into the forest and hid. Until Dante stopped screaming. Until I saw Blackburn get up, blood on his face and hands, and throw the boy I loved into the river. And then I kept running." Her eyes burned. "I haven't stopped."

214

"Uh, yes, you have. That's why you came back to Montana, isn't it? To testify against Blackburn?"

She gave a laugh that had nothing of humor in it. "I'm still a coward. I can't even bring myself to testify against Blackburn. I talked to Ella about it, but . . . I'm just so tired. And . . . I don't know how to fight back. I just want to be safe."

"We all want to be safe, Shae. That's normal."

"Not you. You jump out of airplanes into fire. You want to be a navy SEAL."

"Yeah, but I still want to *live* doing it. Trust me, I'm going to do everything I can to be safe."

She blinked at him. "You are?"

"Of course. I don't have a death wish."

He didn't? And somehow those words seeded inside her, found root. Still, "Then why the SEALs?"

He considered her, saying nothing for a long time. Then, "Well, maybe it's because I'm a coward too."

Right. Her disbelief must have played on her face because his brows rose.

"No. Really. Every time I stood at that open door of my jump plane, a pack on my back, smoke and flame curling up from an inferno below, I thought, *What are you doing, Ned? Have you lost your mind?* For the briefest of seconds, just a millisecond, I panicked. A full-out, mouth-drying scream gathered deep inside me. My hands sweated inside my gloves, my gut dropped. I was terrified."

"What—"

"And it's then I remembered Fraser. And what he taught me about fear, and bullies."

"Bullies?"

"Yeah. See, we're not so much afraid of bullies as we are of getting hurt and what it will cost us. That's what produces fear—the cost. And not being sure we can handle it."

"You were bullied?"

"Oh, I was bullied until about the fourth grade."

Now he was just teasing her. "Right."

"No, I promise. I was bone skinny. And small. I was easy pickin's for this kid named Kostia. He looked like he'd skipped a couple grades and was pretty angry all the time. He made it his personal goal to scare me. It worked. I was terrified to go anywhere he could find me."

She saw him then, scared, with big brown eyes trying not to cry, and everything inside her burned.

"One day, Kostia had me pinned up to the chain-link fence, and a couple of his buddies were kicking me, and my brother Fraser just appeared. He was fifteen, and I'll never forget the look in his eyes."

"Anger?"

"Disappointment. Just a flash of it, but it felt like a blow to my gut. Fraser chased Kostia away, but that night he confronted me. He said I was letting this kid have power over me. But that I wasn't powerless.

"I had no idea what he was talking about because I felt pretty powerless. Fraser said that I could either be a victim or I could fight back and respect myself. See, I'd always been taught that violence was bad. That I should walk away—and yes, that is the best option. But sometimes you can't—especially when the fear or the bullies keep coming after you. He said fear had its own power, and the more I did nothing, the greater my fear would grow. Everybody is afraid . . . but I had to remember two things. First, if I wanted to be free, then I had to stop letting fear win. I had to stop being a victim and fight back with everything inside me."

"And second?"

"That God never intended me to fight my battles alone. That's why he gave me family."

"What did you do?"

"I stood up to Kostia the next time he came after me. And got whupped . . . but I refused to stay down. And he realized he couldn't bully me anymore."

"Fraser is a SEAL, isn't he?"

Ned nodded.

"Did you join because you want to be like him?"

"No. I joined because I want to see what I can do when I don't let fear get in the way. I'd like to impress my family, yes." Ned sighed. "But the truth is, I'd really like to impress myself." His mouth tugged up one side, a little rueful.

She touched his face. "I could love you too, Ned Marshall. So please don't die on me."

Then, because more than anything she wanted to be brave and let go of the safe thing, she moved her grip to the front of his shirt. Tugged.

His grin was sweet and tentative, and he surrendered. Bracing his hand on the sofa above her, he leaned in to move his mouth a breath away from hers. "I'm not going anywhere."

Then he kissed her. His touch was so tender, as if he feared hurting her, and she simply relaxed, breathing him in, letting his mouth soothe, heal, comfort. He didn't try to deepen the kiss, nothing of the ardor he'd showed at the reception. Instead, he lingered, showing her the truth of his words.

Not going anywhere.

She could almost believe him.

The door closed, and Ned jerked away.

Jess had come in. She carried firewood and kindling in her arms, and dropped it on the pile. Then she pressed her hand to the wall, as if to brace herself.

"Are you okay?" Ned said. He gave a little grunt as he rose.

"I found something," Jess said quietly. "I think I know who this cabin belongs to."

217

"That's awesome. Maybe we'll get some help," he said.

"Uh . . . I don't think so." Jess glanced at Shae, then back at Ned.

The way she looked at them sent ice through Shae. "You're freaking me out, Jess."

Jess knelt and pulled out a water-warped magazine from her pile of kindling. "I found about fifteen of these in the wood bin." She handed the magazine to Ned.

"*Sports Illustrated*?" he said, unrolling it. "May 2013 edition."

"Read the back. The mailing label."

As he flipped it over, as he read the words, and as his eyes widened, Jess followed up with her suspicion. "I think this cabin belongs to Sheriff Randy Blackburn."

———— ✛ ————

"Okay, I admit I screwed up." The words took nearly a half hour to work themselves free of the tangle of anger, shame, and yes, heartbreak that lined Pete's chest.

They had come to the river, halted there under a freezing drizzle, the soft, easy patter of rain on pine trees and poplar dying out, leaving behind a fog that lay like doom over the forest.

Just like the cold mist forming in Pete's gut at Felipe's words.

"*It doesn't matter, Peter. She's already gone.*"

Maybe. Yes, probably, given the fact that Jess had turned and walked away from Pete at the barn, not looking back.

How could he blame her, really? Because he might not have cheated on her, not completely, on New Year's Eve, but he had a past that made him flinch. Would make any woman walk away.

If he were honest, he'd *wanted* to cheat that night.

Was still pretty shocked that he hadn't. But he wasn't going to let Felipe get away with blaming him for something he hadn't done. So, "Yeah, I was with someone else on New Year's Eve. But it wasn't what you—and more importantly, Jess—thinks. I didn't . . ." Aw, this felt a little too much like a teenaged girls' confess-all slumber party.

Felipe probably agreed because he turned in his saddle, wearing incredulity on his face. "In what fantasy of yours do you think I want to hear any of this? I couldn't care a whit about what you've done with your time since you broke up with Selene—"

"I didn't break up with her!"

Felipe sighed. "Semantics. Since you let her go. Which, by the way, you *haven't*."

"I can't!" There it was, the bold, brutal truth. "Don't you think I want to? The thought of her . . . and you . . ." Pete hands tightened into fists. "Listen, I've tried. And that's the problem. I can't, okay?"

Felipe shook his head, and if Pete hadn't looked away, he figured he'd also see an eye roll. Because in Felipe's shoes, he'd be doing the same thing. But he couldn't seem to stop this run of his mouth. "I haven't been the same since I met Jess. She somehow made me feel like I wasn't a complete mess." He couldn't look at Felipe. "I guess I figured that if a woman like Jess could love me . . ."

Oh brother. Now, even *he* wanted to give an eye roll. He reeled himself in, found a safer explanation. "Listen. I get it. I've never seen myself as the marrying kind anyway, so . . . not that Jess is better off with you, but—"

"She is," Felipe said, with no emotion.

"What is your *problem*?"

Felipe rounded in the saddle. "You're my problem. You—" He drew in a breath, his voice shaking. "You're always there. Between us. Haunting us. I need you gone, Brooks. Or . . ."

Oh. Heaven help him, inside Pete there was a tiny man doing a fist pump. "Or she'll never be yours?"

Felipe's eyes narrowed. "She's already mine."

The words slapped him. Breathe. Just *breathe*. Pete swallowed and somehow found his footing. He didn't want to imagine what

219

Felipe meant, so he shut out the literal and focused on the metaphorical sense of Felipe's words. *Already mine.*

"Fine." Okay. "But you have to be straight with me, bro. Do you love her? Because I saw the way you looked at that woman at the horse race, the brunette, and . . . well, I'm not blind, and neither is Jess. Is there something going on between you two?"

That got a response. Something raw and stricken flashed in Felipe's eyes a second before he shook his head, the anger returning. "No. Of course not."

"Of course not?" Pete snapped, urging his horse forward and grasping Felipe's reins. "Hold up there, pal. Who was she?"

"Kindly let go of my mount," Felipe said, but Pete shook his head. Beside them, the river roared.

"You can lie to me, and Jess, and even yourself all you want, but I know what it looks like when you can't stop thinking about someone, when they fill up all the space in your head, and what it looks like when you are trying very, very hard not to grab ahold of them and never let go."

Felipe just sat there, looking away, his jaw tight.

How the French drove him crazy with their pride.

"'Selene and I care very much for each other.' That's what you said. Not 'I'm crazy about Selene, I can't live without her. She's my everything.'" Pete's throat thickened as the words took root. "You didn't say you loved her, because you're in love with someone else, aren't you?"

"Selene knows how I feel about her," Felipe said, reaching over to snag his reins.

Pete's grip was unmoving. "I'm sure she does, but fill me in. Because here's the deal." He leaned over, lowered his voice. "I am crazy about Jess. I can't live without her. She is *my* everything, so if you step out on her, if you hurt her—"

"Fine. Yes. It's all a lie." Felipe yanked the reins away and his

220

mount danced back. He reached out to calm the horse, a hand on his withers. Pete noticed that it shook.

"What's all a lie?"

"The whole thing—it's a pitiful ruse. Or at least it started that way . . ."

Pete blinked at him.

Felipe turned his horse to head downstream. And maybe his exit was a good thing, because Jess's words were starting to latch on. *I'm not engaged.*

"What are you talking about?" Pete managed to stay on Lulu, to follow Felipe, but the world seemed like it might be tilting.

Felipe reined in his horse. Beside him the river was a frothy, loud, and dangerous roil of gray-brown water. When he looked at Pete, Felipe appeared tired, a little wrung out and even lost. "It was a ruse. A convenient lie to keep her mother happy."

Pete had nothing. Just the rushing of the river, the ping of droplets from the overhanging trees down the collar of his jacket to accompany the frozen stillness inside.

Felipe gave him a look of annoyance. "Her mother is dying, Peter. Has a fatal disease, and she told Selene that nothing would make her happier than if Selene and I got married. So, we got engaged." He lifted a shoulder.

Like no big deal that Pete's life had been completely dismantled for a lie. "That's what she was calling to explain on New Year's Eve . . ."

"Yes, you idiot," Felipe snapped. His mouth tightened to a dark, unmovable line. "But now . . ."

Now. Pete didn't think it was possible for him to go colder.

"Well, things have changed. Her mother is pressing for a wedding date and . . ." Felipe looked away from Pete, and his voice changed. "We're a good match. Our families have been friends for ages, and with her circumstances, she needs someone who can protect her from scandal. And I . . ." He swallowed. "She's a good partner for me."

Pete just stared at him, his words clicking, finding root. Just like Aimee had been a good partner? "Oh my gosh. Jess is the *replacement*."

Felipe frowned, his mouth tightening.

"You don't love her."

"I love her enough."

No, no, he should not tackle the man, pummel him, finish what they started at Jess's house.

"Because you *do* love someone else more."

Felipe had the decency not to deny it.

"And you're calling *me* the ghost between you? Are you kidding me?" But a tiny flame had sparked inside Pete's chest. Felipe hadn't seen a haunting like the one Pete would give him if he actually went through with this sham of a marriage. "Who is it? Does Jess know?"

Felipe gave him a look of exasperation. "Indeed, she knows. It's just . . . she has accepted it."

"Accepted—what kind of crazy world do you two live in that . . . why would Jess even *consider* this?"

Felipe looked up, his eyes clear. "Because she is not Jess but Selene. And that's my point, Peter. She knows what is best for everyone, including you. You will never fit into her world, and she doesn't belong in yours."

"She belongs with me, whatever world we live in."

Felipe just gave him a sad shake of his head. "I will give her a good life, pay for her education, and she'll become an amazing doctor. I will be her husband. You will be, well, the wild fling."

Pete just blinked at him. "We'll see about that."

Felipe met his eyes, so much calm in them Pete had to look away, across the river to the rim of trees, anywhere to corral the darkness, to keep himself from—"Hey, over there. Do you see that?" Upstream, about twenty yards, under a shaggy pine tree, broken branches lay on the ground, a sort of carpet under the arms of the longer boughs.

As if someone had tried to create a shelter.

"I see it," Felipe said. He moved his horse toward the river, found a crossing place.

Pete followed Felipe's exact path, because he might be furious, but he wasn't stupid. He tried not to clutch his saddle horn like a terrified eight-year-old as they mucked through the water, the river splashing up to soak him even more.

By the time he caught up to Felipe and dismounted, Felipe was already on the ground, heading over to the copse.

Yes, someone had been here—more than one person by the look of the displaced rocks and at least one footprint. Pete knelt, examined the boughs. Ran his fingers along the wetness glistening on the branches. "Blood."

"There's more here," Felipe said, not far away. He pointed to a splatter of blood on the rock.

Pete grabbed his walkie. "Search 2, Brooks, come in."

He met Felipe's gaze.

Ty's voice came over the radio. "Search 1, Search 2, go ahead."

"We made it to the river and found some blood, maybe a shelter. Anything on your end?"

"No. We're . . . half mile from the crow's nest . . . diverting. Kacey . . . spotted a truck . . . switchbacks . . . going . . . check it out."

Pete tried not to let the fact that Kacey had reported in to Ty, not him, put a fist in his gut. Maybe the craggy peaks had cut out the line of communications.

Still, it wasn't like he was in charge. No, this time he was just one of the desperate searchers.

Was sort of beginning to hate it. "How far?"

"Two clicks . . . northeast."

Northeast from where? "We're going to stay on the river. Check in when you find it."

"Confirmed."

Felipe had already climbed onto his horse and held the reins of Pete's mount in his hand. Pete took them from him, got on Lulu.

A shot rent the air and ripped through the hazy mist.

Skewering Pete in the heart.

"Did you hear that?" Felipe said.

Pete was already past him, gripping the saddle horn shamelessly as he spurred his horse down the shoreline.

———— + ————

The sound—sharp and crisp and deadly—ricocheted off the low-hanging, pellet-gray clouds and right into Jess's bones.

Biting at the fragile hold she had on hope.

Ned had thrown the magazine into the stove, and it flamed to life. The cabin had turned cozy over the last hour—at least the temperature. Because the speculation of who this cabin might belong to had turned them all cold.

Jess stood at the window, staring out the grimy pane to the overcast and soggy yard. Maybe fifty feet of cleared property around the house to the tree line. She'd been standing sentry for the better part of an hour.

Just listening to the voices. The ones in her head that simply wouldn't stop talking. Send Ned for help. Barricade the door and hope that the PEAK team might be searching for them. Hike out together. Go for help herself—which seemed like the most reasonable option.

Too many choices, and all of them could get somebody hurt.

"Did you hear that?" Ned stood up from where he was kneeling next to Shae.

Jess nodded.

Ned came over to her. "That was a gunshot."

"I know. I *know.*" She scrubbed her hands down her face and turned to him. "Listen, I don't know, okay? Maybe that wasn't him. Maybe it was the hunters who shot you—"

"*If* it was a hunter who shot me," Ned said. He'd seemed to rally in the last hour. Just getting a can of beans and some heat into his bones had seemed to fortify him. "It could have been Blackburn, and he's tracked us back here."

"Except, why the shot?"

Ned peered out the window. "I don't see anything." He turned back to her. "But I'm not letting him have another chance at killing Shae." He moved past Jess toward the door.

"Where are you going?"

"To get the ax I assume you chopped wood with."

"It's in the woodshed. But Ned—" She put a hand on his arm.

"I'll be back." He met her eyes a moment before he headed outside. Solid brown, a resolve in his gaze. The former pain in his eyes seemed flushed away, as if by kissing Shae he'd found a new inner strength.

Yeah, Jess had seen their kiss as she'd come into the cabin earlier. After she'd dropped the wood, she'd turned away to give them privacy, aching a little. Because she'd give just about anything to have Pete here, to have him to lean against, to feel his hands in hers, or better, tightening around her hair as he kissed her. He had a way of making her believe that they could live through nearly anything. Fire. Grizzly attack. Hurricane.

Funny that she didn't connect those feelings to Felipe, because he'd been a hero to her too. Mostly.

But Felipe never really made her feel like he'd scale cliffs and drive through fire because of his love for her. And she didn't blame him. She wasn't his first choice either.

He loved Gabrielle Martinique. She had to give Felipe credit—he'd kept his cool at the charity event last week when she showed up, carrying his heart in her soft hands.

Jess knew it all, and her heart bled for him a bit.

It only took overhearing the conversation with his father shortly after Pete had left her in Paris to know the truth. She'd come out of her mother's bedroom after checking on her when low voices halted her. Soft whispering out of the library. But with enough edge to the male tones for her to slow, right there in the hallway, not wanting to walk past the open door.

Then, frankly, she couldn't move.

"It's absolutely out of the question, Felipe. Gabrielle is your brother's ex-fiancée. How will it look if you chase after her?"

"Adrien broke up with Gabrielle two years ago. He's dating someone else. I think it's clear they don't belong together—"

"And neither do you, with her. It smacks of scandal, and the last thing this family needs is *more* scandal. Especially now that you've picked up with Selene Taggert again."

"Father, I promise you, Gabrielle didn't love Adrien, and he didn't love her. It's not a scandal—it's just truth. I think she should be applauded for her courage to break it off."

"Which should tell you something, Felipe. There seems to be a pattern here with you. You find women who can't seem to keep their promises."

Jess had winced at that, for Felipe, for her. For all the promises she'd made and broken.

"Gabrielle has a different future now, Felipe, as do you. Settle for what you have, the life that has come back to you. Do not throw away what is good for something that could break your heart. Let Gabrielle go."

A pause, as if he were considering it. Then, poor Felipe voiced her exact thoughts. "It would be just as easy to stop breathing, but thank you for that life lesson, Father."

Admittedly, his tone shocked her. She'd never seen that kind of emotion from him. Then, Felipe's footsteps came too quickly for her to retreat, and he'd caught her in the hall, a rabbit, frozen by his startled gaze.

He must have seen the truth on her face, because he took her hand and led her into an adjoining vacant bedroom. She stood in the shadows, and her heart broke for him as he pressed the door closed quietly.

He walked away from her and stood at the window, his shoulders rising and falling.

"Felipe, I . . ." She'd been about to tell him about Pete. About the engagement, about the fact that she so didn't want to hurt Felipe.

"I'm sorry you heard that." Felipe turned, and she ached at the glistening in his eyes, the way he didn't blink anything back. His gaze found hers. "Gabrielle and I . . . we . . . well, I'm so sorry, Selene. I didn't mean for you to get hurt."

"You two dated while I was in Montana."

He nodded. Ran a hand hard across his cheek. "Well, although she dated Adrien, it was me who she studied with. And rode with and . . . she's a rare woman. It was foolish, probably, but I always thought that Gabrielle and Adrien had broken up because they realized that they didn't love each other. That she wanted me."

He looked away, shook his head, a wry smile edging up one side of his face. "She makes me feel like I won." He gave a chuckle that had nothing to do with humor. "It seems I am, rather, the big loser because Gabrielle told me today that she is being courted by the Viscount of Wessex, a Brit who is interested in buying stock in our stables."

So that was what today's conversation had been about. Her heart wept for Felipe.

"You still love her."

He lifted a shoulder, nodded. "I am afraid I will never be able to extinguish the love I have for her. But my father is probably correct. It looks unseemly to run after Gabrielle after . . ."

"This isn't the Victorian age, Felipe. If you love her—"

"I'm not sure she loves me." He lifted his gaze. "So, there you have it. I've given my heart to a woman who doesn't want it, but I am helpless to get it back. I'm so sorry, Selene. It should have belonged to you."

She came over to him. He was propped against the window ledge, and she stepped close and drew him to herself. Held him. "It did, once."

His arms circled around her. "Yes, it did."

"Settle for what you have. Do not throw away what is good for something that could break your heart."

She didn't know how those words had taken root, but perhaps that was exactly how she ended up on New Year's Eve, agreeing to Felipe's suggestion that they marry. No, *pretend* to be engaged to marry, at least until she could find a way to tell her mother the truth. A truth that became more and more distant with every day of silence until she simply held on to a fantasy of what she wanted.

Just like Felipe was still holding on, despite his words otherwise. She saw the way he looked at Gabrielle, even last week.

"I love you enough."

Jess stood at the window, watching for Ned, remembering Felipe's words.

No, it wasn't enough, for either of them. But maybe it was too late for anything else.

Shuffling sounded on the porch and she spotted Ned carrying the one-sided camping ax. She opened the door, then closed it behind him, wishing they'd hadn't destroyed the lock when they broke in. Maybe they should find a way to barricade it.

Ned set the ax down on the floor, sweating just a little, as if he'd run. But her gaze couldn't move off the tool-slash-weapon.

"What are you going to do with that?"

It took him a minute because he seemed to struggle to process her question. "If he comes in, I'm going to hit him with it."

"Hit him? What—chop his arm off?"

"If I have to, yeah."

"Have you lost your mind? This isn't a Texas Chainsaw Massacre movie. This is real life. You don't just . . . chop someone up."

"I'm not going to chop him up, I'm going to defend us. There's a man out there who is trying to kill us. Hello. It's time we defend ourselves, don't you think?"

Yes, but . . . "Do we have to kill him?"

"I'm not going to kill anybody. But Sheriff Blackburn killed Shae's friend Dante. And has been haunting her for five years. I think we need to get serious."

Jess noticed he hadn't called Dante Shae's boyfriend, but it wasn't anything to squabble about. "We can be serious without killing him. Or chopping his arm off. Let's just . . . subdue him."

"With what? Hot cocoa and a song?" Ned picked up the ax and walked over to the door, then stood behind it. "He comes in, I'm hitting him."

"Not with the sharp end—"

"Fine. Yes. Okay. But I'm hitting him hard enough to take out his knees or break a leg or something to keep him from following us when we take off into the woods."

"We can't leave, Ned. Shae can't be moved."

"Fine. You stay, I'll go."

"It's dark, you'll never find your way—"

Even she could hear her own stupidity, the foolishness of her argument ringing in her ears.

"What is your problem, Jess? We have to do something—we can't just stay here and wait to be killed!"

"I just . . ." She covered her face with her hands. "I'm scared, okay?" She looked up. "I just want . . ." To be rescued. For everyone to live.

For Pete to show up and tell her that it wasn't too late.

And, okay, that kind of thinking wouldn't get them out of this cabin alive, so, "I want everyone to live through this. Including Blackburn, who should be brought to justice."

Ned held up one hand. "Okay, me too. Good idea. So, after we hit him, what's next?"

But they never got past "what's next" because footsteps on the porch steeled them silent. Jess cast a look at Shae, who lay on the sofa, so much terror in her eyes Jess thought she might scream. She shook her head, trying to put enough "it'll be okay" into her gaze to keep Shae silent.

Ned stepped back, raised the ax.

A thump, and the handle moved. Jess stepped back, her breath catching. The door eased open, as if the visitor expected trouble.

She held her breath.

He was sopping wet, wearing a blue rain slicker with the hood pulled up, a wool hat, boots, and—

Ned came at him fast, with a shout and an explosion of fury that erupted a scream from Jess. The man turned, and with instincts she knew he possessed, leapt out of the way of Ned's blow, with the ax landing soundly in the wood floor.

Pete rounded hard and—maybe without thinking, Jess had to give him that—shoved Ned away, separating him from the weapon.

Ned bounced back like he hadn't been shot and came at Pete swinging.

230

Pete caught his fist and pushed Ned up hard, back to the wall. "It's me, man! It's me!"

It's me.

Jess couldn't move, couldn't breathe.

Until Pete turned. He looked at her with such overwhelming relief in his blue eyes that she couldn't stop herself. She launched herself into his arms, a near full-body tackle.

He took a step for balance, then caught her up. "Jess!" His entire body trembled. "Oh, thank God, *Jess.*"

His voice cracked, his breathing rough as he set her down. "I was so worried."

Ned had moved away from the door, and when Pete let her go, she found herself with her back to the wall. He cupped her face with his cold hands, a grip that told her that he was trying not to unravel. But the look in his eyes said otherwise. He wore a hint of a beard, probably two days of golden-red scratch, and the redness in his eyes might be from the wind and rain, but she suspected otherwise.

Especially when he simply leaned down and kissed her. A full-out, push-her-to-the-wall, don't-let-her-go kiss that had her reeling. And running her hands into his jacket to grip it tight, pull her to himself.

Pete.

The past two days dropped away, and she was back in Paris, or in New York, or even caught in the beauty of Glacier National Park, lost in Pete's embrace, the taste of him, the smell of the woods on his skin, an urgency in his touch that swept through her, took possession.

This man. She wanted *this* man, forever and ever, and she made a tiny sound in the back of her throat of longing and pain and desperation.

I love you, Pete. I choose you.

Almost as if her thoughts had stung him, he tore away from her, breathing hard. "I—sorry. I—"

But she had her hands fisted in his jacket, not letting go. "No, I'm sorry," she said softly. "I'm so sorry."

Maybe it was her tone. The quiet pleading that just rushed out of her, raw and honest. But he didn't tear away from her, didn't grab her hands to break her hold, just braced his arms on either side of her head, touching his forehead to hers.

Then he closed his eyes, his breathing rough. "You're safe. That's all that matters. That's all."

Not "I love you, Jess." Her heart fell. Especially with her lips still on fire, her entire body rushing with the longing to pull him back against herself. Needing the solidness and power of his arms wrapped around her.

He finally stepped away, looking at the others in the room.

Who stood quietly, staring at them. First at Jess. Then at Pete. Then . . . what? "Felipe? What are you doing here?"

The hurt that crashed across his face told her exactly why he had trekked across the nation and through the woods to find her in this tucked-away cabin.

"I love you enough."

"I was worried." He offered a quick and tight smile, then he pulled her into his arms. "I was so worried, ma chérie." He was wet and held her like he'd never held her before, tight, his body trembling. Maybe he did love her. He put her away, and his eyes were thick with moisture. "Let's get you all home, and then . . . we can talk."

About how she had practically inhaled Pete? How she still wanted to leap into his arms? Yeah, that would be a fun conversation. But it wasn't as if Felipe didn't know how she felt.

However, by the look in Pete's eyes as she glanced at him, maybe Pete wasn't so sure. Because there was a kiss borne of stress and relief . . . and then there were promises and commitments and broken hearts and . . .

"We need to get out of here," Ned said, coming to life from wherever he'd gathered himself after nearly killing Pete. His words brought them all back to the very real fact that the next person through the door could be murderer Randy Blackburn.

And it was.

11

HE'D NEARLY KILLED PETE.

Ned was shaking, his entire body roiling with the rush of horror.

If Pete hadn't moved, his reaction lightning quick and instinctual, Ned would have brought the ax down on Pete's skull.

Ned folded his arms, trying very hard to hold himself together, still feeling Pete's hands on him, shoving him up against the wall. *"It's me, man!"*

"You okay, bro?" Now, Pete turned to him, a hand on his shoulder. "You hurt?"

Oh. Probably Pete referred to the bloody pants, and yeah, his shoulder felt like it might be ablaze, thanks to Pete's near body slam. In fact, maybe he could thank the weakness from his dislocation for the fact that Pete stood before him unscathed. Because Ned had spent years swinging an ax and normally had deadly aim.

"Not really," he said. "But Shae needs an emergency extraction. She has a pretty bad puncture in her gut."

With that, Pete turned and strode over to Shae on the sofa.

Jess, meanwhile, untangled herself from Felipe's embrace. So this was the other man, the one she'd broken Pete's heart for. Interesting. The man seemed just as worried about her as Pete.

234

Pete sat on the coffee table, reached out and took Shae's wrist to check her pulse. "Hey there, Shae. How are you doing?"

"Not great," she said, her voice weak enough for Ned to worry. More. Worry *more*.

Pete pressed his hand to her forehead. Glanced at Jess. "She's feverish, and her pulse is a little high."

It happened so fast, on the tail end of the commotion, that no one reacted. Just stood silent as a man entered the house. A large man, with wide shoulders, girth, and heft; he wore orange hunting coveralls and a wool stocking cap and filled the space with enough menace to silence the room.

His coveralls glistened from the rain and enough blood spatter to peg him exactly as a murderer. Especially when he pointed the end of his Remington bolt-action rifle first at Felipe, then at Ned and growled. "What's going on here?"

"Hey, hey, easy there, pal," Pete said, rising, his hands held up in surrender. "We don't want any trouble."

It took a second for him to lower the weapon. "Pete Brooks?"

A smile slid up one side of Pete's mouth. "Randy? What are you doing here?" Pete shot a quick glance at Jess, who had turned around, her breath catching.

Ned didn't want to move too quickly over to Shae, but . . . *Randy Blackburn?* He shot Shae a look. She'd closed her eyes, as if trying to just breathe.

Randy lowered the gun and reached out to take Pete's hand. Ned pegged him to be in his late forties, with dark hair, just a smattering of gray around the edges, and a hint of a dark beard. Solidly built, he looked like he might be a handful if Ned decided to launch himself at him.

Pete shook his hand. "What are you doing here?" he asked again, friendly, as if Blackburn wasn't still holding the rifle that had probably ripped a hole through Ned's backside.

235

Did anyone else notice the blood spattering his coveralls?

Weirdly, Jess, too, went over to Blackburn. "Hey, Sheriff."

"Jess?" Blackburn turned to her. "It's great to see you. We've missed you." He gave her a one-arm hug. "What are *you* doing here?"

Running from you!

Nobody was saying that part, or even acknowledging the fact that indeed the Texas Chainsaw murderer had just walked through the front door with a smile.

"It's sort of a long story," Jess said. "We . . . we got lost in the woods, and it started raining, and our friend Shae fell and hurt herself."

The Swiss cheese of explanations, so many huge glaring holes that Blackburn should be able to drive a semi through them. Like Jess's grimy white blouse, and Ned's bloody clothes, and Shae, who lay on the sofa, pale and maybe even dying.

"I'm Felipe St. Augustine," said the man who had watched Jess kiss Pete with a look like he'd been slammed in the gut. And rightly so, because in Ned's recollection of his conversation with Jess about Pete, a lip-lock wasn't on the immediate agenda.

Something was rotten in the state of Denmark. But at the moment, the man with the rifle got the most attention, so while Felipe shook Blackburn's hand, greeting him like he might be his long-lost redneck uncle, Ned decided to sneak across the room to Shae.

If the guy was going to shoot Shae, he'd have to go through Ned.

"We were trying to find them when we heard a gunshot," Pete said, glancing at Ned, meeting his eyes for a second. Interestingly, in that split second, his former teammate sent a world of meaning. *Keep cool, no sudden moves.*

So Pete was simply playing at his easy, hey-neighbor demeanor. He moved aside for Ned to take his place.

Ned knelt in front of Shae and took her hand. Ice cold, but he squeezed it and she tightened her grip around his. Not asleep, just trying not to scream, not to unravel. Cool, no sudden moves.

"That was me," Blackburn said. "I bagged a buck—just dragged him back into camp. I've been here for the past few weeks." He finally set the gun down and shut the door. Ned watched as Pete's gaze glanced off the weapon. "I saw the smoke from the chimney and for a second thought I'd forgotten to bank the fire this morning."

"You've been here for a few weeks?" Jess said, moving over to join Shae.

"With a few runs into town for supplies, but . . . yeah." He unzipped his coveralls, sighed. Glanced at Pete. "I guess you'll hear it from your brother soon enough, but Karin and I are getting divorced. I just had to get away, so I came out here. Since it's deer season, I've been waiting for that nice nine-point buck to cross my stand."

Ned hadn't a clue who Karin might be, but . . . wasn't this the same man who had killed his girlfriend five years ago? Clearly Ned needed a more thorough explanation, but he didn't move. Because the situation felt too weird.

Especially when Blackburn came over next to Ned and took a look at the woman on the sofa. "Hey there," he said, his tone kind, even comforting. Soft. "I'm Sheriff Blackburn. What's going on?"

Shae opened her eyes. And if she wasn't the bravest person Ned knew before this moment, the fact that she blinked, gave Blackburn a slow, almost drugged smile, and mumbled something along the lines of, "I'll be okay," convinced him that if anyone could handle being the wife of a navy SEAL, it was Shae, Miss Calm Under Pressure.

"She has a puncture wound," Jess said. "I dressed it, but it's deep. The sooner she gets medical attention, the better."

Blackburn considered her a moment. And Ned tensed, watching, ready—well, for what he wasn't sure, but the fact that the man showed not even a hint of recognition of Shae . . . then again, she did look washed out, her eyes sunken, not at all the vibrant, beautiful woman Ned knew.

Except for the hold she had on his hand. She might be cutting off circulation.

"Is anyone else hurt?" Blackburn asked. He looked at Pete when he said it.

Pete looked at Jess, who shook her head.

"You look a little roughed up there," Blackburn said, and Ned realized he was talking to him. Well, his pants were shredded, his backside bandaged, and blood saturated his jeans. "Yeah," Ned wanted to say, "because you shot me in the bum." But he lifted a shoulder. "I fell and got scraped up pretty good. It's not as bad as it looks." He could lie with the rest of the crowd.

"Okay, we need to get help," Blackburn said. "You can't get cell service here, but my truck has a CB in it. It's down the path about a quarter mile. I'll hike down and call in the PEAK team, get the chopper out here."

It felt too easy, a sort of miracle that had Ned's head spinning. And not just Ned's, because judging by the look on Jess's pale face, she seemed unable to grapple with their change of fortune.

"I'll be back," Blackburn said as he headed to the door. He didn't even grab for his gun on the way out.

The door closed and the room fell silent.

"What just happened?" Shae said. "Did he . . . was he . . ."

"I don't think he even recognized you," Jess said, her voice thin. "And . . . it didn't seem like he'd spent the past two days stalking us through the forest."

"Wait," Felipe said. "That was the man who forced you off the road?"

"We thought so," Jess said.

"I can't believe he didn't recognize me," Shae said quietly.

"Does he know you?" Felipe said, and Ned realized he wasn't the only one who needed to be caught up.

"No, or yes, but . . ." Shae shook her head. "Do you think—I *couldn't* have dreamed up the fact that he was after me for the past five years, could I?"

Pete knelt beside her. "He chased you down. He killed Dante. He's definitely a killer. But . . . maybe he *didn't* recognize you. It's been years, and you've changed."

"But he knew me before. He was Uncle Ian's friend."

"Maybe he doesn't realize that we know about his crimes. And we don't need to let on. Not until we get you back. Then . . . we'll tell Sam and bring him to justice."

Sam. Pete's deputy sheriff brother.

"You did really well, Shae," Ned said.

Jess had walked over to the window and was staring outside. "What I can't figure out is, if it wasn't him, then there's someone else out there."

"Someone else trying to kill us?" Ned said. "But who—"

The shot barked, fast and sharp, and exploded into the dusk, the sound ricocheting through the cabin.

Jess yelped and ducked away from the window.

Pete launched himself at her, but Felipe got there first, pulling her against him.

Ned watched as she untangled herself fast, turning to join Pete at the window.

"Randy's been shot!" Pete said.

Jess went for the door, but Pete put a hand on it, slamming it.

"Have you lost your ever-lovin' mind?"

She reeled back, staring at him.

"There's no way you're going out there. Jess—someone just

shot Randy. Which means he's here. Whoever has been tracking you has found you."

———— + ————

Pete didn't know where to start with the tangle of panic.

Randy Blackburn, accused murderer, who had just acted—pretended?—to be their best-friend-slash-hero lay crumpled and bleeding, possibly dead, in the yard.

Behind him, Shae seemed to be sinking into a sort of shock.

Ned had nearly chopped his head off.

And Jess. She'd kissed him like she missed him. Desperately. The reunion that he'd dreamed of for nearly a year. Except in his dreams, the reunion didn't include her maybe-fiancé watching, and worse, suggesting that maybe they all needed to go home, sit down, and chat.

Work this out over crepes and mulled wine, perhaps.

Pete had lost his head the moment he'd seen Jess. He'd had no other thought but to yank her away from the drama and pain of the past year and just hold the woman he loved. *Still.* He loved Jess so much his entire body ached.

So yeah, when Jess practically clung to him, Pete dove in, reminding himself of her touch, her laughter, the shape of the future he'd once loosed himself into.

Then she'd whimpered. Or perhaps it was simply shock, but with it, the rude thought flashed that she didn't belong to him anymore.

Maybe. But it was enough for him to pull away, to lean back with apology on his lips.

"I'm sorry—"

"No, I'm sorry." She had grabbed his jacket, as if unwilling to let him go, and it broke his heart because suddenly, as quickly as it had vanished, the pain rushed back. The past year, his stupid mistakes, her betrayal . . . even the confusing fight that had driven her away from him.

He just wanted to start over. But they had too much behind them.

It had to be enough that she was safe. So he braced his arms over her instead of pulling her against him, instead of diving back in for another time-stopping kiss, and told her the truth. "You're safe. That's all that matters." Or mostly the truth.

I love you, Jess. Miraculously, the words didn't slip out as he somehow backed away from her.

It gave Pete the sweetest of petty, satisfactory moments that she'd not given Felipe the same greeting. Even if she did surrender to his embrace.

Yes, maybe they all needed a nice, long, honest chat.

Any hope of this wrapping up without drama ended when Blackburn came through the door. Pete felt the string of tension vibrating between Jess, Ned, and Shae, and with it, the past whispered in his ear—an accusation from Shae that Blackburn had murdered her boyfriend.

Not necessarily something he wanted to throw at the big man carrying a Remington, so Pete had played the easy friend to the man who had worked with him on countless rescues over the past five years.

The man who'd been shot in the yard on his way to get them help.

Pete stood with his hand barring the door, his gaze hard on Jess. "You are not going out there!"

"He's hurt—he might be dead."

"My point *exactly.*" Pete put his back to the door and took her by the arms, his grip on her wrists. "Whoever is out there is not messing around. He's shooting to kill."

That was when he noticed she winced, her eyes tightening around the edges. He yanked his hands away. "You *are* hurt!"

"I landed wrong when we went over the cliff—"

"You went over a cliff?" Felipe said, stepping up beside her.

"When we escaped the truck. We ran through the woods, but it was so dark, we couldn't see and we went right over the edge of a ten-foot drop. Ned dislocated his shoulder."

Really? Pete glanced at Ned, who hadn't moved from his position beside Shae. He looked rough—his jeans ripped and bloody, his shirt grimy—and he bore a brutal scrape on his chin. "You okay?"

"It's Shae we really need to pay attention to here."

No, they needed to get them *all* out of here. Pete grabbed his walkie, the first chance he'd had in all the commotion to call PEAK.

"Rescue 2, Rescue 1, come in."

Static.

He tried again.

Maybe Blackburn had been telling the truth. The river wound through a canyon, and the granite peaks could be cutting off their communication. "I need to get to that radio in his truck."

"If there is a radio in the truck. He could have been lying," Jess said. She had brought her arm into her body, cradling it.

"Let me take a look at that." Pete eased her arm away, gently rubbing his thumb along the bone, watching her face. She met his eyes.

Oh. For a second he couldn't breathe, not with the way she looked at him, a brokenness, a want in her eyes, as if . . . as if wishing him back into her arms.

His throat tightened and he tore his gaze away. "Can you move your wrist?"

She moved it in a circle. "It's sore, but I don't think it's broken."

"Okay. Be gentle with it," he said, noticing Felipe's annoyed expression.

Yeah, well, maybe he should take her up on the wish he'd

seen in her eyes. Or hoped—oh, he hoped—he saw. Sure, they had unfinished business, but paramount in his head was the fact that *he'd found Jess.*

He wasn't going to let some guy out in the yard destroy that, steal her away again.

Pete turned back to the window, scanning the lawn. Blackburn seemed to be still alive, moving slowly across the grass. Maybe. It could also be his imagination.

Shoot.

"I need to go out there and get him," he said, mostly to himself.

"I'll go with you," Jess said.

"Over my dead body," he growled. The sun had started to set and the dusk was upon them, but by the time the shadows had lengthened enough to conceal him, Blackburn would have bled out.

They needed to rescue Blackburn, and they needed to get Shae and Ned to medical help. Pronto.

"Are there any windows here?" The cabin was small—a main room with a stove, another room just off the main. It looked like a bedroom. He walked into it and found a tiny bathroom. A window hung over the toilet. Maybe big enough.

He unlocked it, and with a shove, the window opened. Perfect.

"We can't leave him out there."

He turned and saw Jess had followed him into the room. She stood there, her eyes big, dark, accusing.

"Blackburn?"

"I saw him moving, Pete. We have to get him."

Pete leaned out past her, to see if they had company. Then he pulled her into the room and shut the door.

"What?"

Don't kiss her. How he longed to press her up against the door and just release the hard grip he had on his emotions. Instead, "I

243

know. I have an idea, but you have to promise me that you won't . . ." He closed his eyes, his jaw tight against the constriction of his chest.

"What—"

"That you won't leave!" He drew in a breath, not meaning his outburst.

She just stared at him, and he took a breath before he touched her face, his thumb caressing her cheekbone, wanting, oh wanting . . . "Please don't leave Mercy Falls until I get back."

"Huh?"

"You're right. Blackburn is moving, and we need to get him. But you're not going to like how. Because . . . while I go get him, you're going to go out this back window with Shae and Ned and . . ." He wanted to swear. "Felipe."

Her eyes widened. "No—what? *No!* I'm not leaving you here by yourself! What are you going to do—go out there and drag his body in the house with bullets flying at you?"

That was exactly the plan, and he knew it had crazy written all over it. Maybe that truth showed in his eyes because she shook her head in disbelief, which morphed fast into fury. "Well, you can forget that, Pete Brooks! I didn't come back to Montana to watch you die!"

That stymied him long enough for her to shove him away, reach for the doorknob.

Oh no, she wasn't leaving—he grabbed her arm and whirled her around. "Then why did you come back, Jess? You have your life all figured out. You're going to marry Felipe—he told me everything. Including, yes, your mother, although for the life of me, I can't figure out why you'd let her decide your future. But okay, there it is. So why did you come back? To torment me? Break my heart? Drive me crazy? Remind me that . . . that I was just a stupid fling?"

SUSAN MAY WARREN

"A stupid fling? What are you talking about?" Her voice rasped low. "You were never a fling, Pete. I meant it when I said yes . . ."

"Which yes? When I proposed at your house? Or maybe later in Miami when you said you'd come back to me? Or how about at the Eiffel Tower? When exactly did you mean it? Because from where I stand, I'm very confused. Your yesses feel like *no.*"

Shoot, his voice was shaking, as if he might start crying. He clenched his jaw, fighting the terrible constricting of his chest. No, not here. They just had to get out of here alive.

Knowing she was safe, he might be able to look her in her eyes and bear the truth.

She put her hand on his chest. "I meant it every single time, Pete." Her eyes filled. "But . . . you don't understand—"

"Try me, Jess," he snapped, his hand on hers, not sure if he wanted to hold it there or yank it away.

But really, he should just stop her from talking because her words were destined to wreck him, he knew it in his gut.

"I did try. I called you. On New Year's Eve, and a dozen times after that."

His mouth tightened. "I know."

"You blocked my calls." She said it so softly, a confirmation more than a question.

"Yes. I was just so—"

"I get it."

No, probably not, but now the hurt just poured out. "But if you wanted to explain, there are other ways to communicate. A letter, perhaps? You've heard of those, right?"

"A person has to have a mailing address to get a letter, Pete."

"No good, Jess. You know enough about my life to track me down." He removed her hand from his shirt.

"Okay. Maybe . . ." She swallowed. "I was scared, okay? I knew . . . I knew I'd hurt you. And I didn't know what to say."

245

"How about the truth? Pete, you don't fit into my life. Pete, move on—"

"Oh, you did that just fine without my permission."

Her words were a slap. And Felipe's voice was in his head. *"That's what Selene thought too."*

Jess wiped her hand across her cheek. "And I don't blame you. I saw Aimee. She's cute, and you deserve—"

"I'm not with Aimee," he growled. "I never have been."

Truth, but—

"It doesn't matter." She shook her head.

Except it did. "I didn't move on, Jess. But you were just going to walk out of my life, no answers, nothing?"

"No! I was going to talk to you—"

"When?"

"I don't know!" She swallowed, lowered her voice. "I know I am the queen of avoidance. I hate conflict. I hate hurting people and . . . well, I knew I hurt you and I just couldn't face that." She looked away. "It was easier to pretend that I could wait and then tell you when . . . I dunno—when I saw you next."

He stepped back and raised his hands in a sort of help-me-out-here gesture because he didn't know what to do with that. "As in, what? A natural disaster? A PEAK ten-year reunion?"

Her eyes flashed. "Maybe when my mother died and I could finally come home!"

Oh.

But sorry. For all the grief that hung in her voice, it wasn't enough to stop him from shaking his head. "I would have dropped everything and come to New York City. To be with you, to help you take care of your mother, or whatever else I could do. I loved you that much, Jess."

Loved. Yeah, he heard the word but didn't amend it. He didn't know why.

Well, actually he did. Because it was finally time to face the truth, something he'd already voiced but hadn't wanted to believe.

Jess Tagg simply didn't love him like he loved her. Didn't want to give up her life, the future she could have with Felipe, the world that was, admittedly, safe and comfortable and ordered, for the mess he lived in.

A world without trouble.

He couldn't really blame her, given his history with trouble . . . and with women. It didn't stop the hurt from bleeding into his voice, however, as he probed for the answer he didn't want to hear.

"The truth is, Jess, I don't buy the whole 'I love you but I'm going to get fake engaged' line. You love me, you come back to me. It's as simple as that. So I'm sorry, but you need to be truthful—brutally truthful here, honey. Did you ever really want to marry *me*? Pete Brooks. Because it's not my imagination that I am the complete and utter opposite of Mr. Right out there, and by the way, if he tries to pin our fight on me, you need to know—"

"You had a fight?"

"Of course we had a fight!" He shook his head. "Sheesh, Jess. I'm not playing a game here. I never was. I loved you. I still . . . oh, shoot." He took a breath. "I'm pitiful, I know it, but I still love you. And I think the Jess Tagg I used to know loved me. But what about this one? Selene Jessica Taggert. Does she love me? Or just . . . or just the *thought* of me? The fling she had while she was living a different life in Montana?"

Her eyes filled. "I . . . I'm not the person I left here—"

"That's what I thought." And because he didn't want her to see him cry, didn't want to let her go—well, with it ending with so many ripped, raw edges, he pulled her to himself and held her. "You were the best thing that ever happened to me, Jess. Your love made me a better man. And now, I'm going to make sure you have a chance to live."

He pushed her away and opened the bathroom door.

"Pete—"

But he ignored her and headed out into the main room. "Listen up," he said to Ned and Felipe. "I need to go out there and drag Blackburn into the house. But in the meantime, I found a window in the back. It's big enough to go through, one at a time. Here's what's going to happen. While I'm distracting the shooter, Felipe and Ned are going to take Shae through the window, and then all of you are going to find that truck. And if it's not there, you're going to keep going until you get ahold of PEAK." He unclipped his walkie, walked over to Felipe, and handed it to him. "Send Sam back for me. And don't let me down."

Felipe nodded, glancing at Jess, who had come out behind him. Pete spotted her out of his periphery wearing an expression that he didn't want to get in front of. Well, at least they'd had their closure.

He'd fallen in love with a Jess that no longer existed. And now he could grieve the Jess he'd lost.

"You can't go out there without cover," Ned said. "He'll shoot you."

Pete picked up the Remington, checked the chamber. "Two shots left."

Jess came up to him. "Listen. I know how to shoot. Let me cover you."

"We're not in a movie, Jess. Two shots aren't going to cover me."

"How about smoke?" Ned let go of Shae's hand. "We have a fire here. We could light something—"

"With the rain and oxygen out there, the smoke won't be thick enough."

"Unless we add something to keep it burning. You know fire combustion," Ned said. "The hotter the fire, the blacker the smoke. And these logs are already on fire. We just need to keep them burning."

"With what?" Pete asked.

"How about pine resin? A little napalm?" Jess interjected.

Really? "How did you get resin?"

"You taught me, remember?" Jess said. "I used resin to glue Ned's wound, but I have some left." She went to the stove and grabbed a cast-iron pan. "We could create a fire bundle, light it, and toss it out in the yard. Let it smoke and blaze and then use it as cover." Her voice bore too much excitement.

"Not *we*, Jess." He ignored her look. "But yeah, good idea."

He walked over to the firebox and grabbed out magazines, dried pine needles, kindling, and pine logs. "I need something flammable."

"How about this?" Felipe had gone to the bedroom and now returned with a pillow and a sheet. He handed the pillow to Pete.

While Pete shoved it full with the kindling, Felipe took the sheet and folded it in half, laying it on the floor beside Shae.

"Help her onto it," he said to Ned.

Pete glanced at Jess, who went to help move Shae to the floor. But she looked up, catching his eye, and he knew he had to get her out of here before she did something stupid.

Like chase after him.

No. No, she wouldn't do that. She only ran *away* from him.

Pete brought the fire bundle over to the kitchen and grabbed the pot. The resin sat inside, hard and cool in the bottom of the pan.

"Fuel, oxygen, chemical reaction," Pete said. "If I light this and shove it in the bag, leaving it open, it'll flame. And the resin will keep burning until the pillow and the kindling catch fire. The flashover of heat will cause enough smoke to at least cloud the field of vision, and with the dusk and shadows . . ."

He was talking to no one, apparently, because Ned and Felipe had taken the four corners of the sheet, lifted Shae in it, and started toward the bathroom.

Jess stood in the middle of the room.

He headed toward the door, stopping at the stove.

"Wait." Jess came over to him. "You have to come with us."

He looked at her and kept his voice soft, even took her hand. "Babe. You need to get out of here. I don't know who's out there. But clearly, they're not giving up. And you're right—we can't leave Blackburn to die."

He didn't care so much about Blackburn that he was willing to risk his life for him. This craziness had everything to do with Jess. And needing to cause a distraction so she could get away.

The way she was looking at him, she knew it too. Her eyes filled. "Please, Pete—"

"You need to get out of here, now. Please." Then he leaned over and kissed her, sweetly, on the forehead. *Good-bye, Jess.* "Run and don't look back."

Then he knelt and swung open the stove. Grabbed a log with the tongs and brought it out onto the floor. Shoved it into the mound of pillow, kindling, and resin. Almost immediately, it caught fire, began to smoke.

Jess had moved to the bedroom door. She turned, met his eyes. *I love you.* He offered her a half smile, then opened the door and flung the burning mass into the now dusky yard.

He made the mistake of glancing back.

She was gone.

He went out the door.

———— + ————

What was she doing? Maybe shock had completely taken over her body because Jess saw herself climbing up to the window.

Felipe had climbed out first, hitting the ground and then holding out his arms for Ned to pass Shae down. Ned jumped out behind her and turned to help Jess.

She hesitated, standing on the top of the toilet, one leg in, one leg out, listening to Pete's words rebounding in her head. *"The Jess Tagg I used to know loved me. But what about this one? Selene Jessica Taggert. Does she love me?"*

Yes. The answer consumed her, filled every pore. Every part of her loved every bit of Pete Brooks, from his blue eyes to his wild ideas that usually—*please, God!*—worked.

"Or just . . . or just the thought of me? The fling she had while she was living a different life in Montana?"

Those words now stopped her cold.

The thought of Pete. His presence made her brave. Impulsive.

He'd brought out a side of her that both enthralled and frightened her. She found pieces of herself that she hadn't known existed before she met him.

With Pete she lived with the freedom to taste and believe and live a life that seemed at once exhilarating and terrifying. As if she might be taking a leap off a cliff into a cloudless sky.

But what if . . . what if she simply hit bottom? What if she flung herself into this life and she lost it all? It wasn't as if Pete was safe. He lived life so far on the edge that he barely touched it. He'd already escaped death a few times.

Flirted with it, really.

He'd never been a fling. But in truth, she didn't know if she could live with her heart that far out of her body.

With Felipe, at least, she . . . well, he wasn't the kind of man to run into danger.

Wasn't going to take her heart and live dangerously with it.

"I'm not with Aimee. I never have been." Oh, how could she have so easily believed anything but that Pete was the honorable man she knew. And loved. Oh, how she loved.

She hit the grass. Ned let her go and grabbed the end of Shae's sheet. Felipe worked his way down to the other end, held it behind him. "Let's go."

He started moving toward the edge of the forest where a tiny indent in the waning light betrayed a wide trail, big enough for a four-wheeler.

The air reeked of wood smoke and the soggy loam from today's rain. And over the top of the trees, a blunted sun fought to leave fire in the sky.

She ran after Felipe, toward the trail. *"I'm not the person I left here."*

No, that wasn't what she wanted to say to Pete at all. She was *more* than the person she'd left here. *Because* she'd been here. Because she'd met Pete.

"You were the best thing that ever happened to me, Jess. Your love made me a better man."

And his love had made her more. Jess and Selene.

She wanted them both.

But she only wanted one man.

Her gaze cast over Felipe, good, brave, decent Felipe, as he carried Shae through the darkness. Felipe, who was just as much of a hero as Pete, really. Felipe, who loved her enough to marry her. But who *really* loved someone else, and they both knew it.

Felipe deserved someone who loved him more than enough.

Jess broke away and headed back toward the house.

"Selene!" The voice hissed into the shadows, but she didn't expect him to run after her. He grabbed her arm just as she reached the window. "What are you doing?"

She whirled around, found Felipe large and angry behind her. Behind him, Ned stood holding Shae in his arms. "C'mon!"

"No." She wrenched her arm out of his grip. "Stop, Felipe. You know . . ." Her eyes filled. "You know I can't leave him."

Shae's words in the cave rebounded back to her. *"Someone is going to get hurt here, Jess. And right now, it's everyone. Make a choice."*

She just did.

252

And Felipe knew it. He shook his head, his eyes deepening with hurt. "Don't be foolish, Selene. You need to come with me. Right now."

Maybe she was being a little foolish. But she wasn't so naive not to understand his words. He didn't just mean right now, but forever.

"Felipe—"

"He cheated on you! You were right. He *cheated* on you on New Year's Eve. And probably since then too."

She recoiled. Blinked hard. "No, he didn't. He and Aimee aren't together."

Felipe just gave her a look, something that fisted her heart. "Maybe it wasn't with this Aimee person. Probably it was with someone he barely remembers."

"No." She shook her head, almost fiercely. "And besides, it's not cheating if we weren't together. He thought it was over, that you and I were engaged—"

"No, Selene. He didn't know that then."

She drew in a breath. "I hurt him."

"And he'll hurt *you*." Felipe caught her face in his hands. "Think about it—he's reckless and dangerous and . . ." He swallowed. "I love you."

"You love me enough."

"No. I love you. Period. Not just enough. I see you, Selene. I see how brave you are, beautiful and smart and—"

"I'm *not* Selene. Or not *just* Selene. Not anymore." She pulled Felipe's hands from her face. "I can't be who you want me to be. I love—"

Shots. They cracked the dusky sky. One, then another and Jess jerked away from Felipe. "Go! Please. If you love me, get Shae and Ned to safety!" She pushed him away, ignored his horrified expression, and fled to the front of the house.

The smoke had turned the yard into a ghostly moor of fog, and she could barely make out the figures.

When she did, she stifled a scream, her hand over her mouth.

Two bodies. Blackburn, unmoving.

And Pete.

He lay a few feet from Blackburn, just steps from the deck, the smoking, flaming bundle between him and Blackburn.

Pete!

The sight of him crumpled in the grass simply ignited her entire body. On impulse and grief she raced toward him.

It all happened so fast, she didn't know exactly how to parse it out.

At the smoky edge of the forest, a figure rose, but she kept her focus on Pete.

Who was also rising, gathering his feet under him.

Just as she launched herself at him, he leaped up and tackled her. Arms around her, moving his body to cushion her fall.

They landed with a thump into the grass, so hard it knocked out her breath. But Pete wasn't done. He rolled with her, over and over, until they reached the grassy edge of the woods.

Shots exploded around them. She tried to get her hands over her head, but Pete had her by the back of her dress, pulling her up, clutching her close. He grabbed her hand and hauled her forward even as she gulped for breath.

"Run!"

Into the woods again, this time led by Pete. Somehow she found her breath and stumbled after him.

Then they were running with fury into the shadowy forest, Pete slapping away the trees and brush, without a look behind him.

Another shot shattered bark from a nearby tree, and Pete jerked her in front of him, pushing her now. "Faster, Jess!"

She held her hands out, her heart thundering. A downed tree

tripped her, but Pete grabbed her around the waist, holding her tight to his strong body.

They kept running. Shaggy white pine slapped her face, her arms. They slipped on pine needles, her feet soggy in the wet loam, and not far off she heard the river, loud and raucous. Another shot, this one pinging against a giant boulder that cluttered their path.

Ahead—oh no. The forest opened up into an expanse that suggested a flying leap off a cliff into the abyss below.

Pete skidded to a stop, yanked her hard against himself, breathing in razor-edged gasps. "Okay, okay." He turned, then grabbed her hand and pulled her along the ledge. "There."

A rocky overhang, big enough to hide them.

He ripped off his jacket and threw it around her shoulders, zipped it up. Then he pushed her down, guiding her into the space. "Time to hide."

She climbed into the enclave, and he followed her in, his arms around her, his body hiding hers.

He bent his head to her ear. "Don't make a sound."

She dug her hands in his shirt, beginning to shake. He tightened his hold on her, his own chest rising and falling hard.

Finally, "Why, Jess?" he whispered, breaking his own rules.

And because he'd told her not to make a sound, she touched her hand to his whiskered face, moved it to hers, and without a word kissed him.

He froze. Simply didn't move. Not his breath, not his hands, not his mouth. Just stilled, as if, for the first time in his life, he hadn't a clue how to react.

But his heartbeat betrayed him, practically slamming against her chest. *Yes, that's right, Pete. I can be impulsive, brave, and I choose you.* She put it all into her kiss, ignoring the fact that he couldn't seem to catch up.

Yeah, well her too, because she'd leaped so far out of the Selene, and frankly, the Jess she'd been—and it felt glorious.

Terrifying, yes, but when Pete made a tiny groan in the back of his throat, maybe even in his heart, and began to kiss her back, it seemed exactly right. He pulled her tight against him, his mouth urgent and possessive.

There was the Pete she knew.

She could stay right here, forever—

He pulled away, his lips against her ear. "Jess, I don't think . . . I—"

"Don't make a sound," she said and pulled him back down.

For a long, delicious, Pete Brooks moment, he used everything but words to speak. It seemed he couldn't get enough of her as he ran his hands into her hair, tucking her in close, kissing her with such a fullness that she forgot she was supposed to be afraid.

Because she was with Pete.

He smelled of the forest, the earth, of a man who had fought the elements to find her.

He finally took a breath and pushed away. But in the fading light, the shadows on his face betrayed a sort of panic. "Jess," he whispered. "The way you kiss me. I . . . don't know what's happening here. Why didn't you go with Felipe?"

She was about to answer when his hand clamped over her mouth. He leaned close, his breathing shallow.

Footsteps, a cracking of branches. Shuffling of leaves.

She closed her eyes.

"Brooks! I know you're out here. And I'm going to find you!"

Pete's body stiffened. He lifted his head. And when she opened her eyes, he had his gaze fixed on hers, the realization stark in them.

Whoever was after them was after . . . Pete?

She didn't move, didn't breathe. The footsteps moved away, and Pete bent his head, propped it on her shoulder. He was trembling.

"Who was that?" she whispered finally.

"I don't know," Pete answered on a wisp of breath. "But we need to get out of here."

"Where?"

"Back to the house. We'll barricade ourselves inside and wait for PEAK to show up."

It seemed like the right idea.

"Hold on to my hand, don't let go," Pete said as he eased them out of the enclave.

Never.

12

"I HAVE TO GO BACK." The dome light cast illumination over Felipe, who sat in the driver's seat, breathing hard. He gripped the wheel of the truck they'd found parked down a steep trail, at the edge of a grassy two-lane forest road.

Shae didn't blame him for the tremor in his voice, the way he looked back at them—Ned and her in the back seat of the truck—his expression stricken.

"I can't just leave Selene—and Pete—in the woods."

She got that. She'd didn't know what had gone down between Felipe and Jess, but the poor man had worn an expression of pure panic as Jess ran after Pete. Shae had watched the drama play out and fisted her hand tight into Ned's shirt.

Don't leave me. She was trying very hard to be courageous, but right now she just needed a hold on to something, anything that would confirm that they'd live through this night. That Blackburn wouldn't reappear with an ax or a gun or even just his fists and finish them off like in some sort of horror movie. But Blackburn was dead, or close to it.

Right?

Frankly, the entire thing felt a little anticlimactic. After holding her hostage in her brain for five years, he'd been anything but the monster she made him out to be.

Or maybe that made him even more terrifying.

"I'll be right back," Felipe said. "Can you hold on for one more minute? I just have to—"

"Go," Ned said. He had climbed into the back seat with Shae, settling her inside, then scooting in beside her. She didn't want to imagine his agony sitting on his wound. But he simply pulled her into his arms, cocooning her in his embrace. Warm. Safe. Calm.

Except for the pounding of his heart. She pressed her hand on his chest. "We're almost out of here."

"Not soon enough," Ned said. "I can't believe we left Pete back there."

"He'll be okay."

"He's not invincible, Shae. I worked with him for an entire summer, when I was a rookie. And yes, he was practically a smoke-jumping legend for his ability to stay calm in the middle of a firestorm. He's lived through a few near-death experiences too. Had to run from a fire a few years ago where seven jumpers died."

"Wow."

"Yeah. He's always lived a little on the edge between crazy and brave." He shook his head. "But even the brave can die."

"But that's why you admire him."

Ned looked down at her, frowned.

"Pete and Fraser and even your storm-chasing brother, Jonas. You admire them."

He lifted a shoulder. "I guess."

"For sure. And I get it. It's like what you said—they're willing to abandon their own safety to help others."

"Well, I think Jonas is more about the thrill of the chase, but . . . Pete and Fraser, they're real . . ."

"Heroes?"

"I guess. Yeah. They're the real deal."

"So are you."

"No." He looked down at her. "No, Shae, I'm not. Yet."

She got it then. The smokejumping, the fear of being the weak link, the navy enlistment . . .

"You still feel like the skinny kid in the yard, getting knocked down all the time. Except now Kostia is in your brain telling you that you have to try harder, be more. But you fear that you'll never be enough."

He looked away. "Someday I will be. You just wait."

"Ned—"

Felipe had gotten out but left the door open. Now, he slid back into the front seat.

"Is Jess okay? Are they coming?" Ned asked.

Felipe turned. "I don't know."

Except it wasn't Felipe. The voice was lower, husky and a little frayed. "I saw your friend on the path and he told me to go without him."

Shae turned in Ned's arms and stifled a gasp.

Randy Blackburn was holding his hand to his head, blood oozing out between his fingers.

Ned jerked, too, at the sight. "Are you okay?"

"I think it's just a graze, but it knocked me out for a bit. I came to about the time Jess started screaming, and I got out of there." He leaned over, opened his glove box, grabbed a greasy and frayed towel, and held it to his head. "I got a killer headache, but I'll be okay. I'm good to drive—"

"Wait—what?" Ned said.

Shae was staring at Blackburn, trying to read his eyes. Did he look at her with a spark of recognition? Did he offer a smile of menace?

She shook her head, her eyes filling. She couldn't lose Ned, too. "Please, don't—"

He frowned and she cut off her words. What if he really didn't recognize her? Five years and a whole lot of life experience had changed her. She wasn't the terrified teenager who had fled through the woods, leaving the boy she loved to die. This version of Esme-turned-Shae had rebuilt her life. Returned to Mercy Falls to face her past.

Whatever game Blackburn was playing, he wasn't going to win.

"We need to call PEAK," she said, meeting Blackburn's gaze. Testing.

"Right," he said with a nod, no guile, and picked up his CB. "I'll call 911 and they can relay the message." He turned the dial, and in a moment dispatch picked up.

Shae listened in disbelief as Randy identified himself, as he explained the situation and asked not only for reinforcements but for a message to be relayed to PEAK. When he finished, he turned back to them. "It'll take a while for them to get here. But we don't have that time. We need to get you medical help."

She just stared at him, fighting to keep her eyes from widening, from giving them all away.

"What about Pete and Jess, and Felipe?" Ned said. "We can't leave them."

"Jess and Pete got away." Blackburn shut the door, pitching the truck into darkness. "Felipe said he wants to stay here and look for them." He turned the engine over. "My people will be here soon, but we can't wait."

It cast through her brain that Blackburn might have killed Felipe. Left his body to bleed out somewhere in the woods. As for Jess and Pete—she didn't want to imagine what had really happened.

No. She wouldn't give fear any power.

As Blackburn pulled out, down the bumpy road, she met Ned's eyes and held on.

Pete said nothing, his hand tight on Jess's as they crept through the forest back to the cabin.

Nothing, because anything that emerged from his mouth was liable to be at full volume, and not pretty. The last thing he needed was their—*his*—stalker to come upon them while he was having a meltdown.

But why—sheesh, *why*, Jess? She would be safe if she'd gone with Felipe. And that was the crux of it, something he should probably surrender to.

She was safer with Felipe.

She must have sensed his frustration because she too remained silent as she picked her way through the shadows. The sun had dropped beyond the trees, the darkness growing out of the damp earth. Just the snap of branches beneath their steps betrayed their presence.

He hadn't realized how far they'd run, and if it weren't for a sort of inner natural compass that found landmarks and Vs in the terrain, he might have tangled them farther into the forest. But his years as a smokejumper had honed his wilderness skills, and that radar brought him to the edge of the forest, back to the cabin.

Pete pulled her down into the brush before she could step out into the clearing. "Just wait."

She stayed silent beside him as he scanned the perimeter between them and the cabin. A faint glow of fire, like eyes, blinked at him from the bundle he'd thrown. Beyond that, Blackburn had vanished.

Maybe crawled away. Pete could only hope.

"Okay, we're going to run for it. Stay very close to me." Because then, if any shots were fired, maybe they'd hit him before they'd find Jess.

He took off into the no-man's-land. Heart thundering, his

262

adrenaline spiking, he practically threw Jess on the porch, then slammed into the house, turned, and pressed the door shut.

She was breathing hard, hands on her knees. "It doesn't lock. We broke it."

He walked over to the sofa, got behind it, and shoved it across the floor to pile against the door.

Then he pulled her against him. "We're just going to hunker down until Felipe calls PEAK."

The glow from the stove still flickered light into the room.

"But what about the shooter? What if he comes back and is waiting for them?" Jess asked.

Good question, but right now he didn't have any answers to any of his glaring questions.

Like, how had the shooter known his name? Any number of people knew he was back in Mercy Falls this weekend. But who would want to kill him?

And now Jess was caught in the cross fire. Which wouldn't be an issue if she'd just *listened* to him. He put Jess away from him. Met her eyes, and knew he had nothing of calm or even understanding in his own. "Why didn't you go with Felipe?"

She frowned and yanked her arm from his grasp. "Because I didn't want . . ." She shook her head. "Because I choose you, Pete. I keep trying to tell you that!"

He blinked at her. Shook his head, turning away from her. "You said you weren't the same Jess I knew—"

"No. I'm not, thanks to you."

She walked over to the stove and stood in the dim glow of the heat, radiating her own sort of fire.

She wasn't the only one currently fighting a flashover. "What do you mean, thanks to me?"

"You, Pete. You changed me. You made me . . . I don't know. You got me in over my head time after time—"

"I know, I'm sorry—"

"And taught me how to *get out* of it."

Oh.

"And now . . ." She sighed, her voice falling. She sank down on the coffee table, lifting her hands to the heat. "You said you didn't understand why I let my mother determine my future. The truth is, Pete, that . . . well, it's weird how you can return home and be thirteen and needy all over again. I stepped into her radar and I was right back into the world where my mother . . . well, I never had my own voice, I guess. She's strong willed and determined and . . . I was so glad to see her."

The amber light illuminated her blonde hair. It had fallen out of the bun at the back of her head, and now she pulled it free, and shook it out, running her fingers through it to remove twigs and leaves and dirt.

He wanted to do that. Instead, he shoved his hands into his pockets. Because memory rushed him and for a quick, brutally raw moment he was stretched out beside her in the mossy enclave of the rock, kissing her like a man on fire.

Burning with a way-too-familiar rush of desire.

He didn't want to be that man. Not anymore. And not with Jess. Well, not yet.

He took a breath and stood there, watching her profile in the firelight, his entire body humming.

"She needed me, Pete. For the first time, I think. It just felt so good to . . . well, to be appreciated. To fix the pain I'd caused." She glanced over at him. "I think I just needed to know that what I did to my family wasn't unredeemable."

"You keep forgetting that it wasn't you who did anything to your family. It was your father."

"I know. Or, I'm trying to. It's just . . . well, that was the hard part. My mother was so thrilled to see me and Felipe back together."

"But you weren't back together, right?" He didn't mean his tone, the hint of desperation, but please let her not have lied to him.

"No. We weren't. But to her, it felt like it. She saw us attending social functions together, and it was her idea for us to go to Paris together. I just didn't want to disappoint her." She finally twisted her hair back, tied it into a knot. He wanted to beg her to keep it down, but probably that wasn't a good idea, either. "And then she had her seizure, in Paris."

"Felipe told me everything," he said, not wanting her to relive the pain.

She did anyway—he watched it replay on her face, in the tightness of her mouth, the way she ran a hand across her cheek. She nodded. "The doctor gave her less than a year to live, and the first thing she did was ask me and Felipe to get married."

Pete wanted to ring the old woman's neck, dying or not, because couldn't she see that Jess didn't belong to Felipe? Except, maybe not. Because on paper, yes, Felipe and Selene were a perfect match. And sometimes people only saw what they longed to see.

"It was Felipe's idea. He suggested we pretend to be engaged. And I . . . I didn't want to, Pete." She turned and looked at him then, and her eyes glistened. "You have to believe me, that I didn't want to lie to you. I was going to tell you—"

"I know. On New Year's Eve. Felipe told me that too." His lips pressed together. "I'm sorry I didn't pick up the phone."

A tear dripped off her chin.

So much lost between them because of his stupid pride. Because of the fear of what might happen if he answered her call. Ignoring his pain and balming his heart with cheap rewards felt easier than what she might say.

She drew in a breath. "I understand—"

She looked so wretched he couldn't take it one more second. He crossed the room, sat down on the table, and pulled her to himself.

She was trembling and cold. She still wore his jacket, but it was thin, and under that she had only a flimsy blouse and dress, bare legs, and boots. He climbed behind her on the table and straddled his legs around her, pulling her back against himself, his arms tight around her.

It was a move to keep her warm, but the sense of her sinking against him could unravel him. Still.

She ran her hands along his arms. "I agreed to be engaged to Felipe in appearance only. I didn't give him my heart again, Pete."

He closed his eyes, needing her words to push out the splinter Felipe had shoved into his brain. "Felipe said you . . . well, that you needed to get engaged. And I'm sorry. For a second I thought . . . well, that you, um, *needed* to get married."

She leaned up, turned in Pete's embrace to look at him, and her expression turned his throat tight. "What?"

"You should know that Felipe and I . . . well, before I met you, back in college. We were engaged, for real, and . . . well, we slept together."

His brain wouldn't shut off the sudden influx of images. How he wanted to get his hands on Felipe, strangle the little French jerk for—

What? Behaving with Jess the same way—no, probably better—than Pete had with a dozen other women? In fact, Pete didn't want to do the math. Hadn't kept count, but suddenly he just wanted to close his eyes, push her away.

Jess misread his expression, because she stiffened. "I'm so sorry—"

"What? Oh no, Jess." He reached out and touched her face. "It's not you. I understand. I hate it, but I understand. And believe me, I'm . . . I so don't deserve you."

She drew in a breath then. Searched his face. "Felipe told me that you cheated on me on New Year's Eve."

"No—what? No!" Except the memory of that night bubbled

266

up, and he couldn't bear it. He pushed away from her, got up, and walked away.

"Pete?"

He stood with his back to her, his hand over his eyes, the darkness turning his body to poison.

Her hand touched his back, and he nearly jumped. Instead, he stepped away from her again. Shook his head. "Aw, Jess, I'm so sorry."

She didn't move then.

He turned, aware of the fact that his eyes had filled. "I . . . yes. I was with someone else the night you called."

She drew in a breath.

"I didn't sleep with anyone, but . . ." He clenched his jaw, his chest hot, tight. "I was hurt, okay? I was angry and alone and . . . I missed you so much. I felt like such a fool. I'd raced over to Paris like a lovesick idiot and . . ." He shook his head, swallowed, fighting for a grip on his emotions.

When he cleared his throat, his voice emerged brutal and stark. "I went to a New Year's Eve party with a couple guys from work, and I don't even remember her name. Just some girl with blonde hair, and she reminded me of you and . . ." He couldn't look at her then, the tear that ran down her beautiful face. "I was making my move when you called."

Now he wanted to cry. "It was like some sort of divine retribution seeing your name appear on my screen. And I just . . . I couldn't answer. I couldn't hear your voice, knowing what I was doing. Knowing it would hurt you, even though . . ."

He closed his eyes. "I was just so afraid you were going to break my heart all over again, and I just couldn't . . . So yeah, maybe I did cheat on you."

Her hand touched his arm. "It wasn't cheating, Pete. You thought we were over—"

He scrabbled for composure, but he was too far gone now, tears filming his eyes. "Yeah, it was cheating. Maybe not technically, but it felt like cheating. Because my heart still belonged to you. And in that moment, I felt like I was doing it all over again—letting the old Pete, the one who tried to act like he didn't care, take over."

He looked up then, and found her gaze, soft in his.

It undid him enough for it all to spill out, raw and ugly. "Having you walk out of my life felt a little like walking around with a sucking chest wound. Everything hurt. My body, even my brain. I started making stupid decisions on the job. I was desperate for something good—anything good—in my life."

He pushed past her, toward the stove, opened the door, and threw in a log. Pushed the dying coals to spark a flame. "I was drowning."

He closed the grate and turned to look at her. She stood in the shadows, her arms around herself.

"I nearly did, by the way. Last week. I got caught under a van in a flooded river."

She took a step toward him. "What?"

"Yeah. And when I got out, I was . . . I was done, Jess. So tired of my life and trying so hard to do things right, to prove that I'm not just an impulsive, reckless jerk." He gave a harsh laugh, more a slash-and-burn across his soul than humor. "Which of course is exactly what I am." He ran the palm of his hand almost violently against his jaw. "A man lost his wife during my *gallant* rescue. And if I'd just waited for help . . ." He shook his head. "I don't know. I just know that I am so tired of myself. Of people getting hurt because of me—"

"Pete, stop."

"This summer, a bunch of kids nearly died because I was stubborn and had to have my own way—"

"People don't get hurt because of you."

He stared at her. "Have you been paying any attention? I am reckless. I got my dad killed. I nearly got *you* killed at least twice."

"I remember you saving my life."

"And if we're going to talk about past lovers—Jess, you don't even want to know—"

"No, I don't." She held up her hand, as if to halt his words. "Because you're not that man anymore. You *didn't* sleep with that woman, right?"

"No." He sighed. "But I wanted to. Or, a part of me wanted to want to, if that makes any sense. See, the problem is that the first impulse I had when you called on New Year's Eve was to grab a bottle of Uncle Jack and that leggy blonde and get lost for about a week."

It physically hurt to see her flinch. But maybe it was time for them all to be honest. "And it scares me how much I've wanted the old Pete back. It was like right after my dad died. I just wanted to stop hurting so much. So I ran and lived hard and big, and for a while that saved me. But I was a prisoner, Jess. I was broken and angry all the time. But then I met you and . . ." He lifted his gaze to her. "You broke me free."

She lifted an eyebrow.

"You loved me, despite the Pete you saw, and made me want to be . . . a man worth marrying. And I feel sick that I let you down."

"What? Pete, I let *you* down!" Her voice softened. "You are that man. Worth marrying."

"No, Jess. I don't think so. I'm prideful and impulsive—"

"And dangerous."

He frowned.

"You're *completely* dangerous. You don't give a second thought to running into the fire to save someone. Or hanging off a cliff, or apparently diving into a submerged vehicle. You're so dangerous it scares the breath out of me."

269

He couldn't move. "I—"

"But that doesn't mean you're not *exactly* the man I want to marry."

Oh, he wanted to lean into her words, to breathe them in, but, "I'm not Felipe, Jess."

"I know."

He tried not to wince.

She touched his face. "Because loving you takes courage. Wits. Strength. And yes, that night ten months ago when you didn't answer my call—or any of the ones after that—I was afraid." She winced, caught her lip. "I thought I'd lost you, and Montana. I couldn't lose what I had left. So I agreed to marry Felipe. And maybe I told myself I wouldn't go through with it, but . . . I think deep down I believed that I'd never really have a happy ending anyway."

"Jess—"

"No, Pete. You said you were sick of yourself. You're not the only one. I hated the fact that I'd broken your heart. It's what I do. I broke my mother's heart, and my brother's heart, and even Felipe's heart. I thought I made the right choice to testify against my father, but I left casualties everywhere. I couldn't seem to get anything right and I was paralyzed. Being engaged to Felipe would at least fix a few of them, I thought, but . . ."

It was the *but*, the wry smile that made him reach out and tip her chin up. "But?"

"But I couldn't stop loving you. I think I came back here to see if . . . if you still wanted me."

Oh. And the vulnerability, the truth in her eyes undid him. "Ah, Jess. I have never stopped. I want to protect you and love you and stand beside you and do all the things to help you be exactly the person you want to be. Selene or Jess."

"Or both. I want to be *both*."

He drew in a breath.

"I want to be both, with you." She pressed her hand to his chest. "Because you taught Jess how to climb and rappel and even hold on to you. To trust you. And Selene, well, she knows how to stay calm when you're about to run us down a cliff. And she also knows when you need someone to step in and stop the crazy."

"Crazy?"

"You are crazy, Pete Brooks."

Oh.

"The kind of crazy that makes a girl believe you'll show up to rescue her." She found his eyes, held them. "Please rescue me."

"Always," he said as he reached for her.

———— + ————

"I want to stay here forever." Jess pulled the thermal blanket around her tighter, aware of the heat Pete's body generated as he lay behind her on the floor. The stove was burning through the last of the logs, but he nixed her idea to run out to the woodpile to retrieve more fuel.

So, instead, he'd pulled off the blanket from the bed in the other room and brought it out to the main room, along with the remaining pillow on the bed, and made her a sleeping space on the floor.

"No," he'd said when she offered a space wrapped up with her in the blanket. He'd stood oddly back, his hands in his pockets as she arranged herself in front of the fire. Maybe it had something to do with her suggestion to use the bed to sleep in.

A strange expression washed over his face, and he'd suggested that maybe *she* take the bed. "I'll sleep on the floor."

She'd frowned at him. "No, we'll both take the floor."

He'd fled to the bedroom and had the bedding dismantled before she could reassure him that she'd meant exactly what she said . . . *sleep.*

But he'd been acting weird ever since she curled her arms around his amazing shoulders and lifted her face to his. Since he leaned down and kissed her so sweetly she wanted to weep.

Always.

At his word, her heart had filled her throat, her own tears salting the kiss, but when she started to deepen the kiss, he took a breath and stepped away.

Enter the cold front.

It wasn't until she wrapped up in the blanket, had turned on her side, her head on the pillow, that he finally lay alongside her, his head on his arm, his hand on her hip.

Now, he made a humming noise, almost a grunt of so-called assent to her words about hiding forever, and she couldn't stop herself from rolling over onto her back.

He met her gaze. "What?"

"Why are you acting weird?"

"I'm not acting weird."

"Yes, you are." She rolled over again, now facing him, and when she touched his chest, where his shirt opened at his neck, he caught her hand. "See?"

He kept his hand around hers. "Go to sleep, Jess. I'll watch over you."

"Pete. That is not what this is about. You're suddenly afraid of me touching you. Is it what I said about Felipe? Are you, do you . . . did that disgust you? To know that I, that we—"

"What? No, of course not." He sat up, shook his head. Looked at her with such a pained expression, her throat thickened. "Okay, a little. I can be honest enough to say that the idea of you and him together makes me want to dismantle him, but you're not the one with the baggage here. Sheesh. I just . . . I'm sorry, Jess. For the man I haven't been, that I should have been, long before I met you."

Oh Pete. "It doesn't matter to me. Not anymore. I mean . . .

we were different people then. I do wish that we could start over, you know?"

He leaned down again, propping his head on his hand. He reached out his other hand and caught a strand of errant hair between his fingers, smoothing it. "Yeah, I do. I wish I'd met you before . . . well, maybe I wasn't the kind of guy you would have liked back then, but I wish you'd met my dad. He was pretty awesome. Fun, and although he looked like Sam, he had my propensity to do the wild things. It was his idea to go down the run that day that . . ." He ended with a small shrug.

"Wait. It was his idea, but you blame yourself."

"Yeah, well, I didn't look back. Once I took off down the hill, I didn't even think about him being behind me. I was so caught up in the skiing until I got to the bottom. And he was gone. Just . . . missing. I wish I could have, I don't know, told him I loved him, one last time. I can still hear him, sometimes, whooping behind me."

She touched his face. "I saw my dad in prison and it just about killed me. But he was glad to see me. And he told me he was proud of me."

He pressed her palm to his mouth for a kiss, then tucked it back into his grip. "I wish I'd been there."

"I think I'm just starting to forgive myself a little."

He sighed.

"You need to also, Pete."

He considered her, the firelight turning his face to a warm glow.

"For your dad's death," she said. "It wasn't your fault."

"I know that. I mean . . . in my head."

"But not here." She touched his chest.

He again caught her hand, eased it away.

"Pete, what's going on? Why won't you let me touch you?"

He looked at her. Closed his eyes and rolled over onto his back.

"Because if you do, then . . . well, at the moment, although he's been dead for a good long while, the old Pete is very much alive and roaming around this room. And the more I look at you, the more you touch me, the more the firelight plays on your face and you look so warm and comfortable in that blanket, the more the old Pete starts to win." He looked at her. "I can't get you close enough. But that's the problem, isn't it? I shouldn't." His mouth lifted up in a wry, pained smile. "But I've never wanted you more than right now."

"How I love you," she whispered. "Except . . ." She tugged off his hat. "I miss your beautiful long hair."

He took the hat from her and set it on the table. "I cut it a few months ago."

She reached up and rubbed her fingers through his short hair. "Breakup haircut."

He raised an eyebrow.

"I like it, but . . . I love your long hair. Can you grow it out again? It's really hot."

"You're not helping." He caught her hand and folded her fingers between his. "This is why I'm not kissing you, and I'm praying hard that Sam shows up soon."

She laughed. The way his smile touched his eyes could keep her warm for the rest of her life. "Okay. I'll stop wishing you'd kiss me."

"And looking at me like that . . ." He swallowed. "I'm in so much trouble around you."

She laughed and rolled over, not facing him, and pulled his hand around her waist. He turned, spooning with her. "Better?"

"Thank you from the bottom of my heart."

She watched the stove. "This place reminds me of this cabin my parents used to take us to in the Adirondacks. Just a couple times, but we'd make a fire in the stone fireplace and spend the night playing games. Sometimes we'd just lie on the floor and watch the fire. It was normal. And real. There were no cell phones back then, and sometimes we'd go up early and wait for my dad to drive up from the city. I'd sit by the window waiting for his headlights through the trees. He'd show up, come tromping in through the snow and darkness and suddenly everything was safe and whole and unbreakable."

"That's how a father's love is supposed to make you feel." Pete gave a sort of rueful chuckle. "Sam said that I should start leaning into God's love, start believing it."

"It's hard to do that when we know all the reasons why God shouldn't love us."

"Except I don't have a list of reasons why I love you. I mean, I admire you and respect you and . . . you're so beautiful it makes me lose my head. I think I've loved you since the first day I saw you, Jess. You crept inside me and I would . . . I would die for you."

"Even if I didn't deserve it?"

"It's not about deserving it. It simply is. I love you. I would die to save you. Full stop."

She traced his hand as he went silent.

"If that's how God feels about us, then maybe he's worth trusting," he said softly.

His words found her heart. "Maybe." She traced the sinews in his forearm. "Thank you for proposing, all those times."

He gave a small chuckle. "Should I go for a third?"

"No. My answer's still a yes. But you should know that your love made me stronger. I was in pieces when I first left New York City. Coming out here, making a life for myself on my own, meeting you, discovering that a man like you could fall for me . . . it made me feel like I wasn't quite as breakable anymore."

"You're tougher than you think, Jess."

"Did you know I started taking Krav Maga classes?"

He chuckled. "Good for you."

His words warmed her through, and she wove her fingers between his. He had such strong hands, marked with tiny scars betraying his years as a rescuer. "My mother really is dying, though. And . . . I have to go back to New York City."

He was silent for so long she thought he hadn't heard. Or maybe didn't want to.

Until, "I'll go with you."

"Pete—"

"No. Ty said something to me last summer about how I'd abandoned you. And I never realized that, but . . . I did. Maybe I was afraid that I couldn't fit into your world, couldn't measure up, but . . . I don't care anymore."

She rolled onto her back, a soft smile pressing her lips. "I choose you, Pete. I want to be in your world."

"Aw, shoot," he said softly. "What am I going to do with you?"

His touch wasn't fire and combustion because he wouldn't let it be. But she felt the simmer deep inside him as he ran his thumb along her cheekbone, as he brushed her mouth with his, the taste of desire on his lips, smelling of the woods and the hearth and . . .

He lifted his head. "Do you smell that?"

"There's smoke coming from the bedroom!" She pushed against his chest and sat up.

Pete was on his feet in seconds, a hand over his mouth as he headed into the bedroom.

"Be careful!"

But even as she untangled herself from the floor, she spotted the flames flickering out from the room. Pete came back, shutting the bedroom door behind him. "We have to get out of here. The bathroom is on fire—"

"How?"

He pulled the blanket around her, his face grim, his eyes dark.

"Listen, I need you to stay behind me. Right behind me. Whatever you do, you do not move from behind me unless I tell you to."

"You're scaring me."

He caught her face in his hands, his gaze pressing hers. "I love you, Jess."

This time his kiss was hard, fierce, and everything that she knew he'd been trying to hold back. He let her go too fast and grabbed her hand, tucked her behind him.

She got it. "You think he's out there, don't you? That he started this fire."

"The frying pan is in the bathroom, on the floor. It caught on the shower curtain and the entire room is ablaze."

He moved her behind him. "We're going to go out there, and when I tell you to run, you run and you don't look back, okay?"

"Pete—"

"Jess! Please, for once make me a promise you'll keep!"

She stiffened, but when he looked over his shoulder, his eyes were reddened, his expression so desperate she could only nod. "Okay, I'll run. I promise. But you'd better not die, Pete Brooks."

He pulled her arms around his waist and opened the door. Shuffled out, her on his tail.

The fire bundle that had been smoldering in the front yard was gone, leaving only the cast of the moon upon a glowing pit of embers. Pete moved them off the porch, down onto the grass, his hands holding hers tight around his lean waist.

The forest loomed tall and tangled, skeletal arms reaching into the indigo darkness, the smattering of stars betraying a scrubbed sky. The wind lifted her hair, scurried a chill through her.

"Stop. That's far enough."

The voice emerged from the forest, and in the tone she recognized a hint of a drawl.

Pete stilled, moved Jess between him and the house, completely blocking her body. Oh, how she wanted to peek out, but instead she drilled her head into his strong back, her hands at his waist. His held hers so tight she couldn't have escaped if she wanted to.

"I don't know who you are, or what you want, but whatever I did, I'm sorry," Pete said.

A shot exploded and dinged the house. Jess stifled a scream. Pete jerked but didn't move.

"Nobody has to get hurt here, just . . . I'm all yours, pal. Just keep it cool—oh no . . ."

It was the tiny gasp, the "oh no" slithering out on a fragile breath, the way his entire body went rigid that made her look.

No, *no.*

A man emerged from the edge of the forest, a handgun pressed to the back of Felipe's skull. Felipe held his hands up above his head, and for his part, appeared strangely calm, almost angry.

"Remember your promise," Pete said under his breath.

She couldn't breathe, let alone run.

"What do you want?" Pete said loudly.

"You remember me, Brooks?"

Pete drew in a breath. "Yeah," he said. "Ellis. What are you doing here?"

Ellis?

"You know, at first I thought that petite blonde was your Jess. The way you were dancing together at the party. And then, well, I figured it out. Because my wife and I used to fight like that—so angry at each other that we wanted to rip our hearts out. But it was only because we loved each other so much, had so much to lose. You don't get that angry at someone who doesn't have the ability to break your heart."

"Ellis, man, I'm so sorry—"

"So I figured it out. That's your Jess, isn't it?"

His Jess?

"You got it half right," Pete said, his voice easy. "I did love her. But she broke my heart. She left me for that guy, right there." He pointed to Felipe. "She's actually engaged to him. Ask him yourself."

Felipe did his part by nodding. "We've been engaged for months."

"But you still love her," the man said.

Jess had to close her eyes, to not listen as Pete shook his head. "Not anymore. You can't love somebody who breaks their promises. Who lies to you over and over. I don't even know this woman, not anymore. She's not the woman I loved. She belongs with Felipe now."

Ellis seemed to consider him.

"C'mon, man. You want me, not him. And not her. I get that you're angry, but don't make any more people pay for my mistake."

His mistake?

"Come out here," Ellis said. "Right out here."

Pete unlatched her hands from his waist, held her hand behind him, and crept out into the yard. "Don't shoot." He lifted his other hand.

They stopped a few feet from Ellis. She could see him now. Mid-thirties, dark hair, grimy clothing—jeans, a sweatshirt, a jacket, as if he'd spent the past forty-eight hours in the woods. Something feral in his eyes as he motioned with his chin for Pete to stop. "Get on your knees."

Pete kneeled, one leg, then the other, and raised his hands.

"Wait, no—" Jess started.

Pete hissed at her.

"Hands behind your head, and get all the way down on your face."

Pete didn't move. "Let her go. With him." He looked at Felipe.

Ellis pushed Felipe forward.

"Let them go, and I'm all yours."

Another step, and Ellis stood a yard away. Jess met Felipe's gaze, dark and solid. He nodded.

Her eyes filled.

"Do you love this man?" Ellis said, nodding to Pete, and only then did she realize he was addressing her. She met his gaze and swallowed, finding the voice of Selene, the one she used for lying and pretend. "No. I don't love him. I'm engaged to Felipe."

Ellis narrowed his eyes.

Then he moved his gun off Felipe and turned it to Pete. "Down, now."

Pete bent over, his hands laced behind his neck.

"You two—run."

The voice wasn't Pete's, but it might have been for the way he turned and looked up at her, so much pleading in his eyes that he nearly shouted it.

Run!

She grabbed Felipe's hand and finally kept her promise.

13

PETE KNEW JESS DIDN'T MEAN HER WORDS— had told himself to dig deep, to brace himself.

All that mattered was that Jess was safe. Even if it had to be with Felipe—and Pete knew to the core of his body that Felipe would keep her safe.

So he stayed crouched, his head down, his hands laced behind his neck until he heard their footsteps die. And even then because Ellis put his foot on Pete's hands, pressing his face down into the mud, his gun digging into Pete's skull.

For a moment, Pete debated simply grabbing the man's foot, yanking him down, hopefully dislodging the gun—

Ellis got off him and took a step back. "Get up."

Pete pushed himself off the damp grass.

"Hands where I can see them."

Pete held them up and out. "Okay. See? I'm doing what you told me to. Just take a breath and let's talk about this."

In the glow of the flashlight, Roger Ellis looked about the same as the last time Pete had seen him in a Missouri hospital—wrung out, exhausted, and enough grief in his face to make him dangerous. He recognized a man a hair trigger away from snapping and kept his voice easy.

"You look tired, Ellis. You've been tromping around in these woods for two days?"

"Let's walk," Ellis said. He motioned with the flashlight toward a narrow trail cutting through the trees.

"Where are we going?"

"You'll see."

Pete obeyed, cataloging his options. He could run, although Ellis had already demonstrated that he had no problem pulling the trigger. He'd get about ten feet.

Turn, take Ellis down. But Ellis was at least two steps behind him. He'd probably get shot in the face.

Keep walking, dive into the woods—yeah, maybe. For now, "How'd you find me?"

"I went back to the rescue headquarters and talked to a friend of yours who said you'd left for Montana."

Pete scrolled through the handful of people who knew where he'd gone. Alena, his boss. And Walsh, maybe.

"Then, I just had to ask around. You're a famous guy, Mr. Brooks. Everybody knows you. A woman at some local café said you were going to Benjamin King's wedding reception."

Willow. It had to be. Only she and Sam knew he was coming, and she worked at the Summit Café.

"It wasn't that hard to dress like a local and act like I was invited. I had driven up from Missouri, but I wasn't sure how I was going to get you and that blonde out of the building, and then . . . it just happened, like fate was on my side. I heard you and Jess arguing outside the barn and I knew—she was the one."

Pete's jaw tightened. "Why not just kill me? Why take Jess—and Ned and Shae for that matter?"

"I couldn't take a chance they could identify me. I talked to some hunter at a convenience store on my way north and he told me about the Bob Wilderness area. Said it was remote, and told me how

282

to get back into it. I figured if I left Jess's body in the woods, you'd spend the rest of your days looking for her. Let it drive you crazy."

It would have, not knowing where Jess was, searching for her.

He might have never found her in this wilderness. Pete said nothing, just kept moving.

Except, "What about your daughter, man? Don't do this. She needs a father. I know what it's like to live without a father, and trust me, you can't do that to her—"

"She's dead."

The words punched Pete in the sternum. "I'm so sorry." And he meant it.

"Shut up." He kicked Pete in the leg, and Pete stumbled but righted himself. The light Ellis held scraped back the darkness, and to his right, the rush of the river deepened.

Pete walked, head down. "Listen, Ellis. I know you're hurting. But there's no coming back from this. You kill me, and . . . well, trust me, I know a little about the darkness. About feeling like you're never going to break free, no matter what you do, how far you run. You do this, and it's going to consume you."

"I'm already dead."

Yeah, well, Pete knew that feeling too. "I am sorry your wife died. I did try to save them—"

The shout came from behind him, a scream that ripped through his body because he knew that scream. High and the kind she'd uttered when she'd seen a grizzly barreling down at her.

Jess!

He didn't have time to parse it out, just react as the thunder of hooves bulleted through the darkness. He turned, and his breath cut out at the sight of Felipe charging past Ellis. He held his hand outstretched like he might be in a cowboy flick, an old Western where the hero's chum rides in to save him.

"Grab on!" Felipe said, as if Pete couldn't figure it out, but Pete obeyed, and Felipe hooked him under the elbow, leaning hard to the opposite side. He'd unlatched his foot from the stirrup, and as Pete leaped up, he shoved his foot into the free space.

Somehow, he landed behind Felipe, a circus move that probably looked awkward in the light, but right now saved his life. He hooked his arm around Felipe and grabbed the saddle horn as Felipe spurred his horse hard.

A shot scattered leaves somewhere over his head. The moonlight illuminated the trail, wide enough to see the shape of trees and ahead an expanse that probably opened up to the river.

The next shot bit through his shoulder and made him shout.

"You okay?" Felipe said.

Pete bit back a grunt of pain. "I think he grazed me. I'm fine. Where's Jess?"

"Hidden. She's safe."

More shots, and a horse whinnied as if in fear.

Pete turned around, searching the darkness. A wan light down the path suggested that they'd left Ellis in the dust.

Felipe slowed the horse.

"What are you doing here?" Pete growled, as much for the pain as the roiling emotions. Jess had better be safe,

"Blame Selene. She couldn't leave you," Felipe said, a similar growl to his tone. "I tried. But as soon as we got to the horses, she turned back."

"What were you doing in the woods? I thought you went with Ned and Shae."

"Your friend Blackburn took them to the hospital. I . . ." He let out a word in French. "I couldn't leave Selene behind, either."

Oh. Pete had to give him props for that. "Let's get back to Jess."

Another scream, this time of pain, maybe, as much as fear.

"Go back!" Pete shouted. He grabbed for the reins, but Felipe elbowed him. He jerked the horse around, started back.

No, *no* . . .

Pete slipped off the horse, his hands up, shaking.

Ellis stalked toward them down the path, his hand around Jess's neck, pushing her forward. She limped, blood on her knee, her face.

"I knew it," Ellis said. "She just couldn't stay away from you, lover boy."

Felipe swore, again in French, but Pete understood him perfectly. Especially when Ellis put the gun to Jess's head.

Pete glued his gaze to Jess's. *It'll be okay, babe.*

But it wouldn't. Because he understood Ellis too well. He didn't want to live in a world where Jess wasn't.

Please, please—

Sam's voice picked now to whoosh into his head. *"You gotta start trusting in God's love for you. For Jess. Lean into it. Let it change you. Let it set you free."*

Yeah, he wanted, needed God's love. His freedom. Pete just wasn't sure how to get it. Still . . . *God, if you're serious about loving me . . .*

"Ellis! Let them go. I'm sorry—okay, dude. I get it. Let them go and I won't run." In fact, frankly, he was tired of running. "I know you want to silence the roaring inside, bottle up that wound that just won't stop bleeding. But trust me, this isn't going to make it better. Yeah, it might make you feel vindicated, but it's just going to make the hurt that much deeper."

His words found their way inside, settled there. "There's no replacement for your wife. But you can't heal this on your own. You need help."

Help.

He glanced at Felipe, now climbing off the horse. "Please tell me you still have the radio."

"I do," Felipe said.

"Then turn it on," he said quietly. "Turn it on and pray."

———— ✛ ————

She'd only made it worse.

It had been Jess's fabulous idea to turn back, to use Felipe's amazing horsemanship skills to rescue Pete. For her to be a decoy.

Except, she couldn't be content to just be a decoy, could she? No, she had to break her promise to Pete—and Felipe, for that matter—to stay hidden.

She'd seen Ellis take off after them, and her heart had simply run out ahead of her, a full-out, heedless, no-plan impulse that caused her to run her beautiful mare at the man like it might be a weapon.

Please let the horse not be dead. Please let it simply be terror that stopped the quarter horse and threw her out of the saddle and onto the path.

Her wrist hurt again, and she'd twisted her ankle, which was why Ellis was able to catch her, pull her up by her hair, then grab her by the back of her neck.

She'd let out a scream, of shock more than pain, and immediately wanted to yank it back. *Please, keep going, guys!*

But she knew better and wanted to weep when Ellis's light revealed Pete standing in the path, hands up, already surrendering. Already offering himself for her. Of course.

Because that was Pete. Dangerous and reckless for the people he loved.

"Keep walking, all three of you," Ellis said now. "You too, Eastwood," he said to Felipe, who frowned a second before he put his hands up and followed behind Pete.

Ellis had let her go to hold the flashlight but kept his gun dug into the small of her back.

Pete, it seemed, couldn't shut up as he walked, talking about how he understood Ellis's pain, how he had wanted to die, do anything after he lost his father. And how it wasn't at all like losing a wife, but it still made a person do crazy things. How revenge wouldn't heal anything but just make it worse.

And all the while, Ellis walked them through the forest, the rushing in the air turning nearly deafening as they edged closer to the river.

Trying to save everyone, she'd killed them all.

The forest opened up as they came to the end of the path, and with a start, Jess realized they'd returned to the cliff that she and Pete had nearly run off only hours earlier.

In the darkness, she hadn't realized that it edged a waterfall, sprinkling the night air with mist, the rapids falling into lethal blackness.

Pete just kept talking. About mistakes and trying to numb the pain and healing and love—how love had changed him.

That got her attention.

How he had wanted to be more for the woman he loved. Be the man she needed. And she knew he was relating it to Ellis in some skewed attempt to get him to realize that this wasn't what his wife would have wanted, but really all Jess heard was how Pete had changed, because of her, and that even if he only had that much, it was enough. That he knew what real love felt like and that made all the difference. That he was ready to die because he'd had that, and not even Ellis could take that from him.

Tears filled her eyes. Because she knew, right then . . . she too knew real love. The kind of love that forgave and showed up and chased and forgave again and kept showing up, loving her when she didn't have the courage to love back.

Love pursued. Love forgave. Love believed. Love sacrificed.

She was crying too hard to look at him when Pete stopped at the edge and turned. "Let her go, man. Please."

Ellis walked Jess right up to the edge beside Pete.

She couldn't stop herself from glancing over.

Found Pete's gaze on her. "See, I've already had my happy ending. I've already found the one that my soul loves. And I know I'm not perfect. I make mistakes that end up getting people hurt. I'm sorry about your wife, Ellis. I really am. I know it was impulsive and reckless, but I gave you all I had. I'm sorry it wasn't enough."

It's enough, Pete.

Maybe loving Pete was dangerous, and yes, sometimes people got hurt. But perhaps that was what love looked like too. Not perfect, but raw and jagged and terrifying and wounding . . . and beautiful and overwhelming and completely, wonderfully out of her control.

Because love gave all.

And love would give her the strength to do what she had to do, even if someone got hurt.

She took a breath and stared down into the darkness. The river had widened, turned frothy and thunderous, dropping in a heady whitewater.

Ellis stood a couple steps back. "Jump."

"Please, man." Pete had turned to pleading now. "Please, let her go. Please." She couldn't see Pete now, just heard the shaking in his voice.

She turned around. Looked at Ellis, her resolve tightening, her voice solid. "I get it too. I don't know what happened to you or your family, but I know what it's like to feel trapped and like you don't know what to do or where to go." She took a step toward him, her hands out. "So you panic and you do what you think will protect you. Like hurt someone else." One more step and his gun was level with her chest. Out of her peripheral vision, she saw Pete jerk. *Trust me.* "Or in my case—I ran. I ran away. And then, I ran back to my old world and . . . I'm done running."

That's when she exploded. Redirect. Control. Attack. She pushed the gun to the left and away with her right hand, moving her body to the right. Then she trapped the weapon with her left hand around his grip just as he jerked it—and her—back to himself.

She used the momentum to bring her leg up, kicking him hard, center mass.

He grunted, but he was taller, bigger, and came around with his fist. Instincts more than skill saved her from being clocked in the face. His punch hit her in the shoulder. She ducked her head, kept coming at him, her body in tight as she wrenched the gun backward.

It flew out of his hand. She let her momentum drive her hand up hard into his jaw. His head snapped back, and she bounced away as he stumbled.

She searched for the gun in the darkness. Hands grabbed her arms, pulling her back, and only then did she realize that she'd nearly stepped out into the abyss.

Felipe. He jerked her to safety, his arms around her just as Ellis came up, the gun back in his hands and pointed at Jess and Felipe. "Stop!"

But there was no stopping Pete. He took two steps and launched himself at Ellis.

The gun exploded, and Pete grunted, but he didn't slow down as he pushed Ellis hard toward the edge.

"Pete, look out!"

Ellis tripped, fell back, and his grip closed on Pete's shirt.

Dragging Pete over the edge of the cliff.

Shae was in surgery to clean out her wound and stitch it shut, and Ned was stuck here, facedown on an ER table, his backside, or at least a portion of it, exposed to a third-year intern practicing his suturing.

Ned buried his head in his hands, wishing he was anywhere else. How freakin' embarrassing.

Worse, he couldn't flush out of his system the eerie sense that this wasn't over. The story Shae had told him about Sheriff Black-burn simply didn't jive with the man who had driven them out of the mountains and north to Kalispell Regional Medical Center. Who had turned up the heat full-blast until the truck turned into a virtual oven, who had told them about hiding out at the cabin for the past month, trying to get his head around his upcoming divorce.

As if he might be a real, hurting human being instead of a murderer in sheep's clothing.

Brave Shae simply lay in Ned's arms, a trooper to the bone, barely a whimper as they bumped over ruts and potholes. Surely in agony, she braced herself, no doubt for Blackburn to drive them deeper into the forest, shoot them, and dump them into a gully.

Nope. The man had delivered them right to the front door of the ER and helped Ned carry her out of the car and onto a wheelchair, even alerting the staff as they entered. One look at Blackburn, at his bloody face, shirt, and blood-soaked towel and the entire emergency staff rushed over, but he'd directed them toward Shae as he headed back outside to park his truck.

Yeah, the entire thing felt . . . off.

Except they were safe, finally.

Ned had followed Shae into the ER, stood by her while they undressed her wound and then whisked her off to surgery. He'd wanted to follow, but one of the bossy nurses directed him into a cubicle. Made him lie down, strip off his pants and shirt, and gown up.

Then she'd plopped him facedown on a gurney so the intern could examine the embarrassing, and yes, burning tear in his backside.

He didn't move his head from his arms during the entire inspection.

"What is this . . . stuff?"

"Pine resin," Ned muttered. "It's a Band-Aid."

"It's hard to get off," the intern said, and took about twenty minutes with saline to work the sap free. When he was done, he said, "It's pretty clean. You just need stitches."

"While you're at it, maybe you could also find and plug the hole in his head," said a voice from behind him. "The one that says he should leave town on a whim."

Ned shook his head without looking up. "Fraser. What are you doing here?"

"Oh, I dunno. Something about a phone call." His voice turned falsetto. "Bro, I'm lost in the woods, come and save me."

"I did not say that!"

"Stay still," the intern said.

"Calm down," Fraser said, and Ned turned his head as his brother came up beside him. "I know, sheesh. I'm kidding. We were just worried."

Fraser was the oldest, tallest, and maybe the toughest of the Marshall family, and yeah, Ned still wanted to be like him. He wore his dark hair cut short, although longer than navy regs, thanks to his spec-ops rate, a rash of whiskers that suggested he hadn't shaved in a few days, a pair of Gore-Tex pants, boots, and a fleece pullover. Clearly on leave, apparent by his civvies.

"We?" Ned asked. "Who's we?"

"Me and Jonas and my buddy Ham."

Jonas was here too? Ned didn't know what to do with the sudden rush of emotion. Part shame, part gratefulness.

Fraser leaned over as if to take a gander at Ned's wound. Ned closed his eyes, his jaw tight.

"That's quite an owie you got there."

291

And oh joy, here came the bad jokes. "You didn't have to come all the way out here—"

"Are you kidding me? Bro, we got your back."

Ned winced, and the mumble just emerged. "Nobody has to watch *your* back."

Silence. Ned opened his eyes. Fraser was shaking his head.

"I don't know where you got that idea. I have—had—an entire team of guys watching my back. And me, theirs. You're just lying to yourself if you think you can do it alone, that you don't need any help."

"I don't—"

"Yeah, bro. You do."

"I'm not weak or afraid anymore. I'm not a seven-year-old kid getting beat up—"

"Sheesh, but you can be a prideful jerk. Wow." Fraser shook his head.

"Must be something in the genes," said a voice, and Ned glanced past Fraser to the man behind him, standing with his arms folded over a solid chest. He had dark blond hair cut military short, brown eyes, and a grim set to his mouth that now tweaked up one side.

"You're hilarious, Ham," Fraser said. "Put a sock in it."

Ham raised an eyebrow, but Fraser turned back to Ned.

"You got shot in the bum. That stinks. And it's a little embarrassing. But I also know it hurts like, well, enough to make a grown man cry, and according to the rumors out there, you carried your girlfriend miles through the woods. I respect that, bro. But if you're trying to prove something, it's not necessary."

Ned sighed.

Fraser glanced again at Ham and then at Jonas, who had come up behind Ham carrying a cup of coffee. "Hey there, Swiss cheese."

"Joe, give him a break," Fraser said. Ned shook his head.

Fraser put his hand on Ned's shoulder. "Ham's right. I've learned some lessons over the past few years, the hard way. Ones I don't want you to have to learn. So listen up. It's your pride that makes you weak, not your failures. Not your mistakes."

Ned just stared at him, the words winding inside.

"It's a good thing to know your limitations. To reach out for help."

"I called you, didn't I?"

"And I called Jed, your old smokejumper boss, to find PEAK's number. He told me a little story about a guy I know getting kicked off the team."

Nice. Perfect.

Fraser crouched down beside him, his voice low.

"I get it, wanting to be tough. Wanting to look your weakness in the face and fight it. Hey, I'm the one who taught you that. But I neglected to teach you about letting go. About when it's time to reach out for help, or even give up."

"You don't give up. You don't quit."

"I quit the SEALs."

Ned lifted his head.

"It's a long story, but I'm out. For lots of reasons. But one of them is that it started to get inside my head, and I was taking all the stuff I was seeing—and doing—out there home, living with it, letting it have me. I had to walk away, let it go."

Ned said nothing.

"I guess what I'm saying is that you did good out there, bro. But maybe we could talk about this?"

Ned lifted his head. Fraser held his navy recruit card. "Mom found it in the laundry. Did you enlist?"

"I'm trying to get in the SEAL fast-track program."

Fraser raised an eyebrow, shot a look at Ham, then looked back at Ned. "Really? Oh boy."

"What?"

"Nothing. But . . ." Fraser smiled. "You should have told us."

"I didn't want you to stop me."

"Are you kidding? I'm cheering you on. Hooyah." He made a fist and tapped Ned on the shoulder. "Stop being so paranoid that we're against you. That you have to prove something. We're already on your team." He got up. "Right, Jonas?"

Jonas shrugged. "I'm *mostly* on his team." Then he grinned. "Naw. I'm super proud of you, little bro."

"All finished," the intern said as he took the draping off. "I'll get Dr. Watson, our orthopedist, to take a look at your shoulder."

"What happened to your shoulder?" Fraser asked.

"It's fine," Ned said as he eased off the table, grateful for the painkillers.

"And the ER doc said something about X-rays for your ribs."

"Sheesh," Jonas muttered.

Ned balanced himself on the gurney as the room spun. "I'm fine."

"Although a little breezy." Jonas glanced at the open gown.

Ned clamped his hand on the gap, pulling it closed. "Where are my clothes?"

"Oh, you mean these?" Fraser held a clear plastic bag that betrayed the wreckage of his attire.

"He's about your size, Fray," Ham said. "I'll pilfer something from your go bag." He took off down the hall.

"I need to find Shae," Ned said, moving away from the open door. He peeked down the hall to see if he could spot Blackburn. Maybe he'd already finished being bandaged.

"I'll ask about her," Jonas said.

Fraser turned to Ned as Jonas left. Drew in a breath. "In all honesty, you had us a little freaked out. But I knew you'd be okay."

"You did?"

"Ever since we had that little talk with you and then I saw

you stand up to that Russian kid. You did better the second time around. Kept getting the snot kicked out of you, but you kept getting back up. I so wanted to take that kid apart like I told you we would, but Jonas wouldn't let me. He said you needed to prove to yourself you could do it, beat the hold this guy had over you."

"If I remember correctly, he lit me up pretty good."

"Yeah, but it wasn't too long before you had him down. Just for the record, we had your back. We wouldn't have let him take you apart again. But in the end, we didn't have to jump in." His eyes warmed. "If anyone has what it takes to be a SEAL, you do."

Maybe it was the trauma of the past two days wearing him down, the fatigue, even the softening of his reflexes thanks to the painkillers, but Ned's throat thickened and his eyes burned.

Fraser grinned and grabbed him around the neck, pulling him in tight. "Just remember, you got a team, and I'm not just talking about me and Jonas, or even your fellow frogmen. But . . ." He let him go, pointed up. "Not to sound like Dad or anything, but God has your back too."

Ned stared at him. "Since when did you turn spiritual?"

"Like I said, long story, but trust me when I say that you don't have to prove anything to God for him to join your team. He's already on it. So don't keep him out of the game plan."

Ham returned with a bundle of clothing. "And don't get captured, either. We don't want to have to rescue you."

Ned frowned at him, but Fraser shook his head. "Later."

Ned reached for the clothing—a thermal shirt and a pair of gray cargo pants. He was sliding his bare feet into his shoes when Jonas returned.

"I had to beg, but I got the scoop on Shae. She's out of surgery and on the third floor."

"I'm going up there. If they want a picture of my insides, they'll have to track me down."

"She might still be sleeping," Jonas said. "The hospital is pretty quiet."

"I just want to sit in the room with her." Ned turned to Jonas. "Do me a solid and get me some grub. Last thing I had to eat was a can of pork and beans."

"At this time of night? Dude, I think you're going to have to settle for the vending machine in the lobby."

"Cheetos on the way," Fraser said. "We'll meet you up there. But . . . I have to know. Who is this girl?"

"Oh, I know her," Jonas said. "He met her last summer. She's hot."

Ned shot him a look. "She's more than hot. She's brave and smart and beautiful. And . . . I think I'm going to ask her to marry me."

Fraser lifted an eyebrow. "All right then. Don't let us get in the way."

"Not tonight." Or maybe. No, no. But someday. Because if they'd survived this, they could survive anything.

14

"I'M NOT WAITING." Jess stepped back from the edge of the cliff and started to pull off her boots.

The dawn had just begun to slide across the sky, turning the night from pitch to a layer of smoky gray, the finest slice of gold lipping the jagged peaks to the east.

Enough light for her to see Pete lying thirty feet down, unmoving.

Enough light for her to climb down.

"Wait—what are you doing?" Felipe came up behind her as she kicked the first boot off. "Why are you taking your boots off?"

"I'm climbing down there."

"C'mon, Selene. Have you lost your mind?"

"It's Jess, and nope."

"Okay, fine. I'll do it—"

"No, you won't." She kicked off her other boot, then pulled out her hair, braiding it quickly into a tight knot.

"With bare feet?"

"Pete taught me that. Just so I can feel the rock. I'd rather have climbing shoes but—"

Felipe stood in front of her, his hands on her shoulders, as if

297

he really meant to stop her. "You are *not* going down there. Your wrist is hurt, and you're limping—"

"And the man I love could have a head injury, could be bleeding to death!" And yes, she was shouting. More, she knew her words would hurt Felipe. She touched his face. "Felipe, you know I have to."

"Your PEAK team is on the way. Give them time."

She'd finally gotten ahold of Sierra in dispatch and discovered that Kacey, Ben, and Gage had picked up the transmission on the open channel on Felipe's radio. They were already gearing up the bird, waiting for first light, which meant they were probably just lifting off.

"I know, but . . . if he's dying, I have to be there." She managed to say that, despite the constriction in her throat. She didn't say "if he's dead" because Pete could not be dead.

But he hadn't moved since he went over the cliff. Hadn't roused to her shouts.

"I know it's dangerous. But love is worth the risk, isn't it?"

Felipe's mouth tightened.

She walked over to the edge of the cliff.

Pete lay below, facedown, unmoving on a lip of cliff maybe five feet wide. Another twenty feet below, the falls dropped into a cauldron of churning black water.

A thin line of perspiration coated her hands. She took off Pete's jacket, rolled it up, and tied it around her waist.

"You're right," Felipe said, crouching before her as she stepped out over the cliff. "I don't really know you, *Jess*." She met his eyes. He smiled. "But I'd like to. As friends."

"Yeah. Me too."

She went over the edge.

Pete had taught her some wild climbing techniques over the years, but most of those had been for ascending. Yes, he'd taken her abseiling and taught her how to emergency rappel and even how to descend with just one rope over a long face, but this was more like bouldering.

No rope, working her way around a heavily pocked surface. The cliff wasn't as much perpendicular as it was simply stacked with boulders, too steep to create a trail but not so sheer that she couldn't perch on thick jugs and foot-width ledges, cling to fist-wide cracks and grasp chiseled, protruding edges. She angled away from the slickest, wettest rock near the waterfall spray and took her time, finding the crevices and angles that gave her a secure hold.

Sweat dripped down her back, her muscles quivered in the cold from the exertion.

She looked down at Pete twice. He never moved.

She fought the urge to hurry, to let herself be reckless. There was dangerous and there was stupid.

Okay, this might be stupid.

She continued to move down, her feet working into the rock, finding the holds. She only slipped once but caught herself on an outcropping, scraping her chin.

She ignored the burn of exertion and the throb in her ankle. Probably her wrist wasn't broken after all—just a sprain because she could still use it.

She reached the ledge just as she heard the *whomp-whomp* of a chopper, still unseen deep in the scope of gray.

Pete lay as if dead, his arm under his head—hopefully it had cushioned his fall. Dried blood pooled under his nose, and from the look of his shoulder, he'd dislocated it on the fall. Maybe even broken his clavicle.

But it was the blood pooling under his body mass that had her panicked. She moved over him, assessing his airway.

He was breathing. She wanted to weep. She pressed her fingers to his carotid artery and found a pulse. Faint but steady.

She ran her fingers over his scalp, careful not to move his head, and found some abrasions near his temple. And, behind that, on the left side of his parietal bone, what she thought might be a softness.

No. *No.* She wanted a good look at his eyes, and leaned over him, lifting his lid. Slow, but reactive, although she'd be able to assess better if she actually had a light.

No blood in his ears. Maybe he'd just suffered from a broken nose. Blood was still leaking out beneath his body, however. She longed to straighten him, but not without a neck brace. Instead, she pressed her ear to his chest, listening. Unobstructed air movement, from what she could tell. So wherever the blood was coming from, it wasn't collapsing his lung.

She dragged up his shirt in the back and found a tear in his lower back. A gunshot exit wound.

Ellis's shot hadn't gone wild but instead tunneled through Pete's body.

She untied the jacket, balled it up, and pressed it into the wound. He didn't make a sound.

Somehow, she had to keep him from losing body heat and going into shock.

She had nothing but herself. Climbing over him, she straddled his prone body, wrapping her arms and legs around him, her head against his shoulder. Then she hunkered down over him and spoke into his ear.

"Pete, I'm here. I'm right here. And I'm not going anywhere."

He didn't respond. But he kept breathing. *Please, God.*

She didn't know where the thought, the prayer bubbled out of, but there it was, desperation pouring out of her as she began to shiver, more from panic than cold.

Please, God. You're all we have, and I believe you can get us out of any mess we create. So please, save us. Not because we deserve it, but because we need you . . .

The thump of the chopper against the heavens deepened, but she refused to look up, to take her body heat from him. "I've got you, Pete. I'm holding on."

"Jess!"

She glanced up at the top of the cliff, the rest of her body unmoving.

"It's me, Ty! I'm coming down!"

A rope dropped ten feet from her, and she let the tears escape. A few minutes later Ty landed on the ledge beside her, scrambling over to her. He whipped off his jacket.

"Let him go. We'll get him assessed and packed up."

No. Not ever again. But she backed off him and Ty spread his jacket over him.

Then he pulled out his walkie and called to the chopper that hovered over them.

In moments, Gage lowered himself, a kit, and a basket to the ledge.

"He has a gunshot wound," she said, offering no other explanation as Ty helped Gage to the ledge and took the backboard from the stretcher. "And a soft spot behind his temple."

Gage snapped on a collar, while she gloved up and went to work on the ragged exit wound. She pressed a dressing over it and secured the dressing in place with tape.

Gage was straddling him, getting his vitals, checking his pupils. "A little slow. I'll call my mother and have her standing by."

His mother the neurosurgeon. Jess tried not to cry.

"Ready to turn him?" Ty said, and he and Gage moved Pete onto the backboard.

She dressed his abdomen entry wound as they secured him, then stepped back as they loaded him into the stretcher.

"I'm going with him," she said as Gage clipped himself onto the package.

He considered her a second, then handed her a harness. She climbed in and secured herself to the basket and hoist.

Gage radioed up.

And then she was in the belly of the bird, the sun cascading over the mountains as the PEAK chopper arced them away from the falls, the mountain, and the wilderness.

———— ✚ ————

Clearly Shae had dreamed the entire thing. Built up the chaos and fear in her head. Let it take ahold of her, rule her, make her flee, hide, cower.

Blackburn wasn't out to get her. Had never been, given the way he'd saved her life. She could still hear his voice in the ER. *"We need help over here!"*

What?

Yes, she'd created her own demons. That had to be the only explanation.

Either that, or she'd dreamed the last two-plus days. Maybe the entire escape through the forest had simply been a nightmare, induced by morphine or coma or other drugs and she was just now waking up in the hospital.

The room was still shadowy, the morning peeking through the curtains in a line of soft rose, the room silent. They didn't have her hooked up to any beeping monitors, but an oxygen cannula fitted under her nose, turning the air frosty as it drifted into her nostrils. The IV in her arm pumped in cool saline, antibiotics, and probably painkiller because she didn't hurt anymore. Much. Her bones ached, but the wound in her gut had dipped to a solid three, maybe four on the agony scale.

She moved her hand, found the dressing under her gown. Put her hand over it.

Safe.

She was safe.

That thought burrowed deep. Safe, and not running anymore. She closed her eyes. What if—and she hadn't ever considered this—but what if it wasn't Sheriff Blackburn who'd killed Dante? She'd been so sure—after all, she'd seen him a couple times working out with her uncle Ian. And Dante—he'd mumbled Blackburn's name.

But what if . . . what if it was simply someone who *looked* like Blackburn? He wasn't wearing his uniform—had on a baseball cap, a T-shirt, jeans. He could have been any solidly built hiker with dark hair.

What if she'd falsely accused him, been running for no reason for five years?

Her chest tightened. Oh, the grief she'd put Uncle Ian through. And his entire team. How could she make such a ghastly mistake? Frankly, the immensity of it all made her want to flee all over again.

No . . . she was finished running.

The next step she took would be toward the future. Toward Ned, toward Uncle Ian, toward the life she'd put on hold.

Toward a happy ending, finally.

The door opened and light cast through the room from the hallway. Probably a nurse, checking on her vitals. She pulled the sheet up. "I'm awake."

"Good." A low, familiar voice. As he came into the room, the closing door to the hallway light illuminated just enough of his face for her to catch her breath.

No. She wouldn't jump to panic. "Oh. Hi. I . . . I wanted to thank you . . ."

Blackburn came up to her bed. He wore a bandage across his head, had stripped off his orange hunting coveralls to a pair of jeans and a flannel shirt.

"No, honey. I have to thank you," he said. He picked up the

bed controls and began to press a button. "See, I never thought I'd see you again."

The bed began to lower.

She grabbed the railing. "What?"

"Everyone was looking for you after you vanished, you know. The entire county."

She tried to sit up, but the pain spiked and she collapsed helpless as the bed tilted back.

"I know," she said. "I'm sorry—"

"You're a very slippery young girl. Getting away from me, sneaking out of the park, staying hidden. I didn't even know you'd come back until . . . well, lucky me."

She froze.

"And then suddenly, there you were in the cabin. I had started to think maybe you had died that night. Or maybe you didn't exist."

She drew in a breath, a scream forming, but he clamped a hand over her mouth. Big and sweaty and powerful, it sealed off her breath. She clawed at his grip.

He ripped off the oxygen cannula and put his other hand over her nose, pinching it, cutting off her air.

"But you did exist, and for a second there, I thought maybe you'd recognized me. And then when you started to beg me, back in the truck, well, clearly you remember everything. But I have to give you credit . . . you just played it cool. And I started to think maybe you hadn't told anyone."

The room started to turn black, blotchy.

"But I couldn't take that chance, see? Which meant I needed to finish this. I couldn't kill you at the cabin without also killing everyone else. And now, after everything I did to save you—well, they'll think you died from your injuries. I'll walk away, and the whole thing will be over."

He sighed. "It's better this way. You should have died years ago."

No—not like this!

"If I wanted to be free, then I had to stop letting fear win. I had to stop being a victim and fight with everything inside me."

Ned's words found root, galvanizing her, and she started to thrash.

Blackburn had the girth of a moose and wasn't moving, despite the blows to his face and shoulders, the claws against his hands.

"Sorry about this, sweetheart. Really, I am. You seem like a nice girl."

No—no, she wasn't! Or at least not the kind of girl who went down without a fight. She'd ripped her wound open, she knew that much as the pain cut through the morphine. But oh please, she needed to breathe . . .

In her thrashing she'd gotten her hand around the IV stand, and with everything inside her, with what felt like her last breath, she slammed it against Blackburn's head.

It bounced off him, a nearly useless hit, except it dislodged his hand enough for her to pull in a breath.

She slammed her hand into his face, a scream lifting her lips.

He grabbed her pillow from behind her head. "No, honey. Now it's time you die." Then he smashed the pillow over her face and held it tight.

No, no . . .

"God never intended me to fight my battles alone."

She didn't know why Ned's words roused inside her. Maybe because she had nothing left, but yeah—she'd been fighting her battles alone for years. Running and hiding and even now—fighting alone.

God, please! Help me—

The darkness closed in around her.

———— + ————

For a second, Ned couldn't quite figure out what was happening. He wondered if he'd gotten the right room, and what the man might be doing to the patient in the bed.

And then, Ned saw her thrash, and the realization kicked in.

Blackburn was trying to suffocate Shae.

He launched himself at Blackburn. Yeah, the man outweighed him by a good forty pounds, and had the girth of a grizzly, but Ned possessed enough fury to get his arm around the man's neck, to turn him around.

Before Blackburn could blink, Ned slammed his fist into his face.

Blackburn was a tough old goat because the punch barely fazed him.

He shoved Ned hard.

Ned hit the wall; the air blew out of him.

A word formed in Ned's brain as Blackburn charged him. *Help.* Might have even gotten the word out. Somehow he got his arm up in time to shunt Blackburn's right-hander. It glanced off Ned's chin.

He grabbed the edge of the bed to keep himself on his feet.

Blackburn followed with a left uppercut to his gut that erupted through Ned.

He went over, his knees buckling.

No. Get back up.

His brain was spinning too fast to think beyond instinct, beyond the explosion of fury and fear that caused him to launch himself at Blackburn. He wrapped his arms around his waist, sending him back into the wall.

Blackburn kneed him, but Ned held on, landed a fist to his kidney. Another.

Blackburn woofed out a breath, as if in pain, and Ned backed up, his hand on Blackburn's shirt to deliver a right hook.

The man beat him to it, coming up hard and catching Ned's

chin. Blood filled Ned's mouth, but he threw his punch anyway. Blackburn barely reacted.

Behind him, Shae coughed.

Thank you, God. But if he didn't get a handle on Blackburn . . .

Some version of Fraser's words sliced through him. *God is on your team. So don't keep him out of the game plan.*

Right. "Help!" Ned shouted with everything inside him. "God, help!"

Blackburn's hand grasped his throat and squeezed. Ned hit him in the gut, but Blackburn didn't move and now had both hands clamped on Ned's throat.

He tried to get his arms up between Blackburn's arms, to separate his grip, but the room had begun to blink in and out.

"Hey!"

He heard the voice somewhere down the dark hallway of his brain.

Then, air. Sweet air as Blackburn's hands were wrenched away from him.

Ned stumbled back, gasping as he watched Fraser put Blackburn in a sleeper hold, his arm extended over Blackburn's clavicle, around his neck, the other hand securing his fist against the carotid artery.

Blackburn stumbled back, clawing at him, but Fraser held on.

Ham caught Blackburn's hands, prying them off their grip on Fraser.

Blackburn slumped, and Fraser lowered him to the floor.

Ham set his foot on the sheriff's chest. "Get security," he said to Jonas, who took off.

Ned bent over, breathing in hard to catch his breath, and then stumbled over to Shae.

She had thrown off the pillow, and Ned's hand shook as he tried to fix the cannula back under her nose.

Fraser was right there; he shoved Ned's hands away and sent sweet oxygen into Shae's nostrils.

"Just breathe," Ned said.

"You too." Fraser put his hand on Ned's shoulder. "You okay?"

Ned nodded.

"Good thing you yelled. We decided to hang out in the hall to give you two a little privacy."

Huh.

Shae started crying, and Ned leaned down, his forehead to hers. "I'm here. It's okay. We got him—we got him." He glanced at Ham, who was now flipping Blackburn over and pulling his arm back in a submission hold.

"Thanks," Ned said to Fraser.

"That's what brothers are for." Fraser gave him a wink. Then he backed away as Ned slid onto the bed beside Shae and pulled her into his arms.

And then, because maybe they were all the weak link and needed as much help as they could get, Ned bent his head and let himself cry with her.

15

How Jess wished for Pete's jacket back. But it had been used to stop his bleeding and was probably in some waste bin or in a bag with the rest of his clothing.

Everything had happened so quickly when they reached the hospital chopper pad. Two ER docs were waiting to transport Pete out of the chopper and into the ER. And Gage hopped out, giving Pete's vitals as he passed him over into their care. Pete's heartbeat had dropped precariously low, and Gage had found fluid in Pete's ears.

Dr. Watson, Gage's neurosurgeon mother, had met them in the ER, and while Jess fought the nurses' urging to get medical attention, she listened to Dr. Watson's exam, then walked with Pete all the way down the corridor as they trundled him off for a CT scan.

They'd found internal bleeding, two broken ribs, and a subdural hematoma.

He'd been in surgery for two hours.

Meanwhile, the ER sent her for X-rays and found a hairline cracked wrist. Gage's father, an orthopedic surgeon, came down to set it—mostly out of courtesy, but Gage sat with her, kept her from leaping off the gurney and digging a pacing trench through the waiting area.

Gage had also found her some scrubs, as well as a sweater of his mother's. Jess had showered and brushed her teeth. Busyness to keep herself from losing her mind.

From believing that everything she loved, everything she'd finally decided to hold on to—no, to leap for—was being snatched away.

Please, God. Save us all here. Not because we deserve it, but because you love us.

She stood now at the window, staring at her reflection, a faded, wan image against the shadowed pane.

She probably needed sleep, but her body was on full-out buzz, her nerves frayed so thin she hadn't a hope of sleep . . . well, not until she knew Pete would live.

The door opened behind her, and footsteps made her turn.

Felipe. He looked rugged and worn out. He didn't stop, just came straight for her and held his arms out.

She stepped into his embrace, the warmth of it so familiar.

"How is he?"

"He's in surgery. He has internal bleeding, a broken shoulder, a gunshot wound, and a head trauma and . . ." She closed her eyes. "Felipe, I . . ."

"Shh." He leaned back and lifted her chin. "I can see how much you love him."

"Felipe." She cupped her hands on his face, met his eyes. "Go after Gabrielle."

"Selene, I—"

"I saw the way she looked at you in New York. Pete might know a man's face when he's whipped, but I know a woman who is in love. She loves you, and I don't care what your father says. She's worth the risk, right?"

He drew in a breath.

"You don't want someone who loves you just enough. You want

310

someone who would pursue you . . . all the way to New York City. That's why she was here, wasn't it? Because she definitely looked shocked and upset when you told her we were engaged."

He swallowed. "I think so. She wrote to me and told me she'd broken up with her British viscount, and . . ."

"She told you it was because she loved you, didn't she?"

He looked away.

"C'mon, Felipe. It's time for you to have your happy ending too." She lifted herself onto her tiptoes and kissed his cheek. "You're an amazing fake fiancé. But I'm breaking up with you."

A sad smile creased his face. "I still think we're a better match. Felipe and Selene. But you're right . . . I watched you out there climbing down to him, and it struck me . . . you *are* Jess. You are this amazing, brave rescuer, and yes, you'll always be Selene, but she was . . . she was in a box. Here, you're free, aren't you?"

She nodded. "And it's not just Pete. It's . . . well, when I came out here, it was just me. I discovered who I was. I know I perpetuated a lie, but I also lived in the truth for the first time. I like the me I am out here. And Pete helped me see that."

Felipe pushed a strand of drying hair back, tucking it behind her ears. "No makeup."

She frowned.

"You never went without makeup in New York City. Not in college, not ever."

"I never wear it here."

"You don't need it anyway." He sighed. "What you said out there. About love being worth the risk? You're right." He drew in a breath. "I called Gabrielle on my way here."

"Wow." Huh. "Really, that was—"

"About time, I know. I just . . . I thought, if you could climb down a cliff to the man you love, I could pick up a phone."

"So brave." She winked.

"I woke her up. She's still in New York City. I'm going back. Today."

Jess smoothed her hand over the PEAK jacket he still wore. "You sure? This looks good on you."

"Not as good as it does on you." He took her shoulders and leaned in, kissing her on the forehead. "Are you going to be okay?"

The door opened behind him, and she spotted Ty coming in. He was mud-splattered and road weary but gave her a smile.

"I'm in good hands."

Ty clamped his hand on Felipe's shoulder. Grinned at them.

"We're not engaged anymore," Felipe said.

"Oh, I know Jess's games," Ty said with a wink. "I figured there was more to the story."

Felipe frowned, and Jess gave Ty a little shake of her head.

"Anyone want coffee?" Ty turned to the coffeemaker and grabbed a cup. "By the way, we found the truck. You ran about three miles, if Ned is right about where you camped that first night."

"I wouldn't call it camping." But a strange sense of pride swelled through her. "We were pretty awesome," she said.

"Who knew Selene Taggert had it in her? You're such a toughie." Ty held up his hand for a fist bump.

She met it.

"Seriously! You can't stay out of trouble for one minute?" The voice accompanied the bold entrance of Sierra Shaw. She didn't stop but made straight for Jess and pulled her into an embrace. "Scared us all to death, thank you." Sierra put her away. "And you broke your wrist? Good grief, Jess." But her eyes had filled.

"Hey," Jess said. "I missed you."

"Yeah, well, the upstairs toilet at your house leaks, and they delivered the wood for the back deck roughly a year ago, so anytime you want to pick up your hammer, I'm ready."

Jess laughed. "You don't even live there anymore."

"I'm just relaying Willow's complaints."

"Where is she?"

"She went to pick up Maren. Sam and Chet are on their way up."

"Ian?"

"With Shae. And Ned. And apparently Ned's brothers are here. But even more—Blackburn tried to *kill* her."

"What?" Jess stepped away from her. "Are you kidding me? He was so . . . well, for a bit there, I thought maybe Shae got it wrong."

"Oh no, she got it right." This from Gage, who had come in. "I just talked to Ian. Blackburn is cooling his heels at the county jail. I just got off the phone with Ella. Shae has finally agreed to give her statement about what happened to Dante. And, of course, Blackburn's attack."

"What happened?"

Gage poured himself a cup of coffee. "He tried to smother her. But Ned came in, took him down. Or maybe . . . I don't know. I think his brother might have been there. Ned got roughed up a bit."

"Ned was already roughed up. A lot," Jess said. "If it weren't for him, we might not have made it."

"That's not how he explained it," Gage said quietly. "He seems to think that you're the big hero here. That you made all the tough decisions that saved them."

"I think . . . we just kept moving forward. And trusted that God would save us."

"I've been trying to tell you that for a while now," Ty said.

She hadn't noticed, but Felipe had moved toward the door. He glanced over at her, met her gaze, and offered a smile.

Then he was gone.

Just like that, out of her life. She swallowed back a thickness in her throat.

Ty handed her the cup of coffee. She sipped it, her stomach roaring. But she couldn't eat—not until Pete was out of surgery.

Maren and Chet came in, followed by Sam and Willow. Jess greeted Pete's mother with a hug, and hung on for a long while to Chet. When he stepped away, his eyes were wet.

Willow updated her on the house and showed her the solitaire Sam had given her.

"About time," Jess said to Sam.

"Yeah, well, right back at you." He leaned close. "Please tell me that the fact that I saw Felipe leaving means you and Pete figured things out."

"I think so," Jess said. "No more fake engagement."

Sam frowned, and right about then, the door opened and Dr. Watson walked in. She came over to Maren and Sam.

"Pete's out of surgery and did well. Had some internal bleeding, a couple broken ribs, and a ruptured spleen, but we were able to remove it. The subdural hematoma wasn't as bad as we thought. The bleeding had already stopped by the time we went in to drain it. We'll monitor him for any additional brain trauma, but his prognosis looks good."

Ty touched Jess's elbow, and just in time, because her knees nearly buckled. He pulled her into an embrace, held her up. "See. He'll be fine."

"Can I see him?" Jess asked but glanced at Maren and Sam, just to make sure.

Maren took her arm.

"Follow me," Dr. Watson said.

Jess and Maren followed her down the hallway and into a room. A nurse was logging Pete's blood pressure. "We just brought him from recovery," she said. "He's a bit groggy."

He looked brutal. A gray-black bruise covered one side of his face, and his beautiful blond hair was shaved and his head bandaged. IVs ran from his arm, and an oxygen mask covered his mouth and nose, which was taped, probably broken. His shoulder was wrapped, his arm drawn up to splint it, and so many bruises covered his body that he looked like he'd been run over by buffalo.

"*I love you. I would die to save you.*"

Oh Pete.

She stepped forward and touched his hand. Found it cool. "Pete?"

He didn't move. She stepped closer, leaned down, her mouth close to his ear. "It's me, Jess."

A heart monitor buzzed.

"What's happening?"

"His heart is beating too fast," Dr. Watson said. She moved over to him as Jess backed away. "He's tachycardic, let's—"

The machine flatlined.

Pete!

"Call a code," Watson said. "Everybody out of the way. Now!"

---+---

The breath off the pristine slopes filled Pete's lungs. A chill tightened his nose, brushed his lips, and he suppressed a shiver, despite the layers he wore. Gore-Tex jacket, his black pants, and on his feet, his skis, sharpened and slick.

The glorious day stretched out forever, the sky so blue he could dive in, the jagged peaks of the Rocky Mountains iced with foam and glinting against the brilliant sunshine.

The wind called to him, stirring the trees, swirling through him, and it urged him forward.

Except.

Something. Pete looked around, but in this place, he was alone. On the top of the peak, just the dervishes of snow for company.

He turned back to the slope, pristine and uncut.

Surrendered to the pull.

He shot off fast, straight down, gathering speed as he cut into the powder, his feet tight, together, one elegant form. He leaned, riding back and cutting hard, moving his blades through the frosting, slicing through the thickness. A fluid motion that swelled power through him. He rode the turn over, eased up, and leaned the other direction, repeating the movement.

Snow plumed as he cut, the spray tickling his cheeks. He licked his cold lips, felt the moisture on them.

Overhead, an eagle cried, the only audience, it seemed, to his dance, his freedom.

Except.

He braked, breathing hard, and looked back, his heart pounding, searching. A voice. He heard it call to him. *Pete.*

Nothing but the eagle dipping into the currents overhead. He watched it soar. Listened.

Turned back to the mountain run below.

Shaggy pine trees jutted out of the white, pins in the cushion, and he set himself to gliding between them with arms out.

He emerged onto a jutted rock and crouched into the jump, leaping as he found air.

Flying.

He landed easily, bouncing up into the pillow of snow, gaining momentum.

Pete.

He heard it then. A low voice, deep in his bones. He braked hard, his legs on fire as he skidded through the snow. Breathing in the slick cold, he leaned over his poles. Searched the slope.

Even the eagle had departed. There was nothing but his breath razoring in and out. The thunder of his heartbeat.

"Pete."

He jerked up, around.

Froze. A man stood in the snow, on an outcropping overlooking the mountain.

He wore a blue jacket and black ski pants, and lifted his pole, waving.

Pete's breath caught even as he pushed off, moving toward the man. Dad?

He smiled as Pete came closer. He stood easily in his boots, leaning on his pole.

Dad.

Pete stopped at the edge of the cliff. Snow trickled from the edge into the white.

"I've been waiting for you," his dad said.

Pete just stared at him. Healthy, strong, a hint of a cloud that evidenced his breathing. Alive. "You have?"

"Yeah." He turned, stared out at the horizon, at the towering peaks, at the sun, its rays blinding in their glory. "I wanted you to see this view."

Pete looked down at the cliff's edge.

"No, Pete, look up. At the blue. At the immense glory of the heavens."

Yeah, it was his father, all right, the poet of their family. Once upon a time, Pete had wanted to be exactly like him.

Still did. A warmth started at his core, wrapping around him. Pete tented his hand over his eyes, stared at the heavens.

"It's like flying. Or skiing on a pristine slope."

"What is?"

"Love. Eternity."

Pete looked at him.

"Stop trying so hard, son. Just be still. Rest. Check out the view." His father opened his arm to the horizon. "This is what grace looks like."

Blue, as far as he could see, the glorious mountains rising high, powerful, glistening with a palate of frothy snow, clear and bright and perfect.

317

A hard ball formed in Pete's chest.

Pressure on his shoulder.

His father's gaze met his, unwavering. "You are my son, and I forgive you. You do not have to be afraid anymore. You have been declared not guilty, Pete, for all eternity."

Pete blinked, his throat tight.

"Breathe it in and be set free."

The sun moved into Pete's eyes, and he closed them, aware of the heat glazing them.

"I love you, son. Go in grace."

"Come on, Pete. C'mon—please!"

Not his father's voice, and pain jerked him back into the room, into the harsh light, the screech of machines.

"He's back!"

Pete opened his eyes, breathing in hard. A nurse hovered over him, holding paddles. She backed away, and he took another rasping breath, his body buzzing.

"Welcome back." A familiar face—he couldn't place it, however—leaned over him. She wore scrubs and had her hair tucked into a surgical cap. "You had us scared for a bit there."

He blinked, still hearing his father's voice, and looked past the woman to . . . Jess? She stood at the foot of his bed, tears cutting down her face.

"Hey, handsome," she said. She wore a pair of scrubs, and her hair was damp and clean. She had so much love in her eyes it radiated through him and touched his core.

Go in grace.

"Jess." His voice emerged raspy and dry, and only then did he realize he wore an oxygen mask pumping brisk air into his mouth and nose.

"You had some massive bleeding there, buddy, from your fall, and the doc had to go in and stop it." Sam was standing on the

318

other side of the bed. "Sorry, dude, you're short your spleen. And you've got a hole in your head, which we all knew, really."

Behind him stood his mother, wiping her face, Chet's hand on her shoulder.

"Okay, hero, you keep that heart beating." The doctor—oh yes, he recognized her now. Gage's mother. "I'll be in later to check on you."

"Thank you, Doc," Sam said.

Behind her, the door opened and Gage came into the room, followed by Ty.

Ty held a cup of coffee, his eyes wide. "What just happened?"

"Pete decided to go code blue on us," Sam said. "The jerk." But he grinned and squeezed Pete's leg.

Jess stepped up next to him and took Pete's hand. Held it to her chest. "Don't do that again."

"What?" he managed.

"Everything. Jump off a cliff. Decide to die. Scare me to death."

She was so beautiful looking down at him with those blue eyes that she could probably send him into another heart-stopping event. But he wouldn't mention that now.

This is what grace looks like.

Yes. Yes, it was. He reached up and moved the mask aside. "So. What did I miss?"

Epilogue

"HOW DID IT GO?"

Sam leaned over to Pete, whispering over the hum of conversation in the room. Sam was slicked up in a black suit and tie, with a boutonniere made from a white rose tucked into his lapel. Probably Pete shouldn't mock him because he'd been made to wear the same thing. At least he had a little more hair now. He'd had to cut it all the way down to the scalp to even it out, and after six weeks he still looked like a navy recruit.

Not unlike Ned, he supposed, who sat on one of the folding chairs in the back of the room.

The room was decorated with the colors of Christmas, despite it only being the last week of November. But Sierra seemed to be in a decorating mood, and frankly, she knew this house almost better than the current owners, Ben and Kacey King.

Evergreen boughs wrapped the overhead beams in the great room and adorned the wide mantel of the soaring rock fireplace. Candles flickered in the center chandelier. She'd set up chairs, created a center aisle, and set lanterns lit with candles at the head of each row—all five of them. After all, they hadn't needed many to celebrate this day.

321

Just the important people.

The room was scented with pine and roses, thanks to the creative arrangements at the head of the aisle. Shae's touch, along with the glittering white-and-red-lighted evergreen that sparkled outside the massive picture window. With the sun just starting to set, and against the backdrop of the mountains, well, it just might be a night to propose.

Again.

Except Pete had already slipped a ring on Jess's finger and even gotten her mother's blessing.

Hadn't that been a weird conversation? "I think it went well. Jess introduced me to her mother, who sort of got me confused with her son at times, but I think she liked me. I'm not Felipe, and Caroline really loved him, but I told her I'd love Jess every day of my life and that I'd take care of her, and . . . well, she gave me a little kiss when we left. So . . ." Pete hitched up his shoulder. "We're going back in a couple days for as long as we need to be there. Jess is going to take her Step 1 boards right after Christmas, so it might be a while."

Sam gave him a look, but Pete shrugged. "That's what love does, right? Shows up and sticks around, even for the hard stuff. Keeps its promises."

"Now who's the romantic one?"

"Engaged, bro. Don't forget that."

Sam grinned. "So, I can't persuade you and Jess to move back to Montana to run PEAK?"

"Actually . . . you're looking at the new director of Red Cross search and rescue training. My provisionary disaster search team was such a hit over the past eighteen months, they're deploying two more. Over which I will be in charge."

Sam raised an eyebrow.

"What?"

"Oh, I dunno. More Pete Brooks types out there, saving the world?"

Pete grinned. "You bet." Because maybe the world needed impulsive, sometimes even reckless heroes who stood between danger and death. Who did what they could, holding on to grace and hope.

Maybe he'd also include in the training something about grief counseling and figuring out how to let go of the ones they couldn't save.

"By the way, Ellis's body finally washed up."

Pete gave a tight nod, his gaze drifting to the gang of three, Sierra, Willow, and Jess.

With her dark hair pulled back and wearing a stunning little black dress and white pearls, Sierra looked every inch a billionaire's wife. Except for her bare feet; she was holding her heels as she talked with Willow and Jess, who were both dressed in strapless red dresses.

"Doesn't Willow look amazing?" Sam said.

"Just get married already," Pete said.

But yes, while Willow looked pretty in her gown, Jess could steal the breath from his lungs. She'd done something magical with her blonde hair, pulling it back from her face and curling it, and yeah, he'd had to fist his hands at his sides to keep from touching it when he'd picked her up at the house.

Sierra grabbed her hand then and examined the ring. It wasn't fancy like the ring Felipe had given her, but he'd had it designed. Gold band with a center diamond and two smaller stones, it cost him a couple months' pay. But he'd sell everything he owned to give her the world.

Under all that glitter, she was still Jess, the girl who lived in jeans and a T-shirt, armed with a fixer-upper to-do list, one that apparently included a new deck on her house as soon as the ground thawed.

She caught him watching her and grinned at him.

Yeah, he just wanted to ask her to marry him, again and again. Just to hear her say yes, over and over.

"You clean up well, dude." Ned came up, also dressed in a suit. He shook Pete's hand.

"I thought you were in training for the SEALs."

Ned had stuck around to give his statement about Blackburn and even watch him be indicted, but left for Minnesota not long afterward. "It took me a bit to get back up to speed, but my brother Fraser's been working with me. I just got accepted into the BUD/S program. I go to basic in January."

"Wow," Sam said and also shook his hand. "We're rooting for you."

"Thanks," Ned said. "I'll need it."

Shae came up and slid her arm through Ned's. "He's going to make it," she said, clearly catching the tail end of their conversation.

"Are you back for a while?"

"Just a week. But I had to finally dance with my girl." Ned glanced down at Shae, and Pete recognized the look of a man in over his head.

"Apparently there are happy endings for guys like us." Ben walked over, dressed in a black suit, his own white rose pinned to his chest. He held out his hand, met Pete's. "Right, bro?"

"Listen—" Pete started, but Ben just laughed.

Maybe it wasn't such a bad thing, having Ben King as a stepbrother.

Or . . . weirdly . . . Chet as a stepfather? The older man looked so happy, beaming like he was twenty-five and would live forever.

But maybe that's what love felt like. Abundance. Flinging yourself into eternity for all you're worth, your life abandoned into the arms of a good Father who loves you.

At least that's what Pete was starting to get his brain around. Lean in to.

The music started, the guests took their seats, and the ladies lined up in the back. First Kacey, who also wore a red strapless dress and who should probably grace some cover of a magazine. Beside her walked Audrey, Chet's granddaughter, a spitting image of her mother with that long auburn hair. She grinned at Chet, popping over to kiss his cheek before she joined her mother.

Then came Willow, who only had eyes for Sam. Really, they should just elope because Sam was driving Pete crazy with his wedding plans. In fact, they should both just elope because as soon as Jess started down the aisle, Pete saw himself standing at the altar, saying I do. I will. Forever and ever, amen.

Yes, time to get past the proposals and on to the happy ending.

With a nice long stopover at the honeymoon.

Her eyes widened as she came closer, almost as if she could read his thoughts, and he looked away fast.

But when she stepped up next to Willow, she caught his gaze, her blue eyes twinkling, and mouthed the words "I do." Waggled her eyebrows.

Oh, she was definitely trouble. The kind worth waiting for.

The crowd rose; well, really, it was just a handful of attendees. The PEAK team—Gage and Ella, Ty and Brette, Ian and Sierra, and of course Ned and Shae and a few others from Chet and Maren's church. Pete looked toward the end of the aisle.

And shoot, now he was going to do something completely sappy and tear up. Because his mother stood there beaming, looking so happy, so beautiful in her simple off-white gown with the lacy sleeves. Someone must have done her hair because she wore it puffy, with tiny flowers in it.

She looked positively radiant.

His dad would like this moment. Probably was smiling down

from heaven. Because Chet was a good man. Worth taking his place.

No, not exactly taking his place, but . . . well, adding on. Because Chet had been nearly a father to both Pete and Sam. And he loved their mom. And that was what happy endings were about. Second chances. Trusting in God's love to add on joy in ways you couldn't imagine.

Sam nudged Pete. "Did you bring the ring?"

The ring? "What? No, I thought—"

"Shh," Ben said. "Don't worry about the ring. Sheesh."

"I have it right here," Chet said, patting his pocket.

Pete grinned. Of course he did. The original member of the PEAK team to the rescue.

And then Maren was walking down the aisle to some cello music, and yes, maybe Ben was right after all. It wasn't the ring but the promises that counted.

The promises and the love . . . and the happily-ever-after eternity.

Go in grace.

Author's Note

WHAT A WILD RIDE THE MONTANA RESCUE SERIES HAS BEEN! I hope you've enjoyed the adventures of Ben, Kacey, Sam, Willow, Ian, Sierra, Gage, Ella, Ty, Brette, Shae, Ned, and especially Jess and Pete. Hopefully we'll catch up with them again now and then.

I'm so grateful for the help on this series from the amazing team at Revell. Andrea Doering, my fabulous editor, and Kristin Kornoelje, for smoothing out my words. To Michele Misiak and Karen Steele and the marketing team for their efforts to get the books out to readers. Their ideas, partnership, and commitment to making this series fabulous were a huge encouragement to me!

I could never write a book without my fabulous writing partner, Rachel Hauck. And my daily prayer group, Beth Vogt, Alena Tauriainen, Lisa Jordan (and of course, Rachel!). A huge thanks goes to my walking buddy, Laurie Stoltenberg, who loves to read and brainstorm while we sweat. And, of course, my amazing family, especially my sons, David, Peter, and Noah, who have become amazing storytellers! And to my husband, who so patiently says, "Sure, I'll brainstorm with you." I'm so blessed.

I wanted to write a story about a woman who just didn't want to cause any more problems, didn't want to hurt anyone else, who just wanted everyone to be happy. The problem is, we can't please everyone, and when we try, we end up making a mess. The best thing we can do is live in truth, love others well, and trust in the God who loves us enough to fix our messes.

I fell in love with sweet Pete. He so wanted to be the right guy, and for me, Pete turned into a guy who modeled the reckless love Christ has for us. Even when we break his heart, he just can't turn away from us, just like Pete couldn't get Jess out of his heart. We need to remember this when we look at our mistakes, our messes, and our failures. Instead of running or trying to fix it ourselves—or even band-aiding it with short-term comfort—we need to lean into grace. Lean into love.

God is our rescuer. He won't give up on us until he's found us and brought us home. Hallelujah and amen.

Go in grace, friend.
Susie May

Susan May Warren is the *USA Today*, ECPA and CBA bestselling author of over sixty-five novels, including *Wild Montana Skies*, with more than one million books sold. Winner of a RITA Award and multiple Christy and Carol Awards, as well as the HOLT and numerous Readers' Choice Awards, Susan has written contemporary and historical romances, romantic suspense, thrillers, romantic comedy, and novellas. She can be found online at www.susan maywarren.com, on Facebook at SusanMayWarrenFiction, and on Twitter @susanmaywarren.

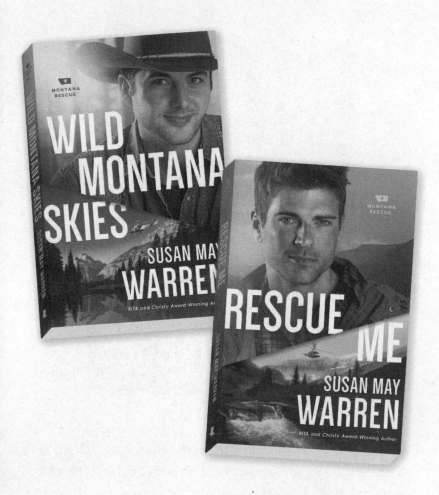

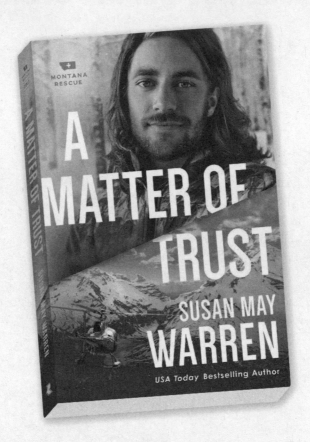

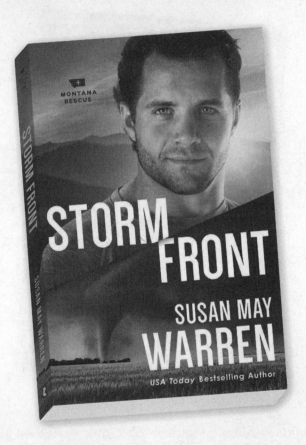

BILLIONAIRE IAN SHAW CAN HAVE EVERYTHING HE WANTS— EXCEPT A HAPPY ENDING.

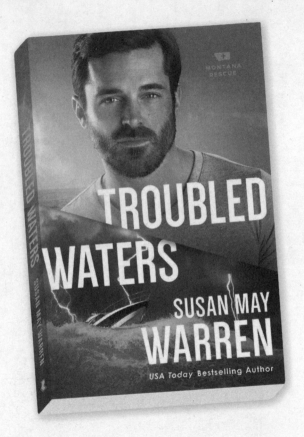

A three-day excursion turns into a nightmare when a rogue wave washes the passengers overboard, leaving Ian and Sierra scrambling for survival. Sparks ignite as they wait for a rescue, but will a secret keep them apart?

Connect with
Susan May Warren

Visit her website and sign up for her newsletter to get a free novella, hot news, contests, sales, and sneak peeks!

www.susanmaywarren.com

 @SusanMayWarrenFiction @SusanMayWarren